Alan Reynolds

Fisher King Publishing

Published by
Fisher King Publishing
The Studio
Arthington Lane
Pool-in-Wharfedale
LS21 1JZ
England

Photograph of the author by
Karen Ross Photography

Also by Alan Reynolds

Breaking the Bank

Flying with Kites

Taskers End

The Coat

The Sixth Pillar

The Tinker

Valley of the Serpent

With gratitude to Rick Armstrong for his
unstinting support, guidance and friendship;
also, to Samantha Richardson and Rachel Topping
at Fisher King Publishing.

Dedicated to my family and friends, and to all
those who have supported me in my writing –
your encouragement is greatly appreciated.
Much love

It is a man's own mind, not his enemy or
foe, that lures him to evil ways
Buddha

Chapter One

It was late spring. Rory Calderwood was seated on a bench overlooking the river, sipping from a water bottle. On the opposite bank, he could see the cricket ground, famed for its iconic cathedral backdrop. It was a warm day but with a threat of rain; there had been plenty in recent weeks.

Everywhere looked green; the riverside trees dipped their branches into the water as if testing the temperature. The fields were speckled with the yellow of dandelions and buttercups. Rory watched an angler land a three-inch Dace and put it in the keepnet, half-submerged in the high-running, fast-flowing Severn. Another twelve of those and he could have sardines on toast, thought Rory, smiling to himself.

He hadn't had much to smile about in the past eight months since leaving the rig. Delta Bravo, the North Sea Oil and Gas platform, had been his life for the best part of twelve years. He allowed himself the occasional retrospection; not that he had much choice, his thoughts would visit him like an unwelcome guest. This time last year, he had a well-paid job, a nice house in a desirable suburb of Aberdeen, a wife and two children. He'd been the statistical aspirational norm.

But now, things were so different. The incident that, in the end, had cost him his job and almost his life, still haunted him. It had destroyed his relationship with Kim, who had tried to nurse him back to health when his demons were at their height. He'd been living with her after leaving the hospital. She'd provided the emotional support he needed until, unable to cope with his mood swings and moroseness, she returned to London. He couldn't blame her; he had difficulty living with himself and couldn't expect anyone else to share his burden.

By that time, his marriage to Janie was already over. He regretted that; she and their two boys had been his life. The strains of fortnightly separation had been too much for her and she'd set up home with her tennis instructor, Geoff. Rory's sons, Matt and Jason, appeared to have settled in too well to their new domestic environment. In his darkest moments, he felt he might as well be dead as far as they were concerned.

The incident on the rig had rekindled memories of his time as an SAS officer. He still could not shake the flashbacks from his army days that awoke him almost every night, haunting him, suffocating him, taunting him. His way of dealing with it was to push himself physically - running, gym, exercise; as if punishing himself for his own failings.

His saviour had come from an unexpected source. It was the regular discussions he'd had with the welfare officer at Petronix, his former employers. Alice Spencer, a motherly figure with the patience of a saint, was a trained psychiatrist, and somehow, she connected with him. The therapy gave him the mental strength that allowed him to come to terms with life and move on. The decision to leave the company was easy; he could never return to his old job as senior engineer stuck in the middle of the North Sea. To ease any financial pain, he received a substantial payoff which included his industrial injury claim.

After Kim had left, he moved into a small flat in Aberdeen but there were too many memories there. So, he made another decision and substituted the wild crags of The Highlands for the gentler hills of Worcestershire.

This was his home territory, having been born and raised the other side of the Malvern Hills in nearby Herefordshire. His only living relative, his sister Anna, had lived in Worcester since leaving university. Unable to think of a better alternative, he called her out of the blue, asking if he could stay with her while he sorted himself out. He'd had little contact with her for some time; Christmas and birthday cards when he, or more likely Janie, had remembered. Although it had been an upheaval, Anna had welcomed him like a prodigal son. "For as long as you need," she said, but without too much conviction.

Janie had taken most of the furnishings from the house,

so it was just his clothes, record collection and some odd bits and pieces that made the journey in a borrowed van from his Aberdeen apartment to his sister's garage.

Rory didn't get on too well with Anna's partner, Sonia, who tolerated his presence with barely veiled hostility; he had disrupted their routine. This had gone on for two months before the inevitable, "how long do you plan on staying," conversation took place. Rory had taken the hint and found himself a small two-bedroomed cottage close to the river; no suggestion of permanency, but it would do for now.

That was over four months ago, but he felt at home in his new abode; there was a familiarity about it, born from his childhood recollections. It was a place of peace and solace which as what he needed right now. His bedroom window looked out across the small unmade road, more a cinder track really, which ran parallel to the Severn. It was a joy to open the curtains each morning and see the river making its way majestically downstream to the sea, almost a hundred miles away, and the rolling fields on the far bank with the Malvern Hills in the distance. Tranquillity it certainly was, and this time of year, at its best.

On moving in, he'd replaced some of the furniture; a new bed, cooker, washing machine and TV; although he was not one to sit still for any length of time. He converted the second bedroom into an office, which he would need to pursue his idea of setting up as a freelance security consultant. Apart from engineering, it was what he knew best. After leaving the Regiment, he had spent three years working for an agency in London before joining Petronix. As a result, he had an extensive knowledge of the shady world of security, particularly close protection, or body-guarding as it used to be called. He'd even run training courses on surveillance techniques and internal fraud. His years in the Regiment had given him a wide knowledge of the more extreme forms of subterfuge.

It was the last week in May 2007, he was beginning to

think more positively about the future. He needed to be doing something; his money wouldn't last forever even though he had his army pension to cushion him. He had monthly maintenance payments for his boys to cover; dipping into his savings to pay the bills was a road to disaster. An income would be required.

His priority was to find some clients. He'd started to ring around some of his old contacts. After twelve years, most had moved on, but he would persevere; something would turn up. Rory knew Worcester was not an ideal base for a security consultant. It was not renowned as a hotbed of serious crime; 'quaint' would be an apt description, but he was happy to travel to wherever the work took him. So, with a website for 'SCI Consultants', his new business name, set up by a friend of Anna's, he was now at least in the marketplace.

He took a final sip from his bottle and dropped it in a litter-bin, then set off back to his cottage, about two miles downstream. There were a few folks about, walking dogs or cycling along the riverside path. There were also fellow joggers. He was approaching Diglis Dock where he would need to take a detour and cross over the Birmingham - Worcester Canal.

A piercing shriek rang out.

"Help...! Help...!"

Rory ran towards the caller, a young woman frantically waving on the river bank.

"Help me, please...!" she pleaded desperately. "My little boy... he's fallen in the water," and she pointed to a small object gently bobbing up and down, being carried out to the middle of the river. "I can't swim."

Rory slid down the bank and into the river feet first. His training taught him never to shallow dive into unknown water; all kinds of hidden objects awaited the unwary. His running Nikes squelched on the muddy bottom making it difficult to move but within a couple of paces, the water was up to his chest. He pushed off swimming hard towards the boy. The cold hit him like a stone, causing him to inhale instinctively. He ignored it and quickened his pace. It was about thirty feet to the centre of the river and the current increased dramatically. Rory was being carried downstream faster and faster, but he was closing in on the lad. It was a race; the canal joining on the left created strange currents. Then there was the weir, two-hundred yards downstream. He needed to catch the boy before he reached that, or the chances of survival would be minimal.

A final effort and he managed to grab the boy's anorak and hold on. The air in his clothing had kept him afloat but it was only a matter of time before the water would be absorbed and the additional weight would drag the lad under.

Rory pulled the boy to him and held his head.

"Hold on son, I've got you."

There was no sound; the boy was either unconscious or paralysed with fear.

Now came the difficult part. There would be no boats on the river this close to the weir. There was no alternative but to head back against the current and hope he reached the bank before his strength gave out. This is where his training and fitness would pay off. Slowly but surely, he made progress against the strong current. There was a boat moored about fifty yards away, one of many parked along the bank further upstream; some had become permanent homes for the owners.

Someone was on deck and, as Rory got closer, he saw a lifeline being thrown. It landed short and the line was reeled in for a second attempt. This time the line reached Rory. The circular lifebelt landed in the water two feet away. Rory made a grab and took the strain as the boatman pulled. It took less than a minute to get Rory alongside the boat. It was as though time had stood still for the boy's mother who was sobbing hysterically on the riverbank as she watched the drama unfold. A small crowd had now gathered, alerted by the commotion. They watched as Rory passed the boy to the man on the back of the boat, and then made his way to the bank. He felt the clinging mud under his feet once again and managed to haul himself up the steep bank. He stood momentarily at the top, hands on knees, to regain his breath.

"I've called an ambulance," said one bystander.

Rory was becoming the centre of attention. "Are you ok?" asked an elderly gentleman with a cross-bred poodle. "Well done, sir," said another, dressed in the uniform of the local rowing club; blazer, cap and short trousers.

Rory stood up straight, water dripping from his clothes and hair, brown silt discolouring the bottom of his jogging bottoms.

"Where's the boy?" he said to nobody in particular.

"On the boat... his mother's with him," was the reply.

Rory made his way over the short gangplank to the open area at the stern where the owner was giving CPR. The boy's mother was standing next to him sobbing. "Save him, please save him, don't let him die," she cried.

"Here, let me have a go," said Rory, turning the lad on his stomach with his head to one side and pressing hard on his back. It was cramped; the small floor area was surrounded by seats and with three people there was not much room to work. Rory continued pushing on the boy's back. There was a cough and a splutter as water was expelled from the lad's lungs.

"What's his name?" asked Rory.

"Kyle," said the frantic woman.

"Hello, Kyle, you're safe. My name's Rory, you're ok... your Mum's here."

The boy slowly opened his eyes. "Mummy?"

He heard an ambulance, then paramedics rushing to the boat and across the short wooden gangway. Rory was still reviving the boy; his mother frantic with worry. The first paramedic took over and placed an oxygen mask over the boy's face. The boatman and Rory moved back into the boat to give the paramedics room. The mother was on her knees cradling her son's head.

"Just breathe normally for me... How old is he?" asked one of the paramedics.

"Nearly three," replied the boy's mother.

Having stabilised him, they lifted young Kyle onto a stretcher and the small party walked back onto the river bank towards the waiting ambulance.

"That was a great job you did there," said the boatman.

"Thanks for the line, I couldn't have held on much longer, the current's really strong," replied Rory.

A spontaneous round of applause broke out as Rory reached the ambulance where the small group of onlookers had congregated, keen to absorb every ounce of drama. Several had their phone cameras out recording the scene. The other paramedic approached Rory with what looked like a giant Bacofoil blanket and wrapped it around him.

"Hi, I'm Stacey, you need to be checked out."

"It's ok, I'm fine," said Rory. "Just need to get out of these wet things. I only live over there," he added, pointing to a group of buildings on the other side of the dock.

"If you're sure," replied Stacey.

She looked into his eyes for any adverse signs. She saw none. "Ok, look, if you feel nauseous or drowsy in the next few hours, call an ambulance. You could be in shock."

"Thank you," said the mother to Rory as the paramedic closed the ambulance door and it sped away, sirens blaring.

"Can I get you a drink?" said the boatman from behind Rory. "I can let you have a change of clothes as well."

Rory didn't want any fuss but to avoid the continued attention of the bystanders, he accepted the invitation.

"Yeah, ok, thanks," replied Rory and the boatman led him back onto the deck and down a couple of steps into the boat. The audience started to disperse, chatting animatedly, comparing notes, swapping stories, recounting events. "Did you see...?" "I couldn't have done that..."

The boat was a cabin cruiser, slightly bigger than many along the river bank with a seating area at the back where Kyle's recovery had been executed. Folding doors separated the living quarters from the small observation area. Rory was not very familiar with leisure-boats but could see it was well looked after and comfortable for the keen enthusiast.

"Nice boat," said Rory.

"Thanks," said the owner. "Here, dry yourself off."

He handed Rory a bath towel.

"Name's Alistair... Alistair Bailey."

"Thanks... Rory... Rory Calderwood." They shook hands.

The boatman opened a cupboard and rummaged around. "Ah yes, here we are," he said as he pulled out a tracksuit.

"Here put this on. I'll leave you in peace," and he went back on deck, pulling shut the doors, providing Rory with some privacy.

After a few minutes, Rory appeared. "Thanks for the loan. I can drop it back to you in the morning."

"No rush," said Alistair. "Here, I've poured you a beer. Bet you could do with one after what you've been through," and he handed Rory a long glass of lager.

"Cheers," said Rory taking a sip, standing in his borrowed tracksuit and carrying his now ruined trainers in one hand and his soaking jogging apparel over his arm. "Lucky I left my iPod at home. Can't get on with it when I'm jogging."

"So, you live around here?" said Alistair. A statement framed as a question.

"Yes, just across the dock... five minutes," replied Rory.

"Lucky you were about, that lad would've drowned. I was below deck and heard the commotion. Came up to see what the noise was all about. That's when I saw you."

"Pleased you did, that current is really strong," replied Rory.

"Yeah, that's the weir, very dangerous, and the river's running on the high side with all this rain we've been having. I tell you this, it's not easy for boats steering down the channel around it, let alone anyone swimming. I don't think I'd have tried it."

"Just instinct," said Rory and he took another sip of his beer.

"So, do you live on here?"

"Well, it's a permanent berth. I use it as a base during the summer; weekends mainly, the occasional bank holiday and days like today, when I just need to escape the office for a while. You were lucky; I wouldn't normally be here on a Thursday."

"Thank goodness you were," said Rory.

"Yeah, that's for sure... No, boating's just a hobby. I live in Birmingham... well, on the outskirts, actually... I've got a small manufacturing business, castings and that sort of stuff."

"Doing ok?"

"Yeah, can't complain. Got a full order book which is more than can be said for some of our competitors," replied Alistair.

Rory was starting to relax, and he viewed his host. He looked the part in his blue and white striped top, navy blue shorts and deck shoes. He was probably in his mid to late fifties with greying hair, long at the back, thinning at the front; fit-looking with a slight tan, evidencing time in the sun. Rory could detect a West Midlands' twang which gave credence to his origins.

"What do you do?" asked Alistair. "When you're not saving people."

"I'm in security," replied Rory.

"Security?"

"Yes," replied Rory without elaborating.

"What sort of security, specifically?" asked Alistair.

"Close protection, internal fraud prevention, investigation, that kind of thing," replied Rory.

"What, on a consultancy basis?"

"Yes," said Rory.

"Now that's very interesting," said Alistair, looking at Rory with a serious expression. There was a pause. "Look, I may have some work for you if you're interested. But now's not the time to talk. Here..." He handed Rory a business card. "Ring me on my mobile tomorrow and we can have a longer chat. You'll be wanting to get back and shower."

Rory was trying to sum up the man. There was an earnestness about him, Rory detected; clearly successful, probably self-made, someone in control.

"Thanks, yeah, I will, and thanks for the drink, and the clothes; I'll get them back to you."

"There's no rush," said the boatman.

Rory put the card in the tracksuit pocket, headed back down the gangway and walked on towards his cottage. The audience had gone; life had returned to normal.

Rory crossed the bridge over the canal dock and along the towpath, a couple of hundred yards to his front door. It was a large converted dwelling, dating back to the turn of the last century, tastefully modernised into three separate cottages; his was at the end. He took his key from his tracksuit pocket and opened the door into a small lounge. He walked through into the kitchen and put his jogging bottoms and T-shirt into the washing machine; his trainers went into the sink to soak. He looked at the clock; it was five o'clock; normally he would be thinking about cooking around this time, but he didn't feel hungry. He went to the fridge and took out a bottle of milk and poured a small quantity into the bottom of a mug along with a teabag. He switched on the electric kettle and waited for it to boil.

He could feel it; the adrenaline rush, then the withdrawal, like coming down from a fix. He knew the signs. It had been like this on every mission; Northern Ireland, Iraq, it was just the same. Personality profiles of SAS soldiers put them in the same category as psychopaths; except they were the good guys. He walked back to the lounge and lay on the sofa.

Within minutes, he was asleep. His mind returned to the firing line; he and his best buddy, Lennie 'The Loon' Arthur. It was so vivid, like watching a movie. The action replayed before his eyes, the barren landscape of the Iraqi desert, the jeep heading back after another successful mission. The rest of the platoon had been air-evacuated back to base; it was just the two of them, dressed in local garb. He was sitting next to Lennie, it was his turn to drive, they were twenty miles from the Saudi border and safety.

Lennie, as his nickname suggested was 'total bonkers' according to all his buddies, but great to be around; always the joker, anything for a laugh. Even driving he would take almighty risks, like cornering fast to see if he could get the jeep on two wheels without it tipping over. Occasionally, Lennie would go too far but everybody excused him. "That's just Lennie," they would say.

Rory didn't know whether he or Lennie heard it first; he couldn't remember. At the later inquest, he was unable to recall the exact sequence of events. There was just sort of a hissing sound and then everything was upside down. He must have blacked out for a few moments. He had no recollection of what had happened, nothing. He just remembered picking himself up off the desert track and seeing the jeep turned on its top, the wheels still revolving as if crazily seeking some traction to drive it forward. He got up and tried to run towards it, but his right leg refused to obey. He dragged himself closer and then there was an explosion as the petrol tank blew, igniting the box of ammunition on the back seat.

Rory shielded himself from the blast as bits of metal hurled through the air; a three-inch shard embedded itself in his arm. He never felt it. He moved closer to the wreck; there was little left. Lennie had been driving and could not have escaped. A roadside bomb, he thought at the time. Rory had been blown clear. Such is the luck of war, totally random. He looked at the charred remains of his buddy at the side of the road and he threw up. He was conditioned to put any emotion out of his mind, but this. He needed to get back to base. "Focus," he ordered himself. He started walking south.

The rest of the squad had landed several hours earlier. They reported Rory and Lennie as overdue which prompted a search and rescue helicopter. It was over three hours before Rory was eventually spotted and picked up, dehydrated and with a broken right ankle, the shard of metal was still embedded in his arm. The pain unimaginable, but he'd managed to block it out as he had been trained to do. He spent a week in a field-hospital recovering, but the hardest part was writing the letter to Lennie's wife, Helen. It wasn't until the inquest that he discovered it had been friendly-fire from an American F16.

Rory woke with a start, jolted by the memory, temporarily disorientated. Then he was back, compos mentis, still on his sofa. These were the demons that returned most nights since the incident on the rig.

The borrowed tracksuit was damp with sweat. He got up slowly and went back into the kitchen and re-boiled the kettle to complete his tea-making. Sitting at the small table, where he would have his breakfast, he reflected on the events of the afternoon as he sipped his beverage. There was something he needed to do. Luckily, he hadn't taken his mobile phone with him on his jog and he retrieved it from one of the kitchen drawers. He looked up a number, then dialled.

"Hi, Worcester Royal...? I want to check on a patient brought in this afternoon. Kyle somebody...he fell in the river. Thank you."

Eventually, someone confirmed that the boy was recovering well; he was out of any danger. Rory felt good about that.

The following morning, he was up at six and back on the towpath for another run, this time down river; he didn't want to face the scene of yesterday's drama. He'd not slept well; his adrenaline levels were still high from the exertion of saving the boy. It was just like returning from an op all those years ago. His trainers had dried overnight but still bore the stain from the river mud. He'd washed the tracksuit borrowed from Alistair, the boatman and, on returning from his run, picked up the business card from the kitchen worktop. He rang the mobile number.

"Hi, is that Alistair? It's Rory, from yesterday… Yes, fine thanks. I can drop the tracksuit back if you're about this morning… Yeah, sure thing, about nine-thirty…? Ok, see you then."

After managing to eat some breakfast, Rory felt better. Just before nine-thirty, he made his way over the bridge that traversed the canal, and along the riverside for his appointment with the boatman. Alistair had seen him coming and was on the stern-deck awaiting his arrival. He beckoned Rory on board.

"Rory, great to see you," he greeted him warmly. "Come on through," and they went down the steps into the cramped living quarters. Rory stopped momentarily, noticing they were not alone.

"Rory, this is Natalie, my personal assistant. Natalie, this is Rory, the man I was telling you about who saved the little boy yesterday."

She held out her hand to Rory. "Pleased to meet you, a hero I think," she said in an accent, clearly not local.

"Pleased to meet you too, but I'm no hero," he replied.

He looked at the woman, late-twenties to early thirties, black hair, high cheekbones, slim with striking blue eyes. Not English; probably Eastern European, from the Ukraine, the Baltic States or possibly Poland, he thought. She was smartly dressed, wearing a white blouse and a dark blue skirt which looked like it was part of a business suit, minus the jacket on this warm morning.

"Natalie's been helping tidy up some detail on a recent contract we're in the process of negotiating, but we've just about finished." Alistair turned to his assistant. "Thanks for coming over, let me know if you've got any questions?"

"Yes, of course," she said, "I'll see you back at the office…"

She picked up her briefcase from the top of the fold-down table and took her car keys from her handbag. As she was walking down the gangplank, Alistair called after her. "Just got one or two things to catch up on here… I'll be in around lunchtime."

She turned and acknowledged him. "Ok, see you then."

Rory watched as she got into a white Audi TT, parked just off the bridleway where he was jogging the previous day. She started it up and roared away.

"Sorry about that," said Alistair. "Needed a quick catch-up with Natalie. I often have meetings here. It's good to get away from the office sometimes, helps me to think. Unfortunately, I do need to go in this afternoon… Friday's always hectic… Here, have a seat," he said, and ushered Rory opposite him onto the wooden bench which went around the stern of the boat; they were separated by a small table.

"Coffee?" asked Alistair.

"Yeah, cheers," replied Rory, and Alistair moved along the boat to a small galley area and boiled a kettle.

"So how are you feeling today? No ill effects I hope," came a shout from his host.

"Fine, no problem, thanks," called back Rory.

Rory looked around; money had been invested in the craft; it appeared to have everything one would need, a real home from home. Alistair returned with two mugs of coffee and placed them on the table then returned with a plastic carton of milk and a sugar bowl.

"Help yourself."

Rory poured a measure of milk into the coffee.

Alistair left again and went to the front of the boat where there were various switches and dials and a large steering wheel. He opened a cupboard to the right of the control panel and returned with a laptop.

Rory was intrigued as he watched the man open his laptop and navigate the keys. He took a sip of coffee.

"Have you worked internationally at all?" asked the boatman.

Rory considered his answer. "Depends what you mean…

not security work, not directly."

"No, I couldn't see anything on your profile," replied Alistair.

Rory looked at him somewhat perplexed. "What do you mean... profile?"

"Ok, cards on the table," said the boatman. He looked up from his laptop and opened a piece of paper lying next to it, then engaged Rory with eye contact. "I've done a few checks..." He read from the note. "Twelve years Petronix, on one of the rigs I believe... Before that, worked for Guardian Securities in London; seven years' army service, awarded Military Medal 1991, little information on army career which makes me think probably SAS, Special Forces. Degree in Engineering."

Rory looked at him in disbelief, and some concern. "Hmm, you are well informed. Where did you get all that from?"

"Oh, I have my sources... It was necessary; as I said yesterday, I'm looking for someone special and I must say your bravery with that young lad yesterday put you in that category. Then, when you said you worked in security, I thought straight away you could be the guy I am looking for, which is why I did the checks."

Rory wasn't sure about the intrusion, but let it pass.

Alistair turned his laptop so Rory could see. It was opened at a website, 'AB Engineering Ltd', nothing flashy, unpretentious even, just an information store really. 'Contact us', 'products', that sort of thing.

"This is my business."

Rory turned his gaze from the man and looked at the screen.

"I set it up around twenty years ago. I was an engineer with GMI, but they lost a big Government contract to the French. All a bit political at the time; so, I set up on my own. The paradox is, they're one of my major customers."

Rory was familiar with Global Metal Industries, the Worcestershire based company specialising, among other things in rocketry and guided missile systems. They used to supply some of the kit he used in his army days.

"What sort of things do you make?" asked Rory.

"Specialist orders, bespoke, mostly Government contracts, which is why I need someone to look after security. The firm I currently use is always swapping people about. I don't know who I'm getting from one job to the next, which is a bit of a worry. I also need someone I know I can trust. As I'm sure you know, the M.O.D. are pretty exacting in their terms and conditions when it comes to security."

Rory was still looking at the website but had heard the reply.

"Ok, I'm interested," said Rory. "How do you want to do this?"

"Come over to the house on Sunday. You can meet some of the team, see what we do. That'll give me a couple of days to set things up."

"Yeah, ok," said Rory. "Where's the house?"

"Near Blackwell, here's the address and directions; I've written it down for you. It's pretty easy to find," said Alistair and he pulled a piece of paper from his pocket and handed it to Rory.

"Have you got a Sat-Nav?"

"No," said Rory, "but it's ok I'll find it."

"Just a minute," he said and went back inside the boat and returned a moment later carrying an A-Z Road Map. He opened the relevant page and detailed the journey.

"Yeah, I'll find it," Rory repeated. "But why international?"

"International?" said Alistair for a moment losing his thread.

"You asked if I'd worked internationally."

"Oh... yes... I did. I'll tell you more on Sunday," he added.

Chapter Two

Two days later, on a rainy Sunday morning, Rory set off for his meeting with AB Engineering. His transport of choice was a three-year-old Toyota MR2, sportier than his previous vehicle, but better on petrol, provided he didn't floor it. He'd sold his 4x4 when he moved down to the Midlands; there was little need for a large car having left the rugged terrain around Aberdeen, and without two boys to ferry about.

He checked his directions, less than twenty miles; his windscreen wipers were keeping his visibility clear. Although he'd never been there, he knew of Blackwell, a very prosperous area south of Birmingham, at the top of the Lickey Hills. Forty minutes later he was turning off the main road onto a long tree-lined avenue with large properties on either side. He checked his note, the house at the end.

In keeping with properties in the surrounding area, it was a 'nice' house, set back off the road with a tarmac drive and guarded by two large wrought-iron gates. The property was surrounded by a ten-foot-high hedge which, on closer inspection, camouflaged some serious fencing with cameras at the entrance, recording the visitor's every move. Rory reached the gate and spoke into an intercom built into a stone pillar, level with the driver's window. A woman's voice answered.

"What name is it?"

"Rory Calderwood."

The gates slowly opened. Rory negotiated the Toyota down the narrow open drive and parked outside the front of the house. The large garden was lawned with flower beds on either side, shrubs in full bloom. Hydrangeas dipped their branches, bowed by the weight of the water-filled flowers, forming a guard of honour to the arriving guests.

There were four other cars parked close to the entrance; a Jaguar, two top-of-the-range BMWs and, what looked like,

Natalie's Audi. Rory went up to the heavy wooden doors but before he reached it, one of them opened and Alistair stepped out. He looked different in smart casual attire, a salmon-coloured shirt and brown chinos. Two golden retrievers scurried by him and ran up to Rory who stroked them in turn. Seemingly satisfied that the visitor posed no threat, the dogs ran off around the other side of the building.

"Come in Rory. You found us ok?"

"Yeah, no problem," replied Rory "Be glad to see the back of this rain, though."

"Yes, it's unrelenting," said Alistair, and led Rory into the house.

It was a reasonably modern property, built in the 70s he learned later, but extensively customised by Alistair. With five bedrooms, the interior was as impressive as the exterior. The entrance hall was large and boasted a fine tapestry to the left where the stairs led to the first floor.

"We're in here," said Alistair, pointing at a door to the right of the hallway. Rory followed him into a spacious room set out as a modern office. Alistair was giving him a commentary. "I tend to use this place for more sensitive meetings, or if I don't want to be disturbed; it can get a bit hectic at the works."

There was a meeting table in the middle; to the left was a large desk with two computer terminals, an office-style printer, telephone and fax machine. Opposite the door, on the other side of the room, was a picture window which looked out over lush lawns; Rory spotted one of the dogs chasing something.

"Probably a rabbit, we get dozens around here," said Alistair, noticing Rory's interest.

There were two flat-screen TVs on the wall to the right, both turned off. He noticed facilities for conference calls linked to a computer under the table. There was a projector pointing towards a screen against the opposite wall; the company logo was projected onto it.

Three other men were sat at the table with open notepads.

Around them were empty coffee cups and the remainder of a plate of biscuits indicating that they had been there for some time. Crumbs were scattered around the plate.

"Take a seat and I'll introduce you to the team. I'll just go and rustle up some more coffee," he said before shouting something towards the next room which Rory assumed was the kitchen.

Rory took the nearest seat and nodded at the other men who returned the greeting. He wasn't comfortable in this environment. Team meetings at the rig were always a chore; he much preferred to be out there doing the business rather than talking about it, but he wasn't nervous; they had invited him and he had nothing to prove.

The group were clearly weighing him up and he suddenly felt under-dressed in jeans, open-necked shirt and trainers. The appropriate dress code was smart-casual judging by the attire of the rest of the group. At least he had chosen to shave which he had sort of regretted; he was getting quite used to the rugged look.

Alistair returned to his seat at the top of the table and made the introductions.

"Rory, this is Steve Lillington, CEO. He was with me when we started; I've known Steve since university." The CEO smiled and nodded in Rory's direction.

"Then we have Marcus Davies, my Finance Director. Marcus has been with us for around twelve years?"

"Thirteen, next month," replied Marcus with an air of pride. He looked the part with his glasses and slicked back hair. He was the only one wearing a tie, Rory noticed.

"And this is Ed Stevens, Technical Director. Ed's been with us for, what…five years… that right, Ed?"

"Yeah, give or take a month," said the technical director.

"I poached him from GMI. He was an apprentice when I worked there but we had the same vision," continued Alistair.

Rory looked at him. A younger man, but prematurely

balding, mid-thirties probably, with a geekish appearance. He reminded Rory of his science teacher at grammar school. He looked at his team, then at Rory.

Alistair continued; "This is my executive committee; oh, except Duncan Wyatt, he's the Sales Director. He would normally be here but he's away in Vienna with a Government trade mission. Between us, we make all the big decisions affecting the company. I've asked them to come here to meet you and give them the opportunity to... how can I put this? Confirm my view that you would be an asset to the business. This is how we've made all our senior appointments and it has served us well. Most of the staff have been with us for over ten years; many since we first set up the business."

Introductions over, there was a knock on the door and Rory was surprised to see a familiar face walk in with a tray of coffee. "You remember Natalie, Rory?"

"Of course, yes, hello," he said and watched her walk across to the table and put the tray down in the middle. She looked at Rory. "Hello," she replied matter-of-factly, rather than any attempt at courtesy.

The other men also seemed to be engrossed in her presence. She was dressed in a smart short dark skirt, white shirt, open at the neck; her dark hair immaculately tied back, business-like, with heavy eye makeup. She reminded Rory of a younger Sophia Loren from the films of the sixties he used to watch as a child with his mother. She sat opposite Rory next to Alistair and opened a large notepad in front of her. There was a move towards the coffee jug and the guests poured cups in turn.

"Sugar?" asked Alistair, passing the bowl towards Rory. "No, you don't do you?" he added quickly, remembering his taste on the boat. Attention to detail thought Rory.

Rory's knack of weighing-up people had never left him; something he'd learned in his army days and something that had kept him alive more than once.

"Right," said Alistair, bringing everyone to attention. He

picked up a remote control from the table and aimed it at the projector and the logo was replaced with a picture of a factory.

"I'm just going to take Rory through our set-up and show him some of our products to give him a better idea of what we do," he said and then turned to Rory. "This is the presentation we give to potential clients," he added, then he switched his attention to the slideshow.

"This is the factory; although we don't think of it as a factory in the traditional sense. It's not your typical manufacturing outlet."

From the outside, it looked like any other industrial unit, anonymous-looking, the type you see in business parks up and down the country, but larger. With the surrounding walls and razor wire, it resembled a prison. No huge garish sign, just a small 'AB Engineering Ltd' in white lettering at the entrance which was controlled by double barriers. There was a turnstile entrance for pedestrians to the right of the vehicle entrance. A service road ran around the side. To the right of the entrance was a small building. Cameras were positioned at regular intervals.

"As you will notice, security is paramount," said Alistair.

"What's that building to the right of the barriers?" asked Rory.

"The security centre... there's a staff of five based there that manages the perimeter and internal security. They control all incoming and outgoing traffic, vehicles and people. Don't worry, that's not how we see your remit," replied Alistair. "But if you have any recommendations we would, of course, be interested."

"How many staff do you have?" asked Rory.

"In total? Fifty-three in production, including research and development, twelve admin, plus the security team and directorate. Then, every year we take on four engineering apprentices and put them through college. It's a tight operation, highly skilled; small precision tooling is our speciality. This is an example."

Alistair continued the PowerPoint slideshow and described the products lines. To the untrained eye, they wouldn't mean a great deal but with Rory's engineering and military background he knew what the various components were. There were parts for rockets, guided missiles, sights for tanks; all of which Rory recognised.

"I am sure you are familiar with some of these products," said Alistair.

"You could say that," replied Rory with a smile. "Had no idea they came from an industrial unit in Birmingham."

"That's the way we like it," said Alistair.

Rory was assessing those around him and was particularly intrigued by the role of Natalie. It hadn't been explained, but she was sitting next to the Chairman and appeared to have been accepted by the rest of the group as part of the team.

The presentation concluded with pictures of the large work area which, as Alistair had said, looked more like a laboratory. Workers wore white coats or smart beige-coloured 'AB Engineering' uniforms rather than the normal greasy overalls. The manufacturing was split into various pods which Alistair explained was for different projects. There were no close-ups of the machines, but the use of robotics was visible.

"I won't cover our work-in-progress and new innovations for now... not for a PowerPoint presentation," he said, and the gathering smiled knowingly.

"Any questions at this stage?" asked Alistair as the last slide left the screen and was replaced by a black square. The projector was switched off.

"No," said Rory. "It looks impressive."

"Yes, we're proud of what we've achieved and, as you might expect, we're very protective about our business... which brings us back to the question of security. I suggest we break for some food and we can discuss our requirements over a sandwich."

The group dispersed. Rory decided to use the opportunity to take a bathroom break.

"There's a toilet over there," said Alistair pointing to a door on the other side of the hallway opposite the office.

A few minutes later another woman appeared with a hostess trolley laden with sandwiches, nibbles and some bottles of orange juice and glasses. "Ah, Dorothy, thank you. This is my housekeeper, I don't know what I would do without her," said Alistair to Rory.

"Will there be anything else, Mr B?" asked Dorothy, in the most extreme West Midlands' accent. Rory had difficulty in understanding her but Alistair was obviously tuned to the sounds and dismissed her from her duties.

"No, that's fine Dorothy. I'll see you tomorrow," he said as she returned to the kitchen.

"Been a godsend, you know," he said turning to Rory. "Doreen, my wife, and I tend to live separate lives. She's got the house in the Cotswolds and spends most of her time down there with her horsey crowd. Can't stand them myself," he said, dropping into a Birmingham twang momentarily. That answered one question Rory had pondered but hadn't asked.

He ushered Rory towards the group who were consuming sandwiches.

"Ah, Natalie, let me introduce you properly. You didn't have much chance on the boat," he said to the enigmatic PA. She put down a vol-au-vent and looked at Rory.

"Natalie has been with us for about... six months, isn't it?"

"Yes, it is just over six months," she confirmed in her Eastern European accent.

"She is, if I can use an engineering term, a cog in the wheel of AB Engineering... fixes things," Alistair looked at Natalie who returned the glance but not with any warmth. She merely acknowledged the remark as any business colleague might do. "Met her at a trade fair in Tallinn. She is, or should I say was, an international lawyer. Among other things, she prepares all my contracts for me and we'll sue the backside off anyone who infringes our designs."

She smiled and looked at Rory; this time with more emotion.

"Pleased to meet you again," said Rory.

"We have a lot of interesting work for you," she said, picking up a glass of mineral water and taking a sip without taking her eyes off Rory. The word "we" was interesting.

"That's good," said Rory, still not quite sure of her actual position in the company; it was clear she did wield a certain amount of power.

"I was trying to place your accent," he said. "Eastern European, Baltic States, possibly?"

"Very good, I'm impressed... Estonia, actually. I was born in Pärnu." Rory was none the wiser. "It's a small town in the south, a tourist centre, lovely shops and beaches," she clarified, doing a reasonable travelogue.

"Sounds nice," said Rory.

"It is," she replied.

There was something about Natalie that didn't quite compute. She was attractive and clearly very smart; with her background, what was she doing working for a small firm in Birmingham and not some multi-national conglomerate earning mega-bucks? Rhetorical questions that had Rory pondering before Alistair broke the slightly uneasy silence. "Come and meet Ed. Probably more in your line with your engineering background," and they approached the technical director.

"Ed is a key member of the team. I wouldn't swap him for anyone. Many of the products are his designs. We wouldn't be where we are without him." Ed looked down modestly; Alistair continued his eulogy. "He's also in overall charge of production, although he does have a good team around him."

In no time, Rory struck an affinity with Ed Stevens. He was his type of man; no pretentions, straight to the point, very clever and not in the least bit geekish as Rory's initial impression of him had been. While Alistair was in deep conversation with Natalie and the other executives, Rory gained more understanding of the technical side of the business from Ed. He was clearly proud of his work. "Some of the new prototypes are ground-breaking," he said.

Once Rory had spoken to each of the directors informally, Alistair called them back to the table.

"We would like to ask you a few questions if we may?" asked Alistair.

"Yeah, no problem," said Rory.

"Why did you leave Petronix?" asked Steve Lillington.

Rory thought for a moment. Instead of saying; "I got bashed over the head by a fucking rag-head," he settled on; "after twelve years offshore, it was time for a change." He didn't elaborate.

It took some time to extract any meaningful information from Rory. He wasn't being deliberately evasive, he just didn't do interviews. He would certainly not disclose any detail of his time in the army, despite being pressed by his inquisitors. His work after leaving the army proved more fruitful for them. He was at home talking about the security briefings he provided for some major clients. After about half an hour of vigorous probing by the directors, Alistair called the meeting to an end.

More coffee was offered, and Alistair led Rory into the spacious lounge, while Natalie disappeared into the kitchen. Despite her position in the company, she had no hesitation in accepting the coffee-making chore which again gave Rory food for thought.

"Do you mind waiting in here for a moment?" said Alistair. "Just want to have a chat with the guys."

"Yeah, ok," said Rory.

The lounge, in keeping with the rest of the house, was well-appointed with high-end, comfortable suites and furnishings. Rory didn't take much notice as he took a seat on a leather settee facing the large picture window. The dogs were sheltering from the rain under one of the trees, seemingly asleep.

After about ten minutes, Alistair returned with Ed, the technical director, followed by Natalie who was carrying a tray with a cafetiére and four cups. He sat on an armchair opposite Rory while Natalie poured the coffee before taking her place next to Alistair in an adjacent armchair. Ed sat on the sofa next to Rory, but without intruding on his personal space. The other directors had also left the boardroom and were mingling in the hallway collecting their jackets and belongings. It had stopped raining. They each waved and shouted "bye" to Rory through the open lounge door as they left; he acknowledged them with no theatrics.

Alistair looked at Rory with a very pleased, almost excited, expression.

"I've been sounding out the team and we're all agreed; we would like to offer you a job with us."

Rory nodded in approval. "Thanks."

"But I'm sure you will be keen to know exactly what we had in mind," continued Alistair.

"I did wonder," replied Rory.

"Before I go into details, let's discuss payment," Alistair said. "I'm offering a twelve-month rolling contract. I'll pay you what you were getting at Petronix plus ten percent. All expenses will be covered and there will be bonuses, depending on the company's performance. It will be equal to the director's bonus scheme and there will be various other perks." He did not elaborate. "You will not, however, appear on the payroll. We've got another small company which we use to fund some of our projects. What's the name again?" he looked at Natalie.

"Hedgeline Securities," she replied.

"That's right. This is all Natalie's idea, tax-efficient apparently… and more secure," Alistair said.

He looked at Natalie again and smiled. "You'll need to invoice them through your own company. I assume you do have one," he added, as an afterthought.

"Yes," Rory replied, still trying to work out the significance of the apparent tax-dodge. Although he had been salaried from Petronix, he'd never formally wound up the security company he used after he'd left the army. It hadn't traded for over twelve years and Rory would have some admin to sort out at some point. He wasn't good with paperwork.

"Excellent," said Alistair, "I need your involvement to be low key; only the team you have met today know of your true role. Are you ok with that?"

"Yeah, no problem," said Rory.

Alistair took a sip of his coffee. "If anyone asks, we'll say you're an engineering consultant or something. How does that sound... ok?"

"Sounds good to me," replied Rory.

"Oh, one other thing... you'll need to sign the Official Secrets Act," said Alistair.

"Yeah, I thought I might."

They shook hands. "Welcome on board," said Alistair.

"Now some details." He put down his cup and moved closer to Rory. "We're engaged in some work which could revolutionise modern warfare," he said. "For obvious reasons, I can't go into specifics but, in broad terms, we are talking about 'stealth technology'."

Rory looked up, "I know the concept."

"I'm sure you do," replied Alistair. He turned to the technical director. "Ed, do you want to explain a bit more?"

Ed took over. "As Alistair said, the technology is ground-breaking and would be of extreme interest not only to our competitors but to other governments and of course terrorist groups."

"What about the Americans?" asked Rory.

"The Americans are, as you might expect, at the front end of this technology but our design is much more effective... and cheaper," continued Ed animatedly. Alistair looked on proudly and smiled as if looking at a favoured child.

"The M.O.D. is testing a prototype as we speak," Ed added.

"So where do I fit in?" asked Rory.

Alistair looked at Ed then back at Rory. "First thing… I need you to do a risk assessment, you know, look at our operation, see where we're vulnerable, and make some recommendations. Not just the physical threat, hijacking, kidnap and so on; but internal stuff like IT systems," he clarified. "Our whole business is built on security; our clients demand it. We can't afford to be complacent. Technology transfer is my big worry."

Rory looked confused. "Technology transfer?"

"Industrial espionage," Alistair clarified.

"Yeah, ok, I can check your protocols and systems, but I'm not an IT expert... not in detail anyway," said Rory.

"No, I understand that, but you'll be able to see things... in the round, as they say. You will, I'm sure, know enough about where to look. You can bring in your own experts if necessary." Alistair looked at Natalie. "But you'd have to fund it yourself."

Rory nodded. "Yeah, ok, let's see how we go."

"We do have a pretty good set up. The M.O.D. have already done checks, but I can't afford to have any gaps. A fresh eye would be very welcome," said Alistair.

Rory looked at Alistair and nodded in agreement. "Yeah, ok."

"Any questions?" asked Alistair.

"When do you want me to start?"

"Soon as you can. Tomorrow?" replied Alistair.

"Yeah, that's ok by me," replied Rory.

"Drop by the house again at eight-thirty. I can go through everything in more detail and then I'll take you over to the works. I'll get one of the girls to draft a copy of the O.S.A. for you."

"I'll be here," replied Rory.

Alistair got up prompting similar moves from Ed and Natalie who looked at Rory and held out her hand. "Look forward to working with you," she said. It was a cold exchange. The suspicion appeared mutual.

Ed was far more effusive. "Drop by when you get over to the works. I'll give you a guided tour of the plant. You'll be fascinated."

"Will do," said Rory.

"There is just one other thing," said Alistair.

Rory looked at him as if waiting for the punch-line of a joke.

"Close protection. You said this is something you could provide."

"Yeah, I've done a bit in the past."

"Good," said Alistair.

Natalie opened the front door. "See you tomorrow," interrupted Ed, again shaking Rory's hand vigorously. Ed headed to one of the BMWs, leaving just the three of them in the entrance hallway.

Alistair continued. "I'll be making some trips abroad. Make sure your passport is up-to-date. I'll need you with me."

"Yeah, ok," said Rory.

As Rory walked out of the door he was almost knocked over by the dogs which had clearly awoken from their slumbers. They shook themselves spraying the immediate area with excess water.

"Get down, Jet!" shouted Alistair at one of the dogs who was trying to jump up at Rory.

The dog dutifully obeyed and skulked off with its companion like a naughty schoolboy suitably admonished.

"See you tomorrow," said Alistair, playing the perfect host waiting for Rory to reach the car before closing the front door. Rory started the Toyota and headed for the gate which opened slowly in front of him.

He had lots to think about.

Alistair watched the car pass through the gates and turned to Natalie. "Well, what do you think?"

"Excellent choice," said Natalie. "Very well qualified."

On the way back to his cottage, Rory stopped off at a small shopping mall to equip himself for his new venture. It was Sunday and families were out in force exploring the various emporia. He made a mental note of what he needed; some new 'business' clothes, certainly.

He found a suitable retailer and purchased three shirts, a couple of pairs of casual trousers and a pair of shoes more suited for the world he was about to join. He also realised his office equipment was lacking and he would need to restock. Priority was a new laptop; his old one was totally unsuitable for his new role. He would also need a printer, a decent internet connection and a smart-phone. A lengthy visit to a computer store was necessary; then he headed on back to Worcester.

There was a lot on his mind as he drove home. The risk assessment wasn't a problem; he'd done many for his security firm before he joined Petronix. The close protection would also be no challenge; it had been a while, but he was still fit, and he knew the drill.

He started mentally assessing the board members he'd met. All appeared competent with lengthy service and he couldn't envisage any security risk there. Alistair had a good team around him that he clearly trusted. His one question concerned Natalie; where did she fit in? He'd had the same feeling back on the rig when he first met Tariq Siddique; he'd done nothing about it and it nearly cost him his life. Maybe that was it, a warning bell. She seemed almost too good to be true; she would be on his radar.

It was early afternoon by the time Rory was easing the Toyota down the cinder track to the cottage. He parked up in a small service road at the back of the house and went inside. There was a musty smell where the rooms had been shut all day and he opened a few windows to let in some fresh air. He went upstairs to his bedroom to change into a pair of shorts and a tee shirt. He would go out for a run later. It took two journeys back to his car to unload his packages.

Task completed, Rory filled the kettle in the kitchen and prepared a mug for a brew. Yesterday's newspaper was still folded on the kitchen table. Rory had not got around to reading it. He made his tea, sat down and opened it.

For someone used to anonymity, the sight of the front page made him recoil in horror.

'Local hero sought', blazed the headline.

'Mystery man saves boy from river', was the sub-heading, with a passable and easily-recognisable picture from someone's smart-phone. There was a full account from the distraught mother who was appealing to the public to help her find the 'white knight' who had saved her young lad. *'I just want to say, "thank you"*, was the message in the narrative.

Rory was in a dilemma. Discretion was a prerequisite in his line of work and he had no idea what the implications would be. His new boss had witnessed the drama and would be well-aware of the possible media interest once the word had got out, so maybe that wasn't going to be an issue. There was nothing he could do about it; he would just ride it out.

Rory had a productive late afternoon and evening; his computer was now set up with everything he would need. He'd even managed to transfer his old files which included all his training notes; he thought they may come in useful. Going through them again had provided a valuable refresher. The whole project had given him a much-needed boost and he was feeling motivated for the first time in ages, certainly since he had left the rig.

Chapter Three

Monday morning, Rory was back on the road to meet Alistair at his Blackwell house. He had arranged to arrive by eight-thirty and, after a further briefing, they would travel to the works in Birmingham. He'd given a great deal of thought to his new role and he used the journey to rehearse some of the questions he had which would help his initial assessment.

The morning traffic was relentless but at least the rain had stopped, and it was reasonably bright, with high cloud. Rory had given himself plenty of time and arrived at eight fifteen. Alistair was waiting for him at the front door as the security gates opened and Rory pulled up outside the house. He picked up his new laptop from the passenger seat and got out.

"Better morning," said Alistair as the two retrievers raced passed him to greet the visitor. Rory patted them hesitantly and they ran off into the grounds to disturb the local rabbit population again.

"Come in, come in," said Alistair enthusiastically. "Dorothy, can you bring us two coffees please?" he shouted towards the kitchen.

"Right you are, Mr B," came the unmistakable tones of the housekeeper.

"We're in the office," he said, leading Rory into the boardroom where the meeting with the directors had taken place the previous day.

"I wanted to go through one or two things before we head over to the works. Once I get there it tends to be Bedlam and we won't have a lot of time to speak."

"Ok," said Rory.

They sat at the end of the table which was more conducive to discussion than sitting opposite each other. Rory appreciated that; here was someone not driven by power. He took the computer from the carry-case and opened it up on the desk in front of him.

"I need to take a few notes if that's ok," he said, seeing Alistair's interest.

"Of course, of course," said Alistair.

Dorothy came in carrying a tray with two mugs of coffee and a plate of Digestive biscuits.

"Thanks, Dorothy," said Alistair, as she placed them on the table, left the room and shut the door.

"Right. Now, where were we…? Ah yes," he said, answering his own question. "Thought I could give you some more background… and I expect you'll have some questions as well."

"Yes, one or two," said Rory.

"Well, why don't you kick off, then I can give you some background as we go along," said Alistair.

"Yeah, ok," said Rory and he picked up his mug and took a sip of his coffee. "I guess the big question is, where do you see the threats? Where do you think you might be vulnerable…? It'll give me somewhere to start."

Alistair put down his mug and thought through the question before answering.

"Well… a couple of weeks ago, I had a meeting with my usual contacts at the M.O.D. They're regular, nothing out of the ordinary, and I've always had a great relationship with them… as you know, they're our best customers… but for some reason, the meeting seemed different."

"In what way? said Rory.

"Normally, I meet up with one of their procurement guys, Major Cummings... well I say 'procurement' because he holds the budget, but he's also part of the strategic warfare committee so, as you can imagine, takes a very keen interest in the products we develop."

"I bet he does," said Rory, taking another mouthful of coffee.

"As I said, it was just a routine meeting as far as we were concerned. You know, updates, delivery times, that sort of thing... I had Ed with me, Ed Stevens." Rory nodded. He remembered the technical director. "He always comes to these briefings, he's got all the details."

He took another drink before continuing. "The Major usually has at least two technical guys with him, but this time there were two chaps we'd not met before... in civvies. He didn't introduce them, I heard the Major call one of them 'Julian'... They just said they had an interest in security and they bombarded us with all sorts of questions... What contingency arrangements did we have in case of an emergency? They wanted details of all my security protocols, too, the works."

"What did you tell them?" asked Rory.

"Everything they wanted to know, pretty much... After the two chaps left, the Major said there'd been a tip-off... a breach in security apparently, with one of their suppliers, but he wouldn't go into detail."

Rory considered this information.

"What do you think that was all about?" asked Alistair.

"Not sure," said Rory. "But there's obviously a problem somewhere."

"Do you think it's something we should be worried about?" said Alistair.

"From what you say, it looks like they've upped their threat level, probably based on some intelligence they've received, but without having access to their information, there's no way of knowing. I mean, we can't be sure if it is your company they're concerned about... But you're right to take precautions... I'll have a better idea when I've had a chance to look at the business in more detail... What about the other directors, are they aware that you're under scrutiny?"

"No, I've not said anything to them. Ed was there, but I've told him not to say anything."

"What about your assistant?" said Rory.

"Natalie?"

"Yeah," said Rory.

"No, I've not said anything to her either," said Alistair.

"Good," said Rory. "Best keep it that way."

Rory had a list of questions which Alistair answered, more detail about the business, other clients and interested parties which he answered. "So, going back to the question, where do you think you are vulnerable?"

Alistair thought before answering. "Since that meeting, I've been thinking a lot about the business... and that question. We've been dealing with the M.O.D for a long time. Much of the work has been sensitive stuff and there has been no problem at all."

"So, what could've changed?" asked Rory.

Again, Alistair was reflective. "That's the point, I can't think of anything... It could be the Hades Project, of course... Now that has really set the hares racing."

"The stealth one?"

"Yes, it's a real game-changer for us, both financially and technologically. The culmination of several years' work. It's streets ahead of anything else on the market and its potential is... well, the sky's the limit... That was another reason why I wanted to get someone from the outside to have a look at things."

Rory was fascinated by it, both from an engineering and a security perspective. "Yeah, I can see that... Look, I'm not expecting you to give me the fine print but, in general, what's the application?"

"Well, imagine your enemy being totally invisible... that about covers it; like a smokescreen, only better. The material is totally permeable to radar so instead of an object reflecting radio waves it absorbs them and makes the vehicle, aircraft, boat, whatever... invisible. That's why we called it Hades."

"Hades?" said Rory.

"Ha, yes, Hades. It's Greek... God of the Underworld, he was given a helmet of invisibility as a gift from the Cyclops... that's the connection."

"Hmm, I see," said Rory. "No wonder the M.O.D. were getting twitchy… I can think of a number of interested parties."

"Well, it's a fact, everybody and his dog would be after it if they knew it existed."

"How long do you think you will be able to keep the lid on it?" said Rory.

"Well, that's something I hope you can help with," said Alistair.

"Well, we can make sure your side is tight, but once the information leaves here, there's no way you can control things," said Rory.

"But surely the M.O.D. won't want its existence broadcast; it defeats the whole object if they're going to start sharing secrets," said Alistair.

"Yes, that's true, but, as I say, it's difficult to control once they get their hands on it; then, of course, the politics start getting in the way."

"Hmm," said Alistair. He knew Rory had a point.

"Going back to your team… they've been with you for a long time…"

Alistair was still pondering Rory's last point. "What…? Oh, yes."

"All except for your assistant," commented Rory.

"Yes, that's true... but Natalie's been such an important part of the team since she got here. As you've seen, we've been working closely together…"

Rory finished his coffee. "Tell me again how she got involved, how was she recruited? You mentioned a trade fair."

Alistair appeared to be recollecting the event. "Yes, we were in Tallinn, with several other companies from across the E.U. It's a regular exhibition, a shop-window, if you like, for defence contracts. We export to other E.U. countries and of course Saudi Arabia, they're important clients."

"You visit Saudi?"

"Yes, occasionally, and The Emirates, about once a

quarter... We supply some of the parts for their weapons guidance systems."

"I see, but going back to Natalie... Can you remember how you met? In what circumstances, specifically, I mean."

"Hmm, yes... she came to our stand if I remember rightly. She was chatting with Ed Stevens, and Duncan Wyatt, the Sales Director, the one you haven't met yet."

"So, she just appeared at the stand... out of the blue, no appointment," said Rory. Alistair was beginning to feel a little uncomfortable with the scrutiny. Rory could tell.

"Sorry, I do need to ask these questions."

"Yes, of course, it's ok. Well, she told us she'd finished university and had qualified as a lawyer. She said she was working in the city... Tallinn... and was looking for new opportunities... She was keen to work in the U.K."

"Then what happened?"

"Well, Duncan was very impressed and asked me to speak to her. I was visiting another stand when she first came over. Duncan asked her to come back, which she did. We'd been using a local firm of solicitors to do our legal stuff, but they didn't have any international trade experience, which of course is what Natalie specialises in."

"So, how come she was given a job offer?"

"She didn't get one at first. When we got back, I spoke to the other directors about the need for her expertise. Then, I invited her over to spend a month with us, expenses only."

"And she agreed to that?"

"Yes, she wanted the experience, she said," said Alistair.

"What about background checks?" said Rory.

"H.R. dealt with all that, quite thorough though... It has to be."

"So, Natalie was with you for a month, what happened during that time?"

"It was a revelation, I don't mind telling you. She spotted straight away our patents were vulnerable... and some of our contracts weren't worth the paper they were printed on."

"Hmm, that's interesting. So, you offered her a job?"

"Yes, her checks were fine, and being an E.U. national, there were no work permit issues. She's on a twelve-month rolling contract, the same as the one you've got."

"Ok, so on a day-to-day basis, what sort of access does she have?"

"Well, nothing of importance... I mean, she's got no access to any of the sensitive projects. There are areas of the plant that are off-limits to unauthorised personnel, I'll show you later... Only those people directly involved can get in. Everything's highly monitored... entry, exit, it's all swipe cards... state of the art kit... Look, I can see why you've taken a particular interest in Natalie, but she's been a breath of fresh air and certainly keeps us on our toes."

Rory took another sip of coffee.

"I'm sure she does... but it strikes me she just seems to be a bit too good to be true. Call it intuition if you like, but I'll keep an open mind. I need to do a lot more work. Thanks for the background."

Rory hesitated and then looked directly at Alistair. "Ok, just one final question about Natalie, which I do need to ask. Look, this is a bit sensitive but are you and she, you know, romantically linked in any way? Only you seemed pretty close on the boat."

"Ah, I see where this is going... the honey-pot angle?"

"Well, it's not a ridiculous idea," said Rory. Alistair seemed a little uncomfortable.

"No, I guess not... but no, nothing like that. She's been on my boat for a couple of weekends nothing heavy, I promise. I think one or two of the younger guys fancied their chances early on, but she gives them short shrift, I can tell you... She's got a fiancé in Tallinn, she told me, seems devoted to him. Speaks to him regularly."

This did nothing to allay Rory's concern.

"Thanks for that, it's been useful," said Rory.

"That's ok, it's what I'm paying you for... Of course, as you said, it might not be us... the breach of security, I mean. They just said one of their suppliers," said Alistair.

"Yeah, I guess," said Rory.

They continued talking for another half-hour or so and Rory made more notes of relevant information. The meeting had proved fruitful from both perspectives, Rory had gleaned a great deal of information that would help him in his role as security adviser. For Alistair, he had found someone with whom he could share information, which was not always possible given the sensitivities; it was a question of trust. He had formed a good impression of Rory and valued his opinions.

Alistair stood up. "Right, we better make a move... We'll go in my car. We won't be late this afternoon. I like to get away well before the rush-hour starts. I can do pretty much everything from here anyway."

Rory made use of the facilities before joining Alistair in the hallway. Dorothy was clearing the cups from the boardroom. "We're off now, Dorothy. Be back this afternoon sometime."

"Right you are Mr B," said Dorothy, and she waited by the front door as the two men went to his Jaguar. Alistair opened the door and Rory got in.

As they left the property, Rory could see Dorothy calling the dogs in and them scampering back into the house.

It was ten-thirty and the traffic flowed freely as the pair continued their discussions; Alistair was giving a running commentary of the journey, one which he could do with his eyes closed. Rory was also forming an impression of his new employer. He liked his enthusiasm, he could see why he made a good leader; people would be inspired by his drive, but with that level of enthusiasm comes naivety and that was a real weakness.

As the urban sprawl of Birmingham enveloped them, progress slowed. "We're based in Washwood Heath," said

Alistair, which Rory already knew. The travelogue continued. "We set up there because the area's got a lot of history in engineering," said Alistair. "One of the major employers was the railway works; Metro-Cammel owned it, but it closed in 2005. Then there were several munitions factories during both world wars. We're carrying on that tradition."

As they entered the suburb, the description did not really live up to the billing. It was not the thriving enterprise zone that Rory had envisioned; in fact, it looked run-down. There were lots of Asian shops and premises, Arabic script ran side-by-side with English. Rory looked at the scene and took it in, parts of it reminded of his time in Iraq. Unpleasant flashbacks coursed through his mind. His brief reflection was abruptly halted.

"We're here," said Alistair.

Rory looked at the perimeter wall with the razor wire running the length; nothing else was visible. It was as austere as he had imagined it from Alistair's earlier briefing. There was the small sign saying, "AB Engineering Ltd" on a board over the top; in front of them a barrier. To the right was the security centre and a guard came out to inspect Alistair's pass. The barrier raised.

"We have gates that close at night and a security guard on site with dogs," said Alistair pointing to two formidable-looking sliding doors either side of the entrance.

Immediately ahead of them was a parking area with bays neatly mapped out and numbered. The last one was number seventy-five. "Plenty of spaces," said Alistair, again seeing Rory's interest.

"How do the staff get in and out?" said Rory. "It must take ages getting through the gates."

"The gates are opened at seven-thirty until eight to allow staff entry, and again at four-thirty until five... They still have to show their passes," Alistair quickly added, in case this was considered as a possible security weakness.

"This is the main admin block," said Alistair looking at the brick building immediately ahead. Alistair parked in the bay next to the entrance. The word 'Chairman' was stencilled across it. Further spaces ran the exterior of the building all depicting ownership; CEO, Technical Director, and so on. They seemed to be in order of seniority, which gave Rory more information on the culture of the organisation. Everyone knew their place and who was the boss.

Immediately through the entrance doors was a reception area attended by an attractive young lady of Asian origin. Alistair approached her. "Any post, Jasmine?"

The girl presented him with a bundle of envelopes. "Any messages?"

"Just two, Mr Bailey," said Jasmine whose attention was suddenly drawn to Rory's presence.

"Can you sign Rory in for me, please?" said Alistair and Jasmine presented Rory with a register.

"Name, company and car registration," she said in the most incongruous broad West Midlands accent. She looked at him and fluttered her eyes.

Rory ignored the flirting and completed the details as requested.

"Just until we get you a pass sorted," said Alistair. "I've spoken to H.R. you should get one later."

The reception area was small but tidy and not particularly welcoming. There were three doors opposite the main entrance; two were male and female toilets, the middle one was more substantial and to the right of it was a small keypad. Alistair approached it and punched in four numbers.

There was a click and Alistair pushed the door. There was an air-lock, just a two-metre corridor, then another door, again security protected. Alistair held up a plastic pass to a sensor pad at eye level; another click.

As Alistair walked through the door, various people approached him wanting advice or approval. He was soon surrounded as if he were a pop star outside a concert hall pursued by autograph hunters, all wanting his attention. He politely asked them to give him ten minutes and they dispersed to their various 'pods'. Rory again took an interest in this behaviour and thought back to his time on the rig. He would have just told them to fuck off.

Rory looked around. It was a large space, open plan, which appeared to be a hive of activity. It was split into work areas and there was a buzz from the myriad of conversations that were taking place simultaneously. He recognised a couple of the directors from Sunday's meeting. The CEO was chatting to a couple of technicians in white overalls, in what looked to be a break-out area. Rory made a mental note of everything that was going on. It was something he had been conditioned to do.

"This is the nerve centre," said Alistair. "All the administration's in here, sales, procurement, health and safety, H.R... I'll get someone to show you around and make some introductions later."

At the end of the administration area, there were two doors. One was labelled, 'Conference Room', the other, 'Chairman'.

Rory followed Alistair into his office. It was a decent size but functional. There was one picture on the wall behind his desk of an anonymous seascape, otherwise, it was just the accoutrements of a working executive - desk, telephone, computer monitor and smaller table in the corner with four seats.

"Make yourself comfortable," said Alistair, nodding towards the table. Rory complied and started opening his laptop. Alistair put the bundle of letters down on his desk and picked up the phone. "Two coffees please," he said as the call was picked up.

Alistair took off his jacket and hung it on a rail in a small wardrobe in the corner.

"Ok," he said, as he approached Rory and sat opposite him. "I thought I could give you a bit more detail, on-site as it were... I'll ask Ed to join us in a minute, and he'll take you around the production area... Any questions so far?"

"No, not really... Where will you want me to work?"

"I've been thinking about that," Alistair replied. "I don't want you in here, in the pods; it's too open, so I've asked Ed to sort you out an office in the production area, next to him. It's nothing special, used to be a storeroom, but I had it kitted out as a spare work area a few weeks ago; we're getting a bit short of office space; but it should be ok… By the way, I've not broadcast your arrival, so you may get some strange looks; I just said that you're a specialist come to help on one of the projects."

"Ok, right, that's fine," said Rory.

There was a knock on the door and another young lady of mixed-race descent entered. She had long black hair and was wearing a smart tee-shirt and a short skirt. Rory noticed a tattoo of a swallow on her left shoulder.

"This is Madeline," said Alistair. "Looks after my expenses, so I have to keep in her good books."

"This is Rory," said Alistair, as Madeline placed the tray and two coffees on the table in front of them.

"Hello," said Rory.

"Hello," she replied with just the briefest of eye contact, then left the two men to their discussions.

"So, what do you think?" said Alistair, clearly proud of his enterprise.

"Impressive," said Rory, realising that Alistair would respond well to positive strokes. He was not sure how he would react to anything critical.

"Thanks," said Alistair. "And the entry procedures?"

"Looks fine," said Rory.

"That's good… as I said, the M.O.D. inspectors were happy," he said. "They did give us some advice."

"I'm sure they did," said Rory.

"Come on, let me take you to see Ed and he'll show you your base," said Alistair, after the pair had finished their drinks.

Alistair got up and Rory followed him out of his office, down the corridor and through the front door. The external area of the works was another hive of activity. Fork-lift trucks were crisscrossing the yard with pallets of items. It was a windy day and bits of dust and debris flew about as they walked. There were still a few puddles from the previous day's rain. Alistair continued to give Rory a running commentary on the works as they went passed the stores towards a new building that was set back from the main administration block, at the rear of the complex.

He went up to the entrance door. A sign read; "Out of bounds to unauthorised personnel".

Alistair used a swipe card and there was the usual 'click' as the door opened.

The hub-bub of the yard was replaced by a quiet calm as they entered an airlock and another security entrance which Alistair accessed via a keypad. There was a slight hum as if coming from a generator. The door opened and the sight in front of him almost took Rory's breath away.

"Now this looks interesting," was all he could say, as he scanned the area. It was much larger than it appeared from the outside, probably the size of a large aircraft hangar, split into various sections where workers in their ABE overalls were tending to machines, or dials, or sat at computers. Some were wearing protective glasses. There was one section where robots were constructing items which were rolling off assembly lines. Each item was being examined by staff who looked like laboratory assistants. There was computer equipment everywhere.

There wasn't the clattering and bangs you would normally expect in a heavy industrial factory; it was noisy, but levels appeared more ambient; not something that would require ear-defenders. Rory took it all in.

"Let me take you to see Ed and he can take over; I need to get on. I'll see you about four and we can head back before the rush."

"Ok," said Rory.

Ed was just exiting one of the production areas with a clipboard in his hand.

"Ed," Alistair shouted as he was about to go into another closed area.

He looked around. "Oh, hi Alistair… Rory. Good to see you again."

"You too," said Rory shaking his hand.

"Can you look after Rory for me? I need to get back," said Alistair.

"Yeah, course… come on, Rory, I'll show you your office."

"I'll see you at four," shouted Alistair to Rory and he left to return to his office in the admin block.

Rory looked at Ed. "A great set-up you have here," he said, still trying to take everything in.

"Thanks, yes, we're really proud of what we've achieved," said Ed. "Follow me," and he started walking to the far end of the factory floor.

Rory followed but was quickly left behind by the fast-walking Ed, fascinated by what was going on around him. There were two rooms side-by-side and Ed was waiting for Rory as he climbed a short flight of wooden stairs to a mezzanine area containing two offices.

"This one's yours," said Ed. "It's not very grand, but it has a phone and internet, so it should do you."

Ed opened the door and stepped to one side so Rory could enter.

"Yeah, it's fine, thanks," said Rory as he walked around the small desk and put down his laptop.

"Would you like a coffee? There's a small kitchen next door with a sink and kettle. I'll fix you up with a mug."

"Cheers," said Rory, and he followed Ed to the kitchen. It was as described, a sink, draining-board, kettle, fridge and a table which had a jar of coffee and a box of teabags. There was spilt sugar on the table top which had Ed tutting. "I do wish people would tidy up after themselves," he said, with an air of frustration. He produced a cloth from under the sink, poured some water on it and squeezed out the excess moisture. He proceeded to clean up the offending particles.

After a couple of minutes, Ed had made the coffee and they were back in Rory's new office.

"So, how do you plan to start your investigation?" said Ed.

"I've already made a start, but I wanted to ask you a few questions if you have a minute."

"Sure, fire away."

"Well, you know this place better than anyone... where would you say you are vulnerable?"

"That's difficult to say... we run a pretty tight ship."

"Yes, but that can lead to complacency, and that breeds vulnerability."

"True," said Ed.

"Ok, let's see if I can help..." said Rory. "In my experience, problem areas generally fall into three categories, people, systems and site."

"Makes sense," said Ed, looking pensive as he drank his coffee.

"The big one is the people; poor recruitment practices, employees with grudges, regular absences, financial problems, that sort of thing. Then we have lax management; most security breaches come from this source... Can you think of anyone who might fit this description?"

"Not off the top of my head," said Ed. "But I'll give it some thought."

"What about systems?"

"Our protocols are top-notch; we've had a lot of advice from the M.O.D... We've got independent servers with their own firewalls. As it stands it's pretty impregnable. I do work closely with our IT people."

"That's good news, although I have to say, I'm by no means an expert," said Rory.

"Well, it comes with the territory if you're dealing with

Government contracts. We use similar protocols."

Rory was taking all this in and watching Ed for any unease in his reactions.

"That leaves, 'site'," said Rory. "Who else has access to the production areas... apart from the production workers?"

"Only Alistair... all the production team have their own badges and access codes... Which reminds me, I've got yours in my office. Julie from H.R. brought them over earlier."

"Cheers," said Rory. He paused for a moment. "What about Natalie? Does she have access here?"

"Good God, no," said Ed, who seemed affronted at the suggestion. "Nor any of the other directors... oh, except Steve Lillington, of course."

"The CEO?" said Rory.

"Yes," confirmed Ed.

They continued talking for another half an hour before Ed excused himself to 'get on with some work'.

Rory started setting his office up to suit his needs and opened his laptop. A couple of minutes later, Ed returned with a set of keys for the office and Rory's security badge. He gave him the access codes to the production area. "Don't write them down anywhere," said Ed as he left and started to laugh.

He stopped at the entrance. "I'll show you the research centre at lunchtime and introduce you to the boffins. Oh, and Des Greenhalgh, the production manager, he'll be back this afternoon; he's out this morning over in Kidderminster."

"Cheers," said Rory.

"About twelve-thirty, ok?" said Ed and left Rory to his report.

At the appointed time, Ed returned; Rory was hunched over his laptop making notes.

"If you're ready, we'll grab a bite to eat and I can show you the research centre.," he said poking his head around the door.

Rory looked up, closed his laptop and left the office. He made a point of locking the door.

The pair walked out of the production area, through the air-lock and out into the fresh air. Rory squinted as the hazy sunshine replaced the artificial light of the factory.

"The research centre's just over here," said Ed, and Rory followed him to another block, smaller than the production area and set back against the boundary wall. Puddles dotted the ground and they both had to take evasive action to prevent their shoes from getting wet.

"What's on the other side of this place?" said Rory.

"What, over the wall?" said Ed.

"Yeah," said Rory.

"Nothing… it's a long drop to a railway cutting and an old canal." Rory was satisfied with the answer.

The research centre was only twenty yards or so from the production unit. There was another small blue sign next to the entrance with white writing. "Research Centre – Authorised Personnel Only."

Ed opened the door with a passcode and they entered another air-lock. There was a different swipe-card to access the next door.

Again, Rory was fascinated by everything that was going on. He counted six staff working in the unit, all wearing white coats and appearing to be engaged in design work of some kind. There was only one woman among the designers, he noticed. There was a large whiteboard down one side of the unit with calculations written in marker pen. The staff all looked incredibly young.

Ed walked up to the nearest operative.

"Hi Will, can I interrupt you for a moment?"

Will was sitting behind a technical drawing board. There was a moveable ruler stretched laterally across the board and various writing implements in a receptacle at the side, more rulers, compass, set squares and everything else a designer would need. There was a drawing being worked on; Rory could see the heading 'Project Hades'.

Chapter Four

"This is Rory; he's doing some consultancy work with us. You'll be seeing more of him, I expect," said Ed.

"Pleased to meet you," said Rory.

"You too," said Will.

The pair shook hands. Rory quickly started to weigh-up the man; late twenties, glasses, looked like one of the mathematicians from the Enigma Project.

"Will's been an integral part of the Hades Project; he and I worked closely on the design and application," said Ed.

"You must be very proud," said Rory.

"Yes," replied Will.

Rory had expected a more animated response, but this was a good sign. In his experience, the more effusive the personality, the more likely to brag about their achievements.

Rory was introduced to each member of the team in turn and was impressed by the array of talent. All had joined straight from university and had passed through the company's vetting process.

After another twenty minutes, Ed led Rory back into the daylight and the admin block. "There's a small canteen where you can get sandwiches, soup and snacks," explained Ed.

They entered the cafeteria which lived up to Ed's description. There were tables and chairs which were nearly all taken as staff replenished their food intake. There was a large TV on the wall showing a news channel and one or two were watching avidly as the sub-titles picked up the narrative. The sound was turned off; it was showing pictures of flooding in some parts of the country. Rory took no more than a passing interest.

Ed and Rory carried their trays to a free table; Rory had chosen a pack of cream-cheese sandwiches, crisps, a yoghurt and an orange drink. Ed had a similar selection.

"So, what do you think?" said Ed as the pair sat down.

"Yeah, so far it all looks fine."

Rory checked there was no-one in ear-shot, took a sip of his drink then continued.

"Tell me a bit more about your product range," he said and tucked into his sandwich.

Ed answered in some detail; Rory listened intently.

"What about stock, do you carry much?" asked Rory.

"No, not really. Most of our orders are bespoke so we tend to respond when the client needs re-stocking. We carry a few spares in case of emergency, but it's an expensive business carrying stock; it can't make money sitting in our warehouse."

"Warehouse?" said Rory.

"Yes, it's at the end, behind the research centre... I'll show you when we've finished."

They continued their discussion and Rory was forming a very favourable impression of the business and Ed in particular. He'd been helpful and open and seemed keen to support Rory in his security assessment. He was also a great ambassador for the company; he seemed to live and breathe it.

After lunch, Ed took Rory to the warehouse which was the only area of the site he'd yet to see. It was again security controlled, smaller than the production facility but larger than the research centre. Everything was immaculate; the stacking system, inventory processes, all controlled by the warehouse manager via its own computer programme. Rory was introduced to Archie Headman, who was in charge. After a brief discussion, Ed and Rory returned to the production centre. Des Greenhalgh had returned from his client meeting and was waiting to debrief Ed.

"Hi, Des, let me introduce you to Rory, who's going to be working with us for a while."

Rory shook hands with the production manager. He looked at him, short, bespectacled, older than many of his team; he was wearing a tie under his brown overalls, which had slipped its knot and was somewhere south of his neck.

Des was clearly intrigued by Rory's presence but fell short of asking the direct question, "what are you doing here?"

He explained his visit to G.M.I. in Kidderminster to discuss some production requirements. Eventually, Des and Ed retired to Ed's office to discuss more detail, leaving Rory to continue his evaluation.

Rory started to pack his stuff away around three-fifty. He had a cabinet to lock away papers but would take his laptop with him. He considered his day and felt a sense of achievement and satisfaction at the state of his new employers; everything seemed fine so far.

He walked back to the admin block to meet Alistair and waited outside his office; the door was slightly ajar. The Chairman was on the phone talking animatedly. Rory heard the call terminate with what sounded like the receiver being forcibly thrust into its holder. Rory knocked on the door.

"What?" barked Alistair, clearly upset at being disturbed. Rory put his head around the door.

"Oh, sorry Rory... come in, I'll be with you in a moment."

"Problems?" said Rory.

"Push the door closed," said Alistair. Rory complied.

"Have a seat," said Alistair and Rory sat down opposite him; he still seemed agitated.

"One of the clients wanting to change specs in mid-production. It'll cost a fortune to reset everything. Ed will blow a fuse."

"But you'll charge them, surely... for changing the specs?"

"Some, but they're disputing the original drawings, which is a nonsense."

"But if they signed up to your designs, they'll have to pay for any amendments," said Rory.

"I need to check with Natalie, it's more her area, I'll get her to speak to the client... Come on, let's get out of here, I need a drink," said Alistair, and he started locking his drawers.

"Talking of Natalie, where is she? I've not seen her about," said Rory.

"What…? Oh, no, she's taken the day off as she was working yesterday."

"Right," said Rory. Alistair could sense his interest, but changed the subject.

"What are you doing a week on Thursday?" said Alistair as he picked up his briefcase and headed for the door.

Rory got up. "Nothing, what do you need?"

"Trade fair… Abu Dhabi, I want you to be around, keep an eye on things," said Alistair, talking as they walked.

"Sure, no problem."

"Ed will be coming and Duncan. You can meet some of our clients, the Saudis for instance; and hopefully vet some new ones for us," said Alistair.

"Ok, fine, how long will we be away?"

"Fly out Thursday, back Monday," said Alistair.

They walked to the Jaguar still talking about the Abu Dhabi trip. Alistair started the car and they approached the front gate. A security guard checked the car and occupants and the barrier rose slowly.

"So, whereabouts in Abu Dhabi is this trade fair?" asked Rory.

"It's at the new Exhibition Centre. We'll have to stay in town, there's no hotel close... I'll get Natalie to arrange one, then you can sort out the security."

"Natalie?" said Rory, somewhat surprised at a relatively minor duty delegated to his legal expert.

"Yes, she knows what we need… Don't worry, she won't mind, she sees to all our travel arrangements."

"So, how does it work… trade fairs I mean?" said Rory. Alistair was weaving the Jag slowly out of the Birmingham sprawl.

"We'll have a stand, so we'll send out the kit we need this week and assemble it when we get there. We can't take it on the plane"

"Yes, but how do you get clients?"

"Ah, I see what you mean... Defence and weaponry trade fairs are private, by appointment only, for obvious reasons. The various delegates will walk around the stands and ask questions and, hopefully, we will get orders."

"So how are the delegates chosen?"

"The fairs are advertised in various trade journals and the applicants get vetted by the organisation host. In this case, it will be someone from the Emirates. The M.O.D. get a list and target those they believe we can do business with. There'll be other firms from the U.K.; British Aerospace, Vickers, Westland, although they're half Italian now, plus some companies from our European partners."

"Competitors?"

"Some of them, definitely, it's quite cut-throat, but that's why we specialise. No-one has our range or expertise."

"Yeah, I get it... You mentioned the Saudi's, any other clients, or prospective clients you can tell me about? I just want to get a handle on the profile."

"Well, obviously, everybody falls over themselves for the Saudis as you can imagine. We'll be meeting some of their buyers and some from the Emirates, although they're not huge clients. Unfortunately, with the line of business we're in, there are countries we can't do business with, Libya, Iran, Iraq, Russia, China. With the new stuff, we're restricted even further. Project Hades, for instance, we wouldn't share with anyone, not even our E.U. partners or the Americans; the M.O.D. want to keep it to themselves, for obvious reasons."

"Just so I'm clear, it will be your basic range you'll be selling, not the experimental stuff," said Rory.

"Good grief, no, that's so secret that most of the Government don't even know about it, except the M.O.D., of course, and COBRA."

"COBRA? Why would they be involved?"

"Well, they're not involved, directly, but at the last meeting, the P.M. was made aware of the development and has asked to be kept informed."

"Hmm, he'll hand it to the Americans, you mark my words... Blair and Bush are all over each other... That was my point regarding leaks, from what I've seen so far, I can't see anything coming from the plant; the problem, if there is one, lies elsewhere."

"Well that's good to hear," said Alistair.

After another twenty minutes, Alistair was outside the gates of his house. He aimed a fob at them and waited patiently as they slowly drew open.

"Ok, you're on your own tomorrow, I've got some clients to contact first thing. You have your clearance and cards, so you'll be able to get into the plant."

"Yeah, no problem, I'll see you tomorrow sometime," said Rory, and he collected his gear from the back seat of the Jag and transported it to the Toyota.

It took Rory another half an hour to reach his cottage in Worcester, the start of the evening rush-hour slowed progress to a crawl for much of the time.

He opened the front door, stowed his laptop and briefcase in his office and changed into his running kit. Six miles tonight, he needed to clear the cobwebs.

Running gave him time to think. As he strode along the towpath of the river, his mind was working overtime. It was a sunny evening, for a change, but the river was unseasonably high. He thought about the day, assessing the people he'd met. He didn't believe any of them were potential security threats, even Natalie, although he wasn't completely ruling her out just yet. The systems and protocols looked fine, especially as the M.O.D. had set them up; they would be as secure as was possible. The site, too, was well-managed and there did seem a security-conscious culture, all positive signs.

It was over an hour before he returned to the cottage; it was almost six-thirty. As he was running along the path next to the house, he could see someone hovering around his front door. He ran passed to get a closer look before deciding whether they posed a threat. He stopped and watched for a moment from behind a tree and got his breath back from his run. His tee-shirt was stuck to his chest from the sweat.

It was a woman with greying hair, wearing a black skirt and casual jacket; as he got closer to the cottage, he thought he recognised her,.

"Hello, can I help you?" said Rory, as he approached the visitor.

The woman shaded her eyes from the sun to get a clearer view of the enquirer.

"Rory?"

"Yes," he said, still not placing his visitor.

"It's Helen, Helen Arthur," said the woman.

"Helen… sorry, I didn't recognise you… come in. You'll have to excuse me, I've just been for a run."

"That's ok, it was just on the off-chance, you're not an easy person to find."

Rory opened the door and ushered in his guest. "Take a seat, it's great to see you… I'd give you a hug, but I'm a bit sweaty… Would you like a drink…? I can make some tea."

"It's ok, you'll be wanting a shower. Show me where everything is, and I'll see to it. Is it still no sugar?"

Rory laughed. "Yes, fancy you remembering that."

"There's a lot I remember," said Helen.

Rory showed Helen the kitchen and filled the kettle. He took out a litre bottle of water from the fridge and took several gulps. "Right, I'll be with you in five minutes, won't be long."

Rory left Helen and went to shower. She found the fridge and took out a carton of milk, then chose two mugs from the mug tree. She washed up the dirty dishes in the sink while she waited for the kettle to boil and left them on the draining board to dry. She made two mugs of tea and took them through to the lounge to wait for Rory. She looked around the room, it was sparse. There were no family photos, nothing to indicate either a past life or a woman's presence currently.

Rory came into the room wearing a pair of khaki shorts and a clean tee-shirt; he was rubbing his hair with a towel.

"Cheers, thanks for making the tea... and clearing the dishes. I would have got around to them eventually," said Rory, laughing. He sat down opposite his guest.

"That's ok, sorry to drop in unannounced but I had no way of contacting you," said Helen.

"No problem, it's good to see you... sorry I didn't recognise you straight away."

"Well, it's been a while... fourteen years since Lennie's funeral." She looked down at her mug in sadness.

"Jesus, where's that time gone?" said Rory. He looked at the woman who had aged considerably since their last meeting.

"So, what are you doing down here? The last I heard you were in Aberdeen, based on one of the rigs," said Helen.

"It's a long story," said Rory.

"What about your wife, what was her name...? Jane, was it?"

"Janie, yes... we split up last year... I left Petronix and moved back down here."

"Oh, that's a shame, you had children I remember," said Helen.

"Yes, two boys," said Rory.

"You must miss them," said Helen.

"Yes," said Rory and took a swig of tea.

"I wondered if anything had happened when I didn't get a Christmas card last year."

"Sorry about that, I don't have the address book, Janie always saw to that."

"I used to look forward to the little messages. It's funny, I never met your wife, but I felt like I knew her."

Helen drank the rest of her tea. "Look, this really wasn't a social call... I need your help."

"Of course, anything, you know that."

"It's Fiona... Fi."

"Your daughter?" said Rory.

"Yes," said Helen. "She's gone missing."

"Missing...? What do you mean missing?"

"Well, we've always been close. You know, during her teens we were more like sisters. She was only ten when Lennie died, but she was a great comfort to me, and of course, I was there for her; we helped each other. In some ways, because Lennie was away such a lot, it was hard to imagine that he was never coming back. It just seemed like one of the normal separations; we'd got used to that, but then we had the funeral and that made everything real... Anyway, Fi moved to London when she started university four years ago and gradually, we spoke less and less. She would still come home for the holidays and we still chat two or three times a week but two weeks ago she stopped answering her phone. I've been going mad with worry."

"So, what does she do?" said Rory.

"She's studying law at Imperial, in her final year. She's got a house in Acton she shares with some other students. I don't have their details I'm afraid, but I do have the address." Helen was starting to get emotional.

"Ok, ok... have you spoken to the police?"

"Yes, two days ago but they just gave me a reference number," said Helen.

"Hmm, yes that's the problem, so many people go missing in London, particularly students and foreign workers, it's impossible to provide the resources."

"Yes, that's when I saw your picture in the paper," said Helen.

"Oh, you saw that?" said Rory.

"Yes, I thought you were so brave," said Helen.

"Thanks... and for not saying anything... about who I was,

I mean," said Rory.

"Well, I guessed you wouldn't want anyone recognising you, given your past. It was the same with Lennie, everything so secret. I still occasionally look under my car for bombs before I get in," said Helen.

"It was a good habit to get into, especially after Northern Ireland," said Rory.

"But how did you find where I lived," said Rory.

"I guessed you would be living around here somewhere as you were jogging. I just described you to a couple of people and one of them said someone who fitted that description lived here, so I hung around and here you are."

"Do you still live in Hereford?" said Rory.

"Yes, we moved to a new house after Lennie was killed, too many memories, but I was ok financially. They paid a decent compensation… What about you, did you get anything?"

"Not a penny," said Rory. "But in fairness, I told them where to stick their money once I'd found out what had happened."

"Yes, such a waste. I still miss him, I think about him every day," said Helen.

"Yeah, me too," said Rory.

"So, how can I help you with Fiona?"

"I don't know," said Helen. "I've got a list of her friends and her address. I gave it to the police, as well, but, as I said, I don't think they'll have done anything."

"Do you want me to go down there and have a look, see what I can find?" said Rory.

"Would you? That would be so good of you, I can pay you," said Helen.

"No, no, you don't have to do that… I do have a problem, though. I've just started a contract with a new client." Rory watched Helen's head drop in disappointment.

"I could give it this weekend, though, just to ask around, see if anyone knows anything," said Rory.

"Oh, that would be wonderful, thank you."

"You better give me your mobile number; do you have one?" said Rory.

"Yes, I got a phone in case Fi called and I wasn't at home. I work at a travel agency in town. It's my day off today," said Helen.

"How did you get here?"

"Car, I'm parked along the track somewhere," said Helen.

"Have you eaten at all? I was going to make some dinner," said Rory.

"No, I haven't... but I've got a better idea, why don't we find somewhere and get a bite to eat, my treat, I insist."

"Yeah, ok, my cold lasagne will keep for another day," said Rory. "There's a pub, not far, they do good bar meals."

"Sounds great," said Helen.

Rory collected his wallet and keys then picked up a jacket from the back of one of the dining chairs. He looked at Helen. He remembered her as a lively girl, a great foil for Lennie. She was one of the few people who could have lived with him, but now, it was as though a spark had gone out. She was three or four years older than him and was certainly showing her age. He felt a well of sadness and cursed the Americans and their itchy trigger fingers.

It was gone ten o'clock before Rory and Helen left the pub. Rory had driven and returned Helen to her car. It was a forty-five-minute drive for her to get home.

During their conversation, Helen had provided Rory with a recent picture of Fiona. She looked like an earlier version of her mum, how Rory had remembered her. Helen also gave Rory some more background on Fiona, where she was studying, who her friends were, just tit-bits that might help the search. Rory gave Helen an update on his circumstances. He told her about the divorce and how he blamed himself for the break-up

They said their farewells. "I'll call you tomorrow and let you know what's happening," said Rory, and he watched as her

Ford Fiesta, bounced its way along the cinder track, towards the main road.

Rory was already giving some thought to how he might approach this. There was someone he remembered who might be able to help him.

The following morning, Rory was on the road early to beat the rush-hour, but it still took nearly an hour to reach the works. He was pleased to see the entrance procedure working which would go in his report; by eight o'clock he was in his office. He'd been awake until the early hours thinking about his new job and Helen's visit. It was time to make a call.

Rory checked his contacts; it had been a while, he hoped he hadn't changed his number. It rang out and Rory was about to hang up when a voice answered. "Swanson."

"Swannie, you old bugger, how the hell are you?"

"Fuck me, Rory Calderwood... you still shagging mermaids on that rusting piece of junk in the North Sea?"

Swannie hadn't changed and the banter was as lively and coarse as ever.

"No, given that up, trying my hand at consultancy," said Rory.

"Really? Well good luck with that," said Swanson.

There was a catch-up for a few minutes then Rory raised the subject of Helen's visit the previous evening.

"I need your help, Swannie. I had a call from Helen Arthur, Lennie's missus, last night, it seems her daughter's gone missing."

"Fiona?"

"Yeah, she's not been answering her phone for a couple of weeks," said Rory.

"That's normal for kids in my experience."

"I don't think so, Helen was very upset... They're very close."

"Yeah, I remember her at the funeral, how old would she

have been?"

"About ten, according to Helen," said Rory. "She's twenty-four now."

"Jesus, where's the time gone?"

"Yeah, you can say that again," said Rory.

"So, what do you want me to do?" said Swannie.

"Well, I said I would come down to the smoke and make some enquiries. It would be great if we could team up."

"Yeah, just like old times," said Swannie.

"Any chance of crashing out at yours. I can get a hotel, but you know…"

"Yeah, course, you've not met Beryl, my wife, have you?" said Swannie.

"No, you were still into camels when I last saw you," joked Rory.

"Ha, ha, The North Sea's done nothing to improve your humour, I see."

"That's true… Have you heard anything from the other guys?"

"Yeah, I keep in touch with Digger, and occasionally Stan, but not Phillips or Bernie, not heard from them in years."

These were the squad members that Rory commanded on the early raids in the first Gulf War; they were a formidable team, all had been decorated for their exploits. Losing Lennie, the only squad member not to return, was a huge blow. Rory often felt guilty that it was Lennie that had died in the incident, not him. He had a wife and family, whereas Rory was single at the time. However, there was nothing that could be done to change things; what's done is done. He knew that they would rally round when one of their own was in trouble.

"Do you think Digger would help?" said Rory.

"Possibly, mind you he lives down on the coast, Eastbourne, or somewhere," said Swannie.

"Have you got his number? I'll give him a call," said Rory.

"Yeah, but don't worry I'll speak to him, see if I can get him up on Friday night," said Swannie.

"Yeah, it'll be great to see him again," said Rory.

"What about Stan?"

"Nah, he's in the States, working with one of their agencies," said Swannie.

"Ok, look I need to go, but I'll call you Friday, let you know what time I'll arrive. I'm thinking of the train if you don't mind doing the driving," said Rory.

"Nah, that's fine, you don't want to be paying the congestion charge."

"Cheers," said Rory. "See you Friday."

Rory left his office and met up with Ed who was catching up with emails in his office.

"Hi Rory, how're things? Like a coffee?" Ed had his own coffee-making facility in his office.

"Yeah, great," replied Rory. Ed got up and did the honours.

"Cheers," said Rory as Ed handed him a mug. "I want to have a look at your IT set up this morning, can you sort something out for me?"

"Yeah, sure I'll just finish off here and introduce you to Vikram; he looks after all our systems."

"Great," said Rory.

"I hear you're joining us in Abu Dhabi," said Ed.

"Yeah, never been to the Emirates," said Rory.

"Interesting place," said Ed. Rory's previous experience in the Middle East was more than 'interesting'.

After a further catch-up, Ed took Rory through the works to a separate pod at the end of the building. Two young men were looking studiously at the innards of a computer monitor.

"Hi, Vikram, got a minute?"

"Sure," said the man, looking up from his labours.

"This is Rory, he's doing some work for us. Can you show him our set-up?" Ed noticed Vikram's quizzical look. "It's ok, he's been cleared for full access. Give him anything he needs."

"Of course," said Vikram and shook hands with Rory.

"Hi," said Rory. The handshake was weak and uninspiring.

"I'll leave you to it," said Ed and left Rory with Vikram and his assistant.

"This is Simon, my assistant," said Vikram and the lad stood up to be introduced. Rory looked at him, tall and gangly, he looked like he needed a decent meal. Probably spent too much time sitting in front of the TV playing computer games, Rory thought.

"Sorry to disturb you guys," said Rory, picking up their frustration at being interrupted. "Can you give me some time just to go through your protocols."

"Yeah, sure," said Vikram. "What are you looking for?"

Rory decided to be straight. "Well, I'm looking at the possibility of cybercrime, fraud, hacking, malware planting, that sort of thing."

He'd pressed the right buttons, Vikram was onboard. It was not often anyone paid them much attention. "Yeah, great... what do you want to know?"

All thoughts of repairing a recalcitrant monitor had gone as Vikram and the lofty Simon answered Rory's questions with enthusiasm. He was impressed by their knowledge and attention to detail. As far as he could assess, the systems that were in place were as robust as could be expected.

There was one other person Rory wanted to speak to today, and after an hour with the IT team he left the production unit and went to the admin block to seek out his quarry.

He hadn't spent any time in the admin centre and, as he walked through, it reminded him of an 80's office, a throwback to earlier times. There was even a typing pool with three girls beavering away on computer keyboards. He went down the corridor to see if Alistair was about, but he was told he was still at the house. Then he noticed Natalie coming out of an adjoining office.

"Ah, Natalie, have you got a minute?"

Natalie looked at him and, for a moment, was caught off-guard.

"Yes, of course, shall we go to the canteen, we can chat over a coffee?"

"Yeah, why not," said Rory.

Rory looked at her, immaculate as ever; power suit, hair tied back, giving her an officious look. It did nothing to lessen her 'ice-maiden' image.

They reached the canteen and ordered their drinks. There had been no attempt at conversation during the short walk.

"That's one-twenty," said Maisie, the cashier, in a broad Midland's accent, as Rory paid for the drinks.

"That's not bad for two coffees," said Rory, trying to make conversation.

"No, we subsidise the cost," said Natalie.

"Right," said Rory, not really able to think of an appropriate answer, but noting her use of the word 'we' again.

They sat in the corner where Rory had sat with Ed the previous day.

"So, what do you want to talk about?" said Natalie, getting straight to the point.

"I would be interested in your role here… and your thoughts about security," said Rory.

She folded her arms, clearly uncomfortable with the scrutiny.

"Look, I'm sorry if this is difficult, but your chairman has given me a job to do, and I intend to carry it out as best as I can," said Rory.

Natalie changed her posture. "No, it is ok, what you are doing it is necessary, I know that. What do you want to know?"

There was a lengthy discussion about her background and her role in the company which, more or less, confirmed what Alistair had already told Rory. He found her shrewd, extremely business-savvy and intelligent, but there was one question he was keen to have answered.

"Just one final question... why here? Why did you join a comparatively small business, based in the back streets of Birmingham? With your background, you could have walked into any of the big firms in London or even the States."

"Yes, that is true... I will tell you why... first, they offered me a job; second, I thought they needed me. When I got here I couldn't believe the state of their contracts, and some of their business practices. They were wide-open to fraud and vulnerable to information transfer. In fact, it was me who suggested we needed a specialist person to look at everything."

This was new to Rory. "Really? So, I have you to thank?"

Natalie smiled for the first time. "Yes, that is true... but there is something else, I do not intend to stay here for a long time. When I have finished my work here, I will move on, but it has been a great experience already."

They carried on talking for a few more minutes; their coffees had been refilled and emptied again before Rory called time.

"Thanks for your time and the information, I'm grateful," said Rory.

"My pleasure," said Natalie. Rory walked out with her, then back to his office in the production unit, deep in thought.

Back behind his desk, he considered the conversation. There was a small detail that didn't exactly collate; Natalie had given him the impression that the company had made all the running to recruit her, whereas Alistair had said she approached them. Just a small point, and he wasn't sure if it was relevant or not. He was, though, beginning to revise his opinion of Natalie. It still seemed too good to be true, but the business may just have made a very shrewd appointment.

Later, Rory managed to grab a few minutes with Alistair who wanted to know how his investigations were going. "So far, so good," said Rory, detailing his discussions with Vikram and Natalie.

"That's good... I've got details of the flights for Abu Dhabi, by the way. It'll be early; we'll need to be at the airport for five," said Alistair.

"Hmm, from Birmingham?" said Rory.

"Yes, there's a direct flight. We'll be in business class, so we can use the lounge there, get some breakfast before we fly," said Alistair and smiled.

"At least that's something; better make sure the alarm clock works," said Rory.

He'd been on some uncomfortable flights in the past; sat in the back of a Hercules was not the height of luxury, business-class would be a welcomed venture.

Rory left the office at four-thirty and endured the slog of the car journey back to Worcester. By five-thirty he was pounding the cinder path alongside the river again. It was another dull evening with a threat of more rain, but nothing that would deter his daily punishment.

He was in the kitchen making his evening meal when there was a knock on the door. Rory was not used to having visitors and the rap put him on alert.

He looked through the window to check. There were plenty of people around on the path, dog-walkers, ramblers, fishermen looking for their next casting spot. He could see a man and a woman loitering at his door; the man had a long-lens camera slung over his shoulders.

Rory opened the door about six inches.

"What do you want?" he said.

"Oh, hi, I'm Laura Kingston, Worcester Gazette, sorry to disturb you have you got a minute?"

Chapter Five

This was the last thing Rory needed. His initial reaction was to tell her to sling her hook but, concerned that that might draw even more attention, he let them inside.

"Thanks," said the woman.

"Take a seat," said Rory shutting the door.

She sat on the settee, her colleague next to her; Rory took an adjacent chair. He looked at her, thirtyish with shoulder length, honey-blonde hair, tied back in a ponytail. She was wearing black jeans, a pale blue tee-shirt, a light jacket and trainers. The cameraman looked like a hippy.

"Is this a good time?" asked the woman.

"For what?" said Rory, which sounded aggressive.

She looked down for a moment, this was not going well; she made eye-contact.

"Well, we've been running a campaign in the Gazette, trying to find the hero who saved a three-year-old boy on Thursday and we think it might be you. We'd like to take a few pictures with the family and get your story."

"Sorry," said Rory. "I can't do that."

"That's such a shame, our readers have been contacting us wanting to know who you are; you have quite a fan club," said the journalist.

"I'm sorry," said Rory.

"Well, weren't you frightened, when you dived in, I mean?"

"Didn't think about it," said Rory.

"Modest, too, that is so attractive," said Laura.

"As I said, I don't want any fuss, no pictures or publicity. I'm sorry I can't help you any further," said Rory, and went to stand up.

"That's a pity. The boy's mother wanted to thank you personally... and recommend you for a bravery award," said the journalist.

"I'm sorry, I can't help… How is the boy, by the way?"

"He's out of hospital, he's fine, thanks to you," said Laura.

"That's good… Look, I'm pleased the lad's ok, but I can't be involved… I don't know what more I can say."

The woman looked at him.

"Yes, ok, I'll leave it then, but it's such a shame to disappoint the family. The boy wanted to say thank you too, you know."

Rory looked down. "I'm sorry, please wish him all the best for me… tell him to make the most of his life."

"Why don't you do that?" said Laura.

"I'm sorry, I can't, it's not possible," said Rory.

"But why?"

Rory felt cornered, he was going to have to provide something.

"Let's just say people's lives are at stake… I can't say anything more. I'm sorry."

Laura was really intrigued now.

"Well, I can't promise anything, I'll have a chat with my editor, see what he says."

She rummaged in her handbag.

"Look, here's my card… If you change your mind please give me a call, yeah?" she said, and passed Rory her business-card.

"I won't change my mind," said Rory.

"That's a shame, but thanks for your time, anyway… Rory, isn't it?"

"Yeah," he said and showed her to the door. He watched as she walked away from the cottage down the path towards town.

Wednesday, Rory was back in the office and at last, he was introduced to the missing sales director, Duncan Wyatt. It was around eleven o'clock when Rory had an internal call, it was Alistair.

"Can you pop over? I want to introduce you to Duncan."

Rory closed his laptop and made his way to the admin

block. Alistair's door was open, and Rory could hear voices coming from inside.

"Ah, Rory," said Alistair seeing him appear. "Close the door and take a seat... Duncan meet Rory, I was just telling you about him."

The pair shook hands. Immediately Rory was evaluating the man; he was different to what he'd had imagined. Sales people usually had an image, brash, confident and, very often, pushy. Duncan, if anything, was the opposite; calm, measured, almost understated. A firm, purposeful handshake, good eye-contact; here was someone used to dealing with people at senior levels. He was smartly dressed in a light-grey business suit, pale-blue shirt and red tie. The immediate impression was favourable.

"Pleased to meet you, Rory. Alistair's been telling me about your exploits on the river. Well done, that was very brave."

"Thanks," said Rory, taken aback by the compliment.

Alistair intervened. "Rory, I want you to bring Duncan up to speed with your findings so far and Duncan can give you some background on our clients... That should keep you both out of mischief for a while."

"Shall we go to the canteen?" said Duncan. "A bit more civilised."

"Yeah, great," said Rory.

The pair left just as another call was being put through to Alistair's extension.

Rory and Duncan chatted for an hour about the Vienna trade fair and the forthcoming Abu Dhabi trip. It was all new to Rory and he was interested to hear all about the process of trade fairs which confirmed Alistair's earlier description.

"What about the new projects, how will you be able to cash in?" said Rory.

"Hmm, it'll take a while. The R & D is expensive, but we get Government grants which cover the development costs. As the M.O.D. is our best customer, it's in our mutual interests. We have the expertise, they have the money."

Rory smiled. "Yeah, let's hope they don't cut the budget."

"Fortunately, defence spending's been pretty steady and everyone's excited about the new development."

"The Hades Project?" said Rory.

"Yes, it should put us in a different league once the prototype's been fully tested and we can get into full production... so they tell me, anyway."

"How long will that be?"

"Hmm, how long's a piece of string? It's the military who drag their feet, takes them ages to make a decision. Having said that, I don't know much about it. I'm not involved in the production side at all. It's still very much in the research stages. All we've been told is the outline application and then we were sworn to secrecy."

"Do you think you're vulnerable to industrial espionage, from your perspective, I mean?" said Rory.

"Good question, I guess it's possible... nothing's a hundred percent, although as you'll have seen, things here are pretty secure," said Duncan.

"Yes, I can't argue with that; the problem in my experience is that once a rumour of a new development gets out, all sorts come crawling out of the woodwork, competitors, rogue states, and, of course, terrorists... They would certainly like to get their hands on some of your kit."

"Absolutely," said Duncan. "Which is why we place so much emphasis on security."

Rory liked the synergy within the company, everybody going in the same direction. He'd not found any dissension which was unusual in his experience. Some company boards, Rory remembered from his training days, were virtually in open warfare about strategic direction; this was a pleasant change.

By six o'clock, Rory was again pounding the footpath. It was an unusually warm evening after recent weeks, the earlier rain had cleared, replaced by high pressure; set to fair for a couple of days according to the weather forecast. He was glad of that; it would give the fields a chance to dry out.

He made light work of the run, another five miles under his belt.

He returned to the cottage, changed and showered. He checked the fridge; his supplies were dwindling, a trip to the supermarket was going to be needed in the next day or so. Not blessed with any culinary skills, Rory tended to microwave most of his meals and occasionally treated himself to some pub-grub; the local hostelry where he'd taken Helen was only a ten-minute walk and the food was ok. Tonight, he decided to take it easy and watch some TV, something he didn't do very often.

By eight o'clock, he'd consumed a shepherd's pie ready-meal and was slopping about in a pair of shorts and flip-flops. He was just finishing washing up when there was a tap on the door.

Rory was ready to confront the source of the interruption, but he was stopped in his tracks.

"Hi, Rory, sorry to disturb you again, I just wanted to give you an update."

"You better come in," said Rory.

"It's ok, I'm off-duty, promise," said the woman.

Rory looked at her, so different from the previous evening. Her blonde hair was loose and seemed to glisten in the evening sunlight which streamed through the window. She was wearing a summery, patterned skirt, fashionably short, and a white blouse that gathered at the neck and buttoned down the front. She had a necklace and was carrying a light-grey jacket.

Rory suddenly felt decidedly under-dressed. "Sorry, you'll have to excuse my appearance, I wasn't expecting anyone."

She couldn't help but notice his lean physique.

"Please, don't worry, I didn't have your number, so I called on the off-chance. As I said, it's merely an update… I just wanted to let you know that the paper is no longer running your story…

I explained to the editor and he was happy to go along with it… We'll cover it by saying you wished to remain anonymous… I think people will understand. We'll say something about your magnanimity… It does you great credit."

"Thanks," said Rory.

"I've spoken to Mrs Clarke too, that's Kyle's mum, and explained that you didn't want any fuss. She was disappointed that she couldn't thank you in person, but she asked me to give you this."

She went into her handbag and pulled out an A5 picture of a young boy; a professional portrait, almost certainly taken by the newspaper. "That's Kyle, he's fine, getting up to all kinds of mischief."

Rory took the picture from her. "Turn it over," said the journalist.

'To Rory, we can never thank you enough for your bravery, love from Michelle and Kyle xx'

Rory was feeling emotional. "I don't know what to say, and I don't deserve this, I just did what I had to do."

"A lot of people would disagree with you, it was special… I think so anyway. The paper has given you a frame to keep it in," and Laura again rummaged in her handbag and pulled out a glass frame.

"That's very kind, thank you."

He looked at her and something took over.

"Look, I'm sorry if I was a bit… off last night, I'd like to make it up to you. Would you like to go for a drink?"

Laura looked at her watch, then at Rory.

"Yes, ok, why not," said Laura.

"I'll just go and change, I'll frighten the punters in this get-up," said Rory.

"Oh, I wouldn't say that," said Laura and smiled.

While Rory was changing, Laura was on her phone checking her messages.

"Signal's not great here," said Laura on his return.

"No, I don't tend to use the phone that much," said Rory, who was now more presentable in a pair of jeans, tee shirt and trainers.

"There's a pub just up the road, it's only a ten-minute walk," said Rory.

"Sounds good, lead the way," said Laura.

Rory opened the door for Laura and locked up.

The sun was losing its intensity, but it was still a glorious evening as Laura walked beside Rory along the river bank to the pub.

"You have a wonderful spot here," said Laura.

"It is on a day like today, it makes a change from all that rain. I heard the cricket at New Road's been abandoned," said Rory.

"Yes," said Laura. "Waterlogged again."

"So, how's the world of journalism?" said Rory, changing the subject.

"Ha, it has its frustrations," said Laura, which Rory recognised was a mild dig at him

"Yes, I'm sure," said Rory, not wishing to be drawn into that area of conversation.

They arrived at the pub; the beer-garden that overlooked the adjacent canal was packed. The smoking ban was only a few days old and having been barred from inside, a great many customers were huddled around the ash-trays provided by the landlord.

"Now, there's a good story for you," said Rory. "How are people coping with the smoking ban?"

"Actually, you could be right," said Laura, looking at the disgruntled punters.

They went inside. It was dark after the comparative brightness of the setting sun and Rory had to stop for a moment to acclimatise his eyes. This was a throwback to his army days on ops when working at night; it was something he was conditioned to do.

It was an old pub with a rustic feel to it, but it had been modernised with a large seating area for food. Rory chose a quieter spot where they could talk. From the window, although you couldn't see the river which was obscured by the bank, there was a view across the plain to the Malvern Hills in the distance.

"What about here?" said Rory. "I'll get them in, what would you like?"

"Yes, this is fine… a glass of red wine please," said Laura.

Rory went to the bar, it wasn't busy; there were more people outside enjoying the evening or smoking than there were in the eating area.

While he waited for the drinks, he looked across at Laura. In a way she reminded him of Kim, his last girlfriend; she was certainly as attractive. He watched as she took out a mirror from her handbag and checked her makeup.

He paid for the drinks and headed back to the table.

"Oh, thanks, that's great," said Laura. "I'm just going to the little girls' room."

"Ok," said Rory and sat down as Laura got up and looked around.

"They're over there," said Rory pointing to the opposite corner.

He took a sip of his lager while he waited and looked at the other customers. It was an older clientele he noticed, very few younger customers.

Rory watched as Laura walked towards him. There was an air of confidence about her, Rory wasn't the only customer who was taking an interest.

"That's better," she said. "Thanks for the drink." She took the first sip of her wine. "Mmm, not bad… some of the pub reds taste like vinegar."

"Yeah," said Rory. "I tend to stick to lager."

"This is your local, then?" said Laura.

"Well, it's the nearest to the house, but I don't get in here that often."

"So, what does our mystery man do, when he's not saving people's lives?" said Laura and she took another sip of her wine.

Rory knew the question would crop up. "I'm in security."

"Ha, that explains it," said Laura.

"Yeah, I guess, sorry if it's a bit vague."

"Self-employed, or one of those creepy organisations?" said Laura.

"Ha, ha, no… self-employed, but I do know some creepy organisations."

"I bet you do," said Laura. "I wish I could get inside your head, I bet there are a million stories in there."

"It's really not that interesting," said Rory.

"Hmm, I bet," said Laura with a hint of sarcasm.

"Have you always lived in Worcester?" said Laura.

"No," said Rory, which reminded Laura to use open questions.

"Where did you live before you moved here?" She tried again.

"In Aberdeen, I worked on one of the oil platforms." This was more like it, Laura was getting somewhere.

"You're not married, I take it."

"Divorced," said Rory.

"Hmm, same here," said Laura, sharing some personal stuff for the first time.

"Any children?" asked Laura.

"Yeah, two boys," said Rory. "You?"

"No, I'm glad to say. I knew after two weeks that it had been a big mistake."

"Sorry to hear that," said Rory.

"It's ok, I'm well over it now," said Laura.

As the atmosphere relaxed, Rory was more forthcoming in his disclosures and Laura was finding a connection.

"Do you live in Worcester?" asked Rory at one point.

"Just outside, near Ombersley. It's a barn conversion; it was the only good thing to come out of my marriage. I managed to raise the cash to buy the bastard out."

"I see… nice area, a bit rural," said Rory.

"Ha, yes, that's for sure, but I was brought up in the country, so I don't mind the seclusion."

"You don't get lonely then?"

"God, no, I've got loads of friends… What about you, do you have a social life?"

Rory considered the answer for a moment. "I guess not. I just go running, and working."

This was true; Rory had shut himself away since he'd returned to Worcester, but he was only now coming to terms with that fact.

"That's a pity," said Laura.

"I think being stuck out in the middle of the North Sea for twelve years might have something to do with it," said Rory.

"Yeah, I guess so. What was it like?"

"Hmm… you just get used to it, two-week shifts, twelve hours on, twelve off."

"Is that why your marriage failed…? Sorry, didn't mean to pry."

"It's ok… Yeah, probably a lot to do with it, when I think back."

Both had finished their drinks. "Can I get you another one?" said Rory. It was nearly nine-thirty. Laura looked at her watch. "Go on then, just a tonic water, I have to drive back."

Laura watched Rory walk to the bar; he fascinated her. She would love to write his real story; there was so much more she was certain. He had said nothing about his time before the rig.

Rory returned with another round and passed the drink to Laura. His eyes caught her gaze for a moment and it was as though time stood still for that fraction of a second.

He sat down; Laura wanted to delve deeper.

"So, before the North Sea, what did you do?"

"In security," said Rory.

"Doing what you're doing now?"

"Sort of?"

"And before that?"

"I was in the army," said Rory.

"Really," said Laura. "That explains it."

"What?"

"Your bravery," said Laura.

He took a sip of his drink; it was a sensitive subject, Laura could tell and dropped the interrogation.

She took his hand. "I've enjoyed tonight."

"Yeah, me too," said Rory.

"No, really enjoyed," she said, emphasising the word 'really'.

"Yeah, me too. We should do it again," said Rory.

"Yes… what are you doing tomorrow night?" said Laura.

"Ha, ha, let me check my social calendar… er, nothing," said Rory, flicking through his wallet, and laughed.

"Would you like to come 'round to mine? I'll cook us a meal," said Laura.

"Yeah, I'd like that," said Rory.

"About seven?"

"Yeah, sounds great, thanks," said Rory.

Laura squeezed his hand. "Let me write down my address, it's easy enough to find. Just off the main road… oh, and you better have my mobile number too."

Laura took out a pen from her handbag and wrote her address on the back of her Gazette business card, then added her phone number.

"Here, you can have mine," said Rory, and wrote it down on another card.

Laura looked at her watch, ten o'clock. "I better get going… work in the morning."

They got up and Rory escorted her to her car, a white VW Golf GTI. It was parked at the end of the tarmac road before it became a cinder track, just a five-minute walk.

"Thanks for tonight, it's been great," said Laura.

"Yeah, it has," said Rory and they kissed, at first hesitantly, then with more passion.

"Whoa, I better go or I'll never get home," said Laura, laughing. Rory pulled her towards him and gave her a hug.

"See you tomorrow," said Laura. She unlocked her car and got in.

Rory watched as she made a U-turn and headed back towards the city. For the first time in a while, Rory felt a sense of elation as he walked back to his cottage.

The following morning, he was back at the works, in his office drinking his first cup of coffee. He'd almost finished his investigation and couldn't find any obvious problems, so far. He had, however, been given all the staff files and was gradually working his way through them. Most were straightforward enough, but as he picked up the next one on the pile, the name leapt out at him, 'Anwar Hussain'. Anyone with a Middle Eastern name would be on his radar given the present state of the political world; he needed to know more.

He looked through the file, starting at the references, a University Lecturer, an Imam, which made Rory shudder but nevertheless would, in normal circumstances, be suitable introductions. He read the citations, 'conscientious, highly intellectual, studious, excelled in engineering and design'. Rory could see the attraction in his recruitment and was trying to keep an open mind, but it was hard. Thoughts of Tariq Siddique raced through his mind, the brilliant engineer who almost killed him on the rig.

He checked his absence record, nothing out of the ordinary. He picked up the file and went next door to see Ed who was in his office.

"Ed, got a minute?"

"Yep, sure, take a pew," said Ed.

"Just going through the files and I came across this guy." Rory opened the file and gave it to Ed.

"Anwar?"

"Yeah, what's his story?"

"Good, very good, in fact... really knows his stuff, bright lad."

"What do you know about his background?"

"Not a lot, he's been with us a while now, been no problem, very conscientious, seems to spend most of his time here, in fact."

This did little to ease Rory's worry. "Works late?"

"Yeah, sometimes," said Ed.

"Really? How often?"

"I don't know, two, three times a week; probably needs the overtime," said Ed.

"Hmm," said Rory.

Ed noticed the concern. "Don't worry he's not on his own. In fact, no one is allowed to work on their own."

Rory looked at Ed. "Well, that's reassuring."

"Would you like to meet him? You can make up your own mind."

"Yeah, ok but not now, I don't want anything formal; I'll just meet him at his workplace."

"Yeah, ok. Just let me know and I'll take you to the area."

"Thanks, Ed, appreciate it," said Rory.

He got up and went back to his office with Anwar's staff file, slightly reassured, but still with some questions.

It was after lunch when his curiosity got the better of him and decided to seek out Anwar.

He called on Ed who took him to the production pod which included Anwar. There were three other operatives working on the production line.

"Have you got a minute, lads," shouted Ed.

The work stopped and the four approached him.

"Lads, this is Rory, he's doing a review of our processes and

I have said you'll show him what we do here… Anwar, can you help Rory, please. The rest carry on, Rory will ask if he needs any more information."

Ed left the group who were now huddled around Rory. "Sorry to interrupt you guys, can you just take me through what you do here?"

It was all very relaxed; Anwar would never have realised he was the target of an assessment. The three guys went back to their places leaving Rory and Anwar together. Rory shook hands; the handshake was fine. He remembered Tariq and his introduction on the rig; it was the weakest he'd ever experienced; like a small child's he recalled. Rory looked at him in his AB Engineering overalls, five-foot-nine, or ten, smart, clean shaven, he was wearing eye protectors and ear defenders.

"Hi Anwar, can you take me through what you're making here?" said Rory.

"Sure," said Anwar, and apprised Rory with the workings of his unit. He was enthusiastic and knowledgeable; Rory was able to use his own experience to ask some technical questions. After about twenty minutes and a brief chat with the other team members, Rory left the pod and went back to his office. After a few minutes, Ed poked his head around his door, anxious to get some feedback.

"What do you think?" asked Ed.

"Yeah, seems a bright lad, enthusiastic, but keep an eye on him and let me know if you notice any changes in his behaviour."

"Such as?" asked Ed.

"His mood, any unexplained absences, conflicts with his team members, those sort of things," said Rory.

"Yeah, will do," said Ed and left Rory writing some notes.

As the afternoon wore on, the prospect of his meeting with Laura started to lift his spirits. He found himself checking his watch every few minutes, wishing time would move more quickly.

He eventually left around four-fifteen and made the slow journey back to his cottage. Just before he took the turn towards the riverside, he called into his local supermarket, a large sprawling complex with an enormous car-park on the corner of the roundabout. All the cars were parked near the entrance leaving swathes of empty spaces. Rory parked as close as he could; he hated supermarkets, but he needed to get a bottle of wine to take with him. As he walked into the store, there was a flower section and for a moment he thought about buying some flowers, something he'd never done before. He quickly discounted the gesture; Laura didn't seem the flower sort, he reasoned.

He contemplated missing his normal run, but it had become so ingrained in his daily routine he found himself changing into his running gear as soon as he got into the house, a subliminal action.

A short two or three miles would get rid of the daily grind and prepare him for the evening.

He showered and changed and checked his route; less than ten miles, but traffic leaving Worcester would be busy. He was wearing a pair of light brown jeans, a casual shirt and loafers. He wouldn't need a jacket; there was no threat of rain, the forecasters had said.

He was glad he'd given himself enough time, it took him nearly half an hour to leave the city and reach open countryside. It was a fine evening, cloudy but with plenty of blue sky and he wore sunglasses to protect his eyes from the low sun. With all the rain over recent weeks, the countryside was incredibly green, the trees and fields verdant and lush. Rory felt good.

Ombersley is a village on the main road that heads out of Worcester towards Kidderminster, on a crossroads where the Droitwich to Holt Fleet road intersects. He consulted his notes as he reached the junction and turned left towards the river, two miles ahead. It was less than half a mile before he was through the village, and he was looking for the first left-hand turn. He slowed as he could see the drive a hundred yards ahead of him. It was a tarmac road leading to a small development, about a hundred and fifty yards from the main road. He reached a large pebbled courtyard which was surrounded by three properties, all converted farm buildings. He could see Laura's VW parked in front of the third house and he parked just behind it. It was a lot like Kim's place in Aberdeen.

Laura was at the window, then disappeared. The front door opened, and she was there waiting to greet her guest.

"You found it ok?" she said as Rory approached; a rhetorical question.

"Yeah, no problem," replied Rory as he was ushered inside. It opened to a small hallway with a door to the right. He presented her with the bottle of wine and kissed her.

"Thank you, that's very good of you," said Laura. "Go through."

She opened the door which led to the lounge. The room was of contemporary design with a spiral staircase in the corner leading to the second floor. The flooring was parquet with scattered rugs, a linen-covered three-piece-suite which faced a flat-screen TV on the wall. A dining table with four chairs was placed against the near-side wall; it was set for two. There was a candle burning in the middle. Opposite the entrance was a large picture window with views across open fields.

"Hey, this is nice," said Rory. "I can see why you wanted to stay here."

"Thanks," said Laura.

"Have a seat, I'll pour a glass of wine unless you'd like something else? I do have some beers if you prefer."

"No, wine's fine," said Rory.

There was a door next to the dining table, which led to the kitchen and Laura disappeared for a moment then came back with two glasses of red. There was a wonderful smell of food;

Rory suddenly felt hungry.

"Thank you," said Rory, as Laura passed him a glass. "Something smells good."

"Thank you, I hope it tastes ok. I've done chicken in white wine sauce with potatoes and veg. I didn't think you were vegetarian." She smiled.

"No, that sounds great... How was your day?"

"Yes, good thanks; I took up your suggestion... We're going to do a piece on the smoking ban."

"Aha, I sense a change of vocation for me," said Rory.

Rory couldn't take his eyes off her; hair down, designer tee shirt, light-blue jeans that seemed to fit where they touched, and slip-on sandals. She looked incredible.

"So how was your day?" said Laura.

"Yeah, good, thanks," said Rory.

"Are you working locally?" asked Laura, another closed question which had the usual short response.

"No," said Rory.

"So, whereabouts, then," said Laura, trying again.

"In Birmingham," replied Rory.

"I don't envy you that commute," said Laura.

"It's not too bad, I tend to leave before the main rush. It means I can finish early," said Rory.

"I'll just go and check on the dinner," said Laura, seeing her guest was settled. While she was gone, Rory got up and looked out of the window. It was west facing, and the sun was making its steady drop towards evening.

"What a great view," said Rory, as Laura returned from her culinary duties. She joined him at the window and put her hands around his waist. Then they were kissing, deep passionate kissing; tongues working overtime. Laura broke away first. "We're not going to get anything to eat if you carry on like that," she said. "Let's eat, you can save that for dessert."

"I like the sound of that," said Rory.

"Take a seat, I'll dish up," she said.

Rory complied but suddenly found his appetite was waning. A couple of moments later, Laura brought in two plates, holding them with a tea towel, "Careful, the plates are hot," she said as she placed one in front of him.

"This looks great," said Rory. Laura went back to the kitchen and returned with her glass of wine.

"Cheers," said Rory, holding up his glass as she sat down.

She clinked glasses. "Cheers," she responded.

Their eyes locked, suddenly Laura didn't feel hungry either.

Chapter Six

There was silence as they picked at their meals; their minds were clearly on something else.

"Tell me about your family," said Laura, trying to make conversation.

"Just a sister," said Rory. "Lives in Worcester. What about yours?" he was being polite rather than being interested.

"My parents have a farm just outside Chaddesley Corbett… my brother manages it," said Laura.

"Nice area," said Rory. It was not one with which he was too familiar, but he knew it was an area of wealthy land-owners. He realised where the money would have come from to buy Laura's house.

The conversation moved to hobbies, which as far as Rory was concerned, consisted of running; Laura belonged to a gym in town.

Eventually, over relatively meaningless discussions, they both managed to finish their meals. Laura looked into Rory's eyes; there was a sexual tension that was almost touchable.

"Would you like another glass?" said Laura without averting her gaze, seeing Rory's empty.

"Just a small one," said Rory.

Laura cleared the plates and took them to the kitchen, returning with the wine bottle. She poured herself a larger measure than Rory's.

"I've made a fruit salad, would you like it now, or later."

"I think later," said Rory. "I don't think I could eat it now."

He got up from his chair and stood behind Laura. He started massaging her neck and shoulders.

"Ooh, that's good, don't stop."

His hands moved lower, down to her shoulder blades, then back up. Then down the front but stopping short of Laura's tee-shirt top.

"Mmm, you have a gentle touch, for an action hero," said Laura.

"Thanks," said Rory.

"Wait," said Laura and she removed her top. She was wearing a black half-cup bra from which her boobs were trying to escape.

Rory was still stood behind her and slid his hands downwards, cupping both her breasts. She started to moan softly, and he took her nipples between his fingers and gently teased them. He slipped the straps of her bra over her shoulders and Laura let them slip down her arms. She reached behind and unclipped her underwear and her breasts leapt free.

She turned in her seat and started kissing Rory who was still giving attention to her breasts. Her hands moved to his jeans and located the zip. She slowly eased the fastener down and reached inside his shorts; Rory's erection bounced free and Laura descended on it. Rory took in the wonderful sensations as she went to work with her tongue. After a minute or so, Laura got up and moved to the settee. She took off her jeans and panties.

"Please, Rory, I want you now," she said.

He manoeuvred her to the edge of the settee; the angle was just right. He held open her legs and entered her. She gasped as he pushed his hardness into her.

"Ooohh, that's so good," she said. "Fuck me, Rory, fuck me."

Rory obliged and within minutes he could feel his orgasm approach. "I'm coming," he shouted.

"Yes, come in me, come in me."

He climaxed and seconds later Laura followed suit.

They lay there together for a moment. "Wow, that was good," said Rory.

"Oh, yes," she said pulling him against her. She squeezed her thighs as if emptying Rory. "That was amazing."

They eventually disconnected. "There's bathroom in the

hall," said Laura. "I'll just pop upstairs."

Rory watched as the naked Laura, went up the spiral staircase, then he retraced his steps to the hall and found the small toilet where he could clean himself.

Rory had dressed and was sitting on the settee when Laura returned wearing a bathrobe.

She walked over to Rory and kissed him.

"Mmm, you smell nice," he said.

"Thank you… would you like your dessert now?"

"I thought that was it," he said and laughed.

"No… fruit salad," said Laura and smiled.

"Yeah, sounds great," said Rory.

A few minutes later they were sat back at the dining room table consuming their fruit.

"This is great," said Rory.

"Thanks, I wanted something quick," she said, then realised the innuendo.

"Not that quick," said Rory and they both laughed.

"Would you like a coffee?" said Laura.

"Yes, I'd love one," said Rory. "I'll give you a hand with the dishes."

"No, it's ok, there's not much to do," said Laura.

"I insist," said Rory and he followed Laura into the kitchen carrying his empty dish.

"Great kitchen," said Rory. It matched the rest of the house with modern appliances, natural wood surround and a large cooking area. Laura loaded the dishwasher as Rory washed up the items that weren't dishwasher-safe.

Every now and then he would catch her eye. There was more kissing as they waited for the coffee percolator to do its thing.

He undid the front of her dressing gown and slid his hands inside. She was naked.

"Ohhh, that's so good," she said as he started exploring her body with his fingers.

She broke away for a moment while she finished making

the coffee.

"We'll drink this and go to bed… how does that sound?"

"Perfect," said Rory.

They took their drinks back to the lounge, Rory sat on the settee. There was a glass-topped coffee table with four coasters which they used for their mugs. Laura sat opposite him.

The curtains were still open; the sun had set and outside was a twilight world of roosting birds and night-time creatures.

"Good job you're not overlooked," said Rory, admiring the view.

"Ha, ha, yes," said Laura, and she got up and moved to the window. Rory followed.

"I love it here," she said. Rory stood behind her, put his arms around her waist then opened her dressing gown. He moved his hands up her body and started massaging her chest. He had his head on her shoulders and started kissing the back of her neck.

"Mmm, that's lovely," she said. "Come on, forget the coffee, let's go to bed."

She held Rory's hand and led him up the spiral staircase. On the first floor, there was a landing and three doors, two to the right and one to the left.

"Bathroom's at the end. Help yourself; I'll be in here," she said and opened the left-hand door which Rory could see was her bedroom.

Rory followed Laura's directions. The bathroom matched the rest of the house and was devoid of any clutter, just a couple of towels hanging from the towel-rail. It looked like a show-house.

Rory freshened up and made his way to Laura's bedroom. She was laying on the bed totally naked.

It was almost midnight before Laura excused herself and got out of bed.

"Would you like to stay over?" she said on her return. "I don't have to go into the office till ten."

"Yeah, that would be great. I didn't bring a toothbrush, though," Rory replied.

"There's a spare in the cabinet, you'll see it. Help yourself," said Laura.

"Thanks," said Rory, and left the bed for the bathroom.

He had already made his mind up not to go into the works on Friday, he could do what he needed to do from home. He would phone Alistair and let him know.

He returned to the bedroom, climbed in next to Laura and held her till she went to sleep. Rory was in a reflective mode and his thoughts shifted to Lennie Arthur's daughter. Whether it was this or not, Rory wouldn't know, but the nightmares resurfaced. It was the trek across the Iraqi desert; it was so vivid as if he was back there; just him and Lennie driving towards the border and safety. Then it was blackness. It was a familiar scene, he'd had this dream many times before. It woke him, and he sat bolt upright.

"Are you ok," said Laura, turning on the bedside light. Rory was sweating.

"Yeah, sorry."

Rory got out of bed and washed himself down in the bathroom.

"Do you want a drink?" said Laura on his return.

"Yeah, please," said Rory and Laura got out of bed and went downstairs. She returned a couple of minutes later with a glass of water which Rory gulped down in one go.

"Thanks," he said, "Sorry if I woke you."

"It's ok," she said and cuddled up to him.

They were woken by the alarm at seven-thirty. It was Laura that stirred first. "Do you want to use the bathroom? I'll make some tea."

Rory took the hint and showered. When he returned to the bedroom, Laura was checking her phone for emails; there was a mug of tea on both sides of the bed.

"I didn't put sugar in it," said Laura.

"No, it's fine," said Rory.

He got into bed and she put her phone down.

"Are you ok?"

"Yeah," replied Rory.

"You were having a nightmare," said Laura.

"Yeah, sorry, they happen sometimes."

"It's ok, I was worried… Do you want to talk about it; it might help?"

"It's ok," said Rory.

"I want to help if I can… don't worry I would never repeat anything you tell me. It's just between me and you."

Rory put his hands to his face and drew them down. "It's ok, it was a long time ago."

"You said someone was dead," said Laura.

"Yeah, sorry. It was a buddy of mine; he got killed… I was with him at the time," said Rory, who had picked up his mug and was sipping his tea.

"You said something about 'ragheads', well actually you shouted, 'fucking ragheads'."

"Did I? Sorry about that."

Laura looked at him. "You were in the army, weren't you? Mmm, Iraq… yes? That would explain the raghead connection. I've got a cousin who's in Afghanistan. That's what he calls the locals."

"I can see why you're a reporter," said Rory. "I really can't talk about it."

"No, it's ok, I can see that… my cousin's the same. He won't talk about his experiences either."

Laura put her mug down and put her arms around Rory. He looked at her and they started kissing; Laura's hand started exploring, and moments later Rory was in her.

Rory left Laura's around nine, declining a cooked breakfast; opting for a couple of slices of toast.

"Do you want to meet up again?" asked Laura as Rory left.

"Yeah, I'd like that," said Rory. "I'm away this weekend on a job, but I'll ring you, see if we can sort something out for next week."

"That would be great," said Laura.

"Look forward to it," said Rory and he unlocked his car and drove back down the drive.

Laura watched with a wave of emotions as Rory's car turned right and headed back to Worcester. It had been the most passionate night of her life. Rory had ignited fires in her she didn't know she had; a powerful, all-consuming elixir which would need replenishing. But there was something dangerous about him that worried her, she wasn't sure if she could handle his insecurities. Time would tell; she couldn't wait to see him again. She shut the door and started getting ready for work.

Rory had also found the experience intense. It had been over six months since Kim had left him and he wasn't sure how ready he was for another relationship. He always seemed to mess things up. At least mentally he was in a better place, except for the odd blip; he'd lost most of his moroseness and spent less time dwelling on past events. His running helped, but he was becoming obsessive with his fitness routine and continually pushed himself to the limit. He still found emotional stuff difficult, but at least he'd learned to control his temper. Anger issues had been a problem following his near-death experience on the rig.

At ten o'clock, Rory called Alistair explaining his work proposals for the day and was given a general update. There was more information about the trade fair which he noted.

Rory had full access to the company's intranet and spent the morning reviewing the clients' list. There was nothing out of the ordinary. HM Government and GMI were the biggest clients but there were other Middle-East connections he would investigate further on Monday when he could review the correspondence in more detail. He would arrange a meeting with Duncan, the sales director.

By mid-afternoon, Rory had completed his intended work schedule and made a call.

"Hi, it's me," he said when the phone was answered.

"Hello me," said Laura. "I was just thinking about you."

"Yeah?" said Rory. "Thanks again for last night."

"It's ok, I hope we can do it again," said Laura.

"Yeah, definitely... I can't talk for long, I'm catching a train at four... do you fancy a drink on Monday?"

"Yeah, ok, that would be great, your place or mine?"

"I'm easy," said Rory.

"Hmm, I hope not," said Laura and laughed.

"Well, what about I come over to you?" said Rory.

"Yeah, ok do you want some food? It won't be any bother."

"Well, yeah, if that's ok," said Rory.

"Of course, seven again?"

"Yeah, great," said Rory. "What are you doing over the weekend?"

"Going across to see my parents tomorrow... Sunday, washing and slopping about," said Laura. "You're on this mystery job, right?"

"Yeah, it's a favour for someone, I'll be back Sunday night."

"Yeah, well, ring me if you get a chance... and take care," said Laura.

"Will do," said Rory and after some goodbyes rang off.

He started packing a small overnight bag with a few clothes and his toiletries. He'd booked a taxi for three-thirty to take him to the station. Right on time, he heard a car-horn outside and he locked up. It took twenty minutes through the afternoon traffic, which would give him ten minutes for his train.

Whenever on a business trip, Rory had always travelled on first-class; it was less busy and gave him time to think. It was worth the added expense. It was a comfortable journey with an attentive steward who was on hand to produce endless cups of coffee and biscuits. As he relaxed, Rory started to feel the effects of the previous night; a couple of times he drifted off to sleep.

As the train pulled into London's Paddington Station around six-fifteen, Rory made his way to the door; the concourse was heaving with people. Rory had a note of Swannie's address; it meant an Underground journey south of the river, Colliers Wood. He'd never been to that part of London before and had arranged to meet his buddy at the Tube Station. It was not a straightforward journey and he would have to change twice to reach his destination. Swannie had given him detailed directions.

It was gone seven when Rory arrived at the station. He approached the ticket-barrier and looked around for his buddy. The Tube had been a nightmare; people crammed in like sardines. How anyone could do that day-in, day-out was a mystery. There were about fifty people trying to get through the gate which was guarded by a surly, uniformed man collecting the tickets. Rory spotted Swannie hovering around the exit.

"Rory Calderwood, you old bastard, how are you doing?" said Swannie, on seeing his former squad leader.

"Swannie, great to see you again," said Rory, which was followed by man hugs.

"I'm parked just down the street," said Swannie, "We're only ten minutes away."

As they left the station, Rory noticed the frontage, a concrete edifice, art-deco in design, probably constructed in the 1920's. Rory was programmed to take in detail. It had saved his life in the past.

The pair caught up with routine gossip as they walked to Swannie's car.

"Parking's a fucking nightmare 'round here," said Swannie, as they reached his one-year-old Vauxhall Corsa; about as anonymous as you can get.

"What's this, Swannie, slumming it a bit, aren't we?"

"My other car's a Ferrari," said Swannie, as they got into the five-door hatchback. "No, I don't tend to drive much in town, this is Beryl's… Anyway, I've been doing a bit of digging since your call. I've found the place where Fiona lives. Not spoke to anyone yet, I thought I'd wait for you to get here, but I hung around for a while to see who was about."

This was standard reconnaissance procedure; check your environment, get information, assess information.

"That's great," said Rory. "Did you see anything?"

"Nah, saw a couple of girls go in, looked like students, that's all."

"Yeah, that would make sense. Helen said Fiona shared with some girls," said Rory.

"How is Helen, by the way?" asked Swannie.

"Hmm, changed a lot, seems to have lost all that spark she had when she was with Lennie," said Rory.

"That's a shame, she was a great girl… certainly kept the reins on old Lennie, God bless him," said Swannie.

"Yeah, that's for sure." There was a moment or two's silence.

"I thought we could wait for Digger to get here, then go and have a look," said Swannie, breaking the mood.

"Sounds like a good plan," said Rory.

Swannie drew up outside a typical suburban house, three-bedroomed, semi-detached, one of many down the street.

"Bring your gear, I'll introduce you to Beryl," said Swannie, heading up the short garden-path to the front door.

Rory was led inside. There was a sitting room on the left, it would have been called a 'front parlour' when the house was built; to the right was the living room where a TV was on.

"Beryl will be in the kitchen, come through," said Swannie.

It was a large room and was clearly where the family socialised and ate their meals; a woman in jeans and a top was tending something on the stove.

She turned. "Hello, you must be Rory… Steve's always talking about you."

"This is Beryl," said Swannie. Rory looked at her, she looked older than her husband and had a 'homely' look about her.

"Hi, Beryl," said Rory and kissed her on the cheek.

"You'll have to excuse the mess… We've just eaten, the kids are watching TV. I've done a meat and potato pie… I did enough for you, and Digger if you want some."

"That's great, thanks," said Rory.

For half an hour, there was a catch-up. "It was terrible to hear about your friend's daughter," said Beryl. "I never knew Lennie, but Steve often mentions him."

"Yeah," said Rory. "He was a great guy."

There was a knock on the door.

"That'll be Digger," said Swannie getting up to let him in.

Rory was still seated and waited for his friend to reach the kitchen.

"Digger, great to see you again," said Rory.

"How's it going, Sarge?" said Digger.

"Yeah, great thanks… you can drop the Sarge, that was too long ago," said Rory.

There were more hugs, and over Beryl's meat and potato pie, they caught up on news.

Rory looked at his buddies. Swannie, as fit as ever, had hardly changed in the fourteen years since they were in the desert together. He was shorter than Rory and wiry. Digger Benson looked more like a prop-forward in a rugby squad, six-foot-two with huge biceps; he'd put on some weight, the wife's cooking was to blame, he said, but he'd kept himself fit.

It was eight-thirty when Rory suggested that they halted the reminiscing and got to work. Beryl was happy to let them borrow the car for the evening. Swannie took Rory upstairs to stow his gear in the spare room. The first floor had three bedrooms, a small 'box-room' which had been converted into a fourth bedroom, and a bathroom. Rory was in the box-room. It was about the same size as his quarters on the oil-rig and would suit his needs, no problem.

The three set off and headed north. Fiona's house was in a residential area of Acton, just off the North Circular Road. It's a desirable area with easy access to Central London; her university was just a few stops on the Tube.

It took nearly half an hour to get to the destination. There was on-street parking and Swannie was able to stop adjacent to the house on the opposite side of the road.

"What do you want to do?" said Digger, who was sitting in the back.

"Well, we don't want to frighten anyone, we just need information," said Rory.

"I'll go and knock on the door, and see if I can speak to someone. I'll call you if I need you," said Rory.

"Yeah, ok," said Swannie. Rory left the car and walked across the road. He reached the front door and rang the bell. He could hear music coming from inside. The front door was heavy wood, patterned and painted white with two stained-glass windows either side of the central panel. Rory could detect movement and rang again.

There was the sound of a chain being attached and the door opened about four inches.

"Hello, what do you want?" said a girl's voice.

Rory had one of his business cards in his hands and passed it through the opening. He was calm and reassuring; he needed to build trust quickly if he was going to get anywhere with this line of enquiry.

"Hi, my name's Rory, sorry to call this time of night but I'm a friend of Helen Arthur, Fiona's mum. She's very worried about her... Fiona's not been in touch for a couple of weeks and her mum's asked me to see if I can contact her. Please, can I come in...? I won't keep you long, I just need some information."

The door was pushed shut and the girl went away, but she returned a moment later with another girl and opened the door.

"You better come in," said the girl, still holding Rory's business card.

"Thank you," said Rory and followed the girls to a sitting room. "As I said, sorry to disturb you, but as you can imagine, Fiona's mum's really worried."

"It's ok. I'm Gemma, this is Olivia." They sat down on an old sofa; Rory sat opposite on a matching armchair.

"So, you are at Uni with Fiona, or do you just share the house?"

"Both, we're on the same course," said Gemma.

"And she's not been to lectures?"

"No, no-one's seen her for nearly two weeks."

Gemma looked at Olivia who took over the narrative. "We've been very worried... we had the police 'round, but they've not done anything."

"Yes, that's why Fiona's mum asked me to see if I could help."

"So, what are you, some sort of private detective?" said Gemma.

"No, but I'm in security, as it says on my card, and I promised Helen I would try to find Fiona if I can," said Rory. "But I really need your help. I need somewhere to start."

"Yeah, ok," said Gemma.

"Look, I've got a couple of associates in the car, we were all friends of Fiona's dad. Is it alright if I ask them in? They may have ideas as well." Gemma looked at Olivia.

"Yeah, go on then," said Gemma. Rory went to the front door and beckoned Swannie and Digger over.

Swannie locked the car and he and Digger walked to the house.

"This is Steve, and this is Digger, we were army buddies of Lennie... that's Fiona's dad," said Rory.

"Thanks for talking to us," said Swannie. "We really

appreciate it."

The three together had an imposing presence, but they were careful not to create any threat. Swannie and Digger sat on the arms of the remaining armchair, opposite Rory.

"So, when was the last time you saw Fiona?" said Rory. He'd taken a notebook from his pocket and was making notes.

"A week last Friday, she had a date," said Gemma.

"A date…? Do you know the guy?" said Rory.

"No. I went home that weekend but Livvy met him, didn't you?" Gemma looked at Olivia.

"Yeah, he came around about seven o'clock… on the Friday night. They were going for a drink, Fi said… She wouldn't have done anything reckless, she was so sensible… and careful."

"Yeah, that's what her mum said… What was he like… this guy?"

"I thought he looked a bit creepy if I'm honest… He was Turkish," said Olivia.

"Turkish…?" said Rory. "Did you get a name, by any chance?"

"Yeah… Mehmet," said Olivia. "That's what he said."

"They're all called fucking Mehmet," said Swannie. Rory gave him a look. "Sorry," said Swannie.

"It's ok," said Gemma.

"Did you tell the police this?"

"Yes, but I don't think they did anything. They've not been back… I thought it might have been them when you called," said Gemma.

"Is there anything you can tell us about this Mehmet?" said Rory.

"Not really, he said his dad owned a restaurant somewhere," said Olivia.

"How did Fiona meet him, do you know?"

It was Gemma who picked up the story. "Fi likes to go to the park at lunchtimes, she says it clears her head… She was sitting on a bench eating her lunch and he just came up and sat beside her."

"Just like that?" said Rory; he looked at his buddies.

"Well, I can't say exactly, but Fi said she'd met this guy at the park and they started chatting... That was earlier in the week, Monday, I think... then she met him again the following day and he asked her if she would go for a drink with him."

"Did she say anything about him?" asked Rory.

"No, not really... except she thought he was good-looking... 'dashing', I think she called him. Mind you that was typical Fi, she has an affinity with Byron," said Gemma and smiled at Olivia.

This was over Rory's head.

Rory recapped. "So, Fiona meets this guy... Mehmet, at the park, meets him again the following day, and he asks her for a date on Friday."

"Yes," said Gemma. "She did seem quite keen... she was certainly making an effort, I lent her some of my mascara, she'd run out."

"What time did he turn up?" said Swannie.

It was Olivia who answered. "He was on time, about seven I think. Fi kept him waiting, although she'd been ready for twenty minutes... She was actually quite nervous."

"Can you describe him to me?"

"He was quite tall, dark with a beard."

"What sort of beard?"

Olivia looked blank.

"Was it bushy or trim?" said Rory.

"Oh, right, it was trim... like Jonny Depp, Pirates of the Caribbean." Olivia clarified, seeing Rory's disconnect.

"She loved that film, said it made her go all gooey," said Gemma.

"Did he mentioned where he worked, or did Fiona say anything more about him?" said Rory. "Please think, this could be really important, anything, any little detail which might help us find this guy."

Olivia looked at Gemma. "I don't think so."

Swannie looked at Rory. "Well, there can't be that many Turkish restaurants in this neck of the woods… The other thing is if he was the son of the owner, why wasn't he working on Friday night? I mean, it's one of the busiest nights of the week, I would have thought."

"Yeah, that's a thought," said Rory. Digger hadn't spoken during the discussion but was taking everything in.

"Did she say where they were going?" asked Rory.

"No," said Gemma.

"She said it was going to be a surprise," said Olivia.

"Hmm," said Rory, digesting the information.

"So, she didn't return that night?" said Rory.

"No," said Olivia.

"Weren't you worried?" asked Rory.

"Well, not really… She used to go out with a boy called Damian and she would often stay over at his," said Olivia.

Rory looked at Swannie and Digger.

"Who's Damian?" said Rory.

"That was her previous boyfriend… they split up," said Gemma.

"When was this?"

"About three or four weeks ago."

"Why? Did Fiona say?"

"Yes, he was getting too 'clingy'… I think was the word she used," said Gemma. She looked at Olivia.

"How long had they been going out?" asked Swannie.

"About six months," said Gemma, looking at Olivia for confirmation.

"Yeah, about that," agreed Olivia.

"Did you meet him?" asked Rory.

"Oh, yes… He used to stay here sometimes?"

"What was he like?" asked Swannie.

"Hmm, I don't like him much; he was a bit of a 'mummy's boy'… Fi even used to wash his hair," said Gemma.

"Yeah, she said he begged her not to leave him, he was quite emotional, apparently... That's what Fi said," said Olivia.

"Mmm, I think we need to speak to him. Do you know where he lives?"

"Yes, he's got a flat in Shepherds Bush. It'll be in Fi's diary," said Gemma.

"Fiona has a diary?" said Rory.

"Yes," said Gemma.

"Can we see it, please...? It may help us," said Rory.

"Yes, just a minute," and Gemma got up and left the room.

"What about her mobile phone? I presume she has one," said Rory.

"Yes, we've been trying to call her, but it's switched off," said Olivia.

"Yeah, that's what her mum said," said Rory.

"When did you contact the police?" said Swannie.

"Not until the following Friday. We were both away that week, Gemma and me. I left on Saturday morning, so I didn't know that Fi hadn't got back... I phoned her a couple of times to see if she was ok, but as I said, it was switched off."

Gemma returned with Fiona's diary. "There's nothing in there apart from her addresses," said Gemma.

Rory flicked through the empty pages. He noticed crosses at the top of the page, every so often.

"What about these crosses?" said Rory.

Gemma looked at Olivia. "Hmm, that's probably a girl thing," said Gemma.

"Oh, yeah, right," said Rory, trying not to appear embarrassed.

The address section at the back had been completed, friends, relatives. There was Helen's address, he recognised. "Ah, here we are... Damian Foster... twenty-nine, Beagle Terrace, Shepherds Bush."

Rory made a note and handed back the diary. There was a phone number which he also noted.

"Do you want a coffee?" said Gemma.

Rory looked at the guys. "No, you're ok, we've taken up enough of your time… Are you about over the weekend if we want to speak to you again?"

"Yes, we're both revising so we're not going out anywhere… You can have our numbers if you want," and Gemma gave Rory the information.

"Thanks for your time, and if you do think of anything that might help, please call me, you've got the number."

"Yes, we will, thank you," said Gemma.

The guys stood up and Gemma led them to the door.

"We'll be in touch," said Rory as he followed Swannie and Digger to the car.

Gemma closed the door. "God, was he fit or what?" she said, and Olivia giggled.

"You can say that again," Olivia replied.

Chapter Seven

Swannie started the car and drove off. "Anyone fancy a pint? I could do with a beer."

"Yeah, go on," said Digger.

"Yeah, sure, I'm in your hands," said Rory.

Within five minutes, Swannie spotted a pub and pulled into the car-park. It would give the guys a chance to compare notes and formulate a plan.

Rory went to the bar while Swannie and Digger found a seat.

The place was almost deserted. The bored-looking barman broke away from watching TV to serve him. "What can I get you?" said the man.

"Three pints of lager," said Rory.

The barman started pulling the first pint. "Quiet, tonight," said Rory.

"Yeah," said the barman. "It's the smoking ban… It'll close us all down the way things are going, you mark my words."

There was a seat in the corner where they wouldn't be disturbed. Rory carried the drinks over on a tray.

"So, what do you reckon?" said Rory, as he sat down.

"Well, we've got the clingy ex-boyfriend or the creepy Turk," said Swannie.

"My money's on the Turk," said Digger. "There's been a spate of kidnappings I've been reading about. Girls being smuggled to the Middle-East as sex-slaves."

"I've told you before about reading the News of The World," said Swannie, and laughed.

"No, it's right enough," said Digger, indignantly.

"It's ok," said Rory. "Digger's got a point, and if she has been taken, she could already be out of the country. It's been two weeks."

"Jesus," said Swannie. "Let's hope not."

"It depends, they tend to ship them in groups to save costs," said Rory.

"You're well-informed," said Swannie.

"Yeah, I keep up with these things," said Rory.

"Look, how about we pay the ex-boyfriend a visit first? That's the easy part, at least we know where he lives," said Swannie.

"Yeah," said Rory. "Makes sense, then if we don't get anywhere, we can still trawl the restaurants, maybe bring the girls with us, at least they can identify him."

"If we call early enough, we may catch our Damian at home," said Swannie.

"What about you, Digger? Can you get over here for, say seven?" said Rory.

"Yeah, don't see why not. I was only planning to clean the pigeon loft."

"Pigeon loft?" said Rory and Swannie in unison.

"You keep fucking pigeons?" said Swannie.

"Well, I don't fuck 'em," said Digger and the three roared with laughter. It was just like old times.

Saturday morning, it was an early start. Rory had slept well in the box room. Beryl and the kids were still in bed as he and Swannie sat in the kitchen drinking tea and eating toast while they waited for Digger.

He turned up around seven-twenty and once again Beryl's Corsa was borrowed for the day. The three set out to find Damian's flat still talking animatedly about the need to find Fiona.

It was another bright summer morning. Luckily, London had been spared the worst of the rain they'd had in the West Midlands.

Armed with an A-Z and with Rory navigating, it was easy enough to find Beagle Terrace and the residence of Damian Foster.

"There we go, number twenty-nine," said Swannie as he drew up alongside a nondescript semi-detached house.

"How do you want to play this, Sarge?" said Digger, still having difficulty getting out of the habit of addressing Rory by his military rank.

"Threat, or stealth?" asked Swannie.

"Oh, I think threat, don't you? From what the girls were saying, this guy will roll over if we exert a bit of pressure," said Rory.

"Yeah, I like that," said Digger. "Threat it is."

"Ok, I'll go to the door and see if anyone's in. If our man is there we rush him and take it from there. Everybody happy?"

"Oh, yeah," said Digger. "Let's get it on."

The three got out of the car and made their way to the front door. It was eight o'clock and Rory could hear music from inside. "Well, someone's in," said Rory and he rang the bell as Digger and Swannie stayed out of sight.

The door was opened by a young-looking man wearing a tracksuit.

"Sorry to bother you, I'm looking for Damian Foster," said Rory.

"Yeah, that's me," he said.

In a flash, Rory had bundled him inside; Swannie and Digger followed and shut the door.

Rory had got hold of the man and lifted him off the floor by the scruff of his neck until his feet were off the ground.

"What do you want!?" he screamed.

"We need a chat about Fiona," said Rory.

"I don't know any Fiona," said Damian. Swannie dealt a swift punch to the solar plexus which took the wind out of him. Rory let him go; he was bent double. "Wrong answer," said Swannie.

"Well, here's how it goes, we can do this the hard way, or the easy way… It's up to you," said Rory.

"What about Fi? We've split up… I've not seen her," said

Damian, getting some of his breath back.

"She's gone missing and we just want to see if you know anything about it," said Rory.

Damian stood up slowly holding his stomach and trying to gain control of his breathing.

He looked at Rory. "Missing, what do you mean, missing?"

"God, this lad's thick, I thought you were at university?" said Rory. "What do you think I fucking mean? Missing, as in, not about."

"I don't know anything about that," said Damian.

"Swannie, give him another reminder, eh?" said Rory.

Swannie was about to aim another blow. "Wait, wait... stop, don't hurt me... there is something. I'll tell you what I know."

"Too fucking right," said Swannie.

Rory lifted Damian off the floor again. There was a room to the right and Digger opened the door. "In here," said Rory. He dragged Damian into the room and threw him onto an old sofa.

"Right, I'm all ears," said Rory.

He started to cry.

"Fucking hell, stop blubbing and tell us what you know," said Rory.

"We'd split up, we'd been going out for six months... she was my world, but she said she didn't want to see me again... It was terrible... I couldn't sleep, or study... I was devastated."

"So, what did you do?" asked Rory.

"At first, I just wanted to die... but then I thought I would try again... try to get her to go out with me. I just wanted to tell her how much I loved her... I would change anything just to be with her again."

He looked at Rory with pitiful eyes. "What did you do?" asked Rory

"I went to her house to see her, but I bottled it."

"You little creep," said Swannie.

"Let him speak," said Rory, the classic 'good-cop, bad-cop' approach.

Damian was still sobbing. "I was sitting in the car watching the house, trying to pluck up some courage but then this bloke turns up in a black car… a Mercedes, and goes up to the front door. He was in there for ages and then she comes out with him and I saw her get in."

"When was this?" asked Rory.

"Friday before last… I've not seen her since."

"What did you do when you saw them drive off?" said Rory.

He looked down. "I followed them."

"Followed them…? Where to?"

"They went to this restaurant in Kensington."

Rory looked at Swannie and Digger. "What restaurant?"

"It was a Turkish Restaurant."

"What was it called?"

"I don't remember. The Medina… I think… something like that." Damian was still sobbing.

"What happened then?" said Rory.

"I waited till they came out."

"How long was that?"

"It was much later, ages. They came out together, hand-in-hand… I was so angry I wanted to kill her."

Rory looked at Swannie, then Digger.

"Then what happened?"

"They went around the corner. I couldn't see that clearly, but she seemed to be struggling with him."

"And?"

"I couldn't stand anymore, so I went to drive off, but then I saw the man she was with walking back towards the entrance of the restaurant on his own… I was over the moon. I thought she must have blown him out and got a cab or something."

"Then what happened?" said Rory.

"Nothing… I just drove home."

"Why didn't you see where she went? You could have given her a lift," said Swannie.

"I did, I looked for her, but I couldn't see her," said Damian.

"And you've not heard from her since?"

"No, I called 'round the next day, on the Saturday but there was nobody in. I tried her phone as well, but it was switched off... I went passed a couple of times to see if I could see her, but nothing, so I just gave up."

"Do you know where this restaurant is?" said Rory.

"Yes," said Damian.

"Ok, we're going for a ride, and you're coming with us," said Rory. Damian looked terrified.

"Don't worry, we won't hurt you. We just want to find Fiona, that's all... Is there anyone else in the house?"

"No, they're away," said Damian.

"Ok, bring your keys, we need to get going," said Rory.

Digger hustled Damian out of the house and into the back of the car. Rory and Swannie were in the front.

"Ok," said Swannie. "Which way?"

"Kensington," said Damian.

Damian was still petrified about what might happen, but he gave the directions when required and in about fifteen minutes they were heading down the famous High Street.

"Here... take the next left, by the supermarket," he directed. "There, on the other side of the road."

Sure enough, there was the Turkish restaurant, 'The Medina Palace'. It was on the corner of a right-hand turn. Swannie drove passed and parked up about a hundred yards on. The shops and retail outlets had gone; it was just residential properties of various descriptions.

"Take us through what happened again," said Rory.

"I was parked on the other side of the road facing the High Street."

Swannie swung a one-eighty and parked again. They were outside a large house which doubled as offices; 'Cecil Bainbridge & Co, Accountants', it said on a brass plaque on the gate post. Next to the house was a funeral director's parlour; there was a sign, 'strictly no parking – 24-hour access', it said.

"Yes, about here," said Damian. "I remember that place," he added.

They were about a hundred and fifty yards from the junction with the High Street. Next to the funeral director was a boutique, then a betting shop, then the supermarket on the corner.

The restaurant on the opposite side of the road looked modern with a facia-board signage depicting the name 'The Medina Palace' with a telephone number. The window had displays of dishes in a montage. The place was dark, no sign of anyone about. There was a left-hand turn immediately after the restaurant and across the road, there was a patch of waste ground with a huge awning advertising a mobile phone company. Behind that were the back entrances to the High-Street shops.

Rory turned around in his seat and spoke to Damian. "Ok, when they came out what could you see?"

"Well, the Mercedes was parked where you were just parked, over there. They came out of the restaurant, holding hands, but instead of going to the car, they turned left and went down that street. That's when I lost sight of them."

"Then what happened?" said Rory.

"As I said, the guy came back on his own."

"And you saw her struggle with him?"

"It looked like it. One minute they were holding hands, then he had his arm around her, but it looked like she was trying to get away. I could be wrong. That's when I thought they'd had a row or something. So, I waited for a bit and saw the man walk back, then I drove off slowly and stopped when I got to that road." He pointed to the left-hand turn. "To see if I could see her, but there was no sign, so I went home."

"What about the bloke, where did he go?"

"He went back into the restaurant."

"Not to his car?"

"No, I'm certain he went back in the restaurant," said Damian.

"This is important, Damian; think… About how long were they out of sight before you saw the man come back alone?"

"Oh, it was less than a minute, seconds maybe… One minute they went around that corner, then the man came back to the restaurant on his own."

"Did you see what he looked like, this bloke?" asked Swannie.

"Not very well, he looked Middle-Eastern… beard, wearing a suit," said Damian.

"A beard… you said a beard," said Rory.

"Yes, a, what do you call them…? Goatee… is that right?" Rory looked at Swannie.

"Ok, thanks for your help," said Rory. "You can piss off now."

"Aren't you going to take me home?" said Damian.

"Sorry, we're going to be busy. Haven't you got your Oyster Card?"

"No," said Damian.

"Then it's going to be a bit of a walk," said Swannie.

Damian got out and slammed the door, then started walking towards the High Street.

"So, what's the plan?" said Digger.

"Well, we can't stay here; we don't want to draw attention to ourselves. Let's find a coffee-shop and have a chat," said Rory and Swannie drove off to find a car park.

A few minutes later, with the car stowed in a multi-story, the three walked down the High Street and found a suitable café. The High Street was starting to get busy with Saturday shoppers and tourists; the café was doing a good trade. Over cappuccinos, the three discussed possible scenarios.

Swannie produced his road atlas and found the appropriate page.

"We need to check out that road, see what's down there… Fenton Street. If what Damian said is right, then they couldn't have got far... My guess, it'll be the back of the restaurant somewhere, but we'll need to check to make sure. It's possible he dragged her through another door, or even into a car; we don't know," said Rory.

"We could stake-out the place for a while, see if anything unusual is going on," said Swannie.

"Yeah, that'll be a start, we need to get the lay of the land, what houses are down there, whether there are any other likely places." This was text-book reccy procedure; check your target.

"We could do with a camera," said Rory.

"There's one in the boot," said Swannie. "Always carry it with me... and a laptop too."

"Great, let's get to work," said Rory. He pointed to a spot on the map.

"We'll drive along the road passed the restaurant and take the first right, here... Musgrove Street, that joins Fenton Street further down. We'll turn right and follow the road back up to the restaurant... We can look out for an obs spot at the same time."

"Right, got it," said Swannie, and for a moment it was just like Iraq, a band of brothers on a mission.

They left the café and headed back to the car. Swannie removed the camera from the boot and handed it to Rory. It was a pocket digital Olympus, ideal for their needs.

It took only a few minutes to get from the car park to the junction. Swannie turned right from the High Street. They passed Fenton Street, then the restaurant; Rory took a couple of pictures. As they'd discussed, they took the next right into Musgrove Street. It was a leafy avenue with nice houses on either side, an expensive place to live. After about half a mile they reached a T junction and they were back on Fenton Street but further down. Swannie turned right and followed the road until they could see the back of the restaurant on the right-hand side.

"Ok, slow down here Swannie, let's take a look," said Rory.

The three surveyed the buildings to the right. On the left were a few terraced houses, then the advertising awning.

The last four houses before the back of the restaurant were in one large block. They appeared deserted.

"These here look empty," said Digger, leaning over from the back seat.

Rory took some more pictures. "Yeah, looks like they're up for redevelopment... Look, there's a sign..." They passed the Estate Agent's signage in front of the block depicting an artist's impression of the modernised houses. 'Twenty Luxury flats', it said. 'Prices from £750,000'.

"Fuck me, have you seen the prices?" said Swannie.

"Slow down a minute," said Rory.

Swannie complied; the car was at walking pace while Rory took more pictures. They arrived at the back of the restaurant. It was difficult to see much, there was a ten-foot high slatted fence around the perimeter with a gate nearest the road for access. It was closed.

"Shit," said Rory. "That's not going to help... We don't want to be shinning over that unless we have to. We'll stand out like a sore thumb."

"We could go around the back, see if there's another way in," said Swannie.

"Wait, I've got an idea," said Rory. "Let's get out of here in case we're spotted."

Swannie accelerated to the junction and turned left towards the High Street. "Take a left and see if we can stop somewhere," said Rory. Swannie obliged and they were soon in another residential area. Swannie parked up in an empty bay in the street.

"So, what's your plan, Sarge?" said Digger.

"Well, we need to have a better look around," said Rory. "But we can't go sneaking around the fence, it'll be too obvious."

"Yeah, that's for sure," said Swannie.

Rory clarified. "That end house overlooks the restaurant; if we can get inside we can set up obs... How do you fancy being a surveyor, Digger?"

"What do you mean?" said Digger, looking confused.

"We'll need to find a DIY store and get you kitted out," said Rory. Now Swannie was looking confused.

"All we need is a Hi-Viz jacket and a hard hat. No-one will suspect anything, and if you do see anyone, they'll just think you're something to do with the houses.... We'll need a clipboard as well, make it look official."

"Yeah, that'll seal it," said Swannie. "Good call."

"Right, let's find a DIY store," said Rory. He turned and looked at Digger. "You happy to do this, Digger...? No offence, mate, but you look more like a builder than me or Swannie."

"Yeah, no sweat, Sarge," said Digger.

Swannie turned the car around and took a left onto the High Street. They didn't have long to wait; there was a large retail park with one of the national DIY chain stores in prime position.

"Right, here we go... Here's twenty quid, get yourself what you need and get back here. Me and Swannie will check the pictures."

Digger got out and headed into the store, while Swannie went to the boot and retrieved his laptop. He got back in the car, switched on the laptop, connected his camera and seconds later the pictures were up on the screen.

"We'll show these to Digger when he gets back, and he can see what's what," said Rory.

It was twenty minutes before Digger appeared with a large plastic carrier bag. He got in the car.

"How did you get on?" said Rory.

"Yeah, got we needed, no change though," said Digger. He opened up the bag and put on the hard-hat, then slipped on his Hi-Viz vest.

"Here, what do you think?" said Digger.

"Bob, the fucking Builder, eat your heart out," said Swannie and they all laughed.

"So, what's the plan?" asked Digger.

"We need to get into that last house, see... there's a window overlooking the back yard," said Rory.

Swannie showed Digger the picture of the house. "Yeah, I can see what you mean," said Digger.

"First, have a look around the outside, as if you're checking out the buildings, then see if you can get in... You'll probably have to force the door," said Rory. "What do you think, Swannie?"

"Yeah, you might want to take the camera, and get some pics. These are the rest of what we've got so far."

Swannie flicked through the remaining pictures enabling Digger to get a wider perspective.

"Yeah, ok, let's do it," said Digger.

"Right, let's get going," said Rory.

It was only a short journey back to the restaurant and Swannie turned right into Fenton Street and parked further down, well away from the eatery and any prying eyes.

"Ok, we should be ok here for a while, we've got two hours parking," said Rory.

"Ok, lads, I'll be back soon," said Digger. He got out in his gear, carrying a clipboard, and walked back up the road.

There were four houses on the block dating from Edwardian times. They had mercifully escaped the Blitz during the Second World War. Digger was nonchalant and confident, giving the impression that he was just doing his day-job. There was another sign, 'Danger building renovations – keep out'. Digger went up to the front door of the first house and looked through the frosted glass; no signs of movement, or anyone living there. He could see builder's tools through the glass. Swannie and Rory were in the car watching.

He did the same to the next two, with the same result. The final house, the one before the back entrance to the restaurant, was next. He again went to the front door and tried the handle.

It was locked, but he started leaning against it with his shoulder. He exerted more pressure, then the lintel gave way and the door opened. He went through and pushed it closed behind him. He went through each room in turn; there was still some old furnishings scattered among the builder's rubble. He made his way upwards; the place was empty, but then as he entered the last bedroom, he found the window which overlooked the back of the restaurant.

Digger crouched low. He had a clear sight of the yard and the back rooms of the building. There were two dumpsters, but otherwise, the yard was empty. He could see the back entrance and above that, were three windows. There was a fire escape leading to what looked like a security door on the first floor. Digger took out his camera and started shooting. He watched for a few minutes but couldn't detect any movement; then suddenly he realised why. Each window was blacked out with something, a material of some kind; not curtains, but just something hung over a rail or possibly nailed. Digger couldn't make it out, but he hoped the pictures would reveal the answer.

He got up and quickly left the building, pulling the door behind him. From the outside, no-one could tell it had been forced open.

He walked briskly back to the car and got in. "You may want to turn around, save going passed the restaurant," he said as he sat down. Swannie turned the car around and headed further down Fenton Street. Then turned left into Musgrove Road, reversing their earlier journey.

"Right, what've you got?" asked Rory.

"Well, I managed to get into the last one, and found the upstairs bedroom which overlooks the back of the restaurant."

"That's great," said Rory.

"Yeah, something's not right, though... I took some pics which should give us more info," said Digger.

Swannie linked up the camera and laptop and accessed the pictures. "There," said Digger. "Can you expand it... the windows."

The three huddled closer to the screen. "Hey yeah," said Rory.

"Fucking strange way to hang curtains," said Swannie. He expanded the picture until the pixilation made it impossible to make out any detail.

"Looks like something's been nailed against the window," said Swannie.

"Yeah," said Rory. "Still, doesn't necessarily mean anything, could just be waiting for new ones."

"True," said Digger. "What about the fire escape…? We could get in and have a look."

The three took a closer look. "Hmm, looks like a security door. We're not going to break in that way without some gear." It went quiet as the three of them considered possible solutions.

"Ok, here's how I see it," said Rory. "It looks like something's going on, but I can't see anyone keeping girls here…it's just too risky. There're too many people about… customers, suppliers, all sorts… If they are involved in trafficking, they'll be somewhere else."

Swannie looked at Digger.

"So, what are you thinking?" said Swannie.

"We'll stake-out the restaurant, at least until it opens, and see what happens… Swannie, you better pop to the supermarket and get some grub... Some sarnies and a couple of stickies, we could be here for a while… Digger, when Swannie gets back, can you get back in the house? You can keep in touch on the phone if you see anything."

"Yeah, no sweat, Sarge," said Digger. "I could do with some binnocks."

"Hang on," said Swannie and he opened the glove compartment. "Here, try these," he said and handed Digger a small pair of binoculars.

"Fucking hell, Swannie, have you got rabbits up your coat an' all," said Rory, seeing more equipment.

"I do a bit of surveillance from time time-to-time," he said and smiled. "Make sure you look after them," he said, looking at Digger.

"Ok, Swannie, get going… we'll wait here, then it's down to business," said Rory.

He gave him a twenty-pound note and Swannie got out and headed for the supermarket on the corner.

It was twenty minutes before Swannie returned holding a plastic carrier bag. He got in the car and passed the carrier to Rory.

"It's fucking bonkers in there," he said and handed out the rations. "There's some drinks in there as well."

"Cheers," said Rory and they started sharing out the food.

"Here, take the bag," said Rory, passing it to Digger.

"Ok, I'll call you when I get settled," said Digger. "I've got Swannie's number."

Digger got out, wearing his hard-hat and vest; he'd left the clipboard on the back seat, and walked up the street to the empty houses. Swannie drove off and turned right, passed the restaurant and parked close to where they were earlier, with a good view of the front of the place.

Rory took a bite of his sandwich. "Ok, here's the boring bit," he said.

Digger, meanwhile, had re-entered the house and made his way upstairs to the bedroom that overlooked the restaurant. He took out the binoculars from the carrier bag and scanned around; all was quiet. He called Swannie.

"Hi. Swannie… it's Digger. In position, all quiet. Will call if I see anything."

"Cheers," said Swannie.

Rory and Swannie exchanged more memories and updates while they observed the restaurant. Digger was keeping a watchful eye on the back, but there was no sign of anyone. After an hour, Swannie called Digger. His phone was set to 'vibrate'.

"Anything?" said Swannie.

"Nah, nothing happening, seems deserted," said Digger.

Just as it turned four o'clock, Swannie noticed a black Mercedes coming towards them from the High Street.

"What car was Jonny Depp driving?"

"A black Mercedes," said Rory.

"Check this out," said Swannie, who was already calling Digger.

"Digger, black Mercedes heading your way, stay on the line and tell us what's happening,"

Digger watched as the Mercedes turned into Fenton Street and stop outside the gates of the back entrance. He started a running commentary.

"Target stopped, opening the gates… driving in… Parked next to the dumpster. Target out of car, closing the gates… walking to rear door. He's gone inside."

"Did you get a look at him?" asked Rory.

"Not clearly," said Digger.

"Ok," said Swannie. "Stay on the line."

"Start the car," said Rory. "I've got a feeling we might be on the move soon."

Swannie complied.

About ten minutes later, Digger was back on the line.

"Target leaving… he's carrying…" He focussed his binoculars. "It looks like takeaway containers… Opening boot, stowing stuff, closing boot, walking to gate, opening gate… Are you going to follow?"

"Yeah," said Swannie.

"Ok, stay put for a moment," said Digger. "I'll let you know when to make the turn… Right, he's out and closing the gate… Ok, now, he's just pulling away."

Swannie drove off and made the left turn into Fenton Street. The Mercedes was about fifty yards in front. Rory took over phone duties keeping Digger up-to-date. "We're right behind him… He's turning right… it's a cul-de-sac… We'll call you back," said Rory, and rang off.

Swannie followed. "Oh, shit, fucking speed bumps. This'll mess-up Beryl's suspension."

They slowed to walking pace and negotiated the first hump. About thirty yards in front, the Mercedes was having similar difficulties.

"Stay back," said Rory. "We're a bit close."

Swannie braked again and went over the next traffic-calmer. To the right, Rory could see, they were behind the High Street. There were more dumpsters waiting for collection and backyards bricked off from the road.

"This looks like a service road," said Rory.

"Yeah," said Swannie, his face deep in concentration as they negotiated more speed bumps.

The Mercedes slowed and parked in front of one of the refuse skips. Swannie drove passed and stopped about twenty yards away on the opposite side of the street. They carefully watched what was happening behind them.

"How's your eyesight, Swannie?"

"Not bad, not bad."

"Does he look like Johnny Depp to you?"

"Haven't a fucking clue," said Swannie. "Don't know what Johnny Depp looks like."

"Well, you're no fucking use," said Rory and started to laugh. "But I think he does, he's got the beard."

The man had exited the car and was retrieving the containers from the boot. He walked to one of the gates and walked through.

"Shit," said Rory. "We've lost him."

"Stay here," said Swannie. "I'll take a butcher's."

Swannie got out and walked towards the back gate where Mercedes-man had entered. He bent down and sneaked forward until he was at the entrance. There were gaps in the wood and he could see Mercedes-man quite clearly. He was knocking on a door. It opened, and another man appeared. Swannie couldn't believe his eyes. He quickly retraced his steps back to the car.

Swannie looked at Rory. "Our man's gone inside, but there was this other guy, Middle-Eastern looking, who opened the door... I swear he was carrying a Barretta, at least that's what it looked like."

"Ok, this could be it. We'd better get out of here, it's a bit conspicuous," said Rory.

"Do you want to wait for Mercedes-man...?" said Swannie.

"Well my guess, he'll head back to the restaurant... Tell you what; let's go back to the junction. He's got to come back this way; it's a dead end," said Rory.

Swannie turned around and negotiated the speed bumps once again. He cursed every time he went over one. As they reached the junction with Fenton Street, Swannie turned right then did a one-eighty so they could see any traffic coming from the service road.

Rory phoned Digger and gave him an update. "Anything happening your end?" asked Rory

"I think someone else has turned up... I saw a light go on at the back."

"Probably the chef," said Rory.

"Stay put for a few minutes; see if Mercedes-man comes back, then we'll have a conflab..."

"The Mercedes," said Swannie loudly, interrupting Rory's call.

"I'll call you back, Mercedes is on the move."

The car turned left, back towards the restaurant and Swannie followed at a safe distance; there was a good line of sight.

"Yeah, just as I thought," said Rory and he called Digger again.

"Can you see him?" said Rory.

"Yes, he's opening the gate... it looks like he's going to work."

"Ok, we'll park up just down the road. Forget the obs for

now, get down here… We'll decide what we're going to do," said Rory.

Chapter Eight

Swannie and Rory were in the car and could see Digger leave the house and walk towards them, still wearing his hard-hat and Hi-Viz vest. He got in the car and Swannie pulled away.

"Where to?" said Swannie.

"Well, I don't know about you, but I feel peckish... Let's go back to the car-park and find a pizza place," said Rory.

"I'm with you there," said Digger. "I could eat a horse."

Within twenty minutes they were sat in a Pizza parlour, drinking lager and waiting for their food. It was packed out.

There was a lot of banter. "Do you remember that night we went to that Italian in Hereford?" said Rory.

"Oh, yeah, how could I forget?" said Swannie.

"What was this?" said Digger.

"Ninety-two, I think. We went out into town for a bite to eat and we found this Italian restaurant. It was me, Swannie, Lennie and a couple of the other guys... Philips, I think... can't remember the other," said Rory.

Swannie picked up the story. "We went in and Lennie asked for a table and the waiter says... 'Have you got a reservation...?' Quick as a flash Lennie says, 'do I look like a fucking Red Indian?'... We were in hysterics."

"Here's to Lennie," said Digger and the three raised their pint glasses. "Lennie," they all said.

It was a welcome break from their mission.

"I'll tell you something," said Swannie. "I'll fucking kill 'em if they've hurt Fiona."

"Yeah," said Digger. "I'm with you there... So, what's the plan?"

"We need to get in that place up the service road and see what's going on. It looks a better bet than the restaurant," said Rory.

"Ok, so how do we do that?" said Swannie.

Rory picked up a napkin and took a pen from his pocket. "Well, I'd like to take a look at the front of the place, but we need to work out which one it is... Pass us the A-Z."

Swannie took the road atlas from his pocket and put it on the table. Rory opened it at the appropriate page. He started drawing the road in more detail on his napkin, using the map as a reference. This is Fenton Street, and this is the service road which comes around here and then straightens at the back of the shops... How far do you reckon?"

Swannie and Digger looked at the map and Rory's drawing. They were interrupted by a waitress with a name badge that said 'Paloma'. She was carrying three plates, with some difficulty.

"Three pizzas, one extra pepperoni, one Hawaiian Special, and one Margarita with extra onions and peppers," she said in a strong Eastern European accent, and placed the meals on the table in front of their respective owners. Rory had moved the A-Z and napkin onto the seat beside him.

He continued his briefing as they consumed their dinner.

"We need to go down the High Street for about three-quarters of a mile, I reckon," said Rory. "My guess is it'll be a kebab shop or takeaway of some kind."

"Yeah, makes sense," said Swannie. Digger was making short work of his Margarita.

It was gone seven o'clock before they left the Pizza place and headed back to the car. It was noticeably darker; heavy clouds had gathered and there was a distinct threat of rain.

From the multi-story, Swannie turned right and they crawled their way towards Hammersmith. The buildings on the left-hand side were mainly offices, then some more shops.

"Wait, what's that?" said Rory. "On the left."

The traffic was slow; red double-decker buses passed in both directions in packs, like hunting wolves prowling for customers. Swannie crawled by the premises, it gave them chance to get a reasonable view.

"A Turkish greengrocer's?" said Digger.

"That's what it looks like," said Rory.

There was a shop front with trays of fruit and vegetables; the signage was in Turkish with the name 'Büyük Import & Export', in English alongside it.

"What do you think?" said Swannie.

"It would be about the right place... Can you park up somewhere, we need a walk-by?" said Rory.

Swannie took a right turn and parked up.

"What've you got in mind?" said Swannie.

"Stay here, anyone want an apple?" said Rory.

"Why not?" said Digger who was always interested in food.

Rory exited the car and walked across the road and up the High Street towards the greengrocer. He stopped outside and pretended to be examining the produce; instead, he was checking out the premises. It was an old building on two floors, with an attic above; two skylights were visible from the roof. The retail outlet took up the ground floor. There were two men at the back of the shop sat on kitchen stools, talking. One of them started taking an interest in Rory who was still viewing the fruit. Seeing the man approaching, Rory picked up three apples and walked through the open door into the shop.

The man looked at Rory intensely, squinting his eyes. Rory would not be intimidated by anyone, but there was something about the man that unsettled him. He ignored the look and handed the man the goods. He handed over a five-pound note. The other man was also eyeing Rory up. He felt like an interloper.

He took his change and left the store with his purchase in a brown paper bag, took one more look at the frontage and headed back to the car.

He got in and handed Swannie the apples. "One each," said Rory.

"So, what d'you reckon?" said Swannie.

"Two guys in the shop look like a right handful... mean as

they come. Door leading to the back but couldn't see anything. CCTV in the shop, alarm system on the outside; open till eleven, according to the notice on the door. It's not going to be our way in."

"So, it's back to the service road and infil from there?" said Swannie.

"Yeah, no idea how many others are in there, but if Fiona's there, there'll be guards for certain," said Rory.

"Let's do it," said Digger. "Apple's weren't bad," he said, winding the window down and tossing his core into the road.

Swannie started the car and drove back up the High Street and turned right at the supermarket, right again at the restaurant into Fenton Street, then the final turn into the service road. It was almost eight o'clock.

"Park a bit further up, we don't want to be visible from the windows," said Rory.

Swannie drove on a short distance and found a service bay. He turned the car around and drove back about twenty yards from the target house, stopping in front of a small office complex; they had a clear view of the property.

"As I see it, the way in is over that dumpster," said Rory.

"Yeah, handy they left it there… fucking idiots," said Swannie.

The perimeter wall was around ten feet high and topped with broken glass and razor wire, but someone had placed a large green refuse skip against the wall just where it joined the neighbouring boundary, reducing the distance to no more than six feet.

"We'll need to watch ourselves on that," said Rory, pointing to the top of the wall.

"I've got a blanket in the back," said Swannie. "We can use that."

Rory looked at Digger and smiled.

"What was on the other side, Swannie, could you see?" said Rory.

"Yeah, there was nothing, just an open space. There's the back door where Mercedes-man went in, fire escape to the second floor... two windows, barred."

Large spots of water started to appear on the windscreen, then the rain gained in intensity.

"Shit, this is all we need," said Swannie, looking up at the skies.

"Looks like we're gonna get wet lads," said Rory.

"Do you want to wait a bit, till it eases off?" said Swannie.

"No, I think we should go now... if the two guys are in the shop then they won't be guarding the girls... that's assuming they're here. They could've been shipped out," said Rory. "Or not here at all; we're just guessing."

"There's only one way to find out," said Digger.

"What's the time?" Rory checked his watch and answered his own question. "Eight-thirty... Ok, let's do it."

The three men got out, it was pouring with rain and the road was deserted. The street lights shone brighter in the gloom of the storm. Swannie went to the boot and retrieved the blanket and stowed his laptop. He rummaged around for a moment and produced a tyre lever.

"This may come in useful," he said.

They walked quickly to the wall on the opposite side of the road which gave them some cover; they could not be seen from any of the properties. On the other side of the road was Beryl's Corsa and behind that, the offices which were unoccupied.

The team edged their way to the dumpster. Swannie was the lightest and made short work of scaling it. It was heavy-duty plastic, but it gave slightly to his weight as he stood up. The top of the wall was within arm's reach and he opened the blanket up, folded it in half and, holding one end, threw it over. The cloth was now covering the jagged obstacles.

He pointed at Rory and made hand signals indicating he was going over and for Rory to follow. The refuse skip would not take the weight of two people.

Using the blanket to protect his hands, Swannie made the leap and disappeared over the wall; Rory was next. Again, the dumpster wobbled but within moments Rory was over too. It was a routine procedure and one they had trained for regularly in their days in the Regiment. Swannie was flat against the adjacent boundary ready to help his buddies. Rory joined him, and they waited for Digger. Just then, he appeared above them, but as he swung his leg over, the bottom of his trousers became snagged on the razor wire. He was lay on the blanket kicking, trying to free his entangled leg.

"Quick, give me a leg up, I'll help him," said Swannie and in a flash, Rory had lifted Swannie until he was stood on his shoulders. He started pulling at Digger's trousers and after a few moments managed to free Digger's leg. Rory gently eased Swannie back to the floor and Digger jumped down beside them.

"Cheers," he whispered and bent down to examine the tear in his trousers. "Bollocks," he said seeing the damage.

It was still pouring with rain and they were soaked, but it was just an inconvenience, nothing more. They kept close to the wall and slowly edged their way to the back of the building, then along to the back door. Swannie had a quick look and turned to Rory. "Opens outwards, looks reinforced, we're not going to smash it down," he whispered.

Rory suddenly looked down; something had attracted his attention, something shiny on the floor. He bent down and picked it up. It was a lady's gold chain bracelet; the letter 'F' was engraved in a swirl on one of the links. He showed the others and put it in his pocket. They nodded.

"Ok, plan B, it is then," whispered Rory. He again made hand signals. Digger was flat against the wall away from the door's swing; Swannie behind Rory. Rory knocked on the door… nothing. He tried again, more urgently. They could hear movement, then a voice in a foreign tongue, Turkish, reasoned Rory. He thought quickly.

"Mehmet," he said in as close to a Turkish accent as he could manage.

There was a rattling of chains and a key was inserted in the lock, then a bolt slid back. The door opened. Digger was through in the blink of an eye and had the man on the floor. He was shouting and kicking. Digger gave him a swift punch to the face and he went quiet.

"Search him," whispered Rory.

Tucked into the top of the man's jeans was a gun.

"Now that's not a friendly greeting," said Swannie and he removed the weapon. The man started to come around. Swannie was holding the gun and pushed it in his face. Rory and Digger were moving forward down a short corridor.

"Where're the girls?" said Swannie. The man shook his head. He was short and podgy and bleeding from his nose.

Swannie pulled the safety catch off and cocked the gun.

"Where are the girls?" he repeated with menace.

The man raised his eyebrows.

"Upstairs?" The man nodded. "You fucking cock-sucker," said Swannie and he crashed the gun down on his skull rendering him unconscious.

There was another heavy door in front of them which Rory slowly pulled towards him. In the background, through a beaded curtain he could see the rear of the shop. Someone was serving a customer. To the right was a set of stairs. To the left, a store cupboard; the door was open. It was packed with crates of fruit and vegetables. There was a squashed tomato, cabbage leaves and other rubbish on the floor, potential hazards to the unwary.

Swannie passed the gun to Rory and he led the guys slowly up the stairs. Rory counted fifteen and they were at the second-floor landing. They could hear a television which was blaring out from the first room on the right; probably why no-one had heard the shouts for help from the first man; that, and the metal door.

Rory got to the doorway and could see the back of a man's head. In front of him was a small TV; he seemed engrossed in a football match. Rory crept in and put the gun to his head and cocked the trigger.

"Get up, now!" ordered Rory. "Slowly."

The man got up. He was around the same age as the one who had opened the door, but slimmer and taller, black wavy hair, thick with grease.

"Turn around," said Rory. Swannie went behind him and grabbed his arms; the man was immobilised. There was another gun on the table next to his seat; Digger retrieved it. Rory put his gun to the man's temple. "The girls... now."

The man spat at Rory, and Digger punched him in the stomach doubling him up. Swannie, meanwhile had let go of the man and was walking down the corridor checking the rest of the rooms.

There was an urgent whisper. "Here guys."

The call momentarily distracted Rory and the man made a grab for the gun. Before he could reach it, Digger was on him and pulled his head back. There was a click from his neck and the man fell unconscious to the floor.

They left him and followed Swannie's voice. They passed a bathroom to the right, which, judging by the pungent aroma, had not been cleaned for some time. It was a short distance to the back of the house where there were two more doors, both were locked. Rory and Digger joined Swannie who was working the tyre-lever wrenching at the lock. There was a crack as it gave way.

Digger watched the door as Swannie and Rory went inside. They were not prepared for the sight or smell that awaited them. There were two single beds with bare mattresses. On top of each was a girl, both had a hood over their head. Their hands were tied behind them and their feet bound together. There was a bucket in the corner.

"Quick, Swannie, untie them," said Rory.

Rory went to the nearest one and removed the hood. It was a woman, early twenties; she had gaffer tape over her mouth. Her eyes were wide with fright.

"I'm going to take the tape off, don't make a sound; we're friends, ok?" he said.

She nodded.

Rory removed the tape and undid her ties. She sat up trying to get the blood circulating to her wrists. She seemed woozy.

"What's your name?" said Rory.

"Alice," said the girl.

"Ok, Alice, you're safe… do exactly what I say… We're going to get you out of here."

Swannie had freed the other girl. "Is it Fiona?" said Rory.

"I don't think so, she's black… what's your name, love?" said Swannie to the girl.

"Etta," said the girl.

"Alice, are there any others?" said Rory.

"N… n… next door, I… I… think," said Alice drowsily.

"Look after them Swannie, be ready to move… I'm going next door."

Rory crashed the door. It gave way at the first attempt. It was a similar scene, but only one bed and one girl.

Rory went to the girl and removed the blindfold and tape. He put his index finger to his mouth. He recognised her straight away.

"Shhhh," he said. "Fiona?"

She nodded. "I'm Rory, a friend of your Dad, we're getting out of here… Can you walk?"

"I… I… don't know… I'll try," she whimpered.

Rory helped her off the bed and supported her as her legs tried to take the weight. She wobbled, then shuffled forward. Swannie and Digger were waiting with the other girls.

"Come on, let's get out of here," said Rory.

They walked slowly down the corridor towards the stairway they had used earlier. They could hear the football commentary coming from further down the passageway. The three men were supporting one girl each. It was dark and dingy. They passed the toilet, then the room where the man Digger had downed was laying on the floor, lifeless. The TV was still blasting out which had, fortunately, covered up any noise they might have made in freeing the girls. Suddenly Rory stopped; he was holding Fiona under her arms, her legs unable to fully support her weight.

"Someone's coming," said Rory. "Quick, the fire-escape," and they re-traced their steps.

"You go," said Digger. "I'll cover you," he handed Etta to Swannie.

Rory and Swannie were now almost dragging the three girls towards the emergency exit. They turned right after the two bedrooms and in front of them was the fire-door. It had a push-bar which Rory hit, and the door swung open. It was an open metal staircase with a handrail on one side. The rain hit them as they exited the building.

Digger removed the gun from the waistband of his jeans; he could hear shouting and footsteps coming from the TV room. He waited and, as the third man turned the corner by the bedrooms, Digger aimed a fore-arm jab. It was more like a karate chop and it hit the man below the chin, the force almost taking his head off. He dropped like a stone, holding his throat and desperately gasping for air from his ruptured wind-pipe.

Digger ran and caught up with the others who were slowly negotiating the metal stairs. He pulled the fire-door shut and descended. Then they suddenly stopped. They could hear a van pulling up outside the gate. They moved quickly, flat against the wall next to the entrance to the yard.

Keys rattled, and the door opened; a man appeared.

"Mehmet," whispered Fiona recognising the new arrival.

"Oh, do I want a word with you... Come here you scrote," said Rory. Mehmet saw the three men and the girls and made a run for the van.

"Digger, call a cab and take the girls anywhere they want to go. Take Fiona to Swannie's," said Rory. "Come on Swannie, we need to catch this bastard."

Swannie and Rory ran across the road to the Corsa. Mehmet, in the white van, had to go in the opposite direction to turn around but having completed the manoeuvre came hurtling down the service road. Swannie started the Corsa just as the van passed them. Although it was going at least thirty miles an hour, it had to slow for the first speed bump. It almost took off as the van negotiated the ramp. Swannie was quickly behind the van, which was swerving from side to side to prevent them overtaking.

The van reached the junction with Fenton Street and turned right; there would be too many people on the High Street.

It roared up the road, passing the junction with Musgrove Street. This was new territory for Rory and Swannie. Suddenly Swannie slammed on the brakes. "What are you doing?" said Rory.

"Fucking speed cameras, Beryl'll go mental if she gets a ticket."

As it happened, the reaction may well have saved their lives. There was a blind left-hand bend ahead and, despite the 'SLOW' warning signs, the van had taken it at ridiculous speed. Swannie approached the bend at less than twenty. As they negotiated the corner, they saw skid marks on the wet road. The van was stationary in front of them, steam coming from the front. As they passed, they quickly assessed the scene. There was a large builders' skip, full of rubble and other debris from a housing development. The van had ploughed straight into it; the front had completely caved in from the force of the collision. The unfortunate Mehmet had not fastened his seat belt in his haste to escape and had gone through the windscreen. His lifeless body was laying in the skip. It was still pouring with rain.

"Come on, let's get out of here," said Rory. Swannie accelerated away and made a left. The car was starting to steam up and Swannie put the heater on to de-mist; there was a whooshing noise as the fan went to full-blast.

Rory was on the phone. "What's happening, Digger?"

"I'm in a taxi. The two girls have phoned their parents and we're dropping them off in Notting Hill."

"What about Fiona?"

"She's ok, she's going to speak to her mum in a sec… We'll be heading back to Swannie's as soon as we've dropped off the others."

"Ok, we'll see you there."

"What about Johnny Depp?"

"It's sorted," said Rory. "Tell you when we see you."

In the taxi it was quiet, the three girls were still in shock and coming to terms with their ordeal. Digger had lent them his phone and they'd manage to contact their families. Both Alice and Etta lived in the Notting Hill area and would be dropped off at their homes.

Alice had a question. "Should we tell the police?"

"It's up to you but you may want to keep this quiet. There'll be some very angry people out there and the last thing you need is for your pictures to be splashed all over the newspapers," said Digger.

This was a brutal, but realistic assessment which did nothing to diminish the shock and stress the girls were experiencing.

"I understand," said Alice.

"So, who are you?" said Etta.

"Just friends of Fiona's dad…" said Digger.

Fiona was still drowsy and had not said anything.

The taxi dropped Alice and Etta off outside their respective houses. Worried parents greeted them wildly as they were reunited with their families. It was still raining.

"We can never repay you," said Alice as she left the taxi. "I don't even know who you are."

"Let's leave it that way, eh. Just glad you're safe now," said Digger.

It was gone ten by the time Digger and Fiona arrived at the house. Swannie and Rory had beaten them by only a few minutes and were drying themselves off with towels. Fiona hadn't said much in the taxi; shock had set in. Digger led her into the house and Rory was waiting in the kitchen with Beryl. She handed Digger a towel.

"Hi Fiona, have you spoken to your mum?" said Rory.

"Yes, she said to say thanks."

"That's ok, have you eaten anything?" asked Rory.

"No. Someone came this afternoon, but they didn't give us anything. They said something about moving us tonight. They spoke Turkish most of the time, so we didn't know what was going on."

Beryl came in. "Sit down, dear. I'll make you some tea, it'll do you good. Can I get you some food? I can do you a scrambled egg on toast."

"I don't think I could eat anything, I feel sick," said Fiona, finding it difficult to take everything in.

"I better get going," said Digger. "It's a bit of a hike back... I'll bill you for the trousers," he said showing Rory the torn fabric.

Rory got up and gave his buddy a hug. "Ha, you do that, mate...Look, thanks for everything... keep in touch, yeah?"

"You bet," said Digger. "Wouldn't have missed it for the world... You take care, Fiona," he added. She smiled at him.

"Oh, just a thought, what about the you-know-what?" Digger said cryptically.

Rory was blank for a moment, then twigged. "Can you dispose safely?"

"Yeah, I'll chuck it in the sea from the pier tomorrow."

"And you," said Rory, looking at Swannie.

"Yeah, sure I'll see to it," said Swannie. Rory knew the

weapons they had retrieved from the Turks would be taken care of.

Swannie saw Digger out as Beryl served the tea.

"I need a bath," said Fiona.

"Of course," said Beryl. "I'll try and find you something to wear as well."

"Thanks, these are a bit…well… they need throwing away," said Fiona.

"Have you phoned your housemates?" said Rory.

"No, not yet," said Fiona.

"Ok, I thought we could get you back to Hereford tomorrow and you could spend some time with your mum while you recuperate," said Rory.

"Yes, that would be good… I still feel a bit strange," said Fiona.

"What did they give you, do you know?" said Rory.

"No, I don't know what it was. They injected me a couple of times, and I was asleep for a long time…"

She took a sip of her tea and looked at Rory. "What about the police… when do we tell them?"

"I think we should leave things alone… most of the men who held you are dead… including Mehmet."

"Mehmet…? He's dead?"

"Yes," said Rory.

"Good," said Fiona quietly.

"Shouldn't she see a doctor?" said Beryl.

"What do you think, Fiona?" said Rory.

"I'm ok, just need to rest and see my mum."

"Well, if you still feel groggy in the morning, we'll get you to a pharmacist or something," said Rory.

"Yes, ok."

Rory remembered something. He rummaged through his pocket.

"Is this yours, by any chance?" he said, and he handed her the bracelet.

"Oh, thank God, you found it," said Fiona and her face lit up.

"It was a present from my Dad… He gave it to me on my last birthday before he died."

"I think the fastener's broken, but I'm sure it can be fixed," said Rory.

"No, that's fine, thank you. It must have come off when they were carrying me."

Fiona finished her tea and Beryl led her to the bathroom. Tomorrow would be a better day.

With Fiona's arrival, there was a change in sleeping arrangements. She had the box room, Rory, the sofa in the sitting room. He found it difficult to sleep, the adrenaline was still coursing through his body. It was the same feeling he had following the rescue of the boy.

Sunday morning and Rory was awake early. The truth was, he'd hardly slept at all; events of the previous day kept running through his mind. The good news was that they had found Fiona, that was what mattered; the collateral was just that. It was something he'd had to accept; it went with the territory.

He was not sure what would happen if the police were to become involved, but, given the nature of what was going on at the house, the chances were, the Turks would just keep it quiet.

Beryl came downstairs to make a cup of tea around seven-thirty; Rory was already sat at the kitchen table.

"I made myself a cup, I hope you don't mind," he said, holding up a mug.

"Of course not, help yourself to anything you want…" She switched on the kettle. "So, what's your plan…? For today, I mean."

"Get a taxi up to Paddington, then get a train back… I'm not risking the Tube," said Rory.

"Swannie'll take you, I'm sure. Just say when you want to go… Do you want me to take Fiona a cup of tea?"

"Yeah, thanks," said Rory.

Fiona hadn't slept well either, her body-clock was all over the place from her time in the house. Being kept prisoner and blindfolded meant she had had little indication of day or night and it had affected her badly. It would take some time before her metabolism would be back to normal.

"Thanks," she said, as Beryl handed her the tea. "Is it ok to shower in a minute?"

"Yes, dear, of course. You help yourself. I've found some clothes, not sure if they'll fit, but should do you until you can buy some more... When you're done, I'll do you one of my special breakfasts... Soon have you right as rain.... How are you feeling? Do you need to see a doctor?"

"That's very good of you," said Fiona. "No, thanks, I'll be fine."

By nine-thirty, Fiona had showered and changed into a sloppy tee shirt and a pair of trousers which were probably three sizes too big. She tied them at the waist and rolled up the trouser legs; they would do until she got home. Fiona enjoyed her breakfast; the best she had ever tasted, she said. Swannie had agreed to take them to Paddington.

There were some fond farewells as Rory said goodbye to Beryl. She hugged Rory, then Fiona. "You take care of yourself, you hear," said Beryl, who was fighting back tears.

"Thanks for everything," said Fiona, and they both waved as the Corsa pulled away.

The previous evening's rain had cleared, but it was a dull morning as Swannie drove Rory and Fiona to Paddington Station where there were further emotional farewells.

"Cheers for everything, Swannie, mate," said Rory as they engaged in a man-hug.

"It was for Lennie," said Swannie. "And you take care, Fiona, love," he said and kissed her on the cheek.

"Thank you," said Fiona, and the pair headed to the ticket office.

There was a half-hour wait for the next train, and they spent the time in a coffee shop. With first-class tickets, it wouldn't be the last caffeine fix of the day.

Rory gave Fiona his phone so she could speak to her mother again and arrange to be picked up in Worcester.

The journey was uneventful, Rory was reading one of the complimentary Sunday newspapers. Fiona slept for much of the journey, her body still reacting to the drugs she had been given. In between naps, Rory was able to get more information on her abduction.

She woke as the attendant brought more coffees and pastries.

"So, when did you realise you might be in danger?" he asked.

"Not until we got out of the restaurant. It was going so well. I was introduced to Mehmet's father, he was a charming man. When we got outside, Mehmet said he needed to get something from the backyard. He started pushing me… I didn't know what was happening. When we got around the corner, there was this car and another man waiting. Mehmet must have tipped them off when we were in the restaurant… Anyway, they just pushed me into the car and I felt a scratch on my arm… then I woke up in the house. I still don't know where I was taken."

"It was a greengrocer's shop on the High Street," said Rory.

"Really?" said Fiona.

"Yeah… Did you meet the other two girls?"

"Not until a couple of days ago… They put us in the same room, but Alice started screaming and they injected her. They told us we were going on a journey yesterday; I think you got to us just in time."

"We had no idea whether we would find you. It was your friend Damian."

"Damian?"

"Yeah, he was stalking you. He followed you and the Turk to the restaurant," said Rory.

"The creep," said Fiona.

"Yeah, but he could well have saved your life, so don't be too hard on him, eh?" said Rory.

"Yeah, you're right," said Fiona.

"Are you going to go back to university?"

"Hmm, yes, I think so. I can't let these people win... I'll just be more careful... I'm not sure what I'm going to tell my housemates."

"Tell them the truth," said Rory.

"Then they'll want to know why I haven't been to the police," said Fiona.

"Yeah, I guess... I'm sure you'll think of something," said Rory.

The train pulled into Worcester Shrub Hill Station around one o'clock. It was spitting with rain again and Helen Arthur was waiting at the exit under cover. There was an emotional reunion.

"Oh, Rory, I don't know how I'm going to repay you... thank you so much," said Helen.

She hugged Rory. "It was for Lennie, we'd do anything for our mates," said Rory.

"Thank you," said Fiona and kissed Rory on the cheek.

"You take care now, do you hear?"

"Yes," said Fiona, and Rory watched as mother and daughter walked towards the car-park, chatting animatedly.

There was a taxi-rank only a hundred yards from the station and Rory took the first available cab back to his cottage.

He unlocked the door and looked around the living room; it felt claustrophobic; he needed a run.

It would be a punishing six miles; it was his exorcism.

Chapter Nine

It was over an hour before Rory returned to the cottage; there was a call he needed to make. He picked up his phone from the table and keyed in the number.

"Hi, it's me... just got back, you ok?"

Rory had texted Laura a couple of times but had not been able to phone.

"I'm ok, you?" said Laura.

"Yeah, thanks. Look, I know this is short notice, but are you free later? I can come over if you're around."

There was a pause. "Yeah... ok... I should be free later... about four, four-thirty?" said Laura. It was a measured response.

"Great," said Rory.

"Ok, see you then," said Laura.

Rory wondered if he should have left it until tomorrow and the agreed meeting, but he needed company. He looked through the window at the clouds; raindrops splattered the window. He could see the top of the river; it was still running high.

He tidied up, showered and was away by three forty-five. He was still high on the adrenaline rush from the previous day. He wondered again if there would be a police investigation at the greengrocer's, but there was nothing he could do about it; he would phone Swannie tomorrow and see if there was any press activity.

He arrived at the barn just before four-fifteen; the roads were much quieter on a Sunday, particularly on such a dismal afternoon, and there was little delay driving through the city.

Laura was waiting at the door.

"Hi," he said and kissed Laura on the cheek as she let him in.

"Hi," she said. "I wasn't expecting to hear from you today."

"I finished earlier than I thought, so I was able to get back," said Rory.

"Would you like a drink? I've got a beer in the fridge… or there's some wine."

"A beer would be fine, thanks," said Rory. "You look nice."

She was wearing a low-cut, V-neck, white tee-shirt and jeans with white sandals.

"Thanks," she said and went to the kitchen.

She came back with the drinks. Rory was sitting on the settee, she sat down opposite him.

"So, how did it go?" said Laura. She leaned forward, showing interest.

"Hmm, let's say we achieved our objective," said Rory, who was staring into his beer glass.

She looked at him, there was something different; he looked pensive and detached.

"Are you ok?"

"Yeah, just a difficult couple of days."

She got up from her seat and sat next to him and put her arm around his shoulders.

"Look, I don't know what security people get up to, but if you want to talk about it, it might help… Don't worry I would never divulge anything private between us, you have my word."

Rory did want to speak, he needed to unload some of his thoughts. He had his head in his hands. He was going through the same emotions he'd experienced after the incident on the rig which destroyed his relationship with Kim. He didn't want this to happen with Laura. Something had to change.

He took a long sip of his lager. "Mmm, I needed that," he said, and turned his head towards her and kissed her. "Yeah, you're right."

"I missed you," she said. "I wasn't going to tell you that."

"Yeah, I missed you too," Rory replied, which wasn't quite true; he'd been engrossed in his mission. Whenever he'd been on a 'job' he was totally focussed, it had saved his life, but he had thought of her and sent her a couple of texts, which, in Rory's eyes, constituted 'missing' her.

Laura, too, had been evaluating the burgeoning relationship. Would it be like a Roman candle, that burns brightly at first, only to fizzle out and die? She had found him exciting and he'd brought her alive in so many ways, but whether this was what she was looking for in a relationship, she hadn't yet decided.

"So, do you want to tell me…? It's up to you, I'm not going to force you," said Laura. "But something's clearly affected you."

She took a sip of her wine, letting Rory consider her words.

Rory looked at her. "It was one of my buddies, from my army days… the one that got killed. His daughter went missing."

"How awful," said Laura.

"Helen, that's Lennie's widow, saw my picture in the paper and managed to track me down. She came to see me last week… frantic with worry."

"I can imagine."

"She'd not heard from Fiona… that's the daughter… for a couple of weeks, and she asked if I could try to find her. It was a no-brainer, we always help our mates."

He looked at Laura and took another sip of lager. She was holding his hand.

"I called up a couple of my old army buddies; we served together with Lennie… They were happy to help, so we met up."

"In London…?"

"Yeah."

"So, what happened?" said Laura.

"It took some time, but we managed to track her down."

"How did you manage that?"

"I can't go into detail, but it did get a bit messy. The good news is, she's back with her mum."

"Well, that's great… Her mum must be relieved," said Laura, her journalistic curiosity had been well and truly aroused, but she didn't pursue it.

"Yeah, she is," said Rory.

Gradually, as they continued talking Rory started to relax, and with the closeness, physical needs started to surface. Once the kissing started, the rest soon followed. Laura started to rub Rory's thigh. Rory slid his hand under Laura's tee shirt. Within moments they were both naked. Laura was laying on the sofa with Rory inside her. Their needs exploded into a crescendo and Rory was on top of her panting with the exertion. She kissed him.

"I don't know what it is Rory Calderwood, but I can't get enough of you," she said and smiled.

All Rory's cares seemed to vanish with the physical release, like a deep cleansing of the soul.

They uncoupled and lay together on the sofa in an air of fulfilment, totally relaxed; the spell was only broken when Laura announced she needed the bathroom.

Rory had washed and dressed by the time Laura returned to the lounge in her jeans and tee shirt.

"I had a thought. Would you like to go out for a bite to eat? There's a lovely pub just up the road in the village; they do fab meals," said Laura.

"Yeah, sounds great, but my treat," said Rory.

The rain had stopped, and it was a dry but cloudy evening; the countryside almost glowed with its lush green colours.

'The Bell' was an old black and white country pub; Rory had passed it a few times but had never ventured in. The car-park was almost full, and the bar was doing a good trade. The rain had stopped meaning the beer-garden was packed with families and smokers.

The pub was a former manor house with the rooms laid out in cubicles and alcoves, which made it ideal for people just wanting to talk and eat with some privacy. There were very few empty seats, but they noticed a couple who were just leaving so they moved in on the vacant table before anyone else could lay claim. A waitress came over and cleared the table and described the 'house rules'.

"Order your drinks and food at the bar and someone will bring it over," she explained.

They perused the menu, made their choices and Rory went to the bar and ordered as required. He returned with an orange juice and a glass of red wine and within half an hour they were eating their meals. As Laura had found, Rory was not a ready conversationalist; he was more of a listener, but they continued to delve into past experiences with Rory describing life on the oil rig. After they had eaten, they were sat enjoying their second round of drinks and Laura asked about his pending departure.

"So, when do you go away?"

"Thursday."

"From Birmingham?"

"Yeah," said Rory.

"What time?"

"Early," said Rory.

Laura was getting frustrated at the one-word answers and tried another tack.

"What will you be doing when you get there?"

"Not sure exactly, it's a trade fair... I'm going with the client I'm working for."

"As security consultant?"

"Yeah," said Rory.

"You mean like a body-guard?"

He looked at her. "Hmm, partly... just looking after security... and it's called 'close-protection' these days."

Laura looked concerned and held his hand. "You will take care, won't you?"

"Yeah, don't worry, The Emirates is a pretty safe place."

"I've never been," she said.

"Me neither," said Rory, and smiled.

"When will you be back?"

"Monday... all being well... flights, I mean," said Rory.

"Oh, right," she said and finished her drink.

It was half-past nine before they left the pub. As they walked to Rory's car, hand-in-hand, Laura looked at him. "Would you like to stay over?"

Rory delayed responding for a moment.

"It's ok, if you don't want to," she replied.

"No, it's not that... but I've got no stuff with me, and I need to get to work early in the morning... I could do with catching up on some sleep as well. You have an adverse effect on me in that area, you know," he said and started to laugh.

She squeezed his hand. "It's ok... yeah, it makes sense."

She wasn't annoyed at the rebuff, she could see the logic.

Rory was driving back to the cottage by ten o'clock. The visit with Laura had been cathartic and he felt much better. He would see her again the following evening.

Monday morning, Rory was back on the commute, but he was in his office before eight o'clock. He'd slept well, but he still had some concerns about possible police involvement regarding the weekend's little escapade. As he drank his first cup of coffee, he made a call.

"Swannie, mate, Rory."

"Hi Rory, you get Fiona back ok?" he replied.

"Yeah, great... Thanks again for your help, I couldn't have done it without you, mate."

"No problem, anytime, you know that," said Swannie.

"Yeah... I just wondered if there was anything about the dead Turks... you know, in the papers?"

"Nah, I checked. If it'd been reported, it would have been across the front pages I reckon."

"Yeah, that's true..." said Rory.

"Oh, there was a bit about that Mehmet bloke," interrupted Swannie. "It just said something about somebody dying in a car accident on Fenton Street and his name. The Old Bill are looking for witnesses, apparently... The skip had got no lights on it so they're after the builders."

"What about your car?" said Rory.

"If anyone asks, we were just driving, but there's no CCTV down there, so I'm not too bothered."

"That's great, just wondered," said Rory.

They finished chatting and Rory went back to work, finalising his report for Alistair. He had a meeting with him later.

As the morning progressed, Rory became more productive and his focus shifted from his weekend exploits. He'd finished his report and emailed a draft to Alistair ahead of his meeting later. His next task was to prepare for the Abu Dhabi trip. It would be a small delegation; him, Duncan Wyatt, Ed and Alistair. Steve Lillington would run the plant in Alistair's absence, which was standard routine and resulted in little disruption to the day-to-day business. Rory had mentioned this as a positive point in his report.

At eleven-thirty, Rory had arranged to meet Natalie.

He approached her office; the door was not fully closed, just enough to prevent anyone looking in.

He knocked and responded to the "come in," request.

"Hi Rory, please sit… how's the report?" she said in her strong Eastern European accent.

Rory sat on the only other seat, on the other side of her desk.

"It's finished… I've sent a draft to Alistair."

"That is good, I look forward to reading it."

Rory looked at her. Her dark hair was tied back, as usual, making her look quite austere; conversely, her white business shirt was open down to her pink bra, giving totally different signals. There was something of a femme-fatale about her; he could imagine men being drawn to her, but he wasn't in the least bit tempted. He wondered about the attention she would get in the production unit.

"I wanted to check arrangements for Thursday," said Rory.

"Yeah, ok, what do you want to know?"

"The hotel, how far away from the venue is it?"

"About ten miles," replied Natalie.

"Hmm, we'll need secure transport to and from the venue," said Rory.

"Already arranged. I spoke to the local police department. They recommended two firms they use for visiting diplomats and VIPs."

"Right… that's good," said Rory, who was now wondering if he was needed at all.

"And the hotel?"

"There is a new hotel called the Emirates Palace which is seven stars. I tried to book you in there but there was no room, so I've made reservations at the Corniche Palace, it is five stars… most of them are over there. I'm trying to get you a floor plan. I assumed you would want one."

"Yes, I need to check the escape routes," said Rory, taken aback by her thoroughness and knowledge.

"Yes, I thought you would… It is not possible to get the guest list I'm afraid."

"No, I didn't think so," said Rory. "What about the material?"

"Everything has been sent… projector, screen and the advertising. Alistair has the presentations on his computer."

"That's great… all taken care of, then?" said Rory.

"Yes, we are used to it; we have done many," said Natalie.

After a brief catch-up, Rory left and went back to his office; something still did not feel right. Years of experience and an uncanny intuition told him so; he would keep an eye on her.

Lunchtime, in the offices of the Worcester Gazette, investigative reporter, Laura Kingston, was sitting at her computer typing the latest copy for the evening edition. Nothing too exciting, just a spate of car thefts on one of the estates. She thought of Rory; in fact, lately, she had barely been able to think of anything else. Nobody had ever made her feel the way he did, and it frightened her. She couldn't wait to see him again but would never tell him; she needed to keep a lid on her emotions for the moment.

She would love to know more about the freeing of his friend's daughter… 'messy,' he said. What did that mean, she wondered? There would be a story there, that's for sure… a hostage…? Possibly. Having finished her piece on the car thefts she made herself a coffee and stared at her monitor. Then searched… *'London Evening Standard'*. The pages of the morning edition appeared on her screen and she scanned the stories, while she ate her pita bread and guacamole. Nothing that she could see. What did 'messy' mean? She was about to log-off the web-page when a 'stop-press' headline caught her eye.

'Police break up a people-trafficking ring in Kensington… three dead in gang-land turf war.'

That's all it said. She needed to make a call.

The world of journalism is a fairly tight-knit community and, having worked in the city, she had a contact at the Evening Standard.

"Can I speak to Vic Trentham, please…? It's Laura Kingston, Worcester Gazette."

There was a pause. "Hi Laura, long time, no speak."

Hi Vic, how're things?" said Laura.

"Yeah, you know, making a living," said the hack.

"Just wondered if you have any more information on the people-trafficking story you've got on your stop-press?"

"Why? Have you got some information?" asked Vic.

"What…? Oh… no, no, I'm doing a piece up here on gangs and stuff and thought it might be useful info."

"You have gangs…? In Worcester?"

"Of course, you don't have a monopoly on villains in the Smoke, you know."

Vic chuckled. "Yeah, ok, well the police haven't said much, but there was some altercation at a greengrocer's in Kensington… three dead, apparently."

"A greengrocer's?"

"Yeah, they got a tip-off and found three bodies and a couple of rooms where some girls had been kept prisoner… that's what my contact said."

"So, what's the line of enquiry, then?" said Laura, now really intrigued.

"Rival gang, so they reckon… They've got nothing to go on. Whoever was being held there had gone. That's about it."

"Thanks, I owe you one… Do you think you can let me know if anything else comes up? I can give you my email address."

"Yeah, ok… Are you sure you haven't got anything here?"

"No… no, just interested in this sort of thing, that's all. Thanks again, Vic… Bye for now."

Laura hung up. What did this mean? It certainly came under the definition of 'messy'.

The meeting with Alistair went well. Rory's report was thorough and made observations and recommendations on the company's security. Overall, he had been impressed with the organisational culture; everyone was aware of their responsibilities, computer systems were robust and communications with suppliers and clients were effective. Access to restricted areas was well-monitored and controlled. He had made some suggestions for improvement, notably around recruitment and the vetting of candidates. Alistair was delighted with the findings and the thoroughness of the investigation. He would be presenting it at the next board meeting on Wednesday evening.

"I would like you to attend… to answer any questions," said Alistair.

"Yeah, of course," said Rory.

"What about Abu Dhabi?" said Alistair. "Where are we with that?"

Rory gave Alistair the latest information. "It's as good as

these things can be. The hotel looks fine, security-wise. Natalie got me a floor plan which is useful."

"Yes, she's very thorough," said Alistair.

"Yeah, you're not kidding… She's also sorted out the travel arrangements. We'll be picked up each morning and returned after the trade fair. We'll also have a car on standby if needed… I've not checked out the drivers, but the company ferries the VIPs around, so we should be ok."

"Ok, thanks. I'll be taking my laptop to do the presentations and Duncan will look after the sales. He knows all the pricing details and Ed will chip in with the technical stuff. I'll introduce you as an engineering specialist if anyone asks," said Alistair.

"Yeah, ok, although I'll have to brush up on the finer points of guided-missile systems," said Rory.

"Ha, I don't think it will come to that," said Alistair. "There is one thing; we'll have to get a couple of the locals to help put up the stand; shouldn't be a problem. There're usually loads of maintenance people hanging about at these things wanting to earn some pocket money, mostly immigrants. We can sort that out on Friday."

"Yeah, sounds ok... What's the latest on the new project?" said Rory. "Hades?"

"No change, everything's with the M.O.D. A couple of our guys have been down to see them today," replied Alistair.

"Will it go to market? Open market, I mean, a trade fair?"

"Good God, no… Certainly not in the short-term anyway. No, this is a British invention and we will just supply the M.O.D once the prototypes have been tested and signed off… That's when we will start to see our return."

"That big, eh?"

"Yes… let me put it into context. It could have the same impact as the Atom Bomb, in military terms. It is that revolutionary… everyone will be after it."

"What about the Americans?"

"Oh, they'll certainly want a piece, but I don't think the

government have forgiven them for playing hardball in 1946."

Rory looked confused.

"Well, they took all our best scientists to help with the Manhattan Project, then after the war, they pulled out of helping us build an atomic bomb, so we ended up having to build our own from scratch."

"Hmm, yeah, I remember that, now you come to mention it."

"Don't worry, we'll do very nicely out of it once it's operational," said Alistair. "And if they want to sell it to the Yanks or the French or whoever, that's not my concern… that's politics and I keep well away from that."

After a cup of coffee and a further chat, Rory returned to his office in the production area. His thoughts returned to Natalie; she seemed too well informed on security matters for an international lawyer. He hadn't yet decided what to do about it but had a germ of an idea.

He returned home and pounded the river bank for three miles. He couldn't help noticing the river was unusually high for the time of year and watching its urgent rush towards the weir gave him an uneasy feeling; he didn't know why. After his exertions, he showered and changed, then left the cottage at six-thirty for his dinner date with Laura.

Once again, she was at the door waiting for him, wearing a light-blue top and white jeans. Rory exited the Toyota and greeted her warmly.

"How was your day?" she asked as he made himself at home.

"Ok?" said Rory.

"Would you like a beer?" said Laura, seeing Rory settled.

"Thanks," said Rory. Laura went to the kitchen and returned with a bottle of lager and a glass of red wine.

"How was your day?" asked Rory, taking his first drink of his lager.

"Interesting," said Laura, cryptically.

"Oh," said Rory.

Laura couldn't hold back any longer; she took a slug of her wine. "I found out some information today from the London Evening Standard... I was doing some research. It was something in the stop-press about some gang-land killings in Kensington; people-smuggling, apparently."

"What did you find?"

"Not much, I spoke to one of my contacts, he works on the Standard... The police think it's gang-related."

Rory looked into his glass, then took another sip.

"I don't mean to pry, but it did make me think about your weekend... You're not in any trouble, are you?" said Laura.

"Nah, what makes you think that?"

"You said it was 'messy', that's all... the weekend."

"Hmm, not that messy," said Rory. He was not giving anything away. He changed the subject. "Something smells nice."

"I've done a home-made curry," said Laura. "Well, I say home-made; the sauce is out of a jar."

She was hoping for more from Rory but didn't want to press it.

Rory was deep in thought; he needed to speak to Swannie.

The revelation changed the mood and Rory was in danger of withdrawing into himself; his way of dealing with pressure.

Laura recognised the signs from the previous day when he was discussing Lennie's daughter.

She put down her drink and moved to join him on the sofa. She put a consoling arm around his shoulder.

"You ok?" she said.

He was looking into his glass and tipped back the remaining dregs.

"Yeah, sorry, got a lot on at the moment," he said and put his glass down on the coffee table.

She kissed him on the cheek. "I'll just go and check on

dinner."

"Yeah, ok... I just need to make a quick phone call."

"Well you'll need to use my landline; there's no mobile signal for miles around here."

"No, it's fine, it's not urgent... it can wait," said Rory.

Laura served the meal and the atmosphere was still subdued

"This is really good," said Rory, after about five minutes, breaking the silence.

"Thanks," said Laura. "It's mostly out of a jar."

Laura watched Rory who seemed to be struggling to finish his food. "Don't worry if you can't finish it. They were big portions."

She put her knife and fork together on the plate, indicating she had finished hers. There was still some rice and chicken uneaten. Rory followed suit.

"Sorry about that," said Rory, looking at his unfinished meal.

"That's ok, but I think we need to talk... something's not right."

She looked at him across the table. He seemed lost in another world. Rory was having difficulty in shaking off the mood.

Laura tried another tack. "Look if you want this to work you need to trust me. I won't judge you or disclose anything you tell me. That's a promise, but unless you can open up, we can't continue... you know that. You will just head into depression... I know I've had first-hand experience."

Rory looked at her. "Yes, I know that... I'm sorry. Part of the problem goes way back."

"The army?" said Laura.

"Yes," said Rory.

"Well, I told you about my cousin... the one in Afghanistan; or should I say, was in Afghanistan. He's back now and suffers from the same problem. I was chatting with his mum, my Auntie, at the weekend and he's been referred to a psychiatrist...."

Rory looked at her. "Sorry to hear that."

"It's ok, the army's paying... His mum told me when he came back, he spent hours in his room just staring at the ceiling, then bursting into tears. He eventually managed to tell his mum about something that happened out there. Apparently, they had some problems on a patrol and a couple of his mates were killed by the Taliban... didn't go into detail. Just like your mate, I guess."

"Yeah, sounds like it," said Rory.

Laura got up and started clearing the dishes. "I'll give you a hand," said Rory. He got up and collected his plate and cutlery and followed Laura into the kitchen.

She opened the dishwasher and started to stack it with the crockery.

"I know you're right," sighed Rory. "A lot of the shit happened years ago in Iraq. I'm fine most of the time, but every now and then, it comes back to me."

Laura handed him a glass of wine. "Come on we can have dessert later, let's sit down and you can tell me what's troubling you this time."

They returned to the lounge and sat together on the sofa.

"Something happened at the weekend, didn't it?" said Laura.

Rory looked into his wine glass. "Look at me," said Laura. "Come on you can do this."

Tough love, they call it, but Laura was not going to let Rory wallow in whatever morass he was buried in.

Rory looked at her. "Yeah, you could say that."

Then he started talking and narrated the course of events that resulted in the rescue of Lennie's daughter.

"That's amazing," said Laura after Rory had told her the story. "You are a very special person, you know that."

"I hadn't thought so," said Rory.

"So, the police involvement might be a problem," said Laura.

"It might, but the girls won't say anything, and we left no

evidence… I don't think the Turks are going to say much either given they were trafficking girls… So, no, I'm not unduly worried."

Laura put her arms around him. "Come on, let's go to bed."

It was gone eleven before Rory left Laura's. The evening had been something of a watershed in their relationship.

Laura sat on the sofa after Rory left, contemplating everything that had gone on. She was still not sure where the relationship was going. She knew it was the physical side that was driving the attraction for her. Rory was so different from her previous boyfriends, tough, self-contained, resourceful; but beyond the hard exterior, there was a soft centre which tonight she discovered. The emotional barriers that had seemed impregnable were starting to come down.

Rory was also reflective as he made the journey back to the cottage though not with an assessment of his relationship with Laura. He was concerned that the police had got involved with the dead Turks. He thought they would be ok, but he needed to speak to Swannie. He was also running through the forthcoming trip to Abu Dhabi, making sure in his mind that he had covered everything. It was just Natalie that bothered him; she was the one question mark he had, and he wasn't sure exactly how he would tackle it yet. He was still mulling over one idea.

The following morning, he was in the office early. With just two days before departure, he wanted to check all the arrangements for the trade fair were in place. He had a couple of phone calls to make before he started work. He picked up his mobile and keyed in the numbers.

"Swannie, Rory, how's it going, mate."

"Yeah, great thanks… I think I know why you're ringing."

"How's that, then?" said Rory.

"You won't have seen the Standard this morning I take it?" said Swannie.

"No, don't get it up here, mate," replied Rory.

"Seems the Old Bill are investigating the Turks... Front page *'police foil trafficking ring'*. More on page two... The good news is that they think it's a gang thing. I've still got some contacts in the Met. They're not looking for anyone else. They raided that restaurant and arrested the owner; he's that bastard Mehmet's dad, according to the paper."

"Well, that should keep them off the track... As long as the girls don't come forward."

"Nah, can't see that. They'll be too scared I reckon," said Swannie.

"Yeah, you could be right."

"Have you spoken to Digger?"

"Yeah, last night... couldn't give a toss. You know what he's like."

"Yeah, that's for sure... Ok, give us a bell if anything turns up we need to worry about. I'm off to The Emirates Thursday, return Monday; I'll call you when I get back."

"Yeah, will do, cheers."

Rory rang off. It was always good to talk to Swannie. There was another call he needed to make but waited until after nine o'clock. He checked his contacts and accessed the number. It rang for a while before it was answered.

"Hello." A slightly anxious voice.

"Is that Fiona? It's Rory."

"Oh, hi."

"Just phoning to see how you were. I wasn't expecting you to answer the phone. I was going to speak to your mum."

"She's gone to work."

"Oh, ok... so how're things?"

"I'm ok... a bit panicky, but getting better. Mum's got me some tablets from the doctor to help me sleep."

"Oh, ok, sorry to disturb you," said Rory.

"That's ok. Thanks again, by the way, for getting me out."

"That's ok, we'd do anything for your dad, you know that."

"Yeah, thanks," said Fiona.

"When are you going back to Uni?"

"Don't know yet... I called my housemates and let them know I was ok."

"What did you tell them?"

"I just told them I'd been taken ill and I'm recuperating."

"Look, I just wanted to let you know that the press in London have got hold of the story, so you may see something if the nationals pick it up."

"So, are they looking for me?"

"No, no, you're quite safe. They'll have no information about you or the other girls... If you get worried, just call me, yeah?"

"Yes, will do, thanks... I'm not going back to London until I'm better... maybe next week., see how I feel."

"Right, I'm glad you're ok. I'll call again, see how you are."

"Ok, thanks for calling, bye."

Rory rang off and went back to his preparation. He decided it was time to sort out the Natalie situation once-and-for-all.

Chapter Ten

Rory had been toying with the Natalie question for some time. He needed to find out more about her so had decided to check out where she lived to see if that yielded anything. Laura said she was going to visit her parents this evening, so he'd taken advantage of the free time.

He had a note of Natalie's address in Edgbaston, an 'up-market' suburb of Birmingham. By six-thirty, following his usual riverside run, he was negotiating the Toyota down the leafy avenues of this desirable suburb.

It was a grey evening and the windscreen wipers were dispersing spots of drizzle. The roads were busy and glistening from the effects of yet another rainy day. Rory had the address but didn't know the area. All the roads in the neighbourhood looked much the same, the houses were two and three-storey terrace and popular with buy-to-let landlords who rented them out to students. It made the area vibrant and, on the weekends, busy. Tonight, it was quiet; partly because of the weather, partly the time of day. People were in their houses eating or watching TV or both.

Rory had an A-Z on his lap and was negotiating the car at the same time as trying to navigate. Eventually, he reached Cairns Avenue. He parked in the only free space on the road, about fifty yards up from the property. Vehicles were parked on both sides of the street making the available driving space barely large enough for two cars to pass each other.

Rory took out a cheese and pickle sandwich pack which he'd bought from his local garage; he took a bite. He could see the house clearly enough; Natalie's apartment was on the top floor and the lights were on. He munched away on his sandwich then opened a packet of crisps and washed them down with an orange juice. The road seemed deserted, not even a dog-walker; not surprising as the rain was now steady rather than intermittent. He put the radio on in the car and listened to the drivetime show. The windscreen started to steam up and he put the blower on to clear it.

By seven-thirty, he was beginning to question the wisdom of his decision to stakeout Natalie's apartment. He had no idea what he was expecting to see, and he could think of more productive ways of passing his time.

Just as he was about to give up, he saw Natalie leaving the building. She waited for a moment on the front step and looked up at the sky before taking a fold-away umbrella from her shoulder bag. Rory watched her press the button on the shaft to open it. She was wearing a jacket, trousers and a pair of high-heeled shoes. There were two more steps down to the short path which led to a wooden gate. She flicked the catch, opened the gate and turned left, walking away from Rory. There was a narrow road at the end of the block, slightly larger than a car's width, and she turned left into it.

Rory suddenly noticed movement from a dark blue Transit van which was parked closer to the apartment and on the same side of the road. Natalie had just walked passed it. Rory watched as a man got out dressed in black combat gear; he appeared to be following her. Rory was out of the car in a flash; he needed to see what was happening. The man had turned left only yards behind Natalie and they were both out of sight. Rory was further back. He took little notice as he passed the van, totally focussed on the immediate threat; he sensed Natalie might be in danger. He quickened his pace trying to keep up with them. Within seconds, he reached the turn, but he still couldn't see anyone. He jogged forward and saw the road serviced garages to the left at the back of the terrace block. The rain was heavy now.

Natalie came into view, about thirty yards away. She appeared to be wrestling with her assailant. Her umbrella was on the ground. Rory watched as she broke away and bent forward, arms in a crossing movement, karate-style. She'd kicked off her shoes and he watched her apply some deft martial-art moves. She was no lawyer. Her attacker took out a knife. Rory was only yards away now and charged at him. In a split second, he had the man on the ground and was landing punches to his face and head. The knife was on the floor and Natalie picked it up. Without hesitation, she bent down and plunged it into the man's neck; blood spurted everywhere.

"Jesus," cried Rory.

"Come on," commanded Natalie. "We need to get out of here." She withdrew the knife, wiped it on the man's jacket and dropped it into her bag, then nonchalantly slipped back into her high-heels. The umbrella had been carried in the breeze and was now stuck in the boundary fence; it would stay there.

The garages ran the length of the block of houses; beyond that, there was a snicket about a hundred yards long which led to the main road. The rain was easing. Rory looked left and right; he hoped they hadn't been spotted. A dog barked in the distance.

"What about your car?" said Rory.

"Too dangerous," said Natalie. "Come on, we must go."

She led Rory up the footpath and onto the main road. Cars crisscrossed on the way to and from the city.

"The pub," said Natalie.

About a hundred yards away, on the other side of the road, was a large steakhouse. They waited for a gap in the traffic and ran towards it. The rain was now no more than a heavy drizzle, but the tarmac was slippery underfoot. Rory checked behind them; there was no one following.

They went inside; both were drenched. Natalie's eye make-up was streaked down her face, her hair lank. There were toilets immediately in front of them. "Wait here," said Natalie and she went into the 'ladies'. Rory ignored her instructions and disappeared into the 'gents'. He checked himself over. He'd got grazed knuckles from the punches, but otherwise, he was fine. There was no blood on his clothing that he could see. He washed his face, dried off with a paper towel and went back out to the foyer to wait for Natalie.

It was another five minutes before she came out and Rory couldn't believe the transformation. She was wearing a blonde wig. Her jacket was inside out, now a pale green colour; not the dark blue in which she had left the apartment block. Instead of trousers, she was wearing a short dress and her makeup had been revived. Her shoulder-bag was bulging, presumably with her discarded trousers.

"Where's your car?" said Natalie.

"Just up the road from your apartment," Rory replied.

"Ok, can you get it? I'll wait here."

"Yeah, ok, I'll be right back."

Rory left the pub and walked down the road. He glanced down the snicket but couldn't see anyone, and although it was some distance, he couldn't see the body of the assailant either. The junction with Cairns Avenue was another fifty yards or so. He turned left and looked down the road. He couldn't see the van; it was just cars on either side; someone had already parked in the spot vacated by the Transit.

He crossed over the road; his Toyota was where he'd left it. He got in and used the service road to turn, then headed back the way he'd just come. He took a quick glance at Natalie's apartment as he passed it but couldn't see anything amiss. He indicated right and could see Natalie walking from the pub entrance. He slowed down and stopped beside her; she got in.

"Have you got anywhere to go?" said Rory.

"No," said Natalie.

"That's ok, you can come back to mine, you'll be quite safe," said Rory.

"Yes, ok," said Natalie, with no other immediate alternative.

Rory pulled away, took the next left and headed for the motorway. It would take about forty minutes to get back to the cottage.

He glanced across at her; he wouldn't have easily recognised her.

"Well, this is a surprise," he said.

"How long have you been spying on me?" said Natalie. "I guess that's why you were there."

"No, I wasn't... well, not spying, exactly. I wanted to see where you lived, check security. I'm doing it with all the directors." It was all he could think of. "Anyway, it's just as well I was here... do you know who it might be who attacked you?"

She looked across at him. "No, I don't... maybe they have the wrong person."

"Hmm, they seemed to know you. It looked like they'd been waiting," replied Rory.

"Yes," said Natalie and the conversation stopped. Rory was in deep thought. He was now convinced more than ever that she wasn't just a lawyer.

He reached his junction and turned off the motorway. "You certainly know how to look after yourself."

"Yes, in Tallinn, I was in the army for two years before I finished university. I was karate champion for my unit... I have done it since I was at school."

That answered one question, but it didn't explain the brutal way in which she dispatched her assailant. That had been cold and calculated; something that was taught in face-to-face combat skills training. Known as slotting; it had not come from any karate handbook.

Fifteen minutes later, he was bouncing along the cinder track alongside the river. The potholes which challenged the car's suspension were filled with water from the recent shower. He parked outside his cottage.

"We're here," said Rory.

It was still light. The rain had stopped, and the clouds had passed; the riverside trees were heavy with moisture and dipping into the river.

"Wait," said Natalie and she walked down to the water's

edge, checked no-one was about and took the knife from her bag, then threw it as far as she could into the river. "You go... I need to call my friend," said Natalie and took out her mobile phone. She waited for Rory to enter the cottage to ensure privacy. It was ten minutes before she followed him in.

Rory had changed into a tracksuit. "Everything ok?"

"Yes, I have spoken to the friend I was meeting tonight to let her know I am ok. I told her I was attacked, and I am staying here... She said she will go to collect my things for me tomorrow from my apartment; she has a key... She will bring them to my office."

"You're going to work?"

"Yes, of course, why not?"

"I would have thought that was obvious... You were attacked tonight. You could have been killed or taken. We have no idea what they were up to."

"No, that is true, but I will feel safe at work until I can make plans... You can take me tomorrow, yes?"

"Yeah, I'll be going in," said Rory.

Natalie looked around the cottage. "Where is the bathroom?"

"I'll show you... there's a spare room you can have. It's not very tidy but it's reasonably clean and the bed's made. I use it as an office mostly."

Rory took Natalie upstairs and showed her the spare room. She put her shoulder-bag on the bed and looked around. It lived up to expectations.

"Bathroom's just there," said Rory, pointing to a door opposite which was slightly ajar. Rory was trying to remember when he last cleaned the shower. It would have to do.

"Have you shampoo I can use...? I need to wash my hair," said Natalie.

"Yes, it's on the shelf, you'll see it. Help yourself. I've got a spare toothbrush somewhere I think... if not, I'll pop down to the garage and get anything you need."

"Thank you," said Natalie. "Do you have a tee-shirt or

something I can wear? I need to wash my things. You have a washing machine?"

"No, I usually go down to the river and bash them on a few stones."

Natalie looked confused.

"Sorry, bad joke… Yeah, in the kitchen, help yourself."

"Thank you."

"I'll sort out some stuff you can wear."

Rory could hear the shower running as he went to his bedroom to find Natalie some clothes. He didn't have a great deal but found an old jogging kit and a tee-shirt.

"I've got some tracksuit bottoms and a tee-shirt you can borrow… I'll leave them on the bed," shouted Rory at the bathroom door.

"Ok," shouted Natalie.

Rory went downstairs and started tidying the kitchen. Suddenly there was a knock on the door. He looked at his watch, ten-past nine. He went to the window and he noticed the car parked just down the track. This was going to be awkward.

"Laura!" he said as he opened the door. "You'd better come in."

She noticed the shoulder-bag on the settee. He leaned forward to kiss her.

"Is this a bad moment?"

"No, no, not at all… there's been some trouble… Have a seat…"

"It's ok, I shan't stop if you've got company," said Laura.

"No, it's nothing like that… Natalie was attacked tonight…"

"Who's Natalie?" said Laura.

"One of the people from work," said Rory.

"So, why is she here?" said Laura.

"She can't stay at her flat. They were watching her…"

"Who were?"

"The ones who attacked her," said Rory. There was a long pause as Laura processed the information.

"How did you get on with your parents?" Rory added.

"Fine, fine... look, I'll go. It looks a bit crowded here," said Laura, clearly upset.

"No, no you don't have to. There's nothing going on... I'm just doing her a favour, that's all."

"Hmm, I've heard that one before," said Laura.

Laura turned and left; the door slammed behind her. Rory thought about going after her when Natalie came down the stairs. He would try and sort things out with Laura tomorrow.

"That was your girlfriend? I have caused problems I think," said Natalie as she entered the living room; she was carrying her washing.

"It's ok," said Rory. "I'll sort things out."

He looked at her dressed in his tee shirt and jogging bottoms, both way-too-big but serving their purpose. She started combing her hair. "Where is the machine," she said holding up her washing.

"In the kitchen. I'll show you," and she followed Rory who provided a brief instruction on the controls.

With Natalie's clothes and underwear safely rotating, she returned to the living room.

"Would you like a drink? I've got some wine, or I can make you a coffee if you prefer," said Rory.

"Some wine, please," said Natalie.

Rory went to the kitchen and returned with two glasses of red wine and sat opposite her on one of the armchairs.

Natalie took a gulp which emptied nearly half the glass.

"So, what are you going to do?" asked Rory.

"Tomorrow you will take me to work, yes?"

"Yeah," said Rory.

"Then, I will ask my friend if I will stay with her until I can arrange things."

"Arrange things?"

"Yes," she said without any further elaboration.

"And you have no idea who would attack you."

"No, not at all," said Natalie.

"Do you think it is about work?"

"I don't know…"

"Because if it is then I need to know about it," interrupted Rory.

"I do not know," repeated Natalie, more aggressively.

Rory looked at her; he had difficulty weighing her up. She had just been attacked; killed her attacker in a most brutal way and didn't seem disturbed in the slightest; everything seemed so 'matter-of-fact'. She showed a cold detachment which either came from training or a personality disorder. His experience with special forces gave him an indication of his preferred analysis, but he was not going to reveal his thoughts just yet.

"What about Alistair? We'll need to speak to him… the other workers may be in danger. At the very least, I'll need to review the security arrangements for the directors," said Rory.

Natalie looked down at her glass and finished her drink. "Yes, that is true."

"There's also the fact that whoever it was, has lost an operative… My hunch is that they will strike again sooner rather than later if only to avenge the killing… It's more likely to be a hit, next time."

"Yes, that is possible."

"You don't seem concerned," observed Rory.

"Yes, I am concerned, of course, I am concerned," she snapped. "But I will not be beaten by these people."

"People?" said Rory.

"Yes, those that want to hurt me," said Natalie.

"Hmm," Rory was certain she knew more than she was letting on. "So, you'll need a plan... to keep you safe."

"Yes, that is what I am doing."

"Well, do you want to share your plans? I could help," said Rory.

"I will let you know," said Natalie. "When will my washing be ready?"

"It will take about an hour, but you'll have to dry them in the airing cupboard."

"What is that?" asked Natalie.

"I will show you later," said Rory. "Would you like a coffee or something. There's no more wine."

"Yes, a coffee, and something to eat please. I have not eaten. I was meeting my friend to eat."

"I'll see what I have," said Rory. "I can go to the garage on the main road and get something if you like. They sell snacks and stuff."

"No, it is ok," said Natalie.

Rory went to the kitchen and managed to rustle up some bread and cheese, enough for a sandwich. With his pending trip, he had not stocked up on food.

He returned a few minutes later and handed her the plate of sandwiches and a mug of coffee. Natalie took it from him and started eating. "Thanks," she said.

"Look, there's no more milk. I'm going to the Minimart, I'll be back very soon," said Rory. "Do you need anything. I have soap and toothpaste you can use."

"No, I have my clothes and makeup. I have what I need."

"Ok, I'll be back in a minute," said Rory and he picked up his car keys and wallet from the table.

It was only seven or eight minutes to the garage and all the while Rory was trying to make sense of the evening. He was also thinking about Laura; he had no idea whether he could repair the damage there. He purchased his milk, a box of Muesli and a toothbrush.

When he returned, Natalie was on the phone but quickly rang off when he walked in.

She looked at Rory rather sheepishly. "It is ok, I have called my friend again; she says I can stay with her tomorrow... I cannot stay here... She said it was ok."

"That's ok, then. Lucky you managed to get a reception, tends to come and go," said Rory

"It was ok," said Natalie.

Rory went to the kitchen, put the milk in the fridge and the cereal on one of the shelves. He handed her the toothbrush, which she acknowledged.

"Your washing's finished," said Rory, opening the machine door and extracting the clothes which were all wrapped up together.

She took her clothes and started to separate them.

"I'll show you the airing cupboard, they'll be dry by morning."

Rory led Natalie back upstairs and opened the airing cupboard door on the landing next to the bathroom. Although it was summer and there was no central heating, the water was hot in the tank which made the cupboard quite warm. Natalie placed her underwear on one of the shelves and hung her blouse on a hanger.

"Thank you," she said. "I will go to bed now, I think."

"Ok, I'll see you in the morning. We'll leave early, about seven."

"Yes, that will be fine."

Rory went back downstairs and picked up his phone. He keyed in Laura's number and heard it ring out, then go through to the answerphone. "We need to talk," he said after the beep.

The following morning, Rory and Natalie were on the road by seven. There was little conversation on the journey. Rory glanced across at her a couple of times and couldn't believe how calm she was, given the circumstances. Looking at her appearance, no-one would have guessed the trauma she'd experienced less than twelve hours earlier; her blouse was creased slightly, but her makeup was as immaculate as ever.

They arrived at the office and Rory walked with her to the admin block. Alistair would be in.

"We need to brief Alistair," said Rory.

"Yes," said Natalie. "You can do that; I have work to do."

Rory could hear a voice as he approached Alistair's office; he was on the phone. Rory knocked on the door and Alistair beckoned him in. Natalie continued walking along the corridor to her desk. "I'll give you a shout if we need you," said Rory which wasn't acknowledged.

Alistair was still talking, and he gesticulated for Rory to sit down as he finished his call.

"Sorry about that, there's always so much to do before I go away."

He looked at Rory and could see his face etched with concern.

"What's the matter?"

"Natalie was attacked last night."

"What?!"

"Yeah," said Rory.

"What happened?" asked Alistair.

Rory explained he was checking her external security, then described the events. He wasn't sure how much information to provide and decided not to say anything about the killing. He just said he chased them off.

"It's a good job you were there," said Alistair.

"It was a stroke of luck; it was a last-minute decision to check out her location," said Rory.

"So, what should we do?" asked Alistair.

"I want you to call a board meeting this morning, as soon as possible. We don't know if it was Natalie they were targeting specifically or if they were looking for anyone in the company."

"Yes, of course, but what about the production area and the R & D team, they could well be targets too."

"Yes, that's possible. I can do a briefing with them this morning after the board meeting," said Rory.

"Yes, of course, whatever you suggest... Where's Natalie now?"

"She's at her desk, I presume; I can get her if you like. She stayed at my place last night; I brought her in," said Rory.

"Well, thank you for that. What is she going to do, did she say…? She can always use the boat if she likes."

"I think she's already made arrangements to stay with a friend," said Rory.

"Ok, let's have a word with her, can you get her in?" said Alistair.

Rory left the chairman's office and went to find Natalie. She was at her desk, typing away on her computer keyboard.

"Have you got a minute?" said Rory.

Natalie logged off and followed Rory to Alistair's office. Rory turned and spoke to her. "I told him about the attack but not the killing."

Natalie understood but didn't acknowledge the comment.

Alistair ushered them into his office and shut the door.

"Rory's just told me about the attack… are you ok?" said Alistair.

"Yes, I am ok," said Natalie.

"Do you need to see anyone…? I can arrange a counsellor if you need one. What about taking some time off?"

"No, I am fine, thank you," said Natalie.

Rory looked at Alistair then at Natalie. "Whoever these people are, they managed to find out where you live. They will probably do so again."

"I will be careful," said Natalie.

"Well, I agree with Rory. Your safety is the most important thing… What about going back home for a while. I'll keep your job open."

"To Estonia?" said Natalie with some surprise.

"Yes, why not. You can stay there until it's safe to return."

"I will think about it," said Natalie. "Was there anything else?"

Alistair looked at Rory; he shook his head.

"I'm calling a board meeting this morning for ten o'clock. Can you get hold of all the directors and get them here… I will need you too?" said Alistair.

"Des Greenhalgh, as well," added Rory.

"Yes, of course," said Natalie, and she got up and left the office.

By ten o'clock, all the directors who were on site had congregated in the conference room. Natalie had arranged coffee and biscuits and people were helping themselves to the snacks. There was a buzz of anticipation wondering what was going on; the original board meeting had been scheduled for six o'clock.

Alistair arrived, followed closely by Rory, and order was called. The group sat down and waited for Alistair to speak. All the directors were present plus, at Rory's insistence, Des Greenhalgh, the production manager. Natalie was also present and taking the minutes.

After a brief introduction, Alistair handed the meeting over to Rory.

Rory stood up; it was not a comfortable environment and, despite his experience in security training, he didn't particularly enjoy public speaking. He addressed the group.

"Right, as you know, Alistair asked me to do a review of the security here and I finished it this week. I think you've all got your copies, yeah?" There were nods around the room. "There were a few issues, but nothing we can't sort out." He looked around at the group maintaining eye contact. "The reason for this meeting, though, is; there was an incident last night... Natalie was attacked outside her flat."

There were looks of concern. Steve Lillington was first to speak. "Are you ok, Natalie?" he said, looking at her. She nodded. "Yes, I am ok."

"Do we know who it was, or why?" said Marcus Davies, the finance director.

"No, we don't," said Rory.

"What do the police say?" said Duncan Wyatt.

"We've not involved the police..." said Rory.

"For strategic reasons," added Alistair. There were looks at each other around the room. Natalie appeared to be doodling on her notepad.

"Maybe it was just a mugging," said Marcus.

"No, it was definitely not a mugging," said Rory.

"I should mention that Rory was doing a security review of the area last night and intervened, otherwise it could have been more serious. We were very lucky," said Alistair.

"What happened...? Did they get away?" said Steve.

"Yes, they ran off when Rory got involved," said Alistair.

This was the story Rory and Natalie had agreed.

"Sorry, Rory, please continue," said Alistair and the group went quiet again.

"As we said, we don't know who they were or their motives, but we can't rule out the possibility it was work-related," said Rory.

"I think we should get the police involved," said Marcus.

"At this stage, we want to avoid anything entering the public domain, the sensitivity of our work is paramount, but I'll be speaking to the M.O.D. later to get their thoughts and advice... Needless to say, your personal safety is our main concern," said Alistair.

Rory was keen not to distress anyone but, by the same token, he needed to get his message across. It had gone quiet again. "I will draw up some personal safety tips for you and let you have them later today... It's a question of being vigilant," said Rory.

"Thank you, Rory... Are there any questions?" said Alistair.

Neither Ed Stevens nor Des from production had said anything.

"What about you, Ed... Des?" said Alistair.

"No, nothing from me," replied Ed looking serious.

"No," said Des.

"I'll speak to the production team later if you like," said Rory. "It's important we don't scare people unnecessarily."

"Cheers," said Des.

Alistair got up and moved back to the coffee area. "Anyone for more coffee?" he said, and the group started to disperse. Steve Lillington went over to Natalie to check she was ok.

Rory was fielding questions from the other directors.

"What about my kids?" said Marcus. "Do I need to take them out of school?"

"No, no that would be an over-reaction," said Alistair, hearing the question.

"Alistair's right… reasonable precautions, being vigilant. If you see anything unusual, let me know," said Rory. "I'll put everything in my note."

After a few minutes, everyone had returned to their work areas. Alistair was chatting with Rory.

"I guess there's more to this?" said Alistair, obliquely.

"Yeah, could be," said Rory.

"What about Abu Dhabi?" said Alistair.

"No, I don't think that will be a problem," said Rory. "But I think you're right to let the M.O.D. know. They might send some people down to help for a few days."

The rest of the morning would be busy for Rory and Alistair; they arranged a working lunch for an update. Rory spent time briefing Des Greenhalgh's team in the production area on personal security and made a similar presentation to the R & D team. He also completed his 'personal safety' advice note and sent it to the entire team.

With all the activity, Rory had completely forgotten about Laura, but just before his lunch meeting, she popped into his mind. He checked his messages; there was no response to his voicemail. He would try and contact her this evening. He also needed to speak to Swannie to get an update on the Turks; he would call him later. He left his office and went across to the admin area for his lunch meeting with Alistair.

He knocked on the chairman's door. "Come in, come in, sit down," said Alistair.

There were two plates of sandwiches and a bottle of water

laid out on the small conference table. Rory sat down, and Alistair updated him on his conversation with the M.O.D. as they started eating.

"They didn't seem unduly concerned," said Alistair. "What was the phrase he used…? Ah, yes… He said they were clearly not 'serious players' because they had run off. The guy I spoke to thought they were probably muggers."

Rory considered this. If they knew the real story they might think differently.

Chapter Eleven

After further deliberations and finalising the arrangements for the trade fair, they finished their sandwiches and Rory returned to his office. He called Natalie on the internal phone to see how she was and get an update on her accommodation.

"It is ok, it is arranged," said Natalie.

"What about your stuff…? At your flat."

"It is ok, my friend said she will go and collect what I need. I will only stay for a few days. I told you, she has a key."

Just as he was about to end the call, a thought ran through his mind.

He'd been going over the events of the previous evening again and there were one or two issues bothering him. The nature of the original attack, which Rory had witnessed, suggested it had been a professional hit. They had clearly staked out her flat and had been lying in wait; they must have gone to some trouble to find her. The perpetrators, whoever they were, had her under surveillance. The area by the garages was much less conspicuous and ideal for a 'hit' but the reason for the attack was unclear.

He was trying to picture the face of the attacker, dark hair, olive complexion; Middle Eastern possibly. He wasn't sure of the relevance. With the instability in the region, there would be numerous factions only too happy to pay serious money for details of Hades or some of the other sensitive projects. Perhaps they had wanted to kidnap her for information or she was intended as a bargaining chip in some way. She wasn't part of the technical team, so she would have no detailed knowledge of any of the projects. It didn't make any sense. The death of the assailant could well have altered things. His assessment was that they would try again, which opened a range of possibilities.

"Has your friend been to your flat yet?" said Rory.

"No, she said she would go on her way back from work," replied Natalie. "Is there a problem?"

"Not sure... I was thinking, they might be watching your flat in case you return."

"What should I do?"

"I'll collect your stuff and bring it here. It might be safer."

"If you think so," said Natalie who appeared happy to be guided by Rory.

"Well, if they are watching they might follow your friend to her place. That would put her in danger," said Rory.

"Yes, that is possible," said Natalie. "I will call her and tell we have changed things... I will give you my key."

"Ok, I'll pop over in a few minutes," said Rory.

At two o'clock, he logged off his laptop, locked his drawers and went over to the admin block to collect Natalie's keys. He had a couple of questions.

"Can you tell me the layout of the apartment?" said Rory. He picked up a piece of paper and pen. "Here, draw me a floor plan... Top floor, right?"

"Yes," said Natalie. "Number five," and she sketched the layout. The front door opened straight into the living room; two doors opposite, one to the kitchen, the other to the two bedrooms and bathroom. Quite compact but functional.

"Thanks," said Rory. "What state was it in when you left?"

"I do not understand," said Natalie.

"Well, was it tidy or was there stuff lying around?"

"Ah, I see. No, it is very tidy. I do not like things everywhere."

"Ok, so what do you need me to collect?"

Natalie detailed her requirements and where they were kept via the map. "There is a suitcase in the cupboard in the bedroom," she explained.

It was almost three o'clock by the time Rory arrived at Natalie's apartment. He drove down the avenue slowly, looking right and left for any possible surveillance vehicles but there were domestic cars only, all empty. He found the next available parking spot about a hundred yards along from the flat, close to where he had parked the previous evening.

It was a bright afternoon as he exited his car and crossed the road to the apartment, being vigilant for anything unusual. It was eerily quiet, but peace would be shattered in a few minutes with the children leaving the local schools for the day.

Rory walked purposefully towards the gate, flicked the catch and went to the front door. He took out the set of keys and found the longest on the link with a red tag attached. He fed the key into the lock and turned. There was a click and the door broke free from its restraint. Rory pushed gently, waited for the door to be fully open, then went inside.

There was a small vestibule with one door to the right with the number '1' appended. Across the small corridor was another, labelled '2'. Rory took in his surroundings; it was text-book stuff. There were five boxes attached to the wall on the left-hand side with slits for receiving mail, numbered 1 to 5; below that, the electricity fuse-box. In front of him were the stairs to the other apartments; there was no lift. He made his way to the top floor, three flights up. He reached the landing and looked around; Natalie's was the only flat on the top floor.

Rory took out his piece of paper with the floor plan from his pocket; a living room, kitchen, two bedrooms and bathroom. He checked the keys again and examined the doorframe for any signs of forced entry. Satisfied, he put the Yale key into the lock and turned it. The door opened inwards. He gave it a sharp push, ducking to the side away from any possible blast, and foiling anyone who may be lying in wait. He peered around the door. It was how Natalie had described it; tidy, nothing out of place. He stood for a moment and looked around taking in the layout. It was a loft conversion, popular in the area, as they created more space for apartments. The ceiling sloped towards the low walls. A two-seater sofa dominated the room, a small dining table against the wall to the left, TV on a smoke-glass and chrome stand. In front of the settee was a fireplace with an electric fire. He could see the doors to the kitchen and bedrooms on the other side of the room.

He checked the carpet around the doorway for any signs of mud or dirt. To the side, there was a course hair mat for visitors to wipe their feet. Then he spotted it; nothing out of the ordinary to an untrained eye; the faint but unmistakable footprints of a pair of trainers. Just a couple of steps before the grime had been absorbed into the carpet and the footwear cleaned as a result. They could have been Natalie's of course, but it was unlikely given the size of the print and her desire for tidiness.

Rory was now on high alert. Whoever had been in the apartment was not looking for anything or the place would have been ransacked. This left the possibility of an explosive device. There were the obvious places he would need to check, toilet, fridge, chairs, but he had no idea whether it would be detonated by weight or trip-wire. Trip-wire would be the easiest to set up and conceal. He looked around more closely to see if there was anything obvious. Doorways were popular, a thin thread across an opening, not easy to spot, particularly at night or if you weren't expecting it. He checked the entrance to the kitchen; the door was open. Clear of wires, he walked in. He went to the microwave, oven and fridge, in turn, gently opening the doors just wide enough to see inside; nothing there.

It would have to be somewhere that would be in regular use so he ignored the kitchen cupboards for now. The main bedroom or bathroom would be his choice.

He moved slowly around the apartment, no sudden movements, checking each step as he went. The footprints had gone so there were no clues he could follow. He carefully opened the door to the corridor leading to the bedrooms and bathroom; again, it was clear of wires. He reached the main bedroom, to the right. The door opened inwards, away from him, which would not be ideal for setting up an effective trip-wire, but he wasn't taking any chances. He pushed it open, little-by-little... nothing. Sweat trickled slowly from his forehead into his eyes. He wiped them with the back of his hand.

He looked around; made-up double bed, no wrinkles, matching pillows on top of the duvet, at the head; bedside cupboards with a small reading light on the right-hand side; to the left, a set of wardrobes with three doors. They were painted white, matching the sparse décor in the room. This is where Natalie kept most of her clothes and where her suitcase was, according to her instructions. Rory thought for a moment. If he were planting a device this is where he would put it. The wardrobe doors opened outwards, towards him. He stopped and planned his next move. It would be simple enough to attach a wire to the door so that when it was opened the wire would pull, thus triggering the detonator. He knew there would be some slack to enable the bomber to fix the wire to the door. He picked up one of the pillows and held it to his face then slowly eased open the first door, the one nearest the bedroom door, an inch at a time.

At about four inches, the gap was wide enough to put his head to the door and scan the inside. He could see the clothes rail with several dresses hanging, handbags on the shelf to the left, then shoes, maybe seven or eight pairs on the floor. The suitcase was in the corner. He focused on the inside of the doorframe; nothing suspicious and he pulled it wider with the pillow still at his face. It was a pointless gesture; any protection it offered would be minimal from the force of an explosive device, particularly if there was shrapnel. The door was open wide now and he rummaged inside slowly taking out the clothes and placing them on the bed. He did the same with the shoes and handbags, then the suitcase, until the cupboard was empty. Two more to go.

He examined the inner connecting panel; it was thin plywood. He had an idea. Anyone planting a booby-trap would have probably used the outer door as the trigger, not the side panel. He pushed the flimsy plywood and it just fell inwards with little pressure. He could see inside the second wardrobe clearly and again there were no signs of tampering; more clothes, jackets, blouses, workwear. He opened the door and removed the items. This left the third wardrobe.

The inside panelling was a similar construction to before and Rory pushed the wood with the same result. He looked inside and stopped in his tracks.

There it was.

Against the wall at the back of the wardrobe was a wooden block perhaps double the size of a mousetrap. On top were two pieces of C4 plastic explosive, Semtex, about the size of two large sausages. There was also a battery and a small detonator which were connected by wire.

"Jesus," said Rory as he tracked the wire from the device. It had been threaded through the tops of the coat-hangers which were holding more clothes on the rail. Anyone flicking through them would set it off. Whoever was responsible certainly knew what they were doing; they were no amateurs.

Rory checked again. There were no other wires which meant he could open the wardrobe door to give himself better illumination and room to work. Careful not to disturb the hangers, he crawled slowly inside ducking under the hanging clothes, mostly jeans and trousers. He stood up behind them, inches away from the bomb. It was an anti-personnel device rather than something designed to blow up the building but was certainly lethal.

Disarming the bomb was not going to be straightforward but, as long as he didn't dislodge the wire from the detonator, he would be ok. He ducked back down and left the cupboard to gather his thoughts. Scissors, he needed a pair of scissors. He went into the kitchen and there was a wooden block on the corner of the work surface with knives used for cooking preparation protruding from it. There was also a large pair of scissors in the set. He removed them from their encasement and returned to the bedroom.

He looked at the scissors; they were larger than he would like and more cumbersome; they would accentuate the shaking of his hands. He took a deep breath and held out his arms in front of him and waited for the adrenaline rush to subside; he needed to be calm. He picked up the scissors and returned to the wardrobe, then ducked under the clothes again. It was a tight squeeze.

Suddenly Rory froze. His back pocket had snagged a pair of jeans and had caused the garment to sway. He pressed himself against the wall and held his breath. The movement had fortunately not been sufficient to disturb the hanger. He waited for less than thirty seconds but it seemed much longer. He was up close and personal with the bomb which was only inches from his face.

He steadied himself and breathed slowly. The firing mechanism worked by the pulling of the wire, so by cutting it there would be no tension; this would remove the immediate danger. Slowly Rory raised the scissors and chose a section half way between the explosive and the clothing rail. He held his breath; snip. He exhaled as he watched the limp wire hanging down from the bomb. The wooden block on which the Semtex was placed had been nailed to the back of the wardrobe. He used the scissors to lever the device from its position.

He took the bomb, placed it on the bed, disconnected the battery and removed the detonator. It was safe. He now had the small question of how to dispose of it, but for the moment he needed to get out of the flat and back to the office. He bundled up Natalie's clothes and put them in the suitcase; he hadn't bothered sorting them; then went to the bathroom. He washed his face and dried off. He took the towel into the bedroom and laid it out on the bed, put the device in the middle, wrapped it up and placed it in a plastic carrier-bag from one of the cupboards.

He carried out a quick sweep of the rest of the apartment, the toilet and spare bedroom. He did not venture into the second bedroom, merely looked through the doorway. It appeared to be a working office with a desk and chair. There was a laptop on the desk but it appeared undisturbed. It was more evidence that whoever had been in the flat was not looking for anything; otherwise, they would have almost certainly taken the computer.

After a few minutes, he left the apartment and headed down the three flights of stairs lugging the, now heavy, suitcase and carrier-bag. He stowed the case and the disarmed bomb in the boot. The street was alive with children making their way home, several dressed in smart uniforms; others, not.

He got in his car and headed back to the works. There were so many thoughts going through his head. Whoever was after Natalie had gone to a lot of trouble to kill her; boobytraps were not your usual modus operandi. He needed to confront her at some point; he also needed to tell Alistair. Natalie was not just a lawyer; that was now a certainty.

It was four-thirty before he got back. He went straight to the admin block and Natalie's office, carrying her suitcase. She was sitting in front of her computer.

She looked up, her expression friendly. "Hello, is everything ok?"

"Yeah, I got most of your stuff. There're a couple of handbags and two pairs of shoes on the bed and I've left your toiletries and make-up."

"Yes, I can buy what I need," said Natalie.

Rory looked at her with some concern. "I think you should leave now and get to your friend's as soon as you can. Whoever's after you may be watching the factory… take a cab."

She looked at him, there was an initial reluctance, but then she agreed. "Yes, maybe you are right. I will phone for a taxi."

Rory was not moving but he discreetly supervised her departure.

"Ten minutes," said Natalie and started packing her things

away. Rory watched closely as she logged off her computer. She didn't have a laptop at work and was using one of the mainframe machines.

Natalie seemed uncomfortable with Rory's presence but said nothing. By ten-to-five she was ready to leave. She was locking her desk just as security rang through to say her taxi was waiting at the gate. Rory escorted her out of the building, carrying her suitcase to the waiting cab.

He opened the door for her and she got in. She had her shoulder bag with her and Rory watched as she rummaged inside and pulled out her blonde wig. She pinned back her hair and put it on.

She turned and looked at Rory. "See you next week," she said as the cab driver shut the door and drove away through the gates.

Rory returned to the offices; he needed to speak to Alistair.

With the trade fair less than two days away and departure to Abu Dhabi in the morning, the Chairman was fielding one phone call after another. Rory stood outside his office; the door was ajar, and he could hear the conversations. He waited for a break. He heard farewells and the phone being returned to its cradle. Rory knocked on the door and went in.

"Ah Rory, glad it's you, I wanted a word," said Alistair. "Can you rustle up a couple of coffees? You can join me."

"Sure," said Rory.

So, coffees duly ordered and delivered, Alistair started detailing his latest thoughts on the trade fair and possible security concerns before Rory could mention Natalie. They finished their coffees and Rory had been able to answer Alistair's questions.

"I think we have a more pressing problem," said Rory, as Alistair appeared to be ending the conversation.

"Oh? What's that?" replied Alistair.

"It's Natalie," said Rory.

"Why, what's happened...? Is it the mugging...? She is

alright, isn't she?" said Alistair.

"It's worse than that... I went 'round to her flat this afternoon to pick up some things for her... I thought it would be safer if I went."

"Yes, I can see that," said Alistair.

"Well, hmmm... it's like this... I found a bomb in her closet. It had been rigged as a boobytrap."

"A bomb...?" said Alistair. "A bomb?" he repeated. "Have you called the police?"

"No," said Rory. "I've diffused it. It's safe."

"But we have to do something," said Alistair.

"Yeah, but first we need to reassess Natalie's role in the company... At the very least she's a security risk; the very worst, a spy of some kind."

"You really think so?" said Alistair.

"I do... Look at the facts; whoever attacked her and planted the device were no amateurs; they knew what they were doing. If she'd opened her closet door, she would have been blown to pieces... In my view, she's an agent of some kind, probably working for a foreign government."

"My God, are you sure?" said Alistair.

Rory nodded. "Yeah, I reckon... no other explanation... There was something else..."

Alistair looked at Rory, a troubled man.

"I didn't want to say anything earlier, but the first attack..."

"What about it...?" interrupted Alistair.

"I said the attacker ran away."

"Yes," said Alistair.

"Well, he didn't... We were grappling on the ground and Natalie picked up his knife and slotted him."

"What?!" exclaimed Alistair.

"Yeah, clean as you like, very professional, straight through the neck. When I checked later, the body was gone... Someone had cleaned up."

"Good God, no..." He put his head in his hands, then looked

up. "I don't know what to say… and to think I've trusted her all this time. She's even stayed on my boat a couple of times." He looked at Rory. It's something that he'd suspected.

Alistair was deep in thought, considering the wider implications.

"What about the trade fair?" said Alistair.

"I don't think that will be a problem… It's what happens here while we're away I'm worried about," said Rory.

"Hmm, yes I can see that," said Alistair.

"It may be worth having a chat with your contacts in the M.O.D. to bring them up to speed. They'll certainly want to know what's been going on… They'll also have connections to other agencies," said Rory.

"Yes, of course, although they'll be at the trade fair, so we can speak to them face-to-face. It'll be too late to do anything now and we leave tomorrow morning."

"Yeah, ok, but in the meantime, I think you should withdraw any access Natalie has to your computer systems; goodness knows what she might get up to while we're away, given the recent turn of events. Personally, I think you should consider letting her go… in the circumstances."

"Yes, you're probably right, but she's been such an important part of the business. She'll be difficult to replace."

"Not if she's been passing secrets she won't," said Rory.

"Hmm, yes… you're right." Alistair was deep in thought. "I still don't get it. I would have trusted her with my life… Do you know, it was her idea to bring in a security consultant? How ironic."

"Yeah, she told me. A smart move, obviously very confident in her cover, that's for sure… But don't be too hard on yourself, she's very good at what she does," said Rory.

Alistair had a lost expression, not knowing how to handle this revelation; it had been quite a shock.

Rory, ever-practical, brought back some perspective. "You might want to check with IT and see what she's been up to.

They'll have details of emails and what records and files she's been accessing. That might give you some idea."

"Yes, ok… Can you speak to Vikram, you have a better idea of what to do? I've got so much here to finish before I leave tonight."

"Yeah, sure…" said Rory. "One final thing, I think we should withdraw her permit, at least until we get back. We don't want her coming in and creating mayhem."

Alistair had an anguished look. "Yes, ok, I'll be guided by you. Do whatever you think is necessary."

"Ok, I'll deal with it," said Rory and he left Alistair and went back to his office.

Within five minutes, Vikram was sitting opposite him.

"So, what's the problem?" said Vikram.

"I've been speaking to Alistair and we need you to do some discreet digging," said Rory.

"Yes, ok," said Vikram, sitting forward in his seat reflecting the seriousness of the situation.

"Firstly, I want you to remove all computer protocols for Natalie Kallaste. On no account is she to be allowed access to any files, email accounts or personal folders… Can you do that as soon as possible?

"Yes, of course." Vikram looked at Rory inquisitively.

"Sorry, I can't go into detail… Then, I want you to start an investigation. I want details of all files she's been working on, particularly anything confidential."

"For how long?"

"Since she started here."

"Yes, ok I can do that… It may take a day or two."

"That's ok, we're away until Tuesday at the trade fair. Can you have it ready for when we get back?"

"Yes, I should be able to," said Vikram.

"One other thing… is it possible she could have hacked into any of the R & D databases at all… the confidential ones?"

"It depends on her knowledge. It wouldn't be easy; the firewalls are pretty robust… She would have had to get hold of the access keys and passcodes."

"Would you be able to tell, if she… or anyone had?"

"Possibly."

"Ok, thanks, see what you can find," said Rory. "Any questions?"

"No… I'll get right on it."

"Thanks, remember, this must take priority over any other work you have." Rory looked at Vikram with a serious expression. "Also, you mustn't discuss this with anyone except Alistair or me. Is that clear? That includes the other directors… If you get any problems refer them to me… I'll need you to let me have an update while we're away. Can you email me…? No, wait; best call me, I'll give you my number; it'll be safer. I don't want any trails."

"Yes, sure, of course."

"Let me know when you've blocked her access?"

"Yes, I'll do that right away."

They exchanged mobile numbers and Vikram left the office. A few minutes later Vikram called Rory confirming that Natalie had been blocked from accessing any company files.

Rory was trying to put himself in Natalie's shoes. If she were a spy, as he believed, now would be the time to get out. He weighed up the evidence. She'd been targeted by a potential assassin, possibly of Middle Eastern origin, and her flat had been rigged with a bomb. Somebody clearly wanted her dead. Did she have information that some other organisation was after? In what way was she a threat, and to whom? Questions to which Rory had no answer.

He had deliberately not told Natalie about the bomb in her flat; he wasn't sure how she would have reacted. His concern was that she might try to sabotage the company in some way; he had no idea of her motives. He was convinced she would have realised she would be under intense scrutiny following the attack on Tuesday night. It was a question of limiting any possible damage she might inflict. With the action he had taken, he hoped he had done enough; there was little more he could do.

He made another call.

"Security? Can I speak to Charlie Forbes? It's Rory Calderwood." Rory waited while the security team leader was found.

"Charlie? Rory... Look, I need you to withdraw Natalie Kallaste's entry permit with immediate effect. If she turns up, ask her to call Alistair or speak to him on his return on Tuesday. I'll confirm by email.... yeah? Thanks, and keep this to yourself, ok? Cheers."

Rory hung up and composed the said confirmation for Charlie, then returned to Alistair's office to update him.

"Thanks, Rory... You know, I still can't take it in."

"No, I can understand that... There was another thing." Alistair looked at Rory in a state of exasperation.

"What's that?"

"I don't think you should mention anything to the rest of the directors, not yet... not until we find out if anyone else has been involved."

"What... all of them?" said Alistair.

"Yes, we've got no idea what she's been up to. Let's wait and see what Vikram digs up, then we can decide."

"Yes, ok," said Alistair. "That makes sense."

"Well, if there's nothing else, I'll get off now and see you in the morning," said Rory.

"Ok... five o'clock, yes?"

"Yeah," said Rory.

He left Alistair's office and returned to his desk; he had one more call to make before he left.

"Swannie, you old bugger, how're you doing?"

"Rory...? Yeah, good thanks."

"Beryl ok... and the kids?"

"Yeah, all good, thanks."

"Just wondered if there's been any more news."

"Nah, nothing in the papers; seems to have gone quiet. The last I heard, there were looking for another gang."

"Cheers, that's good news... Just to let you know, I'm off to The Emirates tomorrow, back Monday, late afternoon sometime, but if anything crops up, you give me a bell, yeah?"

"Yeah, got that, speak to you next week, cheers," and Swannie rang off

Rory was ready to leave. He collected the things he would need for the trip and his work laptop. He checked around his office, then automatically put his hands in his jacket pocket for his car-keys. He could feel another set; it was Natalie's apartment keys. He shrugged his shoulders, took them out, then put them in his desk drawer. He had a feeling he wouldn't be seeing her again anytime soon.

As he drove back, he decided to make a house-call and it would mean a detour.

It was yet another damp and drizzly early evening, around six-thirty, as he drew up outside Laura's house. Her car was parked outside which was a good sign; at least she was in. He wasn't sure of the next bit. He knocked on the door.

There were some noises coming from inside, then the door opened.

"Hi," said Rory.

"Oh, it's you," said Laura. She looked around, left and right as if checking he was on his own.

"You better come in." There was no kiss as a greeting. "What do you want?"

They went into the lounge and Rory sat down, without being invited.

Laura stood for a moment, then sat opposite.

"I wanted to explain about last night," said Rory.

"There's nothing to explain," said Laura.

"Of course there is… you left before I could tell you what was going on."

"It was pretty clear to me."

"Yeah, well you couldn't have been more wrong… I'll tell you the story, what happened. Then it's up to you."

Laura looked at Rory as he explained about Natalie's attack but not the killing or the bomb. "It's what I said last night, I can't go into detail, but it could be linked to the work I'm doing… I had no option last night but to bring her back to the cottage, someone was out to kill her."

Laura's journalistic mind clicked into gear. She would love to know more, but she would stand by her promise not to disclose any information Rory gave her.

"Where is she now?"

"She's staying with a girlfriend," said Rory. Laura was looking down, clearly thinking about Rory's explanation.

"Look, it's up to you… I don't want us to split up, but you will have to trust me," said Rory.

"Hmm, I find that difficult, I've been let down in the past," said Laura.

"Not by me you haven't, I won't do that," said Rory. There was a long pause; she looked at him.

"Have you eaten?" said Laura.

"No," said Rory.

"I'm just making a salad, there's enough for two."

"Thanks," said Rory.

"Do you want a drink?"

"Yeah, a beer would be great, thanks."

Laura went to the kitchen and came back with an opened bottle of lager. "I won't be long," said Laura and went back to prepare the meal.

"I found some quiche in the fridge," she said, as she put the plates on the table a few minutes later. "And there's a jacket potato."

Rory was starting to relax from what had been a difficult

day.

"Thanks," said Rory and she sat down opposite him.

"You have an invitation to Sunday lunch," she said as she tucked into her lettuce and tomatoes. "It was what I came to tell you last night."

"Thanks, that's great," said Rory. "It won't be this week, though."

"No, I told my parents you were away this weekend," said Laura. "The following week, perhaps?"

"Yeah, I should be ok for that. I can let you know for definite in the week," said Rory.

Over the food, the atmosphere gradually changed. "Have you heard any more about London?" said Laura.

"No, I phoned my mate this afternoon, the one who lives down the Smoke," said Rory. "He said there's been nothing in the paper."

"No, I had a look too. I couldn't find anything in the Standard," said Laura. "What do you think will happen?"

"I don't know, but I hope nothing," said Rory.

"What about the girl, how is she?"

"Fiona…? I rang her, and she seems ok, talking about going back to Uni," said Rory.

Laura took a sip from a glass of water. "Is that wise? They may be looking for her."

"Yeah, that's possible, but she's quite determined to put it all behind her… a bit stubborn, just like her dad," said Rory.

They continued chatting over the meal and when they had finished Rory helped Laura clear the dishes.

"So, what time are you going to Abu Dhabi tomorrow?" said Laura.

"Got to be at the airport for five o'clock check-in," said Rory.

"Ouch, that's early," said Laura. "I better make use of you while you're here, then."

She took Rory's hand and led him up the spiral staircase.

It was almost ten o'clock before Rory left Laura's. He was glad they were back on track and had promised to call her over the weekend. He returned to the cottage and parked the car in the usual spot, then opened the boot. The carrier bag containing the bomb was still where he'd left it, undisturbed by the rigours of the journey. He looked around the pathway for something heavy. There was no shortage of stones about and he found one which was large enough, probably seven or eight pounds in weight.

He placed it inside the plastic carrier-bag along with the Semtex and tied the handles tight. Checking it was secure, he walked the short distance to the river bank. It was still running high; the current, fast. There was no-one about. He swirled his right arm in a circular motion to gain the necessary momentum, like a hammer thrower, then he let the bag go. It flew through the air and there was a loud 'splosh' as it hit the water almost mid-stream where he hoped it would stay forever.

He walked back to the cottage and started putting his things together ready for the morning.

Back in Birmingham, trouble was brewing.

Chapter Twelve

Just after five o'clock, Natalie, still disguised in her blonde wig, arrived at her friend's flat in Harborne. The taxi driver carried her case to the front door and she gave him his fare plus tip.

She had met Lorela Beck, an Austrian by birth, in the local library two days after arriving in the UK, just over six months ago. She was also a lawyer, working in the city centre for a large firm of solicitors. They met quite frequently for dinner and, having a spare room, Lorela was only too happy to help with temporary accommodation when Natalie contacted her following the attack.

Harborne is a neighbouring borough of Edgbaston and Natalie's apartment was only a ten-minute drive away. The house was a similar style but slightly smaller; pre-war brick, comprising of three floors that had been converted into four apartments. There was an entrance door with intercoms for each apartment. Natalie rang the buzzer for the ground-floor flat. Lorela answered; she'd left work early to be there for her friend's arrival.

The front door clicked, and Natalie pushed it open then wheeled in her suitcase. Lorela was waiting at the entrance to her flat.

"Hi, everything ok?" she said, then did a double-take. "What have you done with your hair?"

"Oh, that… yes, it is ok, it is only a wig… just a change… Thank you for letting me stay," said Natalie, quickly changing the subject. "Not for too long, I promise."

"No, it is ok, you can stay as long as you need," said Lorela. "Come, I will show you your room… You look so different with blonde hair. I think it suits you."

"Thank you," said Natalie.

Natalie carried her luggage through to the living room, then down a short corridor to the spare room. It was small with just a single bed, a wardrobe and dressing table with a wooden chair.

"I hope it is big enough for you," said Lorela.

"Yes, thank you, this is fine," said Natalie.

Lorela left Natalie to sort out her things. She put her case on the bed and opened it, then removed her wig and changed. She immediately had a problem; she needed her laptop and one or two other items from her flat. She also needed her car.

Natalie went back to the lounge and noticed Lorela's laptop on the dining table. "Can I borrow your laptop?" she said as Lorela came through from the kitchen.

"Of course, it is there... I was working earlier, help yourself. I will unlock it for you."

Lorela logged in, then left Natalie to do whatever she needed to do. Natalie opened the internet browser and accessed the company's website; then tried to log onto the staff portal. 'Please enter your password', said the dialogue box. She complied. 'Access denied - Invalid password', came the reply.

She tried again, same response. Then she twigged; she'd been blocked; it was the only answer. This put a different complexion on the situation. She was now on her own. She logged off the laptop. "I just need to make a phone call... I will not be long," she said.

"Ok, dinner will be another twenty minutes," replied Lorela.

Natalie returned to her bedroom, took out her phone from her bag and dialled a number she knew by heart.

"Epsilon," said the receiver's voice.

"This is Omega... I have been compromised; I need to move. Unidentified attacker last evening outside my apartment, Middle Eastern appearance, query Palestinian."

"Ok, that... What about workplace...? Any news on the project?"

"Negative, no more news, and company computer access has been blocked... it is possible I have been discovered. I have managed to download several files which contains some of the plans, but I am not sure if it is complete, there may be more.

The latest information I have says prototype is being tested by British Government."

"Thank you for update… Status of attacker?"

"Eliminated."

"Ok, head for advantage-point three, we will arrange for your katsa to retrieve the information from you and provide new documents. It's time to bring you home."

Advantage-point three was a code word for a safe-house in London. Natalie knew the number by heart.

"Ok, I will move tonight and contact you when I arrive."

"There is someone is residence… I will let them know to prepare accommodation… Epsilon, out."

Natalie returned to the living room just as Lorela was dishing up the meal. She had moved the laptop and set the table for two.

Natalie needed a favour. She had not told Lorela the full story about the attack, just that she had been mugged and didn't want to stay on her own in her flat. They sat down and started to eat.

"There has been a change of plan," said Natalie after taking her first mouthful of Bolognese.

"Oh," said Lorela.

"Yes, I need to leave tonight but I have a favour to ask."

"Of course," said Lorela.

"I need to go back to my flat and collect some things… and my car."

"But I thought you said it was dangerous."

"I will be careful… and I will wear my wig." She smiled.

"You want me to take you to your flat?"

"Yes please, when we have eaten, if that is ok."

"Yes of course," said Lorela.

It was nearly seven o'clock by the time Natalie lugged her suitcase out of the flat and into Lorela's Fiesta. She had changed into a pair of jeans, short leather jacket and tee-shirt;

it was a warm evening. She was wearing the wig.

"Thank you, for helping me. I will not forget it," said Natalie as she buckled her seatbelt.

The late rush-hour traffic slowed down their progress and it was almost twenty minutes before Lorela turned into Cairns Avenue.

"Wait, slow down," said Natalie. She examined the row of parked cars; nothing suspicious.

"Park outside, I will get out quickly," said Natalie.

Removing the heavy suitcase from the boot of the car meant the operation wasn't as speedy as Natalie would have liked.

Down the road, a plume of smoke from a cigarette puffed out from behind an Ash tree. The smoker was bored; it would be another half an hour before he would be relieved. He peered around the tree, having heard the car approaching and watched the blonde woman exit a red Ford Fiesta with a suitcase. There were farewell exchanges and the car pulled away. He ducked out of sight again until it had passed, then went back to his surveillance. He could see the figure struggling to the front door with the suitcase. He wasn't sure, but it could be her.

He left his post and went down the service road to the garages. Behind the last one, there was a small plot of wasteland; a dark blue Transit van was parked, reasonably concealed from any casual onlooker. The watchman walked up to it and pulled the side door across. Smoke billowed out. He got in. He spoke in Arabic.

"Ahsan, why are you here...? What is happening?" said an overweight, middle-aged man in the passenger seat.

"I have just seen a woman enter the house with a valise."

"Is it her?" said the man.

"I don't know... You said to tell you if anyone went into the house."

"What did she look like?"

"I don't know, it was too far to see."

"What about her hair and clothes?"

"She looked like in business, blonde hair."

"Blonde?" Are you sure?"

"Yes," said Ahsan.

The man thought for a minute. "Hmm, it could be a disguise... I think we should check just in case."

"What about the bomb?" said Ahsan.

"We will go now, see if it is her before she has a chance to set it off... I want her alive," said the weighty man.

There were two other men in the car, the driver plus a younger man with a fashionable beard, who sat in the back. He'd been reading the sports pages of an Arab newspaper.

"What do you want to do, Sayyid?" said the driver.

"Ahsan, Farid, you come with me; Naseer, you drive to the front and wait for us."

The three men scrambled out of the van and walked around to the front of the block as the van followed.

Meanwhile, on the third floor, Natalie had taken off her jacket and put it on the sofa while she went to work; her phone and car keys were in the pocket. She was in the spare bedroom, her 'office', collecting what she needed; concentration level was high. She worked quickly; pulling open the drawer to the small desk and taking it out. She turned it upside down. There was a memory stick stuck to the bottom of the drawer with masking tape; she removed it. She picked up her laptop from the desk and put it in a rucksack with its charger, then dropped the memory stick inside one of the compartments. There were some things in the closet she needed too. She opened the door and took out a couple of handbags which Rory had left. She opened her suitcase and managed to squeeze them in. She had a final check and was about to pick up her jacket and leave when she thought she heard a noise.

Moments earlier, Sayyid, the weighty man, led his two comrades to the front door of the apartment block. He was wearing a dark jacket, trousers and a soiled white shirt opened at the neck revealing untidy grey-flecked chest-hairs.

"Farid, the key."

The younger man rummaged in the pocket of his jeans and handed the man two keys on a ring.

The three went in and started climbing the stairs to the third floor. Sayyid was leading and turned to speak to his comrades in a whisper.

"Remember, be careful, do not go into the bedroom. We should be ok even if the bomb is exploded as long as we are not in the bedroom when it goes off."

They reached the top floor and Sayyid drew a gun from the side pocket of his jacket. Drips of sweat trickled from his forehead and down his double chin. The perspiration dropped onto his white shirt creating a stain. No-one would notice; it was already grubby. He checked the keys and slowly inserted the Yale into the lock and turned it.

They had no idea where Natalie was or if it was even her that Ahsan had seen earlier. He pushed the door slowly, then put his head around it. Suddenly, he was grabbed by his hair and pulled into the room. Natalie slammed her knee into his face then hit him hard with a Karate chop on the back of the neck; he went down, momentarily stunned. Before she could move, Ahsan and Farid were on top of her and had wrestled her to the ground. Natalie was flailing punches in all directions, fighting like a tiger but she was quickly overpowered by the men. Sayyid got up, holding his neck and wiping the blood from his broken nose. He picked up the gun and crashed the butt down on Natalie's head; she slumped to the floor, drifting into unconsciousness.

"We need to get her to the van quickly," said Sayyid, holding a handkerchief to stem the bleeding from his face. "Take her, I need to get the bomb; we can use it again."

Natalie was murmuring incoherently as the two men dragged her down the stairs. Meanwhile, there was a shock in store for Sayyid. He slowly opened the door to the closet; the bomb had gone. He checked the other doors in case he had made a mistake but then he noticed the holes where the block had been nailed to the wall. "What the…?"

Someone had clearly removed the device. He needed to speak to Natalie. He walked back to the lounge and was about to leave the flat when he spotted her rucksack on the table. He opened it and saw the laptop; he put the bag over his shoulder.

Outside, Ahsan checked the avenue; there was no-one about. Naseer was waiting at the end of the footpath with the engine of the Transit running. He saw the men with Natalie, got out and slid open the van's side door. She was still not fully functioning, and the two men were able to drag her into the vehicle without any resistance. It had taken just a few seconds.

"She's starting to come around," said Farid.

"Here, use this," said Naseer and handed Farid a hypodermic.

Quickly, before she was fully alert, Farid held Natalie's arm and inserted the needle. He pressed the plunger and waited for the drug to disappear into Natalie's bloodstream. She was unconscious once more.

Less than a minute later, Sayyid was at the front door, leaving the building. He opened the passenger door of the Transit and got in, still swabbing his bloody nose with his handkerchief. He put the shoulder bag on the seat beside him.

Naseer pulled away.

"The bomb has disappeared!" exclaimed Sayyid.

"What?!" said Naseer. "How can that be?"

"I do not know, someone must have taken it, but whoever it was would have to know about bombs," said Sayyid.

"Was it her?" said Ahsan.

"It must be," said Sayyid. "But I don't know how. She didn't return last night, we know that because we would have seen her, and she wasn't here this morning… What time did we plant it?"

"About six o'clock," said Nasser.

"She must have returned before we got here this afternoon and found it…"

"What about the man I saw?" said Farid. "The one who had the suitcase."

"No, I wouldn't think so. It would be one of the other residents…" said Sayyid. "Have you searched her?"

"Yes, she has nothing."

"What about her phone?"

"No, she doesn't have it," said Farid.

"You know where to go?" said Sayyid, looking across to Naseer.

"Yes, it is not too far."

Alum Rock is a commercial area to the North-East of Birmingham about seven miles from Natalie's apartment and Naseer headed down the back streets to a dilapidated factory scheduled for demolition. The van stopped outside the makeshift corrugated-iron gates. Sayyid got out and pulled them open; Naseer drove through.

There were originally six in the group sent to find Natalie; one had been killed by her, the other, Youssef al-Masri, was at Sayyid's cousin's house in Spark Hill. Sayyid needed someone to stay behind to look after things in case they needed to escape quickly. Youssef was chosen for that task, despite strong resistance.

They had found the derelict property nearly three weeks earlier and they were sensibly switching between it and the Spark Hill house, using them alternatively as bases to avoid any suspicion. Sayyid made a call en route.

"Youssef, my friend, it is Sayyid, we have caught the girl… No, no, you stay, I will call you in the morning… Do not worry we will keep her alive for you. I will even let you have some fun with her… You can be first."

It had taken almost three years to track down Natalie Keim and there was a buzz in the team at the successful outcome of their mission. She was still unconscious on the floor of the van being watched over by Ahsan and Farid.

At the back of the building was, what used to be, a large office. It had been stripped of anything of value and was virtually a shell. Naseer, as well as the driver, was an electrician and computer expert; he had managed to connect the room to an electricity supply. Four sleeping bags were laying side-by-side in the corner and a bench with a microwave oven was situated along the far wall; empty cartons of ready-meals littered the floor. Several old office chairs were scattered around the room. At the far end of the office was a door with steps which led down to a basement, probably an old storage or stationery room.

Ahsan and Farid carried the sleeping Natalie out of the van, through the office and down the stairs.

"She will be out for some time," said Sayyid. "Take off her tee shirt and jeans and tie her to the chair... I want to see what is on her computer. Naseer can you get into it?"

"Yes, of course, it is not difficult," said Naseer, and he followed Sayyid back up the stairs. Sayyid was still holding the back of his neck where Natalie had hit him. He would have his revenge; at least his nose had stopped bleeding

True to his word, it took Naseer less than a minute to hack Natalie's password and start browsing her files.

"Sayyid, you need to see this," said Naseer and Sayyid viewed the screen as Naseer scrolled down a series of what looked like technical drawings.

"What are they?" said Naseer.

"I am not sure... we will need to ask her when she wakes up," said Sayyid. He looked again more closely. "They are weapons of some kind I think. I wonder what a Mossad agent would want with them."

He took out a mobile phone and inserted a SIM card from his pocket. He looked at Naseer. "I need to call Hashem and let him know what has happened."

He dialled a number, 00970… Palestine. The conversation would be in Arabic.

The call rang out for over a minute; it would be around two a.m. there.

"Hashem, it is Sayyid… I have her."

"Y… y… you do…?" The voice sounded sleepy.

"Yes… praise be to Allah."

"Wait."

There was a pause while the man cleared his head.

"What happened to the bomb? I thought you were going to eliminate her."

"Nothing, it has gone…"

"Gone… how?"

"I think she must have found it. I will ask her when she wakes up."

"Hmm, ok," said the man.

"Now we have her, we can execute her on video like we planned," said Sayyid.

"No, no, there has been a change, she is too valuable… we need to get her back here. Call tomorrow and I will tell you where to go… I will arrange it; it will be by ship I think," said Hashem.

"Ok… I have also found a computer with some information on it which looks important. What do you want me to do?"

"Bring it with you, I will get someone to look at it."

"Can I question her?" asked Sayyid.

"Yes… you can question her but don't kill her. We will put her on trial here… then we will kill her. It will be a big celebration."

"But what about Wasim… she killed him. She must be punished."

"Oh, she will be, she will be, beyond anything you can imagine," said the man.

Sayyid dropped the call.

"Come, let us see if we can wake the Yahudi," said Sayyid,

using the derogative Arabic term for 'Jew'.

Sayyid and Naseer went down the stairs and into the basement. The room smelt of diesel oil, cigarettes and some unidentifiable aromas. It was not pleasant. Ahsan and Farid were sat on chairs guarding Natalie who was still unconscious. Her arms were tied behind her with plastic garden ties, then attached to the chair. Her legs were manacled by leather straps which were also attached to the chair.

Her blonde wig had been removed and her hair hung down limply; a trace of blood from the blow of Sayyid's gun had congealed above her eyebrow. She was in her underwear; her discarded clothes lay on the floor.

"Are you going to ask her about Wasim?" asked Ahsan.

"All in good time... all in good time... Fetch some water," said Sayyid.

There was a red fire-bucket on the floor by the door below an ugly mark on the wall where the extinguisher had been wrenched from its housing; a tap was adjacent to it.

Ahsan went over and picked up the bucket and started filling it. Then passed it to Sayyid.

"Let's wake her up," he said and threw the contents of the bucket with some force at Natalie's face.

The sudden shock brought her to her senses.

She opened her eyes and surveyed the scene. She instinctively tried to move but immediately felt the tug of her restraints. She tried to focus.

"Who are you...? Why am I here...?"

"Ah, Natalie, welcome back. My name is not your concern... My colleagues and I have a few questions to ask you."

The water had soaked her, and her underwear was ringing wet and almost transparent. Farid took a picture on his phone. "My friends will enjoy this," he said as he accessed the photo to examine his handiwork.

Natalie had been trained in hostage and capture situations,

but the training could not replicate the sense of fear she was experiencing right now.

"Who are you...?" she repeated. "Who is Natalie? ... I don't know anyone called Natalie."

"Do not insult my intelligence... We have been searching for you for three years... in Israel... then Estonia and now here... You have been very elusive... Maybe you need a little reminder. Farid, fill the bucket."

Farid complied and handed Sayyid the full bucket. Once again Sayyid threw the contents over Natalie, full in the face. Natalie recoiled with the force, and the cold.

"What do you want from me?" said Natalie, gasping for breath and shivering.

"Naseer, bring me my computer."

Naseer went back upstairs and returned with a laptop.

"Bring her," barked Sayyid. Ahsan and Farid lifted Natalie up, still strapped to the chair, and carried her to a small table against the wall. Sayyid set up the laptop computer and turned it on. He hovered over it, searching the files. A grainy video appeared. Sayyid held Natalie's head by her hair and positioned it so she was looking directly at the screen. It was a newsreel video showing a man addressing a large crowd holding rifles and shouting support. A commentator was providing an enthusiastic narrative in Arabic. The man was carrying a Kalashnikov and fired several volleys into the air. The crowd were going wild. Natalie knew exactly who it was... Marwan Zubeidi, the most dangerous man in the Middle East.

The video suddenly changed and sombre music was playing. Crowds were there, beating their chests in grief. Then there was frightening footage; it looked like a prison cell. A man was dragged into the room; he could hardly walk and was clearly injured. His hair was matted with blood; his mouth and eyes like pulp, swollen almost beyond recognition. He was placed on a large wooden board, about seven feet square. His arms were held outwards and upwards against the wood; his fingernails were missing.

"Our brothers can be very creative when it comes to interrogation," said Sayyid.

The prisoner's hands were forced open and a nail gun was pressed against his right palm. Someone out of shot depressed the trigger and a three-inch nail was expelled at lightning speed through his hand impaling him to the board. There was no sound but the pain on the man's face was plain to see. The procedure was repeated with his left hand. There were whoops of joy from the people who were present in the room. Natalie tried to avert her gaze but Sayyid held her head firm. She knew the man; they had been lovers.

The video jumped ahead to a later time. The man was still nailed to the board; it was difficult to know how long he had been there. His head hung down as if he were asleep. There were about five people in the room. A large man with a beard produced a knife and lifted the prisoner's head. It was not a normal knife used for slicing, it had jagged edges like a saw. The victim's eyes gradually opened. The bearded man slowly started pulling the knife backwards and forwards across the neck of the prisoner; his eyes were open, etched with pain. Blood at first oozed, then flowed more quickly as the instrument made slow progress into the victim's throat. It seemed to take several minutes before all the sinews and spinal cord had been severed and the head came away. The bearded man held it up to the camera and smiled a toothy grin. The video stopped. Natalie vomited across the screen and keyboard. Sayyid was furious and hit Natalie across the face with his hand.

"More water," said Sayyid.

Another bucketful was supplied and duly thrown at Natalie; she recoiled again from the shock.

"Naseer, check the laptop, see what you can save," said Sayyid.

Naseer picked up the soiled computer and took it upstairs. Ahsan and Farid carried Natalie on the chair back to the centre of the room. There was blood trailing from her mouth from the blow from Sayyid. She drifted back into unconsciousness.

December 2004, Mossad Operations Room, Tel Aviv

The Kidon is an elite group of expert assassins who operate under the Caesarea branch of the espionage organisation; four of them had been called together for a special meeting. Since joining The Mossad, the group had been through a rigorous training regime on a level equal to any special forces unit in the world. They sat at a desk waiting for their commanding officer to arrive and brief them. No-one knew his real name; his code name was Epsilon.

He walked into the room with an orderly and sat down on another table in front of them. He stopped for a moment and looked at the small group, highly trained and deadly which is why they had been chosen. He spoke in Hebrew.

"We have a dangerous, but vital, mission which has been sanctioned by the Prime Minister himself. A picture appeared on the screen... This is your target."

There were looks exchanged between the group. Marwan Zubeidi, Head of Al-Aqsa Martyrs Brigade, was one of the most famous figures in the Middle East, a thorn in the side of Israel and the peace process which was being brokered by the Americans. The recently deceased Yasser Arafat, the once-reviled figure of Palestinian insurrection, was now being written as a moderate; it was Zubeidi who was calling the shots and thwarting every effort to agree on a ceasefire. His rallies were attended by thousands and they hung on his every word; armed rebellion was the only way, he preached. Any thoughts of peace were going to be difficult while this man was around.

"We have reliable intelligence that this coming weekend, Zubeidi will be visiting this town." A picture appeared on the screen. "Qana."

"Lebanon?" said Meir Hofi, who would be leading the mission. The group knew the town, not far from the Israeli border, about twelve kilometres.

"Yes, you will be leaving Friday. We are looking at a smash and grab raid except there will be no grab. We want you to take him out swiftly and get out again… There is no doubt he will be heavily guarded, particularly that close to the border. However, in the confusion of the hit, it should be possible for you to be able to return safely… speed is the key. I have more information and details about where he will be staying; join me here."

The four left their seats and approached a table in front of the commander where there were maps and diagrams laid out; the briefing took several hours.

Two days later, Meir Hofi, Moshe Yatom, Yossi Harel and Natalie Keim were driving towards the border from their base in Tel Aviv in a ten-year-old Mercedes; a car favoured by taxi drivers. It was about a hundred and thirty kilometres to the outskirts of Tyre, a city on the coast, over the border in Lebanon, where they would turn right towards their destination. Traffic was slight; the weather hot. Friday was the start of the weekend, heralded by prayers.

Qana is a town of about ten-thousand inhabitants and is spread across a large area. As they scanned the surroundings for familiar landmarks, the magnitude of their task was beginning to dawn on them. The mood in the car though, was upbeat, the plan memorised and rehearsed; they were ready. They just needed Zubeidi to show.

"Let's hope Epsilon's intelligence is good," said Moshe Yatom, the youngest of the four, as the car entered Qana. The occupants were looking left and right, checking the landscape. It was one thing seeing the place on a map, even if it was 3D; another seeing it for real.

This group knew each other well; in Natalie and Meir Hofi's case, very well; they had been lovers for three months. That would not affect the mission in any way. Their relationship was not known inside the organisation, by design. They needed to keep everything professional; their lives depended on it. The fourth member, Yossi Harel, was a serious character, quiet and thoughtful. He was, however, a great strategist and in charge of logistics.

They had been on the road for about half an hour from the Tyre turning; it had been slow going. "There it is," shouted Moshe, with youthful enthusiasm, pointing to a large building on the corner of a road junction. Immediately opposite was a small row of houses; in the middle, a hotel bar. That was where Zubeidi was supposed to be heading.

Meir was driving; he turned left and stopped behind the building. There were a few other dwellings dotted around but none in the immediate vicinity. Natalie was in the passenger seat; Yossi, in the back with Moshe. Yossi opened a secret compartment in the central console and extracted the weapons and ammunition, concealed in special holdalls. They were all wearing sunglasses to protect themselves from the glare coming off the white buildings.

It was quiet; this part of town seemed deserted as they left the car with their packages and went inside. The house today would be empty. It was owned by a sympathiser, a Maronite Catholic, who had taken his family to the coast for the day.

Being ninety-five percent Shia Muslims, there were few Israeli sympathisers in Qana. But there was another reason. The deaths of a hundred of its residents under the Israeli 'Grapes of Wrath' bombardment in April 1996 would not be easily forgotten. Evidence of the assault could still be seen on the buildings, pock-marked and shrapnel-scarred, with many derelict, bombed-out houses.

The house was on two floors, with a terrace on the roof. It was sparsely furnished, with just the essentials. The four made their way to the top and looked out. Across the road from the house was the bar which was, allegedly, owned by Zubeidi's brother. According to the source, the visit was a private family one and would not involve any rally or public speaking; as

Epsilon had put it, "Zubeidi has a day off". The information they had been given also indicated he would be accompanied by his family, which was significant. There was to be no avoidable collateral damage, they had been told. This would be purely a sniper operation.

"Ok, let's unpack the weapons and set ourselves up," said Meir. Yossi was the expert marksman and he would be taking the 'kill-shot'; Natalie was to act as back up and would also target any bodyguards or other threat. Their vantage point was ideal; they would be hard to spot, and they had a clear view overlooking the front of the bar.

They did not know when Zubeidi was due to arrive; the source didn't have that detail but thought it would not be until the afternoon due to the distance he would have to travel from Ramallah, the Palestinian capital. The information could, of course, be inaccurate or, worse, a ruse to get four high-value agents into a position where they could be easily captured. Epsilon had vouched for the origin of the information and the group trusted him.

Food and water had been left in the refrigerator in the kitchen and after three hours with little in the way of activity, Moshe was sent to retrieve supplies for the group; it was now almost midday. Their weapons were poised and ready. Yossi's H-S Precision HTR sniper rifle was supported on a tripod to eliminate hand-shake for greater accuracy; everything was in place. The occasional car went by, no sign of Zubeidi. The four were feeling the pressure; perspiration stained the armpits of their shirts. One o'clock went, two o'clock; then at ten-to-three, a large black Mercedes came down the street.

"Look, this could be it," whispered Moshe. Yossi and Natalie were ready; Meir had binoculars on the scene. It would be on his command.

The Mercedes stopped outside the bar. Two bodyguards got out and started scanning the area. The car had pulled up tight to the wall with only a small gap to enable the passengers to get out. Meir could see three heads emerge from the back of the car and go straight into the bar, followed by the bodyguards. The door shut behind them.

"Shit!" said Yossi.

Positive identification, and therefore making a clear shot had been impossible. A contingency would be needed.

There was a 'plan B' but it was far more dangerous than the original. It would mean a hit on the bar itself. There was also another option; hit the car when it left. This would almost certainly result in other casualties, so it would be a last resort.

Taking out Zubeidi in broad daylight was incredibly dangerous, but they had worked out a strategy.

Meir called the group together. "Ok, we need to hit the bar; Yossi, do you have the guns?"

Yossi opened another holdall and produced four Glock 17's, ideal for their task. There would be no body armour which would be too cumbersome and would slow down their escape; they had also decided not to use suppressors. There was going to be a lot of noise, part of the plan to cause confusion.

Meir kept a watch on the bar while the other three chose a weapon in turn and started loading the ammunition. Natalie took over lookout while Meir loaded his gun; Yossi dismantled the sniper rifle; it wouldn't be required.

It was gone three o'clock. Natalie stayed on the roof as a lookout while the remainder returned to the car. Yossi stowed the rifle back in the storage compartment. The group would be split. Moshe, an expert driver and mechanic would stay in the Mercedes ready for a hasty exit. Natalie and Yossi would make the hit, while Meir would act as back up and support. He would provide suppressing fire if necessary.

Meir took over lookout duties from the ground floor and a couple of minutes later Natalie came down from the roof and joined the group. Meir briefed them one last time. He had one more look at the bar; everything was ready.

Chapter Thirteen

The plan was for Yossi and Natalie to walk casually down the road as if they were sweethearts looking for a place to stay for the night. Moshe would have the car ready over the road at the house, with Meir as a back-up, watching and ready to act in case of trouble.

Yossi and Natalie left the house via the back door, heading north away from their base so as not to give away their position. The area at the rear of the property was barren wasteland and not overlooked. There was a burnt-out shell of a building, possibly a shop, before it had been demolished by an Israeli shell. They skirted around it.

Meir was following about fifty metres behind them. After a suitable distance, and well away from any casual observer, the couple re-joined the road about five hundred yards north of the bar. They turned around and started walking back down the slight gradient towards the target; both had their guns tucked into the waistbands of their trousers and were wearing sunglasses.

Within five minutes, they had arrived at the bar. They could hear children playing in the back somewhere. The Mercedes that had ferried the visitors hadn't moved and, as they approached, they could see it was very close to the wall with just enough room for one person to pass. They eased themselves through the gap and reached the bar entrance. The door was shut. Natalie took off her sunglasses, undid two buttons on her blouse and knocked on the door. Not speaking Arabic, they chose English, posing as Australian tourists.

There was no reply, Natalie knocked again. She could hear noises and movement from inside, then a voice in Arabic which she did not understand.

"Please can you help, we need a room for tonight," she said.

"We are not open today," said the voice in broken English.

"But we have been travelling for hours… Can we at least get a drink…? We have money."

There was a releasing of bolts and the door opened a couple of inches. The man seemed distracted by Natalie's chest and the hesitation was sufficient for Yossi to push the door and slam his fist into the face of the host. He dropped to the floor. Yossi hit him again. Natalie checked for a gun; she found none. He was an older man, in his sixties, looking more like a father than a brother. They pulled out their weapons and slowly moved into the customer space. It was a depressing place; old pictures of past political leaders adorned the wall hiding peeling wallpaper. There were six foldaway tables with accompanying chairs and several high stools stood empty against the serving counter. Natalie and Yossi stood for a moment to acclimatise to their environment and the light.

At the corner of the bar was a passageway which led to the back rooms and the garden. Natalie remembered the layout from the briefing. They could hear the children, louder now. Slowly, Natalie edged towards the corridor and the noise; Yossi was behind her. She peered around the doorway into the darkness, and crept inside, flat against the wall; then a voice in Arabic.

"Rafiq, Rafiq."

Someone was concerned at the whereabouts of the older man. Natalie froze. Suddenly the light at the far end was blocked by the shape of a big man. There were some stairs about halfway along leading to the second floor. Natalie quickly slipped up the staircase; just a couple of steps. The man reached this point. His eyes hadn't adjusted to the lack of illumination and he walked passed Natalie's position, almost blind. She was behind him and crashed the butt of her gun on the back of his head. Yossi followed up with two more blows rendering the man unconscious.

It was one of the bodyguards; there was a holster around his chest with a gun encased. Yossi took it out and added it to his waistband; Natalie was almost at the end of the corridor. From her vantage point, she was not visible to those in the garden. She peered around the doorframe. Two women were pushing two young boys on a child's swing; they were giggling and having a fun time. A girl of about four was tugging on her mother's abaya wanting her turn. Three men were sat around a table. One was smoking a hubbly bubbly pipe; the other two were in earnest conversation.

Recognition was immediate. Natalie moved from the doorway brandishing her Glock, quickly followed by Yossi. He moved behind Zubeidi and shot him twice in the back of the head from three or four inches. The bodyguard who was the smoker reached for his gun, but Natalie took him out before he could fire.

There was pandemonium. The man sat next to Zubeidi, was Anwar, Marwan's brother. He was now kneeling holding his fists together as if in prayer towards Yossi, pleading for his life. The children were screaming, the women wailing.

"Quick, away," said Yossi holding his gun at Anwar, covering Natalie's escape. The play area was not large and was surrounded by a ten feet tall, white picket fence. In the corner was a gate which they knew led to the road. Natalie made a dash and opened it. Yossi turned and was running towards Natalie when suddenly Anwar produced a gun from under his thawb and took a shot at him. Yossi went down; Natalie saw what had happened and fired two shots at Anwar, hitting him in the chest; more screaming and wailing. Natalie ran through the gateway and was quickly joined by Meir who had heard the shooting.

It was as though the whole town had woken up. Men were emerging from buildings, carrying Kalashnikovs and handguns; they had stirred up a hornet's nest.

Moshe came roaring alongside the back gate in their Mercedes and shouted. "Natalie, Meir quick, get in." Shots were coming at them from all sides.

Natalie looked at Meir. "You go," he said. "I'll cover you."

Natalie made a dash and opened the passenger door. She turned around to see Meir on the ground. He was holding his leg. Three men were on him in seconds; there was nothing Natalie or Moshe could do.

Natalie slammed the passenger door and the Mercedes roared away from the scene as fast as it could go. Bullets were fired in their direction, some hit the car but merely dented the bodywork.

They had a planned route they would use in case of pursuit. It took them through the mountains, a very deserted area, turning north and eventually reaching the Marjaayoun-Bint Jbeil Road which crossed into Israel, close to the Syrian border. Although it was only a relatively short distance, about seventy kilometres, it seemed to take forever. Natalie was constantly watching behind them, but the road was empty.

The Israeli-Lebanon border is known as the blue line, so-named because it refers to a map that was drawn up in the year 2000 to show a demarcation line for the Israeli army. It is double-fenced, and crossing is tightly controlled. The group were using forged Australian passports and had had no difficulty in entering Lebanon from Israel; the return journey could be more problematic, particularly if the word had got out about Zubeida's murder.

There were some nervous moments as Natalie and Moshe reached the checkpoint and joined the queueing traffic. All their documents were in the car's glove compartment and as they approached the border crossing gate. Natalie rummaged through and retrieved their two passports. She passed them to Moshe, concern etched on her face. He returned the glance and placed a hundred U.S. dollar note in his picture page. He raised his eyebrows as if to say, 'here's hoping'.

A guard approached the car; his waistcoat uniform was old and sweat-stained. Moshe wound down the window and handed him the passports. The man looked at the money and managed a smile; his maggot teeth protruded from his gums. This was it. The man pocketed the money; politics did not put food on the table. He returned the documents and waved the car through.

As Moshe and Natalie entered Israel they breathed a sigh of relief. Moshe turned the car towards Tel Aviv. They were quiet; both reflecting on the events. They had completed their mission, but at what cost. Yossi and Meir were both lost; there would be no way back for them. Natalie was in shock, but grieving would have to come later.

During the following days, there was only one headline in the region's newspapers - the assassination of Marwan Zubeidi; naturally, fingers were pointing at Israel. The Russians protested; the Palestinians were incandescent and promised retribution; the West, in private, were elated but, of course, would never condone murder.

Epsilon had mixed views, he was devastated by the loss of two of his agents; at the same time, it was job done. He knew that the Palestinians would leave no stone unturned until they had identified the remaining perpetrators. Natalie and Moshe were marked and keeping their identity secret would be a priority.

A few days later, with informants reporting that Meir was still alive and being tortured, Epsilon realised that he had to get Natalie and Moshe away. He had been unable to contact Moshe, despite several attempts, but Natalie answered the summons and was in his office at ten o'clock exactly one week after the raid.

"Natalie, we need to get you away... You have relatives in Estonia, yes?" said Epsilon.

"Yes, my grandparents, I was born there."

"Good... we are flying you out to Tallinn this afternoon. This your new passport... you are now Natalie Kallaste, student. We have arranged a place for you studying law at the university, in September. This is what you wanted, according to your last assessment?"

Natalie was momentarily speechless. "Yes, thank you."

"You will be able to finish your masters," said Epsilon with a grin. Natalie had already achieved a qualification before joining the army, a first-class honours degree in Law from the University of Tel Aviv.

"I don't know what to say," said Natalie.

"I have some things here which you will need."

Epsilon produced a holdall which included a new phone, a laptop computer and a blonde wig. Natalie was curious; she picked up the wig and tried it on.

"It suits you," said Epsilon.

That afternoon, while Natalie was in the first-class lounge at the airport waiting for the departure, a call came through to Epsilon's phone. Moshe's body had been found in a warehouse in Jerusalem's Arab quarter; he had been tortured and beheaded.

Natalie's flight was called, and she made her way to the departure gate for the seven-hour journey.

There was another violent splash of water which woke Natalie from her drug-induced sleep.

"Ah, you are back with us, Natalie, my dear," said Sayyid.

Natalie was shivering; any warmth in the evening air was dissipating with every minute; there was a danger of hypothermia setting in.

She was trying to focus; the sleep had refreshed her senses. She recalled her training in capture conditions; compliance, provide some information and importantly look for weaknesses. She looked at her four assailants. Farid appeared to be the youngest of the group, he was the one with the phone, taking the pictures. He could even be Sayyid's son, she thought; he was the weak link. Late teens to early twenties, he was fresh-faced with an attempt at a beard and, Natalie concluded, inexperienced. He would be her target when the opportunity arose; she was certain it would, it was just a matter of time. She needed to stall them for as long as she could.

Sayyid produced Natalie's laptop. "We found this in your bag… What do the drawings mean?"

"I don't know," said Natalie drowsily. "I am a lawyer, not an engineer."

Sayyid threw another bucket of water over her.

"I DON'T KNOW!" she screamed. "It is for work. I was taking it to another solicitor to get the copyright registered." She hoped the pseudo-legal parlance would confuse them. It did.

"Wait," said Sayyid. "Watch her."

Sayyid went back upstairs, took out the SIM card and placed it in his phone. He called the same number again and provided an update. "I asked her about the drawings… I have seen them; they are weapons of some kind, I am certain," said Sayyid.

"What did she say?"

"She said she was taking them to another lawyer… er. for some reason."

"She could be telling the truth," said the man on the phone. "But, no matter, bring the laptop with you. We will give it to our people here. They will know... By the way, I have the information on your passage. Tomorrow you are to go to a place called Felixstowe... There is a container ship going to Beirut, leaving Sunday. Call me when you get to the port and I will give you further instructions. In the meantime, look after the cargo, I am looking forward to meeting her."

"Yes, of course… I don't know this place, how you say?"

"Felixstowe," the man repeated.

"Ok, Felixstowe…" Sayyid said slowly, ensuring his understanding.

"Yes, you will find it," said the man.

"Of course," said Sayyid.

Sayyid rang off and returned to the basement.

He looked at Natalie, who was now in a bad way. It was gone eleven o'clock.

"I have one more question," said Sayyid.

Natalie feigned drowsiness.

"Who took the bomb?"

"Bomb… what bomb?" she said weakly.

Another bucket of water was thrown. The area around the chair was awash. Natalie gasped.

"The bomb in your apartment," said Sayyid.

"What bomb…? There was no bomb… I only returned tonight… you must know that. If there was a bomb, I would be dead."

"Hmm," said Sayyid. He decided not to pursue it further, there was little point now anyway, but it did give him food for thought.

"Naseer, Farid, go upstairs, get some food and some sleep. Ahsan, guard her,"

"What about Wasim…? Ask her about Wasim," said Ahsan.

"Tomorrow… we will ask her. Youssef will be here; it will be his pleasure to ask the questions… Don't worry, there is no rush… She will suffer I will make sure of that," said Sayyid.

He gave Ahsan a revolver. "Do not shoot her unless you have to and whatever you do, don't kill her."

The two associates complied. Sayyid looked at her, then followed the two upstairs. It was just Natalie and Ahsan. She would say nothing; lead them into a false sense of security.

As she dozed, she thought of Meir and wanted to cry but tears would not come. She had grieved for him earlier; now she just needed to focus on her own survival. She slept again but woke up when someone came into the room. It was Sayyid with Farid.

"How is she?" said Sayyid.

"She has been sleeping," said Ahsan.

"Good," said Sayyid. "Farid will take over, go and get some sleep."

Natalie was wide awake now but continued to feign slumber. She waited for Sayyid to leave, then a few minutes for Farid to get used to her presence. She had a semblance of an idea but had to be careful not to do anything that would spook him into running upstairs and fetching Sayyid.

"Ohhh, ohhh," she started moaning. Farid was up like a shot and was in front of her holding the gun.

"I need to pee," said Natalie.

"You can't," said Farid.

"But you can't leave me just to pee in my pants… let me use the bucket. Don't worry, I won't do anything. You have the gun. You can watch if you want…" Farid was wavering.

"You can take a picture with your phone, your friends would really like that," said Natalie.

Farid moved the bucket next to the chair.

"You will need to untie my hands," said Natalie.

"No, I cannot," said Farid.

"How can I sit on the bucket…? Don't worry, you have the gun. I'm not going to do anything stupid. Get your phone, you can tell your friends you have a picture of the Mossad agent having a pee. You will be famous."

Farid took his phone from his pocket and took another picture of her. Her underwear was still soaking wet and her nipples were visibly erect due to the cold." Natalie looked down.

"You like my nipples, Farid, don't you," said Natalie. "You can see them if you like… I'll let you take a picture... Don't worry, I won't tell Sayyid."

She was deliberately using their names; it was personal.

"Come on, Farid, I'm desperate… Look I'm not going anywhere. you've got the gun." There was a pause. "Sayyid will not let you take a picture, will he?" she said, hoping she was pressing the right buttons.

He went behind her and undid the ties to her arms. She was still strapped to the chair by her legs. He stood back and aimed the gun at her. She was wringing her hands trying to get the circulation going, distracting Farid. He moved closer.

"You stand up," said Farid and he lifted the bucket off the floor and tried to position it under her.

It would be his last words. In a split-second, Natalie had grabbed his hair and twisted his neck around ninety degrees. Snap! There was an audible sound as his neck broke. Farid slid limply to the floor. Natalie shuffled forward a couple of feet then bent down and unbuckled the leather straps from the chair; she was free.

She searched the unfortunate Farid, then turned him over onto his back and picked up his phone. It was not protected by any password and she was able to access the camera; she took a photograph of him. It would be useful intelligence. She collected her jeans, tee shirt and trainers which were lying on the floor next to the table. Her legs were stiff, and it was a painful exercise; she ignored the discomfort. She pocketed the phone, then checked the gun. Seven bullets; she would only need three. She rubbed her arms and legs again to help the circulation; now wearing her tee-shirt and jeans, her body temperature would soon recover. She did a couple of stretching exercises then headed for the exit.

She opened the door to the basement and crept up the stairs. There was another door at the top. This was going to be the difficult part; she had no way of knowing what was on the other side. There was a ball handle which she gently turned, then pushed the door firmly in case someone was behind. She was quickly through, her gun in the 'attack' position. Three people were in sleeping-bags in the corner. It was Sayyid who had been disturbed and sat up. Natalie was on him in a moment and fired a shot into his temple. She then dispatched Ahsan and Naseer with equal efficiency before they could move.

She searched her captors for any identity and took their wallets, money and phones. Then she photographed them. She picked up her rucksack and laptop from the table and packed the bag with the items she had collected including Sayyid's soiled computer and the gun. Finally, she picked up the keys to the van and left the building. The van was still parked in the front of the entrance. As she opened the door to the Transit she was almost overwhelmed by the smell of cigarettes. She held her breath and got in, then opened the side windows to try to clear the air before setting off.

She had a decision to make; take the Transit to the safe-house in London or return to her flat for her car and clothes. She paused for a moment; the van it had to be, she couldn't risk returning to the flat. She could always buy new clothes and the car was rented. The first problem; she had no idea where she was.

As she drove away from the industrial estate, she was looking around for any landmarks; nothing, but then she came to a main road and realised she was still in Birmingham. This was not an area she knew at all. She drove down a High Street; boarded-up shops, closing-down sales, not a prosperous area, then reached a large roundabout. She suddenly realised where she was; only a short distance from the works, maybe a couple of miles. There was a signpost; M6, M1 and the South. She pressed on for the capital.

It was gone one o'clock and there was a three-hour journey ahead of her. With the drug still in her system, she was still feeling drowsy. Her mind wandered. There were regrets; it came with the territory. She would be sad to leave England, and particularly AB Engineering. She'd made some good friends and enjoyed her work, but completion of her mission was everything. She had the information or at least as much as she was going to get; she just hoped it warranted the price.

She was very fond of Alistair, there was a certain quality in him which reminded her of herself, a kindred spirit almost, driven and focussed, but with that came loneliness. She reflected on the weekends they had spent together on the boat, special times. She had told him she had a fiancé back in Tallinn to try to prevent any suggestion of a long-term relationship. It also covered up the occasional phone calls to Epsilon.

Then there was Ed Stevens; hoodwinking him had been easy; she knew it would be. She just fluttered her eyelashes, told him that Alistair had authorised her access to the files and he logged on for her without question.

It was over nine months ago when she received the call from Epsilon; she was at her grandparents' house in Tallinn. He was still controlling events from Tel Aviv. He told her they had been tipped off by a 'reliable source' that a small engineering company in the UK had developed a new revolutionary weapon. He didn't go into detail but said it was vital that they had it.

Natalie had, by that time, finished her Master's Degree at the University and was working at a local law firm as a commercial lawyer to get some hands-on experience.

According to Epsilon, Mossad had been tracking the company for a few weeks and had received some information of a forthcoming weaponry trade fair which the company was due to attend. As a matter of course, Mossad always took an interest in arms-sales conventions and the like. This one was in Tallinn which was the reason she had been chosen for the mission. Another agent was dispatched from Tel Aviv with more details and Natalie met him in a coffee house in the old town two days later.

The agent's codename was Romulus. Natalie had previously met him on a training course at the academy, almost five years earlier. She was waiting at a table at the back of the café and watched as he walked in. He was carrying a briefcase. She stood up so he could see her.

"Natalie," he said, walking towards her and they embraced as good friends might do.

"Peter," said Natalie, using his real name.

They ordered drinks and the agent produced a document folder from his briefcase. Over coffee, Romulus gave Natalie a full breakdown of the company and, importantly, details of the trade fair. They spoke in English.

"You will need a special pass to get in, which I have here," he said and produced a badge and a document as identification. "You will be a commercial lawyer investigating potential clients and contacts for the Government if anyone asks."

"Estonian or Israeli?" she said and laughed.

"Ha, yes, Estonian... Don't worry, no-one will check; it is just to get you into the exhibition... Here is a layout of the stands. AB Engineering is number A42, near the door, here." He pointed to the location on the plan. "Not in a prominent position... Probably on a limited budget." This was an accurate assessment.

"So, what happens when I make contact?" asked Natalie.

"We need you to get hired," said the agent.

"Just like that?"

"I am sure with your unique skills you will be able to think of something," said Romulus. "Once you are hired, we will tell you what we need."

This presented Natalie with a huge problem. She had no idea how she was going to accomplish this. She would have to work out a plan.

On the day of the trade fair, she dressed in a smart business suit and took a taxi to the venue. The Estonian Fairs Exhibition Centre is located on the picturesque shore of the Gulf of Finland and is divided into three exhibition halls; only two were being used for this event. There was a line of people waiting at the security check for entry; she showed her badge and was ushered through without any questions.

As she wandered around the exhibition centre, she was fascinated by the various products on display, extolling the virtues of the stand-holders' goods. She had never seen so many ways of killing people under one roof; guided missile launchers, rocketry, videos of tanks, anti-aircraft guns; just about everything you could think of in modern warfare.

Natalie stopped at one or two stands which were of interest, before arriving at the pitch of AB Engineering. It was a modest affair with a few pictures and a video running on a loop, beamed on to the back wall. There was a small seating area inside what was basically an open hut, with three chairs and a table covered with brochures and other sales literature. It was not the most inviting of sales promotion, particularly when compared with two of the French firms which dominated the central floor space. She waited before approaching. There was just one person manning the stand. This was it; she took a deep breath and walked over, picking up one of the brochures. It was like a moth to a flame.

"Hello, is there anything specific you might be interested in?" said the salesman, not the most original opening. "My name's Duncan, Duncan Wyatt, sales director, AB Engineering."

Natalie looked at him, deliberately making eye-contact for longer than was usual, or necessary. She shook his hand.

"Natalie... Kallaste, please call me Natalie... I'm interested in all of it?" Duncan's eyes lit up. "I'm a commercial lawyer and I'm looking for a new challenge... I'd love to work for a company like this." Duncan was captivated.

"Really...? And what exactly would you have to offer us...?"

"A master's degree in International Commercial Law, I can make sure all your contracts are water-tight, make sure you cannot be sued and that someone doesn't steal your designs because of lack of copyright protection... That is so common these days, don't you think? It can break a business, I have seen it happen... and I have international experience, so if you export, I can certainly help you with local laws and regulations. Oh, and I speak four languages, English, Russian, German and French." She omitted Hebrew.

Duncan was considering the company's situation. No-one had ever spoken to him like that before; issues that hadn't really been considered.

"Why don't you wait for a moment and speak to our chairman; he's just gone for a wander around, see what our competitors are up to… Would you like a coffee?"

"Thank you, Duncan. I would love one," said Natalie, deliberately using his name.

They continued chatting over coffee and any thoughts of sales had disappeared from Duncan's mind; she was opening up all kinds of questions. After about twenty minutes he noticed Ed Sevens, the technical director, approaching. He too had got bored with just hanging around and gone for a walk. He entered the stand and Duncan gave the introductions. "This is Natalie, she's been telling me about her work as a commercial lawyer. She's looking for a job and I think she could help us… I want to introduce her to Alistair, have you seen him at all?"

"Yes, he was chatting to some Arabs a moment ago," said Ed who had also poured himself a coffee.

It was another ten minutes and a refill of coffee before Alistair returned to the 'pod' as he called the stand.

"Hi Alistair, have you seen anything of interest?"

"Not especially," said Alistair. He spotted Natalie straightaway.

"Alistair, can I introduce you to Natalie…? Sorry, I can't recall your last name," said Duncan.

"Kallaste, Natalie Kallaste… I'm a commercial lawyer here in Tallinn."

"Natalie's just finished her masters and is looking for a job overseas… she's been discussing ways in which she can help us."

Duncan suddenly became Natalie's sponsor and was explaining the essence of their conversation. Ed was also listening intently.

As Natalie delivered her own sales pitch, Alistair was beginning to see the merits of her experience.

Natalie went for the jugular. "I tell you what, let me work for you for one month, expenses only on a trial basis. If I cannot add value for you, I will return here… Just pay my airfare and hotel."

Alistair looked at Duncan, then Ed. "Can you let us discuss this...? Come back in a few minutes."

"Yes, of course," said Natalie and she got up and walked around the rest of the stands, before returning.

Alistair was smiling as she approached and shook her hand. "We've been having a discussion and we'd like to consider your offer... Do you have your contact details?"

Natalie produced a business card and wrote her private address and her mobile phone number on the back.

"I will call you when I get back to the UK and start the ball rolling."

The rest, as they say, is history. It took a few weeks but, just over six months ago, Natalie arrived in Birmingham. Within a couple of months, she had transformed the business.

As Natalie approached the outskirts of London, she stopped at a motorway service station; she needed to make a phone call. The number rang for several minutes; it was three forty-nine according to the digital clock on the dashboard.

"Hello," said a woman's voice eventually.

"This is Natalie. I had a problem which is resolved; I am at a service station about forty miles from London. I do not know where the house is. What is the address please?"

"Natalie...? We were getting very worried here. Yes, of course, it is in the north, Brent Park... not far from the end of the motorway."

Natalie was given the address but was still none-the-wiser, she would have to buy a map.

"Please call again when you get into London if you can't find it."

Natalie rang off; she needed a coffee.

She opened the rucksack, took out one of the wallets and opened it; three twenty-pound notes. That would do nicely. She put the notes in her pocket and walked into the services. She needed to visit the toilets and clean herself up before going into the café.

She went into the 'ladies' and looked at herself in the long mirror behind the row of sinks. She couldn't relate to the reflection she saw; hair bedraggled, no makeup, a swollen lip and what looked like blood on her cheek and forehead. Her tee-shirt and jeans were stained and dirty from being on the floor. She started working with some toilet tissue and managed to clean her face. She needed to do something with her hair, but without a comb, it would have to wait.

She left the toilet and went into the cafeteria. The place was almost empty; a couple of truckers in the corner and a tired, bored-looking youth at the till. She reached the counter and ordered a black coffee and a large chocolate bar.

"You have a map here?" she asked the lad.

"Only an A-Z... in the corner, by the newspapers." He pointed in the direction and Natalie went to investigate. She found what she needed, then spotted an elastic band on the floor next to the rack of magazines. She quickly picked it up and tied back her hair, then returned to the till to pay for her items.

She took her coffee and chocolate and found a table in the corner. While she was consuming her refreshment, she consulted her map and found the street where she needed to go. She memorised the directions; just a few more miles and she would be safe.

She finished the chocolate and headed for the exit. The cool morning air hit her as she walked back to the car. At least her underwear was more-or-less dry now.

She started up the van and headed out onto the motorway. She had driven about five miles when suddenly flashing headlights appeared in the rear-view mirror, then blue flashing lights.

"Oh my God, no!" she said out loud.

Chapter Fourteen

The click, click, click of the left-hand indicator echoed around the inside of the empty van as Natalie eased the Transit onto the hard shoulder; the police car followed and pulled up behind her about ten feet away.

Her mind was all over the place; she was driving a vehicle she didn't own, she had no documents, and had a gun in her rucksack with which she had just killed three people. The tension returned; she needed to stay calm, but felt far from it.

An officer approached the driver's window. Natalie lowered it.

"Do you know why we've stopped you?" said the man.

"Er... I am from Poland... I speak only little in English."

"Can you turn off the engine and get out of the vehicle please?"

The officer gesticulated to enhance her understanding. Natalie complied.

He shone his torch into her face which made her flinch. He looked at her with some suspicion. The officer led her around the back of the van which was illuminated by the headlights of the police car. She noticed another officer in the driving seat.

"You have a rear light missing," said the officer. Natalie could see the problem.

"Oh, oh, I am, er, so sorry. I did not know that. I could not see it," said Natalie.

"Are you the owner of this vehicle?" said the officer.

"Sorry... I do not understand..."

"Papers... you have papers..."

"No, no papers... er... at... at home, yes."

The officer was looking exasperated. "So where are you going to?"

"Er... Yes, I am... going to... home, yes."

There was a call from the police car; the driver was half out of his seat.

"Brian, urgent shout, mate, been a shooting in Luton… Got to go."

The officer, Brian, looked at Natalie. "You get that fixed… yeah?"

"Of course, yes… tomorrow, I will, erm… fix it, yes."

The officer walked back to the car and got in. Natalie breathed a sigh of relief. The police car roared passed with its lights blazing. That was close. There was a chance she would have had to kill him.

As they headed down the motorway, topping one-twenty mph, PC. Brian turned to his colleague. "I'm sure there was something going on with that van, something wasn't right."

"Well, we'll never know," said his driver.

Natalie pressed on, concerned about her near miss; she would have to dump the van as soon as possible but would need some help. Farid's phone was on the passenger seat. Natalie picked it up and redialled the London number.

"Hello." It was the same voice as before.

"It is Natalie, I need someone to dispose of the van I am driving. The police have just stopped me and it might be a problem."

"Ok, come to the house. We will see to it," said the voice.

"I hope about twenty minutes," said Natalie.

"We are waiting for you," said the voice and Natalie dropped the call.

Natalie's assessment proved accurate and just before four-twenty, she pulled up outside the house. There was movement behind the curtains, then the front door opened; a man left the house and approached the driver's window. "Natalie?"

"Yes," said Natalie.

"Thank goodness you are safe. Please, take everything you need and go into the house. I will see to the van," said the man.

Natalie picked up the rucksack and did a final check

around, including the glove compartment. There was nothing she needed. She walked down a short path to the front door. It was an anonymous three-bedroomed semi-detached, one like a thousand others in the area. A woman was waiting for her at the door and beckoned her inside. She put her index finger to her lips. "Shhh," she whispered. "Don't want to wake the neighbours."

Natalie walked in and the woman closed the door behind her. There was a flight of stairs immediately in front of her which went up then right. She was shown into a small living room with a sofa, TV and a small dining table. There was a sitting room opposite, very characteristic of these properties in North London.

"Thank you… Sorry I don't know your name," said Natalie.

"Rachel, you can call me Rachel. It is ok, I have spoken to Epsilon he wants to get you back to Israel as soon as possible. It won't be today, maybe Sunday or Monday, but you are quite safe here."

"Thank you," she repeated.

"You have the laptop I believe?" said Rachel.

"Yes, and a few other things." Natalie picked up the rucksack and tipped out the contents onto the dining table.

Straightaway Rachel noticed the gun.

"This was the one you used?" she asked.

"Yes," said Natalie.

"Leave it to me. We will see to it."

"We?" said Natalie.

"Yes, my husband, Philip. You have just met him. He will dispose of the van… We have contacts in the motor trade who do not ask questions."

"How will he get back?"

"Oh, he will swap it for another or someone will bring him back."

"What, at four o'clock in the morning?" said Natalie.

"Oh yes, all times. It will not be the first time. At least there are no bodies."

"Hmm, what about those in Birmingham?"

"I don't think we will be able to do anything about them. We will let the police deal with it… You will be out of the country; there will be nothing for you to worry about… Here, drink this." Rachel had poured Natalie a large measure of brandy.

She poured it down in one go and coughed when the effect of the drink hit the back of her throat.

"Leave the stuff here. We will sort it out tomorrow… you must get some rest."

"Thank you, yes," said Natalie.

At about the same time as Natalie was settling down to get some sleep, Rory, unaware of events elsewhere, was in the shower in the cottage trying to wash some energy into his body. He felt heady from the disturbed sleep; the four-a.m. alarm had left him far from alert.

He'd been thinking about Natalie. He had been trying to work out what she might have been doing at the company for the last six months and what damage she might have caused. He hoped Vikram would provide some answers.

By five o'clock, he was walking towards the airline check-in desk at Birmingham Airport. He could see Alistair at the business class reception counter.

"Hi Alistair," said Rory dragging his wheeled luggage along behind him.

"Hi Rory, Duncan's just parking his car. Not heard from Ed but I'm sure he'll be here in a minute… How're things?"

"Aye, ok… bit early for me these days."

"Yes, I don't know why airlines insist on flights leaving at these unearthly hours… Ah, here's Duncan," said Alistair and Rory could see him walking towards them dressed in a suit.

"Morning Duncan, looking very smart if I might say," said Alistair.

"Well, you know, got to keep up appearances… Morning

Rory, everyone here?" said Duncan.

Rory acknowledged him.

"Not heard from Ed yet," said Alistair.

"He'd be late for his own funeral," said Duncan. "Perhaps we should go through to the lounge, I don't know about you, but I could do with some breakfast."

"Yeah, ok, let's go. He knows where to find us," said Alistair.

The three completed the check-in requirements and headed for the Executive Lounge. They registered and after a few minutes, Alistair joined Rory at the coffee dispenser. "I've been thinking about Natalie, you know, it's been on my mind all night. I still can't believe she'd do anything to hurt the business; she's made such a positive contribution."

"Well, we'll see," said Rory, making sure Duncan was out of earshot. "If she turns up on Tuesday we can talk to her. If she is on the level, as soon as she discovers she's been locked out, she's going to telephone you to find out what's going on... In my view, I think she'll disappear as soon as she realises we're onto her."

"Yes, I can understand that; it makes sense... It's a pity we're away just now in the light of everything."

Just then, Ed walked into the lounge. He spotted Duncan and walked over to him.

"Hi, sorry I'm late, the taxi didn't turn up until four-thirty... Not using them again." Duncan was tucking into a full-English but acknowledged the new arrival.

"It's ok, we've saved you a seat, the other two are over at the coffee machine," said Duncan.

They were soon joined by Rory and Alistair.

The journey to Abu Dhabi took almost seven hours and with the time difference, it was gone seven p.m. local time when the AB Engineering contingent arrived. Being in business class they'd been well looked-after; a bit different to some of the journeys Rory had endured to the Middle East in his army days. Hercules aircraft were not known for their comfort.

They landed on time and as Rory left the plane the heat hit him; it was over thirty-eight degrees. For a second he was transported back to a former time, landing at Riyadh, and then the trek into Iraq in the back of a truck or in the belly of a Chinook.

There was a queue at passport control but eventually, the four left the arrivals gate and were mobbed by an army of taxi drivers with various signs. Alistair eventually spotted one displaying, 'AB Engineering'.

"That looks like our ride," said Alistair and, after introductions, the four followed the driver to the carpark pulling their suitcases towards a luxury Toyota minibus.

It was a half an hour's drive before they arrived at the Corniche Palace hotel. On the journey, Rory looked out of the window, deep in contemplation. It seemed different from Saudi somehow, but that could be down to him; the tension was missing. The size of the cars was the same, though. The city was immaculate, no sign of graffiti or decay you see in some places; underpasses with delicate mosaic murals of falcons and the ruling dynasty, an array of building projects. This was a city on the rise.

There was a hit of cold air as they entered the hotel from the drop-off zone where the taxi had stopped; the air-conditioning was necessary and a welcome respite from the thirty-eight-degree temperature outside. Rory checked his watch, nine-ten. Behind the check-in desk, there were six clocks on the wall depicting different time zones; local, London, New York, Los Angeles, Tokyo, Mumbai. Rory checked the exactness with his own time-piece; time was a precious commodity and he had been conditioned in a previous world to ensure its accuracy.

The hotel was busy and a small queue had built up at the desk. As befitting a five-star establishment, waiters were providing complimentary tea and dates. Six reception staff were busy processing arriving guests; four women of Far-

Eastern origin and two men who looked Indian. Rory was taking everything in. He checked the atrium; apart from the arriving guests, it was quiet. Another taxi pulled up outside to be greeted by several porters who piled luggage onto a trolley and escorted the passengers into the hotel.

"Look, it's got a swimming pool," said Ed, pointing in the opposite direction to the entrance. Through the glass door, the shimmering light of the surface water of a pool could be seen in the distance.

"I don't think you'll have any time to use it," said Duncan.

As they stood in line, Alistair turned to Rory. "Most deals are done in hotels," he said.

"Yeah, I can imagine," said Rory.

The group checked in; Rory and Duncan were on the fourth-floor, Ed and Alistair on the third.

"Ok," said Rory. "I'll come with you to your rooms and do a quick check 'round. Ed and Alistair, I'll do yours first; Duncan, wait here till I get back, then I'll do yours."

The directors looked at each other, perplexed.

"Don't worry, just a precaution. Just want to make sure nothing unexpected is waiting for you."

It took a few minutes for Rory to escort the directors and check the rooms. He found nothing out of the ordinary; they would meet at seven o'clock the following morning for breakfast.

Rory was amazed at the luxury of his room and couldn't help comparing it with the basic conditions he had endured on previous visits to the Middle East; freezing-cold dry Iraqi wadis came to mind.

He unpacked and checked his phone for the first time. There was a text message which he accessed. *I have some news. Phone me asap Vikram.*

Rory looked at his watch. It would be around seven o'clock back home. He made the call to Vikram's mobile. He wouldn't be at work, but he might pick up.

It was answered straight away.

"Vikram…? It's Rory... You said you had some news."

"Hi Rory, yes… I've been through the activity on Natalie's computer as you asked and you were right, she has been accessing the confidential R & D files."

"Jesus," said Rory. "How did she manage that? Did you find out?"

"Hmm, yes, that was easy, she was using Ed Stevens' access codes."

"Ed Stevens…? Are you sure?"

"Yes… there's no doubt. The login details match Ed's."

"But how…?" asked Rory.

"She would've had to get hold of his code and password somehow."

"Thanks, Vikram… Can you do some more digging for me, find out what files she's accessed and whether they were copied… Can you do that?"

"Possibly, I'll look into it," said Vikram.

"Ok, do what you can, but don't mention this call to anyone…" said Rory.

"No, of course not."

"You haven't had a call from Natalie by any chance, wondering why she couldn't log-on?"

"No, nothing," said Vikram.

"No, ok… Let me know straight away if she does call, ok? You can get me on the mobile anytime."

"Yeah, sure."

"If you find anything else suspicious, call me, yeah?"

"Yes, will do," said Vikram, and Rory dropped the call. He sat for a moment contemplating the information. Then rang another number.

"Alistair? It's Rory… Fancy a drink…? I've got some news. I'll meet you downstairs in five minutes."

Rory was on the fourth floor and made his way along the corridor trying to make sense of the information. He took the elevator and Alistair was waiting on the ground floor.

"What's the problem?" said Alistair.

"Let's get a drink... I've had a text from Vikram; just spoken to him."

The pair walked from reception to the bar along a short ornate passageway decorated with large pictures of exotic birds. The bar was exquisite but small and, surprisingly, almost empty. They ordered a beer each and found a comfortable seat in the corner.

Alistair took a sip. "Bad news?" he said.

"Yeah, seems like it," said Rory, taking his first sip. "Vikram's been on Natalie's computer and it looks like she's managed to get access to the confidential files."

"What, the R & D?"

"Yeah," said Rory.

"Shit," said Alistair, trying to take in the ramifications.

"There's more," said Rory.

Alistair looked at Rory, concern etched all over his face. "More?"

"Yeah... she's been using Ed's password and codes... That's how she got in."

"What Ed...? Ed Stevens...?"

"Yeah."

"How long's this been going on?" said Alistair.

"Vikram didn't say... If she is what I think she is; she'll only have needed one go."

Alistair was holding his head in his hand. "Do we know what she might have got away with?"

"I didn't ask, but we can assume it will be Hades... I mean that's the valuable one, isn't it?"

"Yes, you could say that..." said Alistair. "To think, I would have trusted her with my life."

"That's the problem when you've got someone that good... and she was good, very good."

"But you suspected her from the start, didn't you?"

"Well, let's put it this way, when something seems too good to be true, it usually is… That's my experience."

"So, what do we do…? What do you suggest?" said Alistair.

"For the moment, nothing."

"Nothing!?" said Alistair.

"For the time being… Vikram's continuing hunting around in case there's any more evidence. I've asked him to find out precisely what files she's accessed and whether they've been copied. I don't know whether he can actually do that or not."

"But how did she get the codes?"

"My hunch is, it will be one of three scenarios. He's either been hoodwinked into letting her have the codes; she stole them from him… or, he's been shagging her…" Alistair raised his eyebrows. "Have you noticed anything going on?" added Rory.

"No, I don't recall anything… although I don't have a lot to do with Ed on a day-to-day basis. I let him get on with things. I do see more of Natalie. She must have been working on it after hours; she did work late quite a bit. I just thought she was being conscientious."

"As I said, she is good."

"You said you had an idea who might be behind it," said Alistair.

"Well, not precisely. There're a number of agencies involved with industrial espionage… the Russians, China, our friends, the Yanks; although I wouldn't have thought it was them, Blair will just hand it over when the trials have been completed anyway. Then we have the Middle East factions, the Saudi's… unlikely, because they will just buy it… that leaves the terrorist States, but I'm not sure how they would have found out about Hades' existence, given the level of secrecy."

"Well, someone's clearly got hold of it."

"There is another party who would be very interested and would certainly have the resources."

"Who's that?"

"Mossad," said Rory.

"What, the Israelis?"

"Yes, they're very active in industrial espionage and have got agents everywhere."

"But how would they know about it?" said Alistair.

"My guess, someone's tipped them off."

"You mean someone from the M.O.D?" said Alistair.

"MI6, more like… the security services are thick as thieves."

"But why…?"

"The usual… money, politics, power… who knows? There'll be some play, some strategy that makes it all worthwhile."

"I don't know what to say… Should we say anything… to the M.O.D. I mean? Only they'll be around sometime over the weekend; they usually are."

"I'm not sure, let me speak to them, then I'll make a decision… if you're ok with that?"

"Yes, yes, whatever you say… You're the expert," said Alistair.

The pair drank their beers in quiet retrospection.

"Do you think we might still be in danger?" said Alistair. "I mean other staff."

"I don't know, possibly. It depends on what's happened to Natalie. Someone clearly wanted her dead and I've got no idea why unless it was to get hold of information about Hades. That would mean someone else must know about it… but, frankly, I can't make that out. Why would they kill her if they wanted information?"

Alistair looked at Rory, a worried man.

"There is another possibility."

"What's that?"

"Well, if she is a Mossad agent, they do have a lot of enemies, especially after the last Palestinian uprising."

"But I thought that had been sorted. Didn't they sign some peace deal or something?" said Alistair.

"Yeah, but there're plenty of old scores to settle… I might

be completely wrong, of course…" He finished his beer. "But if someone is after Hades, then we'll need to be on our toes."

Alistair finished his drink and the pair retired to their rooms; tomorrow would be another interesting day.

Rory made one more call before trying to sleep.

"Hi, it's me," he said as the call was answered. It was good to hear Laura's voice; it brought back some semblance of normality.

Seven o'clock, Friday morning, the start of the weekend locally and Friday prayers. Life in the hotel continued as normal, most of the staff were expats from Europe, Thailand or Philippines.

The four AB Engineering executives were sat at their allocated table sampling the delights of their first breakfast at the hotel; Rory was amazed by the choice and amount.

"What time's the car arriving?" asked Duncan.

"Seven-thirty," said Alistair. "They start early here."

Alistair was finding it difficult to make eye-contact with Ed who was beginning to sense something wasn't quite right but said nothing. Rory noticed the atmosphere and had a quick word with Alistair while Duncan and Ed were at the self-service counter. "We don't want to spook him," said Rory. Alistair acknowledged this but was finding it difficult; it felt like a betrayal.

By seven-thirty the group had finished their breakfasts and were walking through reception to the hotel entrance and the waiting minibus. The heat hit them as they left the air-conditioned building; the temperature was already nearing forty degrees and they had dispensed with suits for what was going to be a setup day. They were dressed in smart casual clothes, short-sleeved shirts and slacks; they carried their jackets. Rory, vigilantly, shepherded his flock into the Toyota. The journey took around twenty-five minutes and he kept a close watch out of the window; sharp-eyed for any possible threat. He noticed the imposing city-scape with its ever-increasing skyline and the hundreds of immigrant workers that were watering the verges and parks keeping the roadsides surprisingly green and lush.

Arriving at the new Exhibition Centre was almost like entering a building site. Plans were well under way for a large hotel with a unique design to be built adjacent to the centre. "It'll be a lot easier when that's finished," said Alistair as they went passed the cranes. It was a dusty hive of activity with hundreds of Thai and Filipino workers toiling in the heat, their heads and necks covered to protect them from the searing sun.

The minibus pulled up outside the trade entrance where dozens of men were ferrying furniture and packages into the building from a fleet of removal vans. The heat was almost unbearable. There was a security screening process and Rory went ahead of the directors to check everything was in order. He removed his sunglasses and presented his documents to the security guard.

Satisfied that the arrangements were secure, Rory went back to the Toyota and beckoned the group to leave. Alistair clarified the pickup time with the driver and caught up with Rory. The group were ushered through by security and a lady assistant wearing a black headscarf was on hand to show them their pitch.

Inside was cavernous, like a large aircraft-hanger, and the noise of building work echoed around the auditorium as the trade fair started to take shape. The assistant checked her map and took the group to the far corner. Their stand was not in a prominent position and Rory wondered if anyone would find them; it didn't seem a good vantage point for sales. Duncan, though, was upbeat and couldn't wait to get started.

The allocated positions were marked out in blocks with white paint, like car parking spaces, about fifteen feet wide by twenty feet long, the size of an average lounge; each was numbered. Stand-holders would be charged by the number of spaces they required. AB Engineering just had one. There was a large crate with several airline stickers appended, placed against the wall; it was stencilled with the company name.

"Our stuff arrived ok," said Duncan. "Must thank Natalie... I don't know what we would do without her." He didn't notice the glance between Alistair and Rory.

Ed was already examining the contents to make sure it contained everything they would need and he seemed happy enough. The stand itself would, however, need constructing; all the pieces were there, they were told, but in a pile, like a giant jigsaw puzzle.

Several labourers were hovering around, anxious to earn some extra money. Alistair was keen to get as much help as possible and he asked Rory to select two to help them.

Within an hour the stand had been erected. Alistair tipped the Filipinos two hundred Dinars each and they walked away happy with their enterprise, looking for more money-making opportunities. Having completed the construction of the stand, all the marketing material was laid out and the projector and screen set up; finally, the chairs and tables where Alistair and his team were hopeful of entertaining new clients were positioned accordingly. Natalie had even remembered the coffee-making machine which was soon put into use.

By lunchtime, the hall was resembling a trade fair with most of the exhibitors appearing ready for the public the following day.

The exhibition centre had its own shops and cafes and Rory and Alistair left Ed and Duncan preparing their pitch to get some lunch.

"I'm not sure how long I can keep this up," said Alistair as they sat down in one of the eateries with a sandwich each.

"No, I understand it's difficult but stick with it, we need to speak to the spooks first... that's if they turn up... before we say anything."

Saturday heralded the start of the trade fair and the AB

Engineering team were at their stand at eight o'clock in good time for the public opening at eight-thirty. Rory wasn't going to be that involved; he wasn't part of the sales drive. He left the others making last-minute checks and adjustments to the pitch and wandered around some of the other stands; some household names were represented hoping for mega deals. Some would be negotiated at government-level and several countries would be sending representatives to source new products. There were rumours that Des Brown, the British Defence Secretary, would be attending, which would entail a significant security presence. Entry was by appointment only, which would reduce any possible terrorist threat. Nevertheless, local armed-police were patrolling the perimeter in their smart khaki and green uniforms with red braiding.

Rory returned to the stand and couldn't help comparing it with the French pitch next-door with their brash colours and attractive female attendants beckoning potential clients their way, armed with leaflets in five different languages. Having said that, there was something 'honest' about the AB Engineering stand; no frills, straightforward; much in line with the corporate culture.

Rory walked over and could smell coffee. Duncan greeted him. "What does it look like?"

"Yeah, great," said Rory. Duncan handed him a mug.

"Cheers," said Rory.

"I was just saying to Alistair, I think we should invite Natalie along to the next one. We could do with a bit of glamour. Have you seen those two girls on the French stand…? We can't compete with that."

Rory reflected on the irony. "Yeah, good idea."

The day dragged for Rory. When he wasn't at the stand drinking coffee, he spent much of the time walking around the trade fair checking out other exhibitors. There appeared to be little in the way of threat; not surprising given the local security presence, although he remained vigilant. The scale of the place was enormous, and it was like the Tower of Babel, buzzing with different languages; delegates from around the world checking-out their defence requirements.

By the end of the day, Alistair was upbeat about how it went. They'd had a serious enquiry from a Nigerian delegation and would be meeting their government's representative over drinks at the hotel later. There were one or two other enquiries, but this seemed the most promising.

Duncan was waxing lyrical about building a relationship in West Africa. "Not done any business in Africa before... Mind you there'll be some restrictions; we'll need to get clearance from the M.O.D. but I think we'll be ok; the stuff they're interested in is just part of our basic range, not classified."

As they were being driven back to the hotel in the minibus, Rory looked at Ed who did not seem to be sharing the same euphoria. It was sad how events had unfolded. Rory had got on well with him and remembered Ed's enthusiasm when they first met at Alistair's house. Ed had been cold-shouldered by Alistair for most of the day, only being consulted when his expertise was needed. There was none of the usual banter you might expect at such an event. Ed, of course, couldn't understand and had become more withdrawn as a result.

That evening after dinner, Rory was asked to join Alistair and the team for their meeting with the Nigerians. In just a short time, Rory had become an important part of the executive team and Alistair's confidante. "I'd like to get your assessment of them; you hear of so much corruption there," said Alistair.

"Yeah, that's for sure. I wouldn't trust any of them... Make sure you get everything tied up. Speak to your M.O.D. contacts before you sign anything."

"Yes, will do," said Alistair.

Duncan and Ed joined them, and Alistair ordered the drinks. They were due to meet the Nigerians at eight-thirty and just a few minutes later a large limousine drove up to the entrance and three African gentlemen got out, immaculately dressed in designer suits and accoutrements. Alistair was waiting for them in the lobby and led the contingent to the corner of the bar which had been partitioned off for them.

There were formal introductions. "I am Doctor Thomas Kwankwaso, head of the Nigerian Trade delegation, representing the Nigerian Government; these gentlemen are my assistants, Godwin Abache, and Sani Kayode." He shook Alistair's hand and Rory couldn't help noticing the large gold Rolex wristwatch which appeared to rattle as the official exchanged greetings with them in turn.

Refreshments were ordered, and the group got down to talks. Rory watched the Africans with some suspicion while Alistair and Duncan engaged the charm offensive. Ed chipped in with technical advice when required. The discussions went on for two hours before they shook hands on orders totalling almost half a million pounds. Alistair and Duncan were ecstatic at the opportunity of breaking into a new and potentially lucrative market. They eventually escorted their guests back to the lobby and Alistair turned and announced, "this calls for a drink," so they returned to the bar. Ed excused himself and went back to his room.

It was just the three of them. "I don't know what's wrong with Ed, he doesn't seem his normal self at all," said Duncan as they sat down.

Rory sensed Alistair was about to say something but intervened. "Probably jetlag, it can really affect some people."

Alistair took a sip of his brandy. "So, Rory, what did you think?"

"Well, if you can tie down the financial side, it looks good. But as I said, these guys are slippery so and so's."

"Yes, I'll speak to the Department of Trade once we've got their written confirmation and the paperwork exchanged, get them involved."

"Yeah, good idea," said Rory.

"Do you want me to email Natalie to get the ball rolling?" asked Duncan.

Alistair looked at Rory. "Let's wait until we get back, we've got another day tomorrow, we may get some more orders."

By eleven-thirty, the three retired to their bedrooms. Rory called Laura when he got back to his room and they chatted for twenty minutes.

"Oh, by the way, I spoke to my friend at the London Standard. No news on the killings, you'll be pleased to hear," she said.

As he drifted to sleep, Rory considered the day. Tomorrow would be more eventful.

Chapter Fifteen

It was Sunday morning, the last day of the trade fair. It was the day the big buyers tended to arrive; the Americans, Chinese and Russians.

AB Engineering was already exporting to The States and was hopeful of adding to that business with more orders; these were their target customers. Then there were the French and Italians. There were also some relationships formed at the Estonian Trade Fare which they were hoping to expand on and turn into orders. Alistair had arranged to meet a buyer from Germany, whom he'd met in Tallinn, to discuss possible business.

The mood at breakfast would have been upbeat if it wasn't for Ed who was still out of sorts. Duncan felt obliged to say something to Alistair while Ed was at the serving counter collecting his full-English.

"What's up with you and Ed? You don't seem to be speaking," he said.

Alistair looked at Rory, there was a brief shake of the head which Duncan didn't notice.

"Nothing, it's fine," said Alistair. "Anyone want any more toast? I'm going to get some."

There were no takers and Alistair got up. With Ed and Alistair away from the table, Duncan confronted Rory. "Do you know what's going on between them? Alistair's been virtually ignoring Ed all weekend," said Duncan

"No idea," said Rory. Any further discussion was curtailed by the return of Ed and nothing more was said.

"Good result with the Nigerians last night, Ed... Should keep you out of mischief for a while once that orders gone through," said Duncan.

"Yeah," said Ed and started tucking into his breakfast. Duncan looked at Rory and shrugged his shoulders.

By seven-thirty, the four were back in the minibus returning to the Exhibition Centre. The journey was spent in silence. Once they got to their stand, Duncan felt he needed to say something and approached Alistair with the subject again. "I don't know what's going on between you two, but we have potential customers arriving shortly and we need to get our act together."

Alistair was taken aback; Duncan was not usually so forthright. The discussion was cut short by the arrival of two smartly-dressed men.

"Alistair, how good to see you," said the first man.

"Julian, good to see you, too," replied Alistair.

"You remember Simon, don't you?" said Julian.

The suits and their air of supremacy gave them away; government men.

Further introductions were made, Ed, Duncan and Rory.

"Ah, you're the new security guy… right?"

"Yes," said Rory.

"We've been hearing good things," said Julian.

"Thanks," Rory acknowledged.

It was gone eight o'clock, nearly half an hour before the doors were officially opened. These rules didn't apply to Julian and Simon who were on 'official business' checking security.

Alistair looked at Rory. "Why don't you and I have a chat with Julian? Ed and Duncan can hold the fort till we get back. The Germans won't be here until gone ten."

There were looks of surprise then acquiescence from Ed and Duncan. "Yeah, ok see you later," said Duncan.

Rory, Alistair and the two men found one of the cafes which was doing a great trade just before opening. They managed to find a table in the corner which was reasonably quiet and secure.

"So, what's the news?" asked Julian, taking his jacket off. Simon followed suit.

"I'll let you explain everything," said Alistair, looking at Rory.

Julian and Simon looked at Rory, expectantly.

"Well, we have a security issue," said Rory getting straight to the point.

Julian looked at Simon then back at Rory. "Go on."

"As you probably know, Alistair asked me to do a risk analysis of security at the works. He told me about the sensitivity of the new research, including the one you're presently testing... Hades."

"So, you know about Hades?" said Julian.

"Not the details but I understand the potential and the technology."

"Of course, you were with Special Forces weren't you... military medal too, if I remember correctly."

"That's correct," said Rory.

"I thought it was appropriate," said Alistair, slightly defensively, in case there were any grounds for criticism. "He has signed the OSA."

"Yes, ok, so you did the review... what's the issue?" said Julian. Simon was watching, weasel-eyed, with interest.

"It seems that someone has accessed the confidential files and almost certainly downloaded copies. We have the IT expert doing further investigations to try and find out exactly what they've done but we know for certain they've got into the files."

Julian glanced at Simon again.

"Who is it, do you know?" asked Julian.

"Natalie, Natalie Kallaste," replied Rory.

"Oh no. Not the delightful Natalie? I remember her from when we visited the factory, such a dear," said Julian.

"Tell them the rest," instructed Alistair.

"Ok, well, there have been two incidents," continued Rory. "The first was last Tuesday; she was attacked."

"Attacked? Where was this?"

"Behind her apartment by the garages. I was there..."

"What were you doing there?" asked Julian.

"I just happened to be in the area doing a risk assessment. I noticed something wasn't right; I could see she was being followed."

"And you… intervened."

"Yeah," said Rory.

"And you just happened to be in the area?"

"Yeah."

"Do I want to know what happened to the assailant?"

"Probably not, but he's not a problem anymore."

"So, you took out this… assailant?"

"Actually, no. Natalie did. Very professional, special forces trained in my view."

Rory looked at Alistair.

"What was he like, the attacker?" asked Julian.

"Middle Eastern, Iranian, Syrian, perhaps."

"What about the body?"

"I checked about ten minutes later, and it had gone." Julian glanced at Simon again.

"I see… You said there were two incidents," said Julian.

"Yeah, I went back to her flat the following afternoon to pick up some stuff for her."

"Sounds all very cosy," said Julian.

"Not quite… there was a boobytrap bomb in her closet."

"What…?! A bomb?"

"Yeah, would have taken out the top floor, I reckon... Semtex, P.E... about half a pound at a guess."

"What did you do with it?"

"I disarmed it… It's at the bottom of the Severn somewhere."

"I see," said Julian. "And where's Natalie now?"

"I don't know, but my guess is she'll have run… We've blocked all her IT access; she can't use the company's email or website or get into the plant. So, that would have warned her something was up… She doesn't know about the bomb though. I never told her."

Rory looked at the two men. "You guys aren't M.O.D. are you…? You're six."

"You are good," said Julian, looking at Simon.

"But I thought you were from the Ministry of Defence?" said Alistair.

"Well, let's just say we do have compatible agendas," said Julian. "We've taken an interest in your Hades project for a different reason which I can't go into… Excuse us a minute."

There were some whispers between Julian and Simon.

"Sorry about that," Julian apologised for the apparent rudeness.

"Do you have any theories, Rory?" asked Julian.

"Well, yes, she's certainly well-trained… and very convincing."

"Yes, I can vouch for that," said Alistair.

"She could be Russian. She's from Estonia and we know what that's like."

Alistair gave Rory a confused look.

"At this moment, there are probably more spies in Estonia than in Germany during the Cold War," explained Rory.

Julian laughed. "Yes, I can vouch for that… but why Russia?"

"Well, they would be very interested in the science… and, they're certainly behind the Americans in stealth technology."

"Yes, you could be right. Although there's no intelligence to support that theory," said Julian.

"That leaves the Israelis… That would be my best guess," said Rory.

"You think Natalie is Mossad?"

"It would certainly fit… and would explain the bomb and the attack. There're still some scores to settle… with the Palestinians."

"Hmm, you could well be right… You could well be right," repeated Julian, deep in thought. He looked at his colleague.

"What do you want us to do?" said Alistair.

"Nothing," said Julian. "We'll take it from here."

"Was there anything else?"

"No," said Alistair.

"No," echoed Rory.

"Ok... well, good luck with the fair. Have you got any new business yet?"

"Yes, the Nigerians have put in some orders," said Alistair.

"Well, good luck with that... most of them are a bunch of crooks. Make sure you get paid upfront," said Julian which did not fill Alistair with any confidence.

They said their goodbyes and then the two agents walked towards the exit. "I think we need to get back and report in. What time's the flight?"

"There's one to Heathrow leaving at thirteen-ten," said Simon,

"Ok, I'll ring Mother, you book the flights," said Julian.

Alistair and Rory returned to the stand. "So, what do we do now?" said Alistair.

"Nothing much we can do. They'll deal with it, I guess. But as soon as we've finished tonight we need to speak to Ed."

"Yes, the sooner the better. He'll not be easy to replace, that's for sure."

"Well, let's see what he says before we jump to conclusions," said Rory.

It was gone six o'clock by the time the AB Engineering foursome returned to the hotel. They did not have to deconstruct the stand, there were people on-site who would do that, but they needed to re-pack their container ready for shipping back to the UK.

Duncan was beside himself with excitement after the day's proceedings. There were new orders from the Americans and Saudis, some firm enquiries from the Germans and an introduction to a French company which would be followed up. Potentially, they had almost five million Euros worth of business. Alistair was still brooding about Ed, but he too was happy with the way the day had gone. Rory was impressed by the expertise of Alistair and the team. Despite the frosty atmosphere, Ed had contributed significantly to the successful outcome. It made the next part harder.

"What time are we meeting for dinner?" said Duncan.

Alistair thought for a moment. "Better make that eight o'clock."

Duncan nodded in acknowledgement and headed for the lift. Ed was about to follow him, but Rory called him back.

"Ed, have you got a minute?"

"Sure," replied Ed suspiciously and he followed Rory and Alistair into the bar. A waiter descended on them.

"Three beers," said Alistair, displaying his key-card. The waiter made a note of the room number and left.

"What's this all about?" said Ed.

"We just need a word about something," said Rory. There was an uneasy silence while they waited for the waiter to return with their drinks.

The bar was fairly quiet again. A couple of guys were sat on stools at the counter. There was a TV showing an English football match in the corner which had attracted a small gathering. There were a few 'oo's' and 'ah's' as near misses were re-run; a cheer went up when one team scored.

Ed took a sip of his drink. "Ok, so what do you want to discuss?"

"What's going on between you and Natalie?" said Rory.

"Eh? What…?"

"We know you gave her your access codes and passwords," said Alistair.

"Yes, I did… She told me you'd authorised it," said Ed.

Alistair looked at Rory,

"So, you admit it," said Alistair.

"Yes, of course… as I said, she told me you'd authorised it.

She said she needed to get some information for you from the R & D files."

Rory watched him; he looked confident, not squirming as he thought he might.

"When was this?" asked Rory.

"Can't remember, a month ago… something like that," said Ed.

"And you didn't think to check with me?" said Alistair.

"No, why? It seemed a reasonable request. She seemed to be… how can I put it… very close to you, Alistair… and I was very busy at the time."

"So, you weren't sleeping with her?" said Rory.

"Ha! Chance would be a fine thing… No, I leave that to Alistair," said Ed, looking at the chairman with some disdain.

This put Alistair on the backfoot and for a moment was quiet.

Rory intervened. "Ok, look, just so you know, we've found out that she's involved in industrial espionage; possibly an agent working for a foreign government. We're not sure who exactly, but we do know she's downloaded the confidential Hades files."

"What!!?" said Ed and his face started to drain of colour. "I had no idea."

"None of us did," said Alistair, whose antipathy towards Ed was quickly waning; he was not the only one to be taken in by Natalie.

"So, what do we do?" said Ed.

"It's in the hands of the spooks," said Rory.

Ed was deep in thought. "Did she get hold of the other files?"

"Other files?" asked Alistair. He looked at Rory.

"Yes… there're two different file sets, precisely to protect against this situation. I was concerned about possible hackers… and integrity issues; you know, computer crashes, software problems, that sort of thing. They're on a different server completely... They're the up-to-date files... We back them up to our mainframe once a month. My guess is whatever she's downloaded will not be the complete picture and possibly useless. I can check when I get back."

Alistair looked at Rory.

"Who has access to the other files?" said Rory.

"Apart from me, only the head of research and the two technicians working on Hades... oh, and Vikram... I certainly didn't give Natalie those codes."

"Vikram...? He never said anything," said Rory.

"No, he wouldn't... As I said it is very secure," replied Ed. "I'll speak to him when I get back."

"So, let me get this straight, whatever files Natalie got hold of might be useless," said Rory.

"Well, yes... on their own; but as I said, I'll need to check when I get back to make certain."

Alistair breathed a sigh of relief. "That's great news... I apologise if I've treated you badly over the weekend."

"It's ok, I can see why now," said Ed.

Julian Burkett found a quiet spot away from the Exhibition Centre exit and called a London number. Simon Mann was calling the airline.

"It's Julian... yes, in Abu Dhabi. Sorry to disturb you, ma'am but I have an update on Hades. Simon and I are catching the one o'clock back to Heathrow, lands around six, UK time. Will you be about later, say, nine? Ok, that's great... I'll call you when we land to confirm... Yes, will do."

He waited for Simon to finish his call.

"Ok, return flight confirmed," said Simon when he eventually rang off. "We'll need to get to the airport fairly sharpish. Check-in opens in five minutes."

"We've got plenty of time... business class I hope?"

"Yes, of course," said Simon. "How did you get on with Mother?"

"The Commander was at home, some lunch party for her kids apparently, but she'll meet us when we get back. She's sending a car to meet us at Heathrow."

"Ok, that's great... so what's our next move?"

"Depends on Mother, but it does seem that someone's taken the bait," said Julian. "Come on let's get a taxi, I could do with a drink," said Julian and the pair headed for the Exhibition Centre exit and a taxi.

Eight o'clock and Rory was in the bar with Duncan waiting for Alistair and Ed.

"Wow, what a day," said Duncan, savouring a lager as if it was the last drink in the world, still on a high from the sales achievements.

"Yes, it sounds as if it all went well."

"Well? No, no, much better than that. We had a target of four hundred thousand and we've smashed that. It should see us in work for two years at least, and we should be able to take on some new apprentices."

"Well, I don't want to put a dampener on things, but I need to mention something to you," said Rory.

"What's that?" said Duncan looking concerned.

"We've found out that Natalie's been accessing the confidential files on Hades."

"What... you mean industrial espionage?"

"Yeah," said Rory.

"Fuck... no wonder Alistair's been a bit strange," said Duncan.

"Yeah, it's hit him hard as you can imagine," said Rory.

Just then Ed and Alistair arrived having patched up their differences.

"I was just telling Duncan about Natalie," said Rory.

"I can't believe it; she was so efficient... what happened? How did you find out?" said Duncan.

"It's a long story," said Rory.

"Yes, I'm not sure I will ever fully trust anyone again…" said Alistair. "Anyway, let's go and eat, I'm starving," he added, changing the subject.

Over dinner, there was no other topic of conversation and the potential ramifications for the business started to become apparent.

"I don't know what the M.O.D. are going to say. It's possible we may not get any more government contracts," said Alistair.

"God, no, don't say that," said Duncan.

"Look, if you want my advice, I would keep this very low key, in fact, there should be no reason for anyone else outside this room to know," said Rory.

"I'll need to tell Steve," said Alistair. "He's CEO, he'll have to know."

"Yeah, ok," said Rory.

"What are we going to tell the staff…? I mean Natalie was well-known, we'll need to say something," said Duncan.

"Just tell them she's been called back to Estonia. She could well be there anyway," said Rory.

"I'll check all the protocols when I get back," said Ed.

"You need to speak to Vikram, he's been doing some digging for me," said Rory. "It was him who found the access breach."

"Yes, I will… I can check again what information she's got hold of… We may have to set something else up," said Ed.

"What about the M.O.D.?" said Duncan. "They're not going to be very happy that a major project has been compromised."

"Take one step at a time, I'm sure the spooks will have spoken to them already," said Rory.

"Rory's right, let's not get carried away here. We can assess things when we get back to the works," said Alistair.

Despite the successful trade fair, the mood was downbeat following the revelation about Natalie's actions. Ed was concerned about the security breach, especially his inadvertent collaboration. "If only I'd checked with Alistair," he kept repeating.

Duncan was worried about the impact on sales. "If this gets out, nobody will buy anything from us." Alistair was concerned about damage limitation, while Rory was still wondering about Natalie and whether there was any residual threat.

"I've just had a thought," said Rory. "Have you got the spook's number?"

"Yes, he gave me a card... I've got it somewhere." Alistair rummaged through his pockets and produced a dog-eared business card. "Sorry about that, it's been in my pocket all day," he said and passed it to Rory. Rory looked at his watch.

"I'll be back in a minute. They should have landed by now."

Rory got up, found a quiet spot and called the number. It rang out and went to answerphone. He redialled.

"Yes!" barked the reply.

"Julian? It's Rory... Calderwood. From the trade fair."

"Yes, of course. What can I do for you?"

"Just to let you know that Natalie didn't get all the files, not the latest ones anyway. The ones she downloaded were out-of-date. I've been chatting with the Tech Director and he says they use two servers. The up-to-date version is not accessible on the passcodes she was given."

"Hmm, well at least that's something," said Julian. "Thanks for letting me know. It looks like we may have limited any lasting damage."

"We?" Rory thought but said nothing.

"Ok, must go, I'll be in touch," said Julian, and he dropped the call. Rory looked at the phone. He went back to the table. They were on their coffees.

With an early start in the morning to get to the airport, the four left the bar around eleven o' clock and went to their rooms. Rory had a call to make. It would be about eight o'clock back home.

"Hi," said Rory.

"Hi, how's your day?" said Laura.

"I wouldn't know where to begin," said Rory. "I'll tell you

when I get back."

"What time's your flight tomorrow?"

"Nine forty-five so it's an early start."

They continued chatting for five minutes about what they had been doing when Laura changed the subject. "Oh, I nearly forgot, there's been a fire in London, a Turkish restaurant… Wait I wrote it down… Yes, here it is, The Medina Palace, Kensington… Does that mean anything to you?"

"Oh yeah, it certainly does," said Rory.

"Well, according to the Standard, they found four bodies, including the owner… Being treated as suspicious, it said. It's being linked to a people smuggling ring apparently… I'll give my contact a ring tomorrow and see if he has any more news."

"Yeah, cheers," said Rory. He would call Swannie tomorrow and see if he had heard anything.

"Would you like me to call 'round tomorrow evening. I can cook something, or we can get a takeaway."

"I'd love to, but I've got some stuff I need to do when I get back. We've got a problem at work I'm trying to sort out… I'm really sorry. Can you make Tuesday…? Tell you what, I'll try and take Wednesday off and we can go out somewhere. How does that sound?"

There was disappointment in Laura's voice which she couldn't hide. "Yeah, ok… I'll see what I can do," she replied, but the lack of enthusiasm was obvious.

"Look, I'm sorry, I really am… I'll make it up to you, I promise… Do you like dates?"

"What kind…? Going out type, or palm type…?" said Laura.

"Palm type?" asked Rory.

"Yes, you get them in boxes at the supermarket," said Laura.

"Ha, yes that sort… I wanted to bring you something back and the place is stacked with them."

The humour had helped to change the atmosphere.

"Not that keen, if I'm honest," said Laura.

"Hmm, it'll have to be the stuffed camel then," said Rory.

"You don't have to worry about bringing me anything back, it's fine., honestly… Ok, Tuesday it is, and I'll try to get Wednesday off, sounds good," said Laura.

They rang off. Rory made a mental note, he would need to do some shopping at the airport.

The two MI6 agents made their way through passport control. Julian took his phone from his pocket as they waited for their luggage at the carousel.

"Hello… Commander? This is Julian. We've landed at Heathrow… You have? That's great, see you in an hour, hour and a half or so, depending on the traffic."

It was six-thirty, rush-hour mayhem was still in full flow.

He dropped the call.

"Spoken to Mother, she's arranged a car to meet us, should be outside," said Julian.

"That's great," said Simon just as their suitcases appeared from the bowels of Heathrow's baggage centre and started the gradual journey along the carousel.

The flight had been half-full, but there were still over one hundred people jockeying for positions to grab their cases before they completed another circuit. Julian looked scornfully at his fellow travellers, and it was Simon who went forward and retrieved the moving baggage.

Outside the arrivals gate, a posse of drivers held cards displaying their passengers' names.

"There," said Simon, pointing to a smartly-dressed man holding a sign; 'Birkett/Mann'.

They followed the driver outside the terminal, dragging their luggage. The car was parked in a VIP area. The driver opened the boot to allow the agents to stow their bags; there was no holding of doors. The driver got in waited for his passengers to belt up and drove off.

While Julian and Simon were making their way into town, there was another passenger waiting in the departure lounge of Terminal 1 for the El-Al flight to Tel Aviv. Natalie twiddled with her handbag nervously; she checked her boarding card and the new passport for the umpteenth time. She kept repeating the new name, Kaplinski, from Haifa; not Kallaste, from Estonia.

She'd been made welcome and comfortable at the safe house but having been cooped up for four days, it was good to get away at last. The injuries she'd incurred at the hands of her captors were healing. She had received daily calls from Epsilon, enquiring about her wellbeing and providing updates on her extraction. He had commended her for completing her mission successfully and obtaining the Hades files. The laptop and memory stick had been taken to the Israeli Embassy in London and was on its way in a secure diplomatic package. Experts were on call in Tel Aviv to examine the information on its receipt in a couple of days. Sayyid's laptop had also been sent on and Epsilon was confident that once it had been cleaned up, it would reveal more information about potential Palestinian terrorists. Natalie's long-term future hadn't been discussed but Epsilon was enthusiastic about future 'projects'.

She kept looking around, alert for any threat, but the other passengers were mostly Jewish, many of the men were wearing the traditional Kippah skull cap. She looked at the boarding gate as the airline assistants prepared to receive the passengers, then she heard the news she had been waiting for: '*El-Al Flight to Tel Aviv is ready for boarding; please have your passports and boarding passes ready*'.

Natalie made her way to the business class queue for the five-hour journey. She would soon be home.

The traffic was horrendous; it took the ninety-minute estimate to reach Vauxhall Cross, the home of the Secret Intelligence Services. Julian looked at the building as they approached, he could understand why it was known as 'Legoland', rather disparagingly, in some quarters; it really did resemble a Lego model.

The building comprises of twenty-two floors and Commander Philippa Jenkins, Head of MI6, was in her office on the twentieth. She stood at her window overlooking the Thames. She was sipping from a bone china teacup. It was an ideal place for thinking and she did a lot of it.

The wood-panelled room was big, bomb-proof and totally secure. There was a large desk with a leather chair behind it. On the desk, immediately in front of the seat, was a leather 'blotter' writing pad with two computer monitors either side and a keyboard. Two chrome office seats were placed facing the desk. There was a larger table towards the inner-wall with six matching chairs either side and three teleconference receivers down the middle, set out for meetings.

Her P.A knocked and entered, disturbing her thoughts.

"Sorry to disturb you, Ma'am. Agents Birkett and Mann are on their way up."

"Thank you, Shelly… You can stay, I may need someone to take notes."

"Ok, will do," and the P.A. started to arrange three seats in front of the desk and waited for their arrival.

There was a knock on the door and Julian and Simon entered.

"Ah, come in Julian, Simon… good flight I hope," said the Commander.

"Yes, Ma'am," said Julian.

"Thank you, Ma'am," said Simon.

"Would you like some tea or coffee?" said the Commander.

Julian looked at Simon. "Two teas, please," said Julian, and Shelly was sent to do the honours.

"So, what's the latest on Hades?" said the Commander.

"Well, there's some good news and bad news… The bad news is that the Hades files were hacked into at the factory by one of the staff there, a woman called Natalie Kallaste."

The Commander gave the pair a scornful look.

"Hmm, ok, so what do we know about her?" said the Commander.

Julian continued the commentary. "Been with the company just over six months, graduate in International Law from Tallinn University."

"Tallinn? Well that should have alerted somebody," said the Commander. "So, Hades has gone tits-up?"

"Well, no, not really, that's the good news. I think we've managed to limit any damage... quite clever, actually... The technical director there set up two systems to prevent possible hackers from getting hold of the complete data. Whoever accessed the files did not get the full picture."

"I see, well that is good news. So, this Natalie woman, where is she now, do we know?"

"We think she's almost certainly out of the country. They've blocked her access to the company's internet and the plant, so she'll know something's wrong. From her perspective she already has the files so there's nothing to hang around for... Unless of course, she was trying to get more information... But there's something else."

"What's that?" said the Commander.

Shelly arrived with the teas and sat down next to the agents with a notepad. Julian picked up his cup, tipped in two spoons of sugar and stirred, then continued.

"They have a new security consultant at the works, a guy called Rory Calderwood, ex-regiment; impressive, I have to say. He's been brought in to check their procedures; it was him that picked up on Miss Kallaste... Apparently, last... Tuesday, if I remember correctly, he foiled an attempt on her life. She was attacked at the back of her flat." He looked at Simon for confirmation, he nodded. "And he... 'intervened' was the word he used."

"Intervened?" repeated the Commander.

"Yes, it seems between them they 'neutralised' the threat."

Julian made the double inverted comma sign with his fingers. "According to Calderwood, it was the girl that dispatched the assailant... very professional, so he said."

"What happened to the body?" said Shelly.

"We don't know, but as it's not been reported, that I know of... We can assume it was cleaned up."

"I see, so someone was after this Natalie woman?"

"Yes, but there's more... Apparently, Calderwood returned to the flat the following day to get some things for her and found a bomb in her closet... Semtex."

"Really...? Now that is interesting... What does that tell us?"

"Well, either someone else is after Hades or after Natalie Kallaste. My guess is the latter, I mean why would they try to kill her if they wanted Hades...?" replied Julian.

"Unless, they knew she already had the information," said Shelly.

"Yes, but they would try to kidnap her, surely, not kill her," said Julian. "They certainly wouldn't have booby-trapped the apartment."

"Yes, that makes sense... So, assessment... What do we think?" said the Commander.

"Calderwood came up with a suggestion that I like. He thought it might be the Israelis."

"You mean, Miss Kallaste is Mossad?" said the Commander.

"Yes, as I said, it makes a lot of sense. We know the Israelis are active in knowledge transference and they would be very interested in the technology... Plus, that would explain the attempted hit, I mean it would be a chance to take out a Mossad agent."

"I can see that," said the Commander.

"The other thing is... it also tells us who leaked the information, which is why we got onboard with Hades in the first place."

"Hmm, yes, it does... Hamilton... Well, I did have my

suspicions," said the Commander.

"What do you want to do about him?"

"Nothing… now we know who it is, we can manage him… I might even have a new assignment for Mr Hamilton…. Shelly, can you get Guy Hamilton here for nine tomorrow morning. I need to speak to him."

Shelly was writing furiously. Julian smiled at Simon. The Commander was deep in thought.

"Wait a minute, wait a minute… Shelly can you get a projector and the laptop," said the Commander.

They finished their drinks as they waited for Shelly to set up the equipment.

Chapter Sixteen

The Commander was becoming quite animated. "Something came in this morning, I don't know whether it's relevant or not... four murders in Birmingham."

"But that's plod, surely...?" said Julian.

"No, the victims were on our radar; Palestinians," said the Commander.

The laptop burst into life and the Commander took charge of the mouse. She clicked on a couple of files and some grizzly pictures appeared on the screen. Four men, three with gunshot wounds to the head, the fourth with no visible injury.

"Four men found dead in an abandoned factory in Birmingham, Thursday morning... Three, shot in the head, one bullet each, the fourth had his neck broken. We've identified them all. Farid Darwaza is the one with the broken neck; the others are Ahsan al-Hasan, Sayyid Al-Wazir and Naseer Said. We've been doing a CCTV search and it seems they entered the UK into Birmingham from Frankfurt, just over three weeks ago. There were originally six of them... Here they are... a real barrel of fun."

Six men appeared on the screen from CCTV footage. The Commander paused it frame by frame.

"It was this man we were particularly interested in... Sayyid Al-Wazir, son of Khaled Al-Wazir, also known as 'the father of Jihad'."

The screen zoomed in on the target man. Julian looked at Simon and raised his eyebrows.

"A dangerous man," said the Commander, "But not on our watch list. We didn't even know he was in the country. Seems he was using a false passport... Otherwise, he would never have got in."

Julian looked at the Commander. "Let's join the dots... Can we tie this to Natalie Kallaste?"

"Possibly, we've got pictures of the crime scene from SOCO in Birmingham… This might interest you," said the Commander.

The Commander clicked on a file and a video stream appeared. It was the derelict factory; the picture panned the room. It was the upstairs showing sleeping bags; the bodies of the three men were visible.

"Not this bit… wait…here," said the Commander. The video picture went downstairs and entered the basement where Natalie had been held. There was a chair in the middle of the room with ties and straps on the floor. There was the body of a young man next to it.

"The body of the youngest of the group can be seen here, next to the chair. His neck was broken," said the Commander. "There are traces of blood on the floor and chair; the DNA does not match any of the four men."

"Natalie?" said Julian. "You think the Palestinians kidnapped her?"

"Quite possibly; it would fit. They were clearly after her from what your guy Calderwood said. Seems whoever was held had been there for some time and possibly tortured with water. The floor was awash. It appears they managed to escape, killed the boy, took his weapon then went upstairs and shot the others. That's the theory anyway."

Julian looked at Simon, then his boss. "But surely, we can match her DNA, we know where she lives, or at least Calderwood does. If we pay her place a visit, we can soon collect some samples…"

"Hmm… yes, ok… Julian, speak to Calderwood and get someone up there to have a look."

"It's ok, I'll go. I'll take Simon too," said Julian. "We can head up there tomorrow."

"Yes, ok do that, and report back straight away; let me know how you get on," said the Commander.

"Ok, will do…" Julian paused for a moment, thinking. "But

what I don't understand is, if it was Natalie then why kidnap her? They could have just taken her out, I mean they did try to bomb her apartment."

"Yes, that's true... Well, it could be Hades... but, thinking about it, my guess is that they had a change of plan. If her attacker was Palestinian, he could well be one of the two from the CCTV that aren't accounted for. If she did kill him, then the others probably decided to ship her back to Gaza, Ramallah or somewhere to give her a show trial. The propaganda value would be immense," said the Commander.

"So that could explain how the four men died and possibly who killed them, but that leaves us with a problem," said Julian.

"Go on," said the Commander.

"Well, if we assume that the Palestinians came here to go after Natalie Kallaste, then one was taken out in the attack Calderwood told us about, then these four were eliminated... that leaves one other."

"Yes, and we need to find him," said the Commander.

"Do we know who he is?" asked Simon.

"Well, it's either Wasim El-Serag or... Youssef al-Masri, according to border control. They're not known to us, so I sent a request to the Israelis earlier to see if they had any information on them... They emailed back about an hour ago. They don't know El-Serag, but got very excited about al-Masri... Palestinian, aged thirty-two, parents were killed in an Israeli airstrike in 2003, a real hard-liner. No wonder he wanted along. The Israelis are definitely interested in him."

"What about SOCO...? What do we tell them?"

The Commander looked at Simon and Julian with a serious expression. "Nothing yet, but I will tell them not to issue any further press statements without my say-so on the grounds of national security. Unfortunately, they've already released some details as part of their investigation; they've been trying to get witnesses to come forward, so we can assume that El Serag or al-Masri, whichever it is; will be aware of what's happened to his accomplices. Heaven knows what his reaction will be, and that's my main concern. I'll give them an update once we get more information…If we're right it'll save SOCO a fortune on an investigation."

Monday morning, Grayling Avenue, Spark Hill, Birmingham

Earlier that day, in an anonymous back street, in an anonymous area of Birmingham, Youssef al-Masri was trying to come to terms with the loss of his five colleagues. He'd help bury his good friend Wasim after they found him lying on the ground by the garages behind Natalie's flat, stabbed in the throat. Now, this. He read the newspaper report again, front page; 'a massacre' the Express and Star had called it; a 'gang-land hit', posed the Sunday Mercury. He vowed revenge.

He thought again about Wasim, so brave, so headstrong. On the night of the first attack, it was him, Wasim, Naseer and Sayyid; the two youngest, Farid and Ahsan, had stayed behind. He was driving. There had been an argument in the van about who was going to kill the Mossad agent. Wasim had lost his brother in an Israeli air raid and insisted he should be the one to take out Natalie on his own… for his brother, he'd said.

He probably would have been successful, but no-one had considered an accomplice. Youssef had seen the man walking quickly passed the van and continued watching him from his door mirror. He saw the man turn left following Wasim to the garages at the back of the flats.

At first, they thought nothing was amiss; Sayyid was nervously checking his watch for the umpteenth time. Then after about five minutes, he announced, "something is not right… Come, let's see."

The three got out and went down the service road but no-one was there. It was just Wasim lying on the muddy, cinder-strewn ground with blood spurting from his neck. Sayyid checked him over while Yousef went back for the van. They managed to get

Wasim inside, but he was already dead.

In Birmingham, there was no shortage of sympathisers willing to provide board and lodgings to the six Palestinians. It was Sayyid's cousin, Ismail, who offered to help. He too was devastated by the slaughter of his fellow countrymen and promised his support to Youssef in finding the perpetrator. It had to be Natalie Kallaste, she was the number one target.

Ismail walked into the small kitchen, Youssef was staring into space, daydreaming, still devastated by recent events and twisted with anger.

"Why has this happened…? I should have been there… I may have been able to stop this," he said as Ismail entered the room.

"You mustn't blame yourself, Sayyid needed someone to stay behind and look after things in case you needed to escape quickly, you know that. It was the will of Allah that it was you."

"Insha'Allah," said Youssef.

"Yes," said Ismail. "What do you want me to do?" added Ismail, seeing his friend in such anguish.

"I need to find the woman who did this," said Youssef.

"But we do not know where she is," said Ismail.

"We know where she lives, we know where she works… we will find her," said Youssef.

"Have you spoken to Hashem?"

"Yes, I told him what has happened. He said Sayyid called him twice on Thursday morning, very early to say that they had captured Natalie and found a computer with designs for weapons. Hashem wanted to get hold of them, but I fear they are gone."

"You told him she has escaped?"

"Yes, and I told him Sayyid and the others are dead… He wants her found, whatever it takes, however long it takes," said Youssef. "Tomorrow I will go to where she works and watch for her."

"But she may not be there," said Ismail.

"And then I have wasted one day; I am in no hurry. If she is not there, then I will look somewhere else," said Youssef.

Rory drove up the cinder track alongside the majestic Severn, which today looked angry and brown. Several of the fields on the far side of the river were flooded. The potholes along the path were full of water where the weekend's heavy rain was still sitting; the river was running high. The undulation tested the Toyota's suspension as he bounced down the track towards the cottage. He was glad to be home; the air was fresh and the trees a vivid green, a proper green, not the manufactured colour of a thousand immigrant workers in the Gulf States.

He reached the cottage and went inside. Immediately, as he was inclined to do, he opened the windows to freshen the house after being shut up since Thursday morning. There was not much in the way of food in the refrigerator and he was beginning to regret declining Laura's offer to cook for him. What he hadn't told her was he just wanted to be on his own. He needed some private space to clear his head and reboot.

He checked the time; his watch said six o'clock, but his body-clock was three hours off. He felt tired despite managing to nap on the plane. A run would sort him out.

Ten minutes later he was in his running gear pounding the path. It felt good, the enzymes coursed through his body, enriching, revitalising; it was as though he was floating on air. It was cloudy with a threat of more rain, but quite warm and, despite the height of the river, there were still people fishing, making the most of the light summer evening. He ran passed the weir which was an awesome sight; the normally steady flow was replaced with a mighty roar as if the river gods were angry at having to manage the excess water. Rory completed another three miles before returning to the cottage and showering.

He returned to the kitchen and poured himself a large glass of water, then called Laura.

"Hi," said Rory.

"Hi, you ok? How was your journey?"

"Long," said Rory.

There was a catch-up, then Laura mentioned the Turks again. "Not much more information, investigation ongoing is all it says in the Standard… You still ok for tomorrow?"

"Yeah, looking forward to it," said Rory.

"Yeah, me too," said Laura.

There was more chat then Rory called time; he had another call to make.

He dialled the London number. "Swannie…? Rory."

"Hi Rory, I was going to call you later… You heard about the Turks?"

"Well, yeah, bits and pieces… the restaurant's been torched I heard."

"Yeah, it was all fuckin' kicking off. I met up with a pal of mine from the Met last night… a couple of beers and he was all over it," said Swannie. "They still think it was a rival gang, apparently there's been trouble over some girls. That's what was going 'round. They're not looking for anyone else according to my buddy; which means we're in the clear. He was over the moon, reckons they've smashed one of the biggest trafficking gangs in the country."

"That's great news," said Rory. "Have you spoken to Digger?"

"Yeah, rang him, last night. Wasn't a bit bothered, typical Digger."

"Yeah," said Rory.

"How's the girl?"

"Fiona…? Spoke to her a week or so back and she was hoping to go back to London soon. Definitely got her Dad's guts, that's for sure," said Rory.

"You can say that again," said Swannie. "I can't imagine how she must have felt…. I'd have gone fuckin' mental."

"Yeah, you're not kidding," said Rory.

"How were things in the Emirates… kill any more

ragheads?"

"Nah, bit eventful though, I'll tell you about it next time we meet up," said Rory.

"Yeah, and don't make it too long, eh?"

Tuesday morning, Vauxhall Cross, London, Commander Jenkins was at her desk; she called her P.A on her intercom. "Shelly, did you get hold of Hamilton?"

"Yes, Ma'am, he said he would be here at nine."

"He's cutting it a bit fine," said the Commander.

"Yes. Ma'am," said Shelly. "Oh, by the way, we've had some pictures sent in by Border Control from yesterday afternoon… It looks like Natalie Kallaste has left the country; she was travelling under the name of Kaplinski."

"Thank you, Shelly… Where was she was going, as a matter of interest?"

"Tel Aviv."

"Hmm, it looks like our Mr Calderwood's hunch was right," said the Commander.

Flat 23, Napier Gardens, Chelsea, an hour and a half earlier, MI6 agent Guy Hamilton was in his apartment preparing for his meeting with Commander Jenkins. It was an unusual summons and he had no idea what it was about but as he once said, when 'she who must be obeyed' called, you ran.

He checked his suit, then thought about a carnation in his buttonhole; he would see if there was a flower-seller outside the Tube station. He looked in the mirror one last time, straightened his tie and picked up his briefcase from the kitchen table. It was a cloudy morning with more rain expected, but he'd decided against a mac, his rolled-up umbrella would protect him from any inconvenient showers.

He opened the door to the apartment and was about to leave when he was knocked back inside. He sprawled on the floor completely taken by surprise. The disorientation would be temporary; the attacker took out a Glock 17, complete with a suppressor and shot the unfortunate agent in the temple before he could focus.

The assailant turned, left the apartment and closed the door behind him; the whole event took less than a minute. He pocketed the gun and walked purposefully to a black BMW, parked just along the street; he got in, drove away and disappeared into the morning traffic. He headed to North London to change the car, then it would be back to Brent Park. Once at the safe house, he made a phone call.

"Epsilon…? The loose end has been dealt with."

"Excellent, excellent… I am meeting Natalie this morning we have much to discuss."

Rory was up early and on the road by seven o'clock heading for the office. It was pouring it down again and the weather forecast was warning of more to come. For a moment, he wished he was enduring the heat of The Emirates, but the thought quickly left him. He would take a rain-lashed Worcestershire any day.

Even this early in the morning, the roads were busy with others making the daily slog into Birmingham. The windscreen washers were at odds with the beat of the music coming from the car radio, adding more stress to the journey.

As he drove, Rory was thinking about everything that had gone on over the weekend; he thought too about Natalie and wondered where in the world she would be. He had no hope that she would turn up at work. Wherever she was, she could still be in danger and he speculated what her paymasters would do when they realised the Hades information was next to useless.

He arrived at the works and stopped at the barrier. He needed a chat with the security gate supervisor. "Has Natalie turned up, do you know?"

"Not on my watch," said the supervisor. "And I'm pretty sure she wasn't on any of the others, but I'll check and let you know."

"Cheers, Dave," said Rory. "I'll stop by later," and he drove off to his parking space.

He went straight to Alistair's office; he was pretty sure he would be in. The door was ajar, and he could hear a voice coming from inside. It was Ed's voice; Rory knocked on the door.

"Come in" shouted Alistair.

"Ah, Rory, glad it's you, come in, I've just been talking with Ed, there's been a development."

Rory sat next to Ed in front of Alistair's desk. Ed seemed dejected.

"So, what's new?" said Rory.

"Well, Ed was in at five this morning… Checked all the access codes and it seems he was right, Natalie's got hold of the archive files… I mean, don't get me wrong, they would be useful to a competitor or someone already working on a similar project, but she didn't get all the information."

"Well, that's a relief," said Rory. "The M.O.D. will be pleased."

He noticed Alistair was not as elated about the situation as he should have been.

"Is there something else?"

"Yes," said Alistair and looked down.

"I had an email late yesterday evening from the M.O.D… They're pulling Hades."

"What!?" said Rory.

"Yes, they've decided not to pursue it further… They mentioned budget cuts or some such nonsense… I'll send you the email, you can see it," said Alistair. "I'm calling a board meeting at ten; you can join us if you like."

"Yeah, ok… sorry about Hades," said Rory.

Ed was in a state of shock. "Five years' work, down the fucking drain."

"Yes," said Alistair. "But we can't sit here licking our

wounds... we've got plenty of other stuff to be getting on with."

"Not like Hades," said Ed. "The guys in the department will be shattered."

"Yes," said Alistair. "Bring them up to speed on the orders we got at the weekend. That should help... There's plenty of research opportunities there, I'm sure."

Ed got up and left to brief the research team on the news.

Rory also stood up. "Oh, nearly forgot... Is your boat ok...?"

"As far as I know... why, is there a problem?"

"I hope not but the river's running very high. Not seen it this high at this time of year before. If we get much more rain, it could go over."

"Really...? Hmm, well I can't get down there before the weekend, there's too much to do here. Do you mind nipping over and having a look for me? It's battened down pretty well, but if it slips its moorings it could end up over the weir and that would be that."

"Yeah sure, I'll check it out tonight. I'll call you if there're any problems."

"Thanks, Rory, for everything you've done, by the way. I'm not sure what would have happened without your input."

"Cheers," said Rory. "Sorry about Hades though, I thought that had real potential."

"So did I, Rory, so did I."

"No news on Natalie I take it," said Rory.

"No, nothing," said Alistair.

"I checked with the gate, they've not heard from her. I'll speak to them again this afternoon," said Rory. "Catch you later... ten o'clock, the meeting?"

"Yes," said Alistair and Rory left the chairman's office and headed to his own in the production unit.

Seven o'clock in Spark Hill, Youssef was planning his day.

"Today, I will watch the factory until it closes and then I

will watch her apartment."

"But you don't know where she will be, she could be anywhere," said Ismail.

"But someone will know, we need to find her," said Youssef.

Later, he too was winding through the rush-hour traffic towards the works using Ismail's ten-year-old Suzuki Swift. It was going to be a boring day, but you never know he just might strike lucky. That's what he told Ismail before he left.

He reached the factory and parked up, armed with a flask of coffee and some sandwiches. He was about fifty yards away from the gates and could see the entrance quite clearly from his vantage point. He watched as the cars queued at security for access. It was an ideal position, they had to pass him to enter the works. He could see the car park and realised that some people were already in the building before he had arrived, but he was sure he would catch them leaving.

Youssef al-Masri was a product of Jabalia on the Gaza strip, his upbringing around the refugee camps and Palestinian hard-liners were bound to lead him in his present direction. His hatred for the West was only bettered for that of Israel, which he cursed with every part of his being for killing his parents; innocent people who had harmed no-one. That was four years ago.

He thought again about Wasim. Youssef still felt guilty and berated himself for not being firmer with his friend, but Wasim was so adamant he wanted to do it. He was strong and a great soldier; Youssef was sure he would carry out the mission.

Youssef was a patient man, a day observing the factory would be no hardship.

Inside the works, unaware of the happenings outside, Rory was reading the email from the M.O.D. when a call came through on his mobile.

"Rory Calderwood…?"

"Yeah."

"It's Julian, Birkett… six. I'm heading your way with Simon… will you be around later, say midday-ish?"

"Yeah, should be," said Rory.

"Oh, that's great… wondered if you would be so kind as to take us to our friend's apartment. You don't have a key by any chance?"

"Yeah, I do as it happens."

"Oh, that is convenient, it will save a lot of messing around…. Don't worry about picking us up we'll get a cab from New Street. Should be with you about twelve-thirty… We'll call at the gate, ok? Cheery bye."

"Yeah," said Rory. 'Cheery bye?' who talks like that these days, thought Rory.

Rory checked his watch, it was time for the board meeting and he made his way across to the admin block. It was the same line-up as the first meeting he attended at Alistair's house, with the notable exception of Natalie. The atmosphere was muted as Alistair entered the boardroom with a pile of papers.

He thanked everyone for attending and introduced Sonya, one of the secretaries who had been drafted in to take the minutes. Alistair had spent much of the morning with Steve Lillington, the CEO, briefing him on events so he was up to speed with the Natalie situation and the news from the M.O.D.

The Chairman kept the meeting brief; he merely announced the Hades decision and highlighted the potential impact on the business. His tone was relatively upbeat, certain that the sales they had acquired in Abu Dhabi would go a long way to off-setting this set-back. He was quick to point out that the rest of the government contracts were not affected. No-one mentioned Natalie or her indiscretions, but word had got around. Alistair eventually closed the formal meeting and, over coffee, Marcus Davies, the finance director, approached him.

"So, is it true about Natalie?" he said. He was the only executive not fully in the picture about the industrial espionage.

"What have you heard?" said Alistair.

"Something about accessing the Hades files," he said

"Let's just say Natalie is no longer working for us… and keep it to yourself, I don't want anything getting to the press."

"Yes, of course," said Marcus. "Mum's the word."

At twelve-twenty, Rory was sitting at his desk when a call came through on the internal phone.

"Gate here, Rory, two gentlemen to see you; said you were expecting them."

"Yeah, ask them to take a seat, I'll be with them in a couple of minutes."

He went to his desk and took out Natalie's keys, dropped them in his jacket pocket and left the building. The rain had not eased at all. His Toyota was parked in its normal place in the executive car park and he made a dash for it. His jacket and trousers were spattered by the time he'd unlocked the door and got in. He headed for the exit where his guests would be waiting and parked outside the security gates. He went inside the small 'guard-house', as it was known, where Julian and Simon were sat opposite the counter where visitors were registered. Rory went up to them, shook hands and exchanged pleasantries.

"Good journey?" asked Rory.

"Yes, quite fine actually," said Julian. "A lot of flooding up here I noticed from the train… I was just saying to Simon. Quite bad in places."

Simon, who was carrying a leather briefcase, just smiled. "Is it ok if we go with you, save another cab fare; you know, budgets and all that?" said Julian.

"Yeah, sure," said Rory.

Youssef was still watching the gate. He had seen the two men draw up in a taxi and hurry to the security cabin out of the rain. A Toyota approached the gate and the driver got out. He looked familiar. Youssef was straining his eyes to get a better view. Then he saw the man go into the building. Moments later, he exited with the two other men and the barrier rose to let the car through. It stopped at the entrance to let a car go by. The driver was looking left and right to make sure the road was clear. There was no mistaking… "It's him!" Youssef said to himself.

He started the car and pulled away, following the Toyota. He had no idea where it might be going, but he suddenly thought they may have Natalie somewhere.

Keeping pace with them was not difficult; travelling across the city, the traffic crawled for much of the way, partly due to the road conditions. Youssef could easily keep them in sight without being seen.

In the car there was polite discussion, Rory was interested in what they hoped to find in Natalie's flat. "Just want to have a look around," said Julian, "I expect you've heard about the bodies."

"Bodies?"

"Yes, thought you might have read about it in the papers," said Julian.

"No, not seen the papers while we were away."

"Four Palestinians found dead last week in an old factory not far from your works. Three shot, one with his neck broken."

"And you're connecting this to Natalie?"

"Just a line of enquiry," said Julian.

"Well, she didn't show up for work today," said Rory.

"No, she was tagged at Heathrow yesterday; using the name Kaplinski."

"What… you caught her?" said Rory.

"No, unfortunately, we were too late."

"Where was she going?"

"Tel Aviv," said Julian. "Looks like your theory was correct,"

"Hmm," said Rory, now deep in thought.

Once they had reached Edgbaston, Youssef figured out where they were heading; Natalie's apartment, it had to be.

Sure enough, the Toyota pulled into Cairns Avenue. Youssef decided to hold back and let them park before making the turn, to ensure he wasn't spotted.

Rory pulled up outside the flat and the three of them got out and went to the front door. Rory passed the key to Julian who opened it. They were in the entrance hall.

"Top floor," said Rory and took the lead. They quickly went upstairs to the third floor. Julian unlocked the door to the apartment and opened it slowly. Rory couldn't believe the sight that greeted him. There were signs of struggle, the carpet was stained with blood and a chair was tipped over.

"Well someone's had visitors," said Julian. "Ok, Simon, try the bathroom."

Simon placed his briefcase on the settee and opened it. He put on a pair of rubber surgical gloves and took out a phial and what looked like a long cotton-bud. Finding traces of Natalie's DNA was not going to be an issue and various items were sealed in containers, labelled and returned to the suitcase. Simon walked back into the lounge where Julian was on his hands and knees, also gloved, swabbing the carpet blood stains. This too was labelled and sealed in a container.

"Well, she definitely left in a hurry, she even left her toothbrush," said Simon and showed Julian the evidence.

"That's excellent, we should have more than enough," said Julian.

Rory had already worked out what was happening. "So, you're going to test for her DNA?"

"Yes, if we can match it with what was found at the factory then it will confirm our theory," said Julian. "It should give us a clear picture of what happened."

"Well, she also left her clothes… that's the suitcase I collected for her," said Rory pointing to Natalie's luggage on the floor next to the settee. "Her jacket's there as well." He went through the pockets and found her phone and keys.

"I'll take the phone," said Julian. "It certainly looks like the kidnapping theory holds up."

Rory gave it to him and Julian put it in his pocket.

Youssef had stopped further down the road but could see the entrance to the flat. He saw the men exit and get into the Toyota. Youssef set off in pursuit.

"Can you drop us off at New Street, there's a nice restaurant there? We can get a bite to eat before we catch the train back," said Julian.

"Yeah, ok, I wasn't busy," said Rory with a hint of sarcasm which Julian didn't notice.

It was a tedious journey into the city centre, dropping off Julian and Simon at the station.

"We'll be in touch," said Julian as he left the car.

Then it was back to the works; it was after two o'clock before Rory returned to his desk and it was still raining. He'd called in at the canteen to get a sandwich.

Youssef meanwhile had parked up again outside the works, close to where he had parked earlier. He was in a dilemma; was Natalie back at the flat? Who were the men and why were they visiting the apartment? He wasn't sure whether to continue watching the works or return to the flat and see if she was there.

He decided that the man in the Toyota held the key. He was almost certainly involved with Wasim's murder and would know where Natalie was. He decided to wait; he took out one of his sandwiches and started to eat.

Julian and Simon arrived back in London and took a taxi back to Vauxhall Cross. Julian phoned the Commander and outlined what had happened. "We have plenty of material... The kidnap theory seems the most likely."

"I'll have someone standing by to process the DNA as soon as you get back," said the Commander.

By five o'clock, Rory was ready to leave. He was looking forward to seeing Laura again. it would give him a chance to unwind. They had decided on getting a takeaway, there was a Chinese restaurant only ten minutes' drive away from the cottage and neither felt like cooking.

He reached the Toyota and before getting in, he looked up at the sky; it had stopped raining for the moment, but with heavy clouds around, more was forecast later. He turned on the car radio to get the latest and the news items were starting to issue flood warnings in the Severn Valley; the river had already breached its banks further north.

Youssef was vigilant as the daily exodus of cars left the works; there was only one he was interested in. His patience was rewarded as he saw the red car approach the security barrier. Youssef had already turned the ignition key in the Suzuki.

He was half-expecting the car to return to Edgbaston and Natalie's apartment; maybe he was living with her, but instead, the car continued to the motorway. This would possibly give Youssef a problem, there was no way the ancient Suzuki could keep up with the Toyota. The name 'Swift' was a misnomer.

Fortunately, the spray from other vehicles precluded any fast speeds. It meant Youssef could keep pace with Rory without difficulty and, with visibility severely restricted, he would not be seen to be following.

The Toyota took the Worcester turning off the Motorway and Youssef followed. He had no idea where he was or where he was going.

On reaching the riverside, Rory could see the once majestic Severn; it was now a raging torrent. The noise was audible from inside the car, above the sound of the music on the radio. It had risen at least two feet since the previous evening and was almost level with the top of the bank; it was still rising, an eerie sight. The local news said that the cricket ground and racecourse were already under water. Jogging was not going to be on the agenda tonight.

He drove slowly down the cinder path towards the cottage. To his right, boats were straining at their moorings and were colliding with the riverside trees; some of the over-hangs were already completely submerged; the power of the river was awesome. He suddenly remembered he needed to check Alistair's boat, although what he could do about it was open to conjecture.

He parked in his usual spot; he didn't notice the Suzuki pulling up about fifty yards away. Youssef watched Rory go to his cottage; he would think of a plan.

Chapter Seventeen

Rory went into the kitchen, made a mug of tea and then called Laura.

"Hi, it's me… Look, I don't know if you've been watching the news, but I don't like the look of the river; it's almost breaking over and it's pouring it down again."

"Hi… yes, it's flooding at Holt Fleet," she said, referring to a small riverside community, about two miles up the river from her house.

"What do you want to do?" said Rory.

"Well, you could come here if you like… it might be safer."

"Yeah, good call, sounds like a better idea. We can nip up to the pub for something to eat; I don't expect they'll be very busy in this weather."

"Good idea… but don't be long or I might start without you," she said and started to laugh.

"I won't, I'll just take a shower and I'll be on my way," said Rory.

"Great, I'll put something special on for you."

Rory rang off and took his shower. He changed into a pair of jeans and a shirt. He checked outside; it was still teeming down with rain; he would need a jacket. He checked his wallet, keys and phone were in his pocket and left the house. He held his jacket over his head rather than put it on in the conventional way, to keep the rain from his hair. He was about to make a dash for his car when he remembered his promise to Alistair. He would make a quick detour and check out the boat. As he got to the cinder track, he noticed the route was cut off. Water was backing up and starting to lap the track. At this rate, he would be completely cut off in a few minutes

He abandoned the good deed on the grounds of sensibility and headed for his car. The sight of the river lapping the path was disconcerting, but he estimated he should be able to just get through. He was feeling good at the thought of meeting up with Laura again and what was going to be on offer. He reached his car and was about to open the door when, from nowhere, came an unexpected force. He was pushed against the car and he could feel something sharp against his neck.

"Where is she?" said a voice. The accent was strong, Rory recognised it straight away; he'd heard enough Arabs speaking English in his time.

"What the fuck are you on about?" said Rory, as aggressively as he could, letting the assailant know he was not going to be a pushover.

"The girl, Natalie, the Yahudi?"

"I haven't the faintest idea, mate... probably out of the country, if she's got any sense."

Rory relaxed, the blade was still at his neck, he could feel it, but he needed to get the attacker to drop his guard.

"I do not believe you... Why you go to her apartment today?"

"We thought she was sick... She's not been at work; we wondered where she was. We just checked to see if she was at home," said Rory.

Must keep him talking.

"Look, if I knew where she was, I'd tell you. I don't know about you, but I'm getting fucking soaked here, mate."

Rory could feel the attacker relax; he sensed the man didn't know what to do... Any second, he would have him... Now!

In a flash, Rory had ducked and wrapped his jacket around his arm; he was now stood a yard away and facing his assailant. The rain was still coming down. The man made a lunge with the knife and Rory parried it with his jacketed arm. The man was off balance. Rory managed to slam the side of his hand across the back of his neck; the infamous rabbit punch, seen in all the best movies but rarely effective unless you knew what you were doing. Rory knew what he was doing. He followed up with a kick in the ribs. This would take the wind out of the attacker's lungs and make it difficult for him to stand. Rory landed a fist on the side of the attacker's face in a bid to render him unconscious. The knife was nowhere to be seen; Youssef had dropped it somewhere.

Youssef tried to get up, but Rory landed another kick, this time to the groin area, another sensitive spot which would temporarily disable his opponent. Surprisingly, Youssef somehow regained his strength and made a dive at Rory. Rory was caught off-guard and suddenly found himself on the ground rolling in the mud. Youssef made another move and was on top of Rory with his hands around his neck. Rory kicked hard, causing the man to lose his grip. The next thing Rory knew they had rolled off the cinder path and were in the water.

He couldn't feel the bottom and suddenly a branch of a tree crashed into him. He was being swept along faster than he could run; it was like a water slide at an Aquapark. More debris; the top of a caravan went by, branches, litter, a cow, mooing frantically trying to save itself. Rory could see the head of his attacker being carried along, but he was now ten feet in front of him and heading for the weir. There was nothing to stop him. He could hear him screaming for divine assistance. Rory made a grab for an overhanging branch; he held it for a moment, but the force of the current broke it away, leaving Rory holding thin air.

Rory kicked hard but the force of the water was incredible. He needed to go left to reach the channel that bypassed the weir. Normally, it would be at least thirty feet from the river surface to the walkway running above, but now the water was almost at the top. The rain continued to pour. The cold started to become a problem now. Rory was swimming hard. 'Go left, go left' he willed himself; but the current was relentless and took him inexorably towards the weir. Another caravan crashed into the bank to his left with a crunching noise and broke into pieces. Rory could see people on the bank; some were taking pictures.

The weir was in front of him fifty yards, thirty, twenty; he gave one almighty kick. The momentum took him somewhere mid-channel. In front of him, there was a boat; it was in a strange position, floating sideways. It had hit the metal post in the middle of the river where it divided into the safe channel and the weir. He could see the sign; 'Danger Weir' with a large pointer to the right.

Somehow the boat had become wedged against it and the force of the water was preventing it from going anywhere. Rory couldn't stop himself and slammed into the side. The mooring rope was hanging loose, and he made a lunge for it. The incredible speed of the water carried him almost horizontally as he held on.

Unfortunately, the sudden impact had shifted the small cruiser from its involuntary mooring; he could feel the current slowly starting to push the boat to the right, towards the weir. The stricken vessel was moving but behind it, there was small eddy where the current couldn't escape. The warning post rose just above him. Rory let go of the rope and made a lung-bursting effort to grab it and hold on. The boat rolled, then tipped right over and was swept away towards the weir.

Rory had nowhere to go; he had his arms wrapped around the metal post, hoping it would hold his weight. He started to shiver, whatever protection his clothes had afforded him had gone. He thought about trying to shin further up the post to try to get to the dock in the centre of the river that divided the safe channel from the weir, but the gap was too large, at least six feet; he would never make it.

He didn't know how long he'd been hanging on when he heard a noise; it was loud, above the sound of the weir and water. A sudden blast of air; the whirring of rotors, and there he was, like a guardian angel, hanging from a metal line. It was around seven-thirty and officially still daylight, but the rain and cloud made it dark and gloomy. The Hi-Viz jacket reflected the beam of a searchlight like a beacon. The spray was incredible, but the rescuer managed to swing himself alongside Rory and secure a life jacket around his waist. Rory felt himself being lifted, fast. It made his stomach turn. Then he was inside the chopper wrapped in a 'Bacofoil' blanket just as he had been when he saved the boy. A paramedic checked him over.

"You ok?" said the medic.

"Yeah, just a bit wet... Thanks for the lift," said Rory. "Where're we going?"

"Worcester Royal... just to get you looked at," said the man.

"Thanks, have you got a phone I can use by any chance? I need to call someone," said Rory.

"Sure," said the medic and handed him his mobile.

"Cheers," said Rory and dialled the number. "Hi, it's me," he shouted.

"I can't hear you," said Laura.

"I'm in a helicopter."

"What are you doing in a helicopter?"

"I'll tell you later, can you collect me from Worcester Royal?"

"What, the hospital...? Yes, of course... Are you ok?"

"Yeah, I'm ok. I'll see you later... I've got to go, I'm on someone's phone," said Rory. He hung up and handed the mobile back to the medic.

"Cheers, and thanks for getting me out; I couldn't have hung on for much longer," said Rory.

"I don't know how you managed to survive in that. We've already had a report of a body the other side of the weir."

Within five minutes the helicopter was making its landing adjacent to the hospital. Rory was led to the emergency ward by an awaiting paramedic; he turned and watched the chopper take off again.

Rory was taken to the resuscitation ward and given an initial assessment.

"Can't see anything major, just some bruising and mild

hyperthermia, but I would like to keep you in overnight as a precaution," said the doctor.

"It's ok, I'm fine," said Rory. "I'll come back if there's any problem. I just need to get out of these wet things."

Rory had warmed up, but his clothes were still wet, and he was uncomfortable. He discharged himself and went to the front entrance to wait for Laura.

It was half an hour before he saw her car approaching. He waved, she pulled up alongside him and opened the door.

"God, you're all wet," said Laura as she leaned up to kiss him.

"Yeah, decided to go for a swim," said Rory.

"Ha, ha, no really, what happened, not playing the hero again?"

"No, not this time… I'll tell you later, but I could do with going back to the cottage to get a change of clothes."

"Ok," and she left the hospital and turned left towards the cottage,

"Thanks… I don't know if we'll be able to get down there, the river's broken over, but my jacket's by the car somewhere; it's got my keys and wallet… oh shit, and my phone, it's in the pocket."

"Ok, let's have a look."

It took about ten minutes to get there; the cinder track was now completely under water and there was no way of getting through. He was beginning to wonder about the cottage.

"Leave it, we can't get through this," said Rory.

"God, I've never seen the river like this," said Laura.

"That's for sure," said Rory.

"Let's get you back to mine; we can sort out something tomorrow," said Laura.

She reversed and headed back to her house.

"I've really missed you," said Laura, and she grabbed his hand.

"Yeah, I missed you too," he said. He realised it was true.

It took about twenty minutes to get to Laura's, the rain was easing slightly, but the road was flooded in places making the journey hazardous.

Back at the house, Laura could see the state of Rory more closely.

"You've got blood on your shirt," she said. "Have you hurt yourself?"

"No, I'm fine."

"Ok, let's get you out of those wet things, I can wash them through and have them ready for you in the morning."

"You say all the right things," said Rory and smiled.

"Later, let's get you sorted out first... You can have a shower if you like," said Laura.

"Yeah, great," said Rory.

"Wait, I'll get you a dressing gown." Laura went upstairs and returned with the said item. Rory was just standing there in his shorts.

"You want me to wear this?" he said, as she handed him the garment.

"Pink will suit you," she said and started to laugh.

Rory removed his shorts and put on the dressing gown. Laura was in hysterics.

"Well, you've certainly found your feminine side," she said, still laughing.

Rory handed her the rest of his clothes. Laura went to the kitchen and fed them into the washing machine, then heard the water start to run in the shower upstairs. She finished seeing to the washing and poured two glasses of wine, then headed for the bathroom. She pushed open the door and could see Rory's naked body covered in soap.

"I've bought you a drink," she said and held it up so he could see it. The shower cubicle was full of steam.

"Thanks," he replied and continued his ablutions. The warm hot water flowing down his body was therapeutic. Laura sat on the toilet seat for a couple of minutes watching him.

"Would you like me to scrub your back?" she said.

"Sounds good," Rory replied.

Laura stood up and stripped off her clothes.

She opened the door to the shower and got in behind him. She wrapped her arms around his body and slowly rubbed his chest. Rory could feel her breasts pushing against his back. Despite his recent ordeals, Laura's touch was having a stimulating effect. He turned around and they began kissing. Water continued to cascade onto them as their love-making grew more urgent. Laura leaned back against the wall of the shower to give Rory an angle; then he was in her.

It was so powerful; Laura screamed as Rory reached orgasm. He was breathing heavily for a few moments, then they disengaged and stood holding each other; the water still running over them.

"God, that was good," said Laura.

"Yeah, that's for sure," said Rory.

Laura turned off the water, opened the shower and grabbed a couple of bath towels from the rail. She passed one to Rory.

"What are we going to do about food?" said Laura and started to laugh.

"Well, I can't go to the pub like this…" he said, with the towel wrapped around his waist. "Unless you can lend me some clothes."

"Hmm, I don't think they'll be quite ready for that sight… It's ok, I can fix us up with something," she said, handing him her dressing-gown.

Laura went downstairs while Rory finished drying; he could hear the sound of pots and pans rattling.

Youssef couldn't remember anything after being struck with something as he went over the weir. He'd got tangled in some branches which had kept him afloat and found himself snagged on the opposite bank. Below the weir, the current was in a trough creating mini-whirlpools; it was this momentum which had propelled him to the bank or at least what used to be the bank; the river had breached its confines for several miles. He was in a field; the water some three feet deep. He eventually managed to find a foothold and half-crawled, half-walked through the cloying mud. Dry land was about fifty yards away and a hedge marked the border of a farmer's land. He summoned his strength and headed for the gate in the corner; he was freezing cold.

The other side of the gate was a lane and for the first time since he went in the water, he could feel solid ground beneath him. He thanked Allah for his deliverance. His tee-shirt and jeans were caked with mud and his hair was matted with twigs and other river debris. It was this sight that greeted the approaching tractor-driver. Youssef flagged the vehicle frantically, forcing it to stop.

"You alright, there?" said the driver in a rural accent.

"Can you help, please…? I fall in water, there, many miles." He pointed upstream. "I am saved here; Alḥamdulillāh."

"I don't know about Allah, but you's a lucky so and so, make no mistake… Hop on, I'll get you up to the farm," said the tractor-man. Just then a helicopter flew over towards the river, its search-beam scanning the fields and riverbank

It was about a mile up the lane when they reached the farmhouse. A typical rural cottage, nineteenth century but modernised. The farmyard was littered with old machinery and chicken droppings. There was an old VW parked next to, what looked like, an old barn. Youssef was shivering uncontrollably.

"We'll soon get you warm, don't yer worry," said the farmer seeing his distress.

The tractor pulled up against the barn.

"Come on, you best come with me. I'll see if we can find you a change of clothing and get you cleaned up," said the farmer. "You can get warm, too."

He walked in through the front door and immediately two Border Collies were surrounding him wagging their tails.

"No, you go in, you can't go out tonight," he said to them. They obeyed without question. "Peggy, are you there?"

His wife came in from the kitchen; homely-looking, round with a ruddy complexion, her greying hair was tied back in a bun; she was wearing an apron.

"Just as we thought, river's topped... lower field's gone... I found this chap wanderin' up the lane... Gone over the weir, or so he says... Come in, come in," he said to Youssef, who was standing in the doorway. It was still raining.

Youssef entered the cottage and closed the door.

"My goodness, look at you," said Peggy. "You should be in 'ospital."

She went to him for a closer look. Blood in his hair and down his arms; there was a gash on his forehead. His clothes sopping wet. He started to shiver again.

"Dan can drop you off, can't yer?" said Peggy. "The 'ospital... I tell you what, Dan'll find yer some dry things and then he can take yous into town, how's that sound...? Would yer like a sandwich or summat? It'll be no problem."

"Yes, a sandwich, good," said Youssef. Dan went upstairs on the search for some clothes.

"You're not from 'round 'ere are you?" said Peggy.

"No," said Youssef.

"Where're yer from, then?"

"Birmingham, yes, Birmingham," said Youssef.

"Yeah, I 'eard they got all sorts there, now... Sit yerself down, Dan'll be back shortly."

Peggy went into the kitchen followed by the two dogs. Youssef was sitting on the settee but feeling anxious and ill-at-ease. He thought one of them might be contacting the police. He stood up and went to the kitchen door. He could see Peggy making a cup of tea. The breadboard and loaf were on the table, a large kitchen knife with serrated edges used for cutting bread was next to it.

In a moment Youssef had entered the kitchen. Peggy was at

the sink and turned around.

"Don't yer go worrying, you go and sit yerself down I'll bring it through," she said.

Peggy continued to fill the kettle and before she could turn around, he'd picked up the knife and plunged it into her neck. There was a gurgling sound and then she fell to the floor. The kettle dropped into the sink with a clatter. The two dogs started barking furiously.

Dan had heard the dogs and the noise and came downstairs. There was no sign of Youssef.

"Peggy…! Is everything alright?"

He went into the kitchen and could see his wife laying on the floor; a pool of blood was spreading outwards from the top of her body. He froze instantly. Youssef was behind the door and brought the knife down on Dan's back. He stabbed again, then again, and again. It was a frenzy. The dogs were still barking at Youssef, sensing something was wrong, and without a second thought, he grabbed them in turn and slashed their throats. The kitchen was awash with blood, the floor a deep red. Youssef's clothes were covered from the splatters.

He went back into the lounge and picked up the dry clothes that Dan had brought for him, a pair of old jeans and a pullover. Youssef quickly changed. He went back to the kitchen and found an old plastic carrier-bag in one of the cupboards. He looked at the bodies of his victims; the blood was now covering virtually the entire kitchen floor. Back in the lounge, he put his blood-stained clothes in the plastic bag and tied the top together with the handles. He looked down at his muddied trainers which were now also covered in blood. There was nothing he could do about that.

Dan's jacket was hanging up behind the door, Youssef picked it up, checked the pockets and found what he was looking for, a key-ring with a VW label. The jacket engulfed him; it was about three sizes too big, but he would manage. He picked up the carrier bag with his clothes in and left the house. He stopped at a puddle and tried to wash the blood off his trainers, then crossed the yard to where the VW Polo was parked. He unlocked the car and got in, putting the carrier-bag on the passenger seat. The car smelled like wet dogs. He turned the ignition key, the engine coughed and then fired.

It was almost dark now, but at least the rain had stopped, replaced by a murky mist. The headlights illuminated the yard, the beams standing out in the gloom. He passed the tractor that had come to his rescue and drove out of the farmyard into the lane. He turned right, away from the river. The narrow road meandered, the headlights reflecting the hedgerow and the red sandstone bank. Every so often there were gaps in the roadside verges and water poured through from the fields, flooding the road. He ploughed through the rushing water, causing cascades left and right.

He eventually reached a T junction. A white signpost with black lettering informed him that Worcester was 5 miles to the right and Upton, 8 miles to the left. He turned right; he knew he needed to go through Worcester if he wanted to get back to Birmingham. After a couple of miles, he reached the main road; right to Worcester, it said. He waited while several cars went by going in the same direction, then made the turn.

The bridge across the Severn was miraculously still open; everywhere around was flooded, including the riverside properties. Shops, cafés and pubs had been swamped and it would take many months for them to re-open. For some, that would never happen; it would mean the end of their businesses. There were crowds of bystanders watching the deluge, a once-in-a-lifetime experience. Arc-lights, lit up the river, newscasters were giving pieces to cameras against the backdrop of the bridge and the torrent below. It was an awesome sight; the water had risen to the top of the arches of the bridge forcing the water through at tremendous speed.

Youssef crossed the river slowly behind a small queue. Police were at the far end directing traffic away from the flooded areas and up the hill out of town. Youssef held his breath as he passed them, but they were far too busy to notice anything amiss. Then he saw a sign for Birmingham, he followed the directions. Before reaching the motorway, he spotted a lay-by and pulled in. There was a large rubbish-skip into which he discarded the carrier bag containing his bloody clothes.

Wednesday morning, Laura turned over and kissed Rory on the cheek. "Would you like a cup of tea?"

"Hey, yeah… what time is it?" he said drowsily.

"Seven-thirty… you were very restless last night."

"Sorry, had some bad dreams."

They were the usual ones, the ones which haunted him when he was under stress. His near death experience the previous evening came under that category.

"Well, you can have a lie-in if you like, then I'll take you back to your house, see what the damage is."

"Thanks," said Rory.

A few minutes later Laura returned with two mugs. "Just been watching the news; it's terrible. Upton's flooded, Tewkesbury is completely cut off; just the Abbey surrounded by water, looks awful, those poor people."

"Shouldn't you be covering this?" said Rory, sipping his tea.

"I've already sent in one piece, but I will need to go in later if that's ok," said Laura.

"Yeah, of course, no problem. It looks as though I'm going to have some cleaning to do in any case," said Rory.

"You can call over again tonight if you like… We might even make the pub."

Just then Laura's mobile phone rang. "It's my editor," she mouthed seeing the caller's name on the screen.

She listened.

"What!? When…? Last night…? That's terrible. Yes, of course… I can be there about nine," said Laura.

She dropped the call and looked at Rory. "You don't mind, do you? There's been a double murder over at Linton, a farmer and his wife… and their two dogs, it sounds horrific. I'll drop you off at your place on the way."

"No, that's fine, I'll get a shower if that's ok. I don't even know if I'll have any water. Hmm, how ironic will that be."

By eight-thirty the couple were on the road. The rain had stopped and there were patches of blue sky. Evidence of the previous night's deluge was everywhere; branches and twigs were strewn across the road where the water had gushed through from the fields. They reached the cinder path leading to the cottage. The river was still flowing very fast, but had receded and was just at the top of the bank; the level appeared to be dropping.

"It's ok, I can walk from here," said Rory, as they reached the path.

"Ok, I'll call you later, about midday… You can give me a report," said Laura.

"Yeah, ok, chat later." He got out and watched Laura turn and head back; he waved.

He surveyed the scene, total devastation. Several boats were out of the water, some on their side, others still gamely holding onto their mooring ropes as the current tried to sweep them away. Then he remembered Alistair's cruiser; he could see it just ahead. He skipped over some large puddles and reached it. Luckily it was still in the water, although it was difficult to tell what condition it was in. It had become wedged under an overhanging tree but was still tethered to its post. He would ring Alistair and let him know.

There were none of the usual dog-walkers or joggers; it was ghostly quiet, just the roar of the mighty Severn a few feet to his right.

He reached the cottage. The first thing he needed to do was to find his jacket, otherwise, it would mean breaking a window.

He saw the Toyota; the wheels were caked with mud and

there was a line at the bottom of the sill indicating where the water had reached. There was a brick wall the other side of the car about three feet tall which separated the cottage grounds from some other land. It sloped downwards towards the cinder path; the water had clearly breached it in places. He walked along its length, and then there it was, stuck in a small gully snagged on a nail. He picked the jacket up; water poured from the garment. It was going to be a write-off. He checked the pockets; both sets of keys were still there and his wallet. His phone was there too but that would be unusable.

He went back to the car and opened the door. There was water in the foot-well. He put the ignition key and turned. It coughed and spluttered for a moment and then sprang to life. He said a silent thanks to the Japanese car-maker. He would leave it running for a moment to dry it through and clear any remaining water. Inside smelt stale. He opened all the windows.

Then he noticed a Suzuki. He realised straight away that it must belong to his attacker; there were no other cars around. He made a note of the registration and went into the cottage.

Luckily, the water had not penetrated the house but it had been close. There was a damp feel about the place. He opened all the windows and the front door to let some air in. The sun was now shining. He looked across the other bank and the fields beyond, the terrain completely transformed, lush green fields had been replaced by huge lakes.

As he looked towards the distance, he could see one or two houses dotted along the landscape. There was something on his mind; it was something Laura had said... Linton, a double murder. The hamlet of Linton was not visible from where he was, but it was not that far along the other bank; about three, maybe four miles as the crow flies. He thought about the weir and how far someone would be carried before ground fall.

He went inside and switched on the TV, the news channel was reporting live from a helicopter circling Tewksbury but there was lots of footage further upstream. It showed the racecourse and cricket ground below the Cathedral which was regularly flooded. It had become a bit of a joke in cricket circles. 'Are you batting with, or against the tide today?' was the tag.

He listened to the commentary. *"Despite the carnage and unbelievable damage wrought by this ancient river, mercifully there have been no reports of fatalities."*

"So, either his body hasn't been found, which is quite possible... or he survived," Rory said to himself.

The news report switched to a breaking story. *"The bodies of Dan and Peggy Fletcher and their two dogs have been found at their cottage in the small village of Linton early this morning by their son. Police are saying that they were brutally killed but are releasing no further details at this time... We will update you as soon as we have further news."*

The narration continued with a short background on the couple, farming there for forty years; there was a helicopter shot of the cottage with several police vehicles in attendance. The tractor was still in the yard.

Rory had a hunch. If his attacker had survived, would he be capable of killing a farmer and his wife in cold blood? The answer was a categorical 'yes'. His kind were ruthless and would definitely have no qualms committing murder if it meant achieving their aims.

He needed to make a call but with his mobile out of action, he would need to go to the supermarket and buy a replacement.

He locked up the cottage. The car engine was still running, and he got in and headed down the path. The river was level with him to the left and it felt weird. He was glad when he reached the road.

He was able to get a new phone without too much hassle, then he returned to the cottage. He noticed Alistair's boat again; he needed to call him first. He went into the kitchen and retrieved the SIM card from his old phone and placed it in the new one, then plugged it into the charger.

He waited ten minutes to allow enough charge to make a couple of calls. While he was waiting he checked his address book and found Alistair's mobile number.

"Alistair, Rory... just an update on your boat. Sorry, I haven't got back to you sooner, but I've had some problems I've had to sort out... No, nothing serious, just the insurers, a bit of damage from the flood. Speaking of which, your boat is still upright, but it looks like it's got wedged under a tree, you might want to come down here sooner rather than later and check it out. Yeah, I'll be around... Yeah, see you about two."

He went back to the kitchen drawer and took the business card that was rolling about loose. He dialled the number.

"Birkett!"

"Julian, it's Rory... Calderwood."

"Oh, hello Rory. How are things...? Looks a bit damp over your way."

"Aye, you can say that again... Listen I've got some information which may or may not be of interest, but bear with me... Last night I was attacked by someone... Middle Eastern origin for sure... asking about Natalie."

"Go on."

"He had a knife at my throat, wanted to know why we'd been to her flat, so he'd obviously been following us."

"I see, so where is this man now... You've not taken him out have you?"

"Well, no, not exactly... We ended up in the river. I got picked up by a chopper, but he went over the weir."

"Oh, that's a shame. We really wanted to talk to him."

"Well, that's why I'm calling. Have you seen the news... the murders near here... farmer and his wife? They've not given all the details yet, but they were killed last night. So, say if the bloke who attacked me did survive and managed to get out of the water, he would be looking for a car... right?"

"Yes, that makes sense."

"And we know these bastards are ruthless enough to kill an

innocent farmer and his wife?"

"I can see where you're going with this," said Julian.

"There's another thing… the bastard's car's still here. It's parked behind mine, I can give you the registration number."

Rory gave Julian the details. "I don't know what you want to do with all this, but it occurred to me that if you were to trace the owner of the car, you may find your man… or at least someone who knows where he is."

"Yes, I like your thinking Rory, I like your thinking… Listen, leave it with me, I'll be in touch to let you know what we find."

He rang off and made an internal call. "Ma'am, I've just had Rory Calderwood on again. I think we may have a lead on our missing Palestinian."

Chapter Eighteen

Julian looked up a number on his laptop and made another call. "Can I speak to the investigating officer, please? I have some information regarding the murdered farmer in Worcester."

There was a delay and much rustling of paper, then a voice. "Superintendent Charles, who is this please?"

"Oh, hello, my name is Julian Birkett, calling from Vauxhall Cross."

"I see," said the officer. "And how can we help Special Intelligent Services?"

"We have a particular interest in two Palestinians, we believe are involved with acts of terrorism in the Birmingham area. We have received information that last night one of them attacked a member of the public which resulted in our Palestinian ending in the Severn. We believe he survived and got out of the river near your farmer's place. If he was looking for transport to get away, he could well have killed the couple."

The Superintendent was getting interested.

"Is the couple's car missing, by any chance?" asked Julian.

"Yes, we believe it is," said the officer.

"Ok, here's something else for you... We believe the attacker was driving a Suzuki Swift." He gave the officer the number. "The car has been abandoned in Worcester." And again, Julian provided the address.

"Now, my best guess is, if you can find the owner, at the very least he is either the murderer or knows where the murderer is."

"Thanks for that, do you have a name by the way?" said the officer.

"He is one of two, Wasim El-Serag, or Youssef al-Masri, they're not on any watchlists at the moment and we don't have any fingerprints or DNA, but I can let you have a photograph."

"Thank you," said the officer. "We really need to catch whoever did this. It was a dreadful murder, the worst I have seen in my thirty years."

"I hope this will help. I'll get the pictures to you straight away. Please keep me in the loop."

Julian gave the officer his mobile phone number and rang off.

Back at the cottage, Rory called Laura for an update. He needed to give her his new number. He told her about the car and the cottage; he had been lucky. They arranged to meet later.

At just turned two o'clock, Rory heard a car pull up; it was Alistair's Jaguar. He went out to greet him.

Alistair got out of the car and shook hands with Rory. "Jesus, the track's a bit hairy."

"You're not kidding; you should have seen it last night," said Rory. "Would you like a coffee?"

"Yes, why not," said Alistair and Rory led him inside.

"Nice place," said Alistair, looking around the cottage.

"Yeah, it serves its purpose... not a long-term project. How're things at the factory?"

"Yes, ok, considering. Young Vikram and Ed have been working on the I.T. trying to prevent any more problems."

"It's not the I.T. that's the problem, it's the people," said Rory.

"Yes, I think you're right there," said Alistair.

Rory made them both a drink and handed Alistair a mug. "Oh, before I forget, I had a conversation with our friendly spooks and it seems Natalie caught a flight to Tel Aviv on Monday from Heathrow."

"Really? So, you were right then," said Alistair.

"Looks like it, although I don't think much to her chances in Israel; she'd been better off going back to Estonia; that's what I'd have done."

"I find it all so sad, this business. I'm not sure I will ever trust anyone again," said Alistair.

There was a pause while they sipped their drinks.

"So, what's next?" said Rory.

"What do you mean?"

"For the business, now Hades has been ditched?"

"We'll continue with our bread and butter stuff, and hope that the enquiries we got at the weekend start to bear fruit. Duncan's been going flat out... In fact, between you and me I think he's working a bit too hard. I've told him to take a holiday, but he keeps putting it off."

"Hmm... I see... Well, while you're here, I wanted to ask you a question," said Rory. Alistair looked at him.

"Of course."

"How do you see my involvement with the business... I mean, without Hades in the picture?"

"I can't say I've thought much about it," said Alistair.

"Well, I have," said Rory. "And I can't see there's much of a role for me as things stand. I don't want to be sat twiddling my thumbs, that's not me."

"No, I know that," said Alistair. "So, what are you saying?"

"To save you some money, why don't I work on a consultancy basis, you know, daily rate, as and when?"

"I always honour my contracts," said Alistair.

"Yeah, I know that. I'm just offering you a cheaper option."

"I appreciate that. Tell you what, let me speak to Steve and we can chat some more."

"Yeah, ok, shall we go and sort out this boat of yours?" said Rory.

"Yes, let's," said Alistair.

They left the house and walked towards the riverbank. The river had dropped a few inches and was below the top now; hopefully, the worst was over. They reached the stricken boat, it hadn't moved very much since Rory had last seen it. It was wedged between the branches of an overhanging tree, still tied to the mooring. Alistair looked at the boat.

"This side looks ok. I can't see the other side, it could have been hit by something and holed. Maybe best to leave it where it is for the moment and wait for the river to drop."

Just as he said that another caravan drifted by, crashed into a submerged tree and broke up.

"See what I mean."

"Yeah," said Rory.

Alistair checked the rope. It was still secure.

"I've got another rope in the car. I'll lash a second line just to make sure."

He went to the car and returned with a length of rope. With Rory holding him, Alistair leant across and managed to thread it through the safety rail at the back. Then tied it to a docking point on the bank with a double knot, then looped it through again.

"There, that should do it," said Alistair. It was as secure as it was going to be.

As Alistair was about to leave, two police squad cars came bouncing down the track. Alistair waited for them to get by him and then drove off. The cars pulled up outside the cottage and four officers got out. Rory went to see them.

"That's the car you're after," he said to the leading officer.

"And you are?" said the officer.

"Rory Calderwood... I reported it this morning. Looks like it's been abandoned."

"Right thanks for that, you can leave it to us now," said the officer and the four men surrounded the Suzuki, looking at it with some suspicion. Rory went into the cottage and left them to it.

Thirty miles further north, a different operation was underway, led by Detective Inspector Shaun Proctor.

Grayling Avenue, Spark Hill was surrounded and cordoned off. A drive-by had already revealed the farmer's VW Polo parked at the bottom of the street. Youssef had not had time to dump it.

It had been late by the time Youssef returned to Ismail's house the previous evening. He was starting to feel the effects of his experience. On his way back from Worcester he'd developed a blinding headache which was affecting his vision. A couple of times he'd had to swerve to avoid other cars. Despite this incapacity, he had had the presence of mind to park away from the house, just to be on the safe side. He would get rid of the car later.

Ismail was waiting for him. "You are very late. I have been worried about you," he said as he opened the door for his guest. "I will make you a drink." They went through to the kitchen.

"Yes, I am sorry. The car, it has broken down. I will return tomorrow to fix it. I had to get a lift from someone." Ismail accepted the explanation without question. He looked at Youssef more closely in the light of the kitchen.

"Are you alright? You don't look well… and your clothes…"

"Yes, I got very wet, someone loaned them to me …"

"I see," said Ismail, but he was not entirely convinced.

"Are you sure you are ok? You have blood on your face and in your hair… I think you should go to the hospital."

"No…!" said Youssef, forcefully. "Sorry… no, I will be ok… I just need to sleep."

Youssef left Ismail deep in thought and went to bed.

There were about ten armed-response officers walking up the street crouching in the lea of the boundary wall. They had done their homework; a similar number went around the back of the block to make sure there was no escape.

The leading group reached the door of Ismail's house. The first officer had a short battering ram and pounded the door. It gave way and sprung open. The leading four officers, dressed in their combat gear stormed in. Ismail was in the kitchen.

"Armed officers… on the floor!" shouted the lead officer. Ismail complied. The other officers fanned through the house then up the stairs. Youssef was in the bedroom. He was not in a good way, still suffering the effects of a concussion. He tried to get up but immediately lost his balance. An officer entered.

"You, out of bed… on the floor… NOW!" he shouted.

Youssef held his hands up and meekly dropped to the floor. He was roughly handcuffed and dragged downstairs. His eyes were vacant.

"Don't like the look of this one, Sarge," said the officer. "He's either on drugs or something's wrong with him. Best go steady, yeah?"

Youssef was taken to an awaiting van while the scene of crime and forensics took over.

Epilogue

The forensics team found overwhelming evidence that Youssef al-Masri had killed Dan and Peggy Fletcher. His trainers were beside his bed, still bloodstained, and they were soon able to match the DNA with that of the famer and his wife.

The brutal murders made headline news across the country and Laura's articles were picked up by several of the nationals which did nothing to harm her journalistic reputation. A few weeks later, she received a call from the editor of the Telegraph, offering her a position as an investigative reporter.

She tried to persuade Rory to go with her, but he was keen to stay closer to home and there was a mutual parting of ways.

Rory continued to work at the factory just two or three days a week. He'd become close friends with Alistair and once the river had dropped to more-or-less normal levels, Alistair took him out one Sunday down to Gloucester and back. The boat was none-the-worse for its encounter with the flood, apart from a few scratches to the hull; nothing that a lick of paint wouldn't cure. After leaving the mooring, they soon approached the weir. Rory could see the post where he was stranded in the flood and shuddered at the thought. He had no idea how he'd survived.

In Vauxhall Cross, Commander Jenkins was delighted with the capture of al-Masri who, after receiving treatment for concussion in hospital, would eventually be sentenced to life imprisonment with a minimum term of forty years for the brutal murders. There were pleas from the Israelis who wanted him deported, but the Commander insisted he would serve his UK sentence; then they could have him. She was less inclined to be accommodating given she was certain they had killed her agent, Guy Hamilton, and they had been engaged in industrial espionage on British soil.

The name Rory Calderwood came up several times in discussion whilst MI6 reviewed the lessons from the Hades affair; he'd impressed Julian with his intuition and practical thinking. Just after Laura left for London, Rory was in his office at AB Engineering when he received an unexpected call.

"Mr Calderwood…? Rory Calderwood? My name's Jenkins, Felicity Jenkins. I work for Special Intelligence Services. I've been hearing good things about you. I may have some work right up your street. Would you be interested?"

"Yeah, I would," said Rory, without hesitation.

"That's great. Can you get down to Vauxhall Cross tomorrow, say midday? We can have a little chat. I do look forward to meeting you."

"Yeah, ok… I'll see you tomorrow at noon."

Sunday, November 18th, 2007, Natalie Kaplinski was walking through Hayarkon Park, Tel Aviv, with her cousin and her two children, heading for the zoo. They had parked in the parking area the other side of the Yarkon River and crossed the footbridge with dozens of others. It was always busy on weekends. The children were naturally excited at the thought of seeing the wild animals. As they got nearer, the sounds of a lion roaring could clearly be heard, adding to the anticipation.

There was no traffic allowed, but suddenly Natalie could hear a motorcycle; it seemed to be getting closer and closer. She turned around to see what it was, just as the bike drew alongside the family. Suddenly the pillion passenger pulled out a gun and shot Natalie three times in the head at point-blank range; the bike roared away.

THE END

Postscript

The summer of 2007, May-July was the wettest in England since records began in 1776. The estimated cost of the damage has been put at between £3.5 and £6.5 billion with many parts of the country affected. Average rainfall in June was around 5.5 inches, more than double the June average. 4.7 inches of rain fell in one day – 18th July. The rescue effort was described as the biggest in peacetime Britain. By July 23rd parts of Worcestershire were under six feet of water.

Alan Reynolds

"**...story left me with a racing pulse, jangling nerves and a real want for a follow up book.**"
- *Jacque Gerrard*

"**This book has everything.** The characters really come to life and I cannot wait for the next in the series!"
-*Sara Seastron*

"**Brilliant read, thoroughly enjoyed it**. Just waiting for your next publication"
- *Sarah Knight*

"**...one of those books you cannot put down... gripping tale.**"
- *Anna-Marie Dreyfus*

"...currently reading Flying with Kites **CAN'T WAIT TO GET HOME TO READ MORE!**"
- *Keeley Edge*

"**...David is raving about Flying with Kites. He's half way thru and already sees it's potential for a film...**"
- *William and Victoria Restaurant - Harrogate / book club*

"... It will make you gasp, sigh and laugh out loud... Alan Reynolds has the ability to make this happen all on one page, absolutely superb... **a definite five stars!**"
- *Lynette Machin*

"**A Brilliant Read...** I'm never normally gripped so much by storylines but this kept me in suspense throughout. Just couldn't put it down!"
- Anita Flowers

"**Gripping stuff...** This story had me hooked from the outset. I'm sure that my pulse rate must have increased as I progressed through it and circumstances, decisions and fate all began to take effect. I recommend this book to fans of Ruth Rendell and I don't think for one moment they will be disappointed."
- Anne Ulah

"**Awesome read...** I don't read very much at all and it's not the type of story I would have chosen but I could not put this book down. The whole story is totally believable. Towards the end I just could not leave it and sat all night reading to find out what happened."
- Claire Setchel

"**I recommend it as a must read book...** Having read Flying with Kites I was eagerly waiting for Reynolds next book to be published. It was well worth the wait. Psychological thrillers are my favourite genre and this is one the best I've read for some time."
- 'Snow Leopard'

"**I couldn't turn the pages fast enough to find out what was going to happen...** After reading Flying With Kites I was excited to read Alan Reynolds new novel, Taskers End, and I wasn't disappointed.
- Heather McLaren

"**...recommended.** Having worked in the banking system I can relate to the background culture that was prevalent in 1990s / 2000s, and in other sectors, and I feel I have met the characters. ...a roller coaster of emotion, excitement and despair, hedonistic fun and shattering sadness."
- Richard King

"**A riveting read...** Alan's writing is very engaging and keeps you enthralled from start to finish. Would definitely recommend for anyone with a curiosity about the inner workings of branch banking."
- Sally Turgoose

"**I couldn't put the book down...** Larger than life" characters are portrayed set in a ruthless and stressful environment; but are there elements of truth here? One is left wondering, particularly in the light of the recent banking crisis and recession! This book would lead to an interesting discussion in any book club."
- CBL

"**Brilliant and insightful...** It would probably have been less risky to have taken our money to the casino than to the bank. Brilliant and insightful into just what was going on from the government downwards. No wonder we finished up in the mess we did."
- John Leach

"**This book is one I could not put down...** As the title suggests, the storyline is set within a banking background. By the time I had finished, the reason the banks hit a crisis sending us into economic free fall became much clearer!"
- Kate Goddard

"If you love an intriguing plot, this book is for you..."
– *Lynn Newhart*

"Can't wait for the next!... Loved it, a gripping story line, this is yet another book from Alan Reynolds that has enthralled me!"
– *Chris Wren*

"The Sixth Pillar is such a brave book... Terrorist attacks are something that many of us will find entirely unthinkable and horrifying. Yet in this novel, Reynolds gives enough insight and impetus to show how someone could perhaps choose that route. Not that he condones it; Tariq is still a hard character to like, though you may sympathise at times."
– *Nikki Mason*

"...captivating read from the first chapter... The author gives you an insight into what it must have been like during the war in Iraq and also the war on terrorists in our own communities at home. I found the book to be a thought provoking read and as with his other books I didn't want to put it down."
– *Sarah K*

"I look forward to reading more of Mr. Reynolds fine work... Reynolds literary prose and timing are impeccable as he takes you from the deserts of southern Iraq to an oil platform off the coast of Britain. What makes a young person (Tariq) become so enamoured in sacred ideals that he is eager to commit suicide if given the opportunity to strike a blow against what his religious faction deems a Great Evil? Reynolds answers this most-often-asked question of our times and many more in this superb suspense novel."
– *Randall R Peterson*

"**Another Reynolds classic...**
Don't want to spend time giving
away the plot etc., you can
read the synopsis and reviews
elsewhere… The book's superb,
just buy it."
– *C James*

"**…a writer whose work rivals
any author…** In my review of
Flying With Kites, I concluded that
Alan Reynolds had raised the bar
for all writers. Any trepidation I
might have had as to whether he
could live up to that standard with
The Tinker, quickly disappeared.
Once again, he has skilfully woven a unique and thoroughly
enjoyable story that continues to place Reynolds up there with
the best of them"
– *Alex Jones*

"**From the moment the story starts you realize something
special is taking place between you and the words written
between the covers…** The quiet village of Drayburn is the
perfect place to relax while on holiday or before drifting off
to sleep at night with this book and a hot cup of cocoa on
your bedside table. And you do relax. You become part of
the village, a friend to Michael, like all the rest. But there is a
growing tension surrounding this unusual, seasonal, handy-
man, you feel it from the fist time you meet him… You will not
want this book to end but you will keep turning the pages"
– *Deep Reader*

"**Exceptional…** I've loved reading all Reynolds books and
awaited the publication of this one with bated breath. The wait
was definitely worth it. The characters are well portrayed and
the storyline was tantalising in its mystery. I absolutely loved it
and wholeheartedly recommend it."
– *Snow Leopard*

www.ingramcontent.com/pod-product-compliance
Lightning Source LLC
Chambersburg PA
CBHW020949030726
47496CB00005B/1429